THE BONE YARD

MARK SENNEN

avon

HarperCollins PUBLISHERS
— Since 1817 —

This novel is entirely a work of fiction.
The names, characters and incidents portrayed in it are
the work of the author's imagination. Any resemblance to
actual persons, living or dead, events or localities is
entirely coincidental.

AVON

A division of HarperCollins*Publishers*
The News Building
1 London Bridge Street
London SE1 9GF
www.harpercollins.co.uk

A Paperback Original 2017

First published in Great Britain by
HarperCollins*Publishers* 2017

Copyright © Mark Sennen 2017

Mark Sennen asserts the moral right to be identified as the author of this work

A catalogue record for this book is available from the British Library

ISBN-13: 978-0-00-758790-2

Set in Minion 11/14 pt by Palimpsest Book Production Limited, Falkirk, Stirlingshire

Printed and bound in Great Britain by Clays Ltd, St Ives plc

MIX
Paper from
responsible sources

FSC
www.fsc.org **FSC™ C007454**

FSC™ is a non-profit international organisation established to promote
the responsible management of the world's forests. Products carrying the
FSC label are independently certified to assure consumers that they come
from forests that are managed to meet the social, economic and
ecological needs of present and future generations,
and other controlled sources.

Find out more about HarperCollins and the environment at
www.harpercollins.co.uk/green

Acknowledgements

Book six in the DI Charlotte Savage series almost wrote itself. Once I had the charismatic Malcolm Kendwick, I knew the way the story would pan out. I simply had to watch as the words appeared on the page. Of course, once finished, others had to put in considerably more effort to lick the manuscript into shape. In short, the story couldn't have been told without the following people:

Editors Eloise Wood and Rachel Faulkner-Willcocks saw the book through from the messy first draft to the (hopefully) polished final copy. Thanks also to the unseen army at Avon/ HarperCollins who work with little acknowledgement, but much dedication.

Claire Roberts, my agent, deals with matters of contracts, rights, and royalties. A world where knowledge of both the dark arts and higher mathematics is essential.

Talking shop with fellow authors Simon Kettlewell and Neil Vogler has led to an increased intensity (not to mention perversity) in my writing. Thanks guys!

The best line in the book was served up by Kate Campbell, Rob Longworth and their son, Sachin, over Sunday lunch. More, please! (Both lunches and lines.)

My wife and daughters gave their love and support. Writing is not a nine to five job and putting up with me wittering on at all times requires endless patience (or earplugs).

Finally, thank you to all the readers of the series, from those who've been with Charlotte from the start, to those who've just climbed aboard. Many of you know her better than I do.

To Niamh and Morgan
In a sky filled with stars, you are the brightest

Prologue

She looks up at the trees. Huge, towering sequoias looming over her. Mist swirls in the canopy high above, a distant sky just visible through the dense tangle of leaves. Like ancient sentinels, the trees stand watching but taking no part in events. They've stood here for centuries, since long before the invaders with white skins came from the west and changed the continent forever. The oldest specimens were alive over two thousand years ago, when a man was nailed to two pieces of wood and left to die in order to save mere mortals. She reaches up, touches her neck and finds the slim silver chain. She runs her fingers down to the cross and then brings it to her mouth and kisses the figure of Jesus. He is her last hope.

She moves to one of the wider trunks, pushing herself up against the rough bark, sensing the patterns press through the thin material of her dress. She shivers, feeling vulnerable in the light summer frock because she's nothing else on. He made her remove her panties and bra and her shoes too. Part of his perverted game.

She peeks round the side of the tree, hoping she's lost him. For now, it looks as if she has. She shivers and then stares down at her feet where blood trickles from several gashes. There'd been rocks earlier and an area of scree leading down from the forestry track where he'd released her . . .

The trunk of the car had opened and she'd closed her eyes against the brightness.

'Get out,' he said. He held a pistol in his hand, the barrel pointing at her chest. 'Get out and then I want you to take everything off but your dress. And when I say everything, I mean everything, your underwear included.'

She clambered over the lip of the trunk and stood in front of him. Pleaded. He shook his head and waved the gun.

'Off or I'll shoot you in the leg.' For a moment he turned the gun away into the distance and then he fired, the retort echoing off a high bluff. 'Your choice.'

She took her time to remove her bra from beneath the dress and then she slipped her underwear down. He gestured at her sandals.

'Those too.'

She bent and removed her shoes and then stood before him.

'Now, you're going to run.' Once again he waved the gun, this time in the direction of the treeline some thirty paces from the track. 'I'll give you a hundred seconds head start and then I'm coming to find you. And when I do, you'll lie still and we'll have some fun, right?'

'You don't have to do this. You don't—'

'Oh, but I do.' The man smiled. 'And I'm going to start counting now. If I was you, I wouldn't waste a second. Not. A. Second. Of course, it's your choice. One, two, three . . .'

Which was when she'd scrambled down the scree at the side of the track, cutting her feet on the sharp stones, before disappearing into the shadows beneath the tall trees. She'd half expected to hear a shot, feel a bullet implant itself between her shoulder blades. But she'd reached the treeline unharmed, stumbling into the quiet of the forest, the only sounds that of her breathing and her feet rustling in the dead wood and leaves as she scampered away from him as fast as she could.

Now she's worn out, the huge tree not just something to hide behind, but something to cling to, to slump against as she tries to recover her breath. She doesn't know how far she's run, only that it's all been downhill. Twice she'd fallen and sprawled in the soft loam, tumbling over and over. The hundred seconds are long gone and now he must be coming after her. She wonders about heading off to the right or left and following the contours. Perhaps that might confuse him. At least the change of direction would give her a fifty-fifty chance.

She pushes herself away from the tree and bears off to the right. She trots along a narrow animal trail which weaves among the sequoias. At each trunk she pauses for a moment to listen. There's nothing. She moves on. She pauses again. Nothing.

Up ahead a gash of grey stone slices through the hillside. She walks forward to where a ravine blocks the trail. The sides are steep and the bare rock sharp. There's no way across. She has to turn left and forge her way downhill once more.

She catches her foot on a bare root and trips again, rolling in the dirt before pushing herself up and following the edge of the ravine towards the valley bottom. Down, down, down through the lines of trees until all of a sudden the rocks spill out onto a flat plateau. The trees are fewer here, but taller. And they're still watching. Watching over . . .

She shivers at the sight. Dozens of rusting automobiles lie scattered amongst the trees. Several trucks. A school bus with yellow paint peeling away from decaying panelling. An old sedan has a wide grille and empty holes where the headlamps have fallen out. Like the trees, the car is watching. Next to the sedan, a young sapling sprouts from the bed of a pickup. Where there are no vehicles, scrub creeps across the ground. Snaking through the scrub are pathways where the vegetation has been cut back. Someone comes here. Someone tends this place.

She steps forward, a glimmer of hope rising within. She reaches for the cross again. Perhaps her prayers have been answered. Perhaps this isn't the wilderness after all, but a park somewhere on the edge of a town. As if in answer to her thoughts, a figure steps from behind one of the metal husks. In the shade of the trees she can't make out his features, but he's not as tall as the man who kidnapped her. He's older, too. Her heart begins to pound, sensing a relief from her troubles.

'Help me!' she shouts out to her saviour. She begins to trot over towards the man, winding her way along one of the paths. The man nods, a smile forming on his lips. She realises she must be quite a sight. Her dress torn up the side and front, her body half smeared with mud and leaves. She crosses her arms, trying to cover herself. 'I've been attacked. Help me!'

'Sure, lass,' the man says, his accent strange and unfamiliar. His smile grows and she feels his eyes feasting on her exposed flesh. 'No problem.'

She slows as she reaches him. Hesitates now she's just a few steps away. She turns to look over her shoulder, but there's no sight of her pursuer. And when she turns back, the older man fades from view, stepping deep into the shade of a tree.

'Hello?' She slides forward on the grass. 'Please help me!'

'Found you!' The man who abducted her dodges up from behind an old Volkswagen Bug, his hands outstretched. He grins at her and laughs as he claws at her dress. The material falls away as another seam rips. Then she's screaming and hollering as he pushes her to the ground. He's on top of her now and his strength is frightening. She kicks and she scratches but it's no good. 'Keep still!' he shouts. 'Now you've run, I want you still!'

For a second she wonders about complying. Perhaps he won't harm her if she does what he says. Then, from the corner of her eye, she sees the older man again. He's walking over, a

4

large knife in his right hand. He kneels beside her, the knife poised. He reaches out with his left hand, the fingers brushing her face.

'Lovely,' he says. Then he grasps the chain round her neck and with a tug, wrenches it off and throws it away. 'But we don't need that getting in the way.'

She sees the cross spinning in the air, catching the light as it tumbles over and over and over, a glint from the silver figure on the cross mirrored by a flash from the knife as the man lowers the blade.

'Now then, the boy told you to be still,' he says as he slices at her neck, cutting deep into flesh and sinew. 'So you best be still, right?'

Chapter One

Near Bovisand, Plymouth. Saturday 15th April. 7.43 a.m.

Detective Inspector Charlotte Savage woke to an aroma of hot croissant and fresh coffee. A blinding glare too, along with a swish as the curtains swept open and sunlight came streaming in through the window. She shielded her eyes against the rays, squinting through her fingers.

'Surprise, Mummy!' said a small figure on the far side of the room. 'Breakfast in bed!'

A tray clicked down on the table beside her, the rattle of cutlery against crockery.

'Jamie,' Savage said, propping herself up on one elbow. 'Darling, how sweet.'

'It was his idea.' A taller figure stood next to the bed. Pete, Savage's husband. He removed a cup, plate and a cafetiére from the tray and then pressed down the handle on the coffee pot. 'But all my work. That's parenting, I guess.'

'There's a price to pay for everything.' Savage sat up and Pete plonked a couple of pillows behind her back. She looked at Jamie as he climbed up onto the bed and slipped beneath the duvet to give her a cuddle. He was seven years old but still as needy as a toddler. Not that Savage minded. She ruffled his short, black hair and smiled at him. 'I think it's worth it, don't you?'

'That all depends on which one you're talking about.' Pete poured the coffee and handed Savage the cup. He nodded in the direction of the bedroom door. 'Samantha's in a right strop.'

Savage nodded. Samantha was her daughter. She'd just been dumped by her boyfriend and, being fifteen and full of hormones, the event had turned her world upside down. Pete and Savage were, unfathomably, largely to blame for all her woes.

'She'll get over him.' Savage followed Pete's gaze and then looked to the window. Outside, beyond their garden, she could see the waters of Plymouth Sound. A deep blue punctuated by the occasional snowflake of white sail, the early sun dancing on the gentle waves. 'It's a beautiful day, so why don't we all go into town and grab something for lunch? If there's any chance of a bit of shopping, especially with us paying, Sam will go for it. I'm sure that will cheer her up.'

An hour later, Savage regretted her suggestion. Detective Superintendent Conrad Hardin had phoned and lunch was most definitely off. She was wanted urgently at the station. She enquired as to what was pressing enough to require her presence on a Saturday. There hadn't been a murder or any other serious crime, had there?

'No, not yet,' Hardin said cryptically. 'And I can't tell you what this is about on the phone. This is strictly a need-to-know situation. I don't want anything getting out.'

Savage protested, exasperated at Hardin's notion of phone taps, conspiracy theories and leaks to the media. He ignored her and refused to divulge any more information.

'Oh,' he added at the end of the call. 'And pack for an

overnight stay. You're going on a little trip. You'll be back tomorrow afternoon.'

'Sir, tomorrow's Easter Day.'

'Off to church, are you, DI Savage? Seen the light?'

'No, but—'

'As I said, you'll be back tomorrow afternoon. If all goes well.'

'If all goes—?'

The DSupt ended the call, leaving Savage to apologise to her children and pack a few things into a bag.

'So?' Pete said. 'Going to fill me in?'

'I haven't a clue.' Savage shrugged as she stuffed some underwear into a side pocket on the bag. 'An essential training course, I shouldn't wonder. Probably some other lucky bugger has cried off and Hardin needs me to fill their shoes. Assuming, of course, that he isn't intent on taking me on a dirty weekend.'

'That's not even remotely funny.' Pete eyed a matching pair of black knickers and bra. 'Are those new?'

'Yes. I bought them especially for the DSupt. I'm calling them my promotion set.'

'Stop it.'

Savage continued to rib her husband until Samantha came into the room and started a raging argument about parents and broken promises and how life really couldn't get any worse. Savage tried to console her daughter, but the more she tried the more heated the conversation became. Eventually, she zipped up the bag, slung it on her shoulder and left Pete to bribe his way out of the situation.

The journey to the station was stop-start, the Saturday shopping traffic into Plymouth backing up across the Laira Bridge. Savage didn't mind. She'd taken her little MG, a classic car older than she was, and with the mid-April morning being bright and warm, she'd put the hood down. She sat in the queue, enjoying the sun and watching the waterskiers on the expanse of estuary north of the bridge. Eventually, she cleared the traffic and headed up the A38 with the wind in her hair, arriving at Crownhill at a little after twelve.

After poking her head into the deserted crime suite, she went up to the DSupt's office. She knocked and entered, surprised to see Detective Sergeant Darius Riley seated on one side of the desk. Shocked, too, to find herself thinking about the black underwear. She immediately censored herself.

'Ma'am,' Riley said with a smile. Hardin was over the far side of the room pouring coffee into three grotty looking mugs. Riley made a silent theatrical sigh and shook his head. 'Hope you packed your toothbrush.'

Savage glanced down at Riley's feet where he'd parked a small rucksack. She unshouldered her own bag and dumped it on the floor, before taking a chair.

'Yes,' she said. 'Although I'm itching to know the destination for our little magical mystery tour.'

Riley nodded but said nothing more. He shifted in his seat and ran a finger up to his shirt collar where the bright white material met his black skin. The DS was, as usual, immaculately turned out, with his hair neat and short, his attire spotless. Savage had always figured that Riley had to go the extra mile to prove himself in a force which was overwhelmingly white. And prove himself he had. He'd been instrumental in the success of several operations including the capture of a multiple murderer which had nearly cost him his life. He'd also helped Savage track down the person who'd been involved in the hit-and-run which had killed her daughter, Samantha's twin sister, Clarissa. Riley had become more than just a work colleague, he was a confidant and, she liked to think, a friend.

'Ah, Charlotte.' Hardin spun round, coffee slopping from the three cups as he tried to hold them in two hands. He squeezed his considerable bulk behind his desk and set the coffees down, before sinking into his chair. 'Ready for the off?'

'If I knew what the "off" was, it would be helpful, sir.'

'In good time. I was hoping DC Enders would be here by now, but we'll proceed without him. He's only your driver so it's not as if he needs to hear this briefing. You can fill him in later.'

'Our driver?' Savage glanced at Riley, but the DS only shrugged. He appeared to know little more than she did.

'Malcolm Kendwick,' Hardin said, rolling his eyes and shaking his head. Savage and Riley sat there in silence for a minute while Hardin shuffled through a load of papers on his desk. He pulled a stack of documents from a large FedEx envelope. Several of the documents bore a header with the graphic of an eagle. Below the eagle, large text with the words *US Department of Justice*, marched officially across the envelope. 'As I was saying, Malcolm Kendwick. Know who he is?'

Savage nodded. 'Yes. Sort of.'

'Sort of' meant she'd read the headlines in the tabloids, the longer pieces in the quality press. Malcolm Kendwick was, if you believed the paper who'd bought the rights to his story, an innocent British citizen abroad. Framed for the murder of several young women in the US, he had surely faced the death penalty until he'd been let off on a technicality. Several other newspapers naturally took the opposing viewpoint. For them, Kendwick was a serial killer who, with his good looks and charm, was following in the footsteps of

11

Ted Bundy. What's more, he was going to be deported from the States, which meant he'd be returning to the United Kingdom where he would undoubtedly wreak havoc. No female within fifty miles of wherever he ended up would be safe.

Hardin snorted. He picked up a sheaf of papers and waved them at Savage.

'Funny, isn't it, how when one of our own is in a foreign country they're innocent, and yet when a foreigner commits a crime over here they're guilty as sin.'

'Sir?' Savage was keen to get to the bottom of what Hardin was on about, why she and Riley had been called in.

'Well, Charlotte, according to this Kendwick *is* guilty.' Hardin waved the papers once more to emphasise his point. 'It's a transcript of the confession Kendwick gave to the cop. You've read the story, what was her name . . . ?'

'Janey. Janey Horton.' Savage hadn't cared much about the Kendwick case, but she had kept up with the news on Officer Horton. 'Tough cookie. Dedicated.'

'Trust you to know her name,' Hardin said. 'Five thousand miles but peas in a pod, hey?'

Officer Horton had been with the Fresno Police Department in California. Her daughter, Sara, had vanished, and Horton had become convinced that Malcolm Kendwick was responsible. Evidence – hard evidence – had been in short supply, but that hadn't stopped Horton. She'd kidnapped Kendwick and imprisoned him in the basement of her house. Over a period of several days she'd extracted a confession from him along with the location of her daughter's body. Leaving Kendwick tied up, she went out into the wilderness of the Sierra National Forest to find her daughter.

'She did what any parent would do, sir.' As she spoke, Savage was aware of Riley casting a glance in her direction.

'Horton simply wanted the truth about what happened and justice for the man responsible.'

'Well, she didn't get it, did she?'

No, Savage thought, but not for want of trying.

Horton had spent two days searching, eventually discovering the corpse of a woman a good while dead, but definitely not her daughter. She returned to her house to find Kendwick had escaped. She hurried round to his apartment, but he'd fled from there too. Using contacts in the police department, she traced his credit card to a motel on the outskirts of Sacramento. She drove to the place intending to recapture Kendrick, but the owner of the motel grew suspicious when he saw her dragging Kendwick screaming from his room.

Local officers, responding to a 911 call from the owner, arrived and Kendwick pleaded innocence, claiming Horton was carrying out a vendetta against him. The officers were all for arresting Horton until she showed them a video on her phone. The video was the confession from Kendwick and once they'd seen it they arrested Kendwick instead. And that should have been that, the whole thing done and dusted. On the video, Kendwick admitted killing Horton's daughter and several other girls. A forensic team hurried out into the wilderness and quickly located the remains of five women, including those of Sara Horton. All that remained was a lengthy trial and, hopefully, a minimal number of years on death row before Kendwick crapped himself as he was strapped to a gurney and given a lethal injection.

It wasn't to be.

The evidence on the phone was inadmissible. No room for doubt. This wasn't some obscure technicality which Kendwick's lawyer had come up with. It was obvious. Horton had tortured Kendwick and filmed herself doing so. She'd sliced him with a knife and poured battery acid on his feet.

Held a gun to his head and threatened to kill him. Anything Kendwick had said in the video couldn't be used as evidence, couldn't even be used as a lead to point to other evidence. Kendwick was untouchable.

Still, Fresno detectives worked double shifts for no extra pay trying to sift through the material Horton had gathered in her initial search for her daughter. The material which had led her to Kendwick in the first place. The problem was much of the evidence was circumstantial: Kendwick had been spotted at a park where Sara Horton often hung out with friends. He'd been seen jogging past the clothing store where she worked. He had a membership at a gym where she once had a part-time job. None of which was particularly incriminating. It looked at first as if Officer Horton had followed a hunch, used a dollop of female intuition, perhaps consulted the grounds in her morning coffee. Then Horton told her fellow officers about a rucksack she'd found in Kendwick's car. Inside were handcuffs, a full-face balaclava and a pair of gloves, a roll of gaffer tape, some rope, a hammer and several trash bags. Kendwick claimed the items were nothing special, but Horton told the detectives they comprised a rape kit. It didn't matter. Horton's search of the car was ruled illegal and the evidence couldn't be used.

All hope of a conviction now rested on a scrunchy discovered in Kendwick's apartment, a single strand of blonde hair entangled in the shiny red material. A blonde hair which DNA analysis proved belonged to Sara Horton.

Kendwick was questioned about the scrunchy, but, as advised by his lawyer, said nothing more than he'd picked up the hairband in the park one day. Since Kendwick had long hair himself, which he kept tied back, the explanation was all too believable. Short of water boarding, which several detectives were keen to try, Kendwick was on the home straight. There was just a matter of another four girls linked with Kendwick, but while he couldn't provide specific alibis, nor was there any direct evidence to suggest he'd been involved in their disappearances. After a year in limbo, the case against Kendwick was finally dropped on the provision that he wouldn't bring charges against Fresno Police or Janey Horton. His lawyers advised him to get out of the country pronto, before circumstances could change.

'That's why this is short notice, Charlotte.' Hardin was waving another piece of paper at Savage and Riley. This time Savage could see the initials NCA at the top. The National Crime Agency. The closest thing the UK had to the FBI. 'We've got to make arrangements. We don't want a media circus and we certainly don't want a lynch mob. On the other hand, Kendwick needs to know that we're watching him, that if he puts one foot out of line we'll have him.'

'Arrangements?' Savage didn't know where this was going. What could Malcolm Kendwick's affairs have to do with Devon and Cornwall Police?

'Yes.' Hardin had begun to gather the papers together again. He slipped them back into the FedEx envelope. 'The arrangements at Heathrow. Security on the journey back. What to do once the man is here.'

'I don't get it, sir.' Savage turned to Riley but he could only shrug his shoulders again. 'What do you mean, *here*?'

'There's no mystery, DI Savage. Here means here. Malcolm Kendwick is returning to the county of his birth. The fucker's coming to Devon.'

'Devon?'

'Yes.' Hardin stuck his tongue out over his bottom lip in consternation. 'And you, DS Riley and DC Enders are the lucky buggers who have to go and get him.'

* * *

As he looked down from the plane, he could see the mountains below. Grey peaks poking above green forest. There were a million acres down there. A million acres of woodland and rock and dirt. Hundreds of streams and rivers, thousands of miles of tracks and trails, untold numbers of gullies and ravines and caves. By any measure, the Sierra National Forest was a true wilderness. A wilderness you could get lost in, a wilderness you could hide things in, a wilderness where searching was pretty much a waste of time. But they didn't do much of that in the US anyway. Searching. Not in a country with well over ten thousand homicides a year. What was another handful to them? Nothing, that's what.

Malcolm Kendwick eased himself back in his seat and thought about the horrors which had happened down there. The girls who had been murdered. Their faces had been all over the media. TV, newspapers, websites. Pictures culled from their friends and family or from the internet. Their names and biographies were indelibly fixed in Kendwick's memories.

All five of them.

One: Stephanie Capillo, a student from Santa Barbara. Blonde hair. Slim, leggy, and with small, pert breasts. She'd been twenty-one. An English major at UCSB. Liked dogs and children. Helped out at an animal refuge. Went to church. Wore a purity ring. A fucking do-gooder by any standards.

Two: Amber Sullivan. A year younger than Stephanie. Long hair. Also blonde. A little chubby. Not quite the perfect all-American girl since she worked in a cheap burger joint and had a citation for smoking grass. Still, her mother's pride and joy.

Three: Chrissy Morales. About as far removed from Stephanie as you could get. The most used image was one of the girl in leather thigh-highs and a PVC miniskirt. Petite and very cute and, yes, blonde again. Chrissy usually worked the streets near Highway 99 in Bakersfield. A hooker – the fact even acknowledged by her parents – she was inevitably at the bottom of any list of victims the media chose to display.

Four: Jessie Turner. Seventeen. Her pictures showed a fair-haired cheerleader with pom-poms and a lovely smile or else the news outlets played a video where she sang in a school musical. She'd auditioned for *America's Got Talent* and, to hear her family talk, she was but one step away from superstardom.

Five: Sara Horton. Nineteen. Footloose. Had spent a year in South America. Just about holding down a job in some fashion outlet. Like all the others, blonde and a real beauty. Everything to live for, according to her mother.

Her mother . . .

He cast a glance at the window once more. The mountains were falling away now, the green forests gone as the aircraft crossed the state line and entered Nevada airspace. He shook his head. He wouldn't see the wilderness again except in his memories. His life from now on would be like the land below: dusty, arid and dull. He sighed and then leaned back in his seat, closed his eyes, and slept.

Malcolm Kendwick was thirty-two years old. He'd lived in the US for ten years, moving from the UK when the internet start-up he'd founded had been bought up by a company in California. That company had itself been subsumed into the workings of one of the software giants and he'd moved on to another tech firm. He'd grown bored of that after several years and, having plenty of money, he'd jacked in the job and pursued other interests. A new start-up, some time spent catching waves on the coast, several months just bumming around. Now though, he was heading back across the Atlantic, and not through choice.

Janey Horton.

Sara's mother had been blonde but she hadn't been young. In her late thirties, Kendwick considered Janey Horton flesh gone sour, a world away from the smooth-skinned beauties who'd died down there in the wilderness, five miles below. Horton was one of the ones who *did* bother to search. But then you would, wouldn't you? If it was your daughter who'd gone missing.

Sara had vanished from the small town of Morro Bay some one hundred and fifty miles up the coast from LA. Kendwick had been amused to hear she came from a little hamlet called Harmony a few miles along the Cabrillo Highway. Not that there was anything harmonious about her mother.

When her daughter had disappeared, Janey Horton had looked far and wide, but instead of finding Sara, she'd found him. And he hadn't had any answers for her. Not at first. Later, when she'd begun to torture him, he'd blurted out stuff. About her daughter, about the others. Anything he could think of really.

And once she heard what he'd had to say, she'd decided to kill him.

You fuckin' piece of crap. I'm goin' to cut your fuckin' dick off and feed it to you, understand?

He could well understand. She'd already carved three slices across his chest using a box knife, the thin blade like a razor the way the cuts opened up. Bloodless at first and then a weep of red painting thick lines down to his abdomen. He'd struggled, but try as he might, the ropes she'd secured him to the chair with held him tight. He'd opened up to her then, just like the cuts. Poured out what had happened, made up some story about how he'd been abused as a kid. Begged for his life. She wasn't interested. She left him while she went to search for her daughter's body. He'd been in that chair for two days. Crapping, pissing, bleeding. Crying, even.

Kendwick awoke from a fitful sleep. The horrors of the long hours he'd spent in Horton's basement still haunted his dreams. He shivered and then pressed his face to the plane's window once more. The aircraft had met the night now and straight out there was nothing but a winking of a light on the wing tip, beyond the light, blackness. The interior illumination made it impossible to see the stars, but peering down beneath the wing, a glow marked a small town. Surrounding villages and hamlets spread out below as if somebody had flicked fluorescent paint across a black canvas.

Or made a cut and watched blood spatter on the concrete floor of a dingy basement.

The girls had bled too. All over a vein of pure white quartz high in the Sierra Nevada, miles from any highway. The dried blood had been scraped from the rock by men and women in white suits, taken back to the lab and analysed. The blood belonged to the five missing girls, the DNA results said. According to the coroner, the sheer quantity suggested they'd died there.

You killed her, didn't you? You raped her and then you fuckin' killed her. Admit it, Malcolm. Tell me the fuckin' truth! Tell me where my daughter is!

He hadn't wanted to tell her anything. Not at first. He pleaded with her, tried to convince her she had the wrong man.

'I didn't do it. It wasn't me. For God's sake, you've got to believe me.'

19

'I don't believe you. You killed Sara, I know you did. Just like you killed Stephanie, Chrissy, Amber and Jessie.'

'Honestly, I didn't do it!' Kendrick said again, in a vain attempt to convince Horton. 'I never killed those girls!'

'We'll see about that . . .'

At which point she'd started to use the box knife on him. Not the chest to begin with, his right calf. Slicing the skin as if she was descaling a fish. Peeling back a layer and then digging the knife into the exposed muscle. Rotating the blade until—

'Excuse me, sir?'

Kendwick flicked his eyes from the window. A hostess leaned in from the aisle. Gestured at the overhead locker. Reached across to open the locker and push back the strap of his bag which had jammed in the door.

He smelt the perfume and glanced up through the trans-lucent material of her blouse at the magical swell of her breasts. Swallowed.

You fuckin' piece of crap. I'm goin' to cut your fuckin' dick off and feed it to you, understand?

Kendwick managed a half smile at the girl and then looked away again. He stared into the dark sky beyond the wing tip and for a moment wished he was out there in the thin air. Falling, falling, falling to the ground below where the safety of death and oblivion waited.

Then he turned back and watched the hostess walk away down the aisle. Took in her nylon-encased legs, the wondrous shape of her hips beneath the navy-blue skirt, the way her long blonde hair lay curled in a bun beneath her cap. Wondered about letting the bun free so the golden strands could brush over her shoulders as she stood before him. Realised that oblivion wasn't what he wanted at all.

*   *   *

20

The journey up had been easy. Saturday afternoon, light traffic, just a bit of a snarl-up at Cribbs Causeway in Bristol as those who had nothing better to do headed for the stores on a warm spring day. Nothing better to do such as driving to London to pick up a suspected serial killer.

They'd booked two rooms at the Premier Inn at Twin Bridges in Bracknell, Enders and Riley sharing, Savage on her own. The hotel was attached to a three-hundred-year-old coaching inn, now remodelled as a Beefeater. As they pulled into the car park and unloaded their overnight bags, Enders was keen to point out the name.

'Twin Bridges, ma'am. Like Two Bridges back home on the moor.' He stared out at the busy A322 where cars streamed past, their windscreens glinting in the late-afternoon sun. 'Only not.'

'Only not.' Savage repeated Enders' words as she wondered what travellers past would have made of modern-day developments.

Enders raised a hand and tousled his mop of black hair. He looked wistful for a moment. Unlike DS Riley, he'd come dressed casually and wore brown cords and a mustard-coloured pullover over a green T-shirt. Such sartorial blunders were common with Enders, but the DC was in his twenties and his youth, his cheeky boyish face and the Irish lilt to his voice allowed him to get away with the clothing mismatch.

'Bet Darius feels at home though.' Enders nodded across at Riley. 'Don't you, sir? Back to your roots?'

Savage laughed as Riley shook his head. 'I'm not exactly sure where Darius' roots are, but I'm pretty sure they're not here.'

'Battersea,' Riley said, pulling his bag from the boot of the car.

'Battersea?' Savage raised her eyebrows.

'My dad was a lawyer.' Riley shrugged an apology. 'Still is, actually.'

'We're obviously in the wrong end of the business, ma'am,' Enders said. He gestured at the hotel. 'The cheap-as-chips end.'

Later, that's what they had: fish and chips in the Beefeater. Several pints of bitter for Enders. Then a discussion about the main event. Savage and Riley had been over the plan earlier when they'd been briefed by the DSupt, but after they'd finished their meal, Savage laid out the agenda for the next day.

'Kendwick's plane lands at nine-forty, so we'll aim to be in the terminal by nine. That will give us time to meet the NCA officers. I'll sit in on the interview and then Patrick will bring the car round and we'll set off. I don't reckon we'll leave until twelve at the very earliest, meaning we won't get back to Devon before four.'

'And we're dropping Kendwick off, right?' Enders plainly didn't like the idea and he'd not stopped moaning about it for most of the journey up. 'A door-to-door limousine service paid for by the taxpayer. All while we're having to lay off staff.'

'We're taking him to his new place in Chagford, yes.'

'Chagford? How the bloody hell did he afford that?'

'His grandmother had a cottage there. She's now in a home and Kendwick's sister has been letting the place out. Kendwick's going to use the cottage while he finds his feet.'

'Finds his . . .' Enders shook his head. 'Forgive me, ma'am, but he's the one who should be in a home. You'll be telling me we're giving him a job next.'

'I don't think he needs one. There's talk he's going to sign with one of the tabloids and he's already got a book deal. Probably be six figures in all.'

'What's the book called, *Serial Killing for Dummies*?'

'I might remind you he's innocent in the eyes of the law. We can't touch him.'

'Bloody lawyers.' Enders smiled across the table at Riley. 'Explains how your old man got rich.'

'Business law,' Riley said. 'The City. Not defending the likes of Malcolm Kendwick.'

'OK folks,' Savage said. 'That's enough. Tomorrow you both need to be on your best behaviour so you might as well start practising now. The last thing we need is Kendwick bringing some kind of harassment charge against us. Our job is to ferry him home and, while we're doing so, get a measure of the man. Make him realise that if he puts a foot out of line we'll be onto him.'

'Well, let's hope he *does* put a foot out of line,' Enders said. 'Any excuse to clock him one and believe you me I'll—'

'You'll do nothing of the sort. Anyway, guilty or not, he's not going to want to cast suspicion on himself. Not now. He'll want to lie low, write his book and enjoy his freedom. Remember, he's been incarcerated for over a year and all that time he's had the possibility of a capital trial ahead of him. I don't think he'll want to cause any more trouble for himself.'

'So that's where old serial killers end up, is it? Retire to the country and live happily ever after? Sounds like the punchline to a bad joke. Only it's not funny. How did it fucking come to this?'

'Well, there's nothing we can do to change the situation. California is a little way out of our jurisdiction and they've washed their hands of him.'

Enders glowered and then reached for his pint. Riley tried to start a new topic of conversation, but the evening was done. A little while later Savage called it a night, reminding Riley and Enders not to stay up too late.

Back in her room, she made herself a hot drink using the miniature kettle and the instant coffee and UHT milk provided by the hotel. She sat on the bed sipping the coffee and reading the material Hardin had given her. The coffee was disgusting and she put the cup aside. Without the cup in her hand, she found herself nodding off. When she jerked awake she caught sight of herself in the mirror on the wall opposite the bed. She stared into her own eyes, thinking about what they had to do tomorrow and recalling DC Enders' statement from earlier in the evening.

How did it fucking come to this?

She shook her head, put the notes away and got ready for bed. Five minutes later she was asleep.

Chapter Two

Seventy-five miles due west of the Isle of Barra, Scotland.
Sunday 16th April. 6.02 a.m.

There was a rim of light beyond the wing when Kendwick awoke and slid the blind up. Dawn creeping from the east, the plane rushing to meet the new day with an eagerness which he didn't much share.

Around him bodies stirred. An hour or so until they touched down. An hour until he walked away from the nightmare of the last twelve months.

We'll be waiting for you, Mr Kendwick. Airside. We'll take you through passport control and hand you over to officers from Devon and Cornwall Police. They'll whisk you out of the airport without the press so much as getting an inkling of what's going on. OK?

OK? No, it wasn't OK. But the alternative to a little impromptu interrogation by National Crime Agency officers was a full-on assault by the British media. And they made the cops in the US look like kittens.

Kittens.

He turned his head, scanning the aisle for the blonde hostess. The one with the translucent shirt and the long hair in a bun. She was nowhere to be seen. Perhaps she'd taken

25

herself off to business class to give those who'd paid more for their ticket a breakfast treat.

He sighed and stared ahead not wanting another conversation with the person next to him. The man with the BO and the persistent chit-chat about his work, his family, his car, his fucking boring life which Kendwick wasn't the least bit interested in hearing about.

'Back home soon.' Too late. The man had noticed Kendwick's gaze move to the aisle in search of the hostess. 'The Chilterns, me. Goring. Handy for the M4. Know it?'

Kendwick nodded even though he'd never heard of the bloody place. 'Nice,' he said.

'You?'

'Devon.' Kendwick turned his head to the window, hoping the message that he wasn't interested in talking would get through.

'Lovely!' BO seemed impressed and not at all put out by Kendwick's failure to continue to make eye contact. 'Long way though. Bit of a hike. But worth the journey. Me and the wife were down there a couple of years ago. The Rick Stein place. Padstow. Stayed in a little holiday cottage right on the harbour. Pretty as a postcard. Beautiful.'

Padstow was in Cornwall, not Devon, but Kendwick kept quiet. He wished he'd just named a random London borough. Then again, the man would have probably found something to say about that too.

'Tell you what,' BO continued. 'My car's in the long-term parking. I could give you a lift as far as Reading. I normally take junction twelve, but I could just as easily go off on ten and run you to the station. You could catch the Paddington train there. Save all that nonsense at the Heathrow end, wouldn't it?'

Kendwick turned back. Tried hard not to tell the moron

to fuck off. Said instead: 'Thanks, but no thanks. I'm being met at the airport. I've got a lift all the way home. Now, if you don't mind, I'm going to try and get another hour or so sleep, OK?'

BO hesitated for a moment. 'Sure,' he said, nodding and swivelling in his seat and then muttering. 'Only trying to be friendly. Some people.'

Yeah, thought Kendwick. Some fucking people.

Savage was pissed off. They'd got up and breakfasted in good time so as to arrive at the airport by nine as planned. However, as they'd parked the car she'd phoned her contact in the NCA, DCI Kevin Rollins. He told her Kendwick had taken a different flight.

'United 901,' Rollins said. 'Direct from San Francisco instead of via LAX. Landed a little after seven o'clock. We're all done and dusted and your man's just waiting to be picked up. We'll bring him round to the VIP arrivals lounge.'

Rollins hung up before Savage could say anything.

'Ma'am?' Riley read the displeasure on her face. 'Everything all right?'

'No it bloody isn't.' Savage slipped the phone into her pocket. She explained to Riley what had happened. 'The NCA are playing games with us. They knew we'd stayed over and must have known Kendwick was on an earlier flight. Rollins thinks we're no better than a taxi service.'

Fifteen minutes later and they were striding across the near-empty VIP lounge. In one corner, two men in suits and a third in a Coldplay T-shirt sat at a low table. Savage recognised the man in the T-shirt as Kendwick. Early thirties, with a muscular, well-defined torso. Long black hair tied in a ponytail, the hair with a sheen like something from a men's toiletries commercial. As he laughed at a joke one of the men had made, his lips parted to show perfect teeth. American teeth. He was good-looking, for sure. Quite a charmer.

As they approached, one of the men in suits turned and then stood.

'DI Savage?' he said. 'DCI Kevin Rollins. Sorry about the mix-up with the flights. No harm done and all that, hey?'

Rollins was at least a decade or so older than Kendwick and a bit flabby round the edges. A bald patch poked from greying hair. By his swagger he plainly fancied himself, but alongside the younger man he was nothing.

Kendwick didn't bother to get up. Savage could see he was well aware the handful of passengers in the lounge were looking their way and assuming he was some kind of star, the two men in the cheap suits his bodyguards.

'Ah, my chauffeur,' he said. 'Or should I say, chaperone? Someone to stop me getting into trouble, right?'

'Detective Inspector Charlotte Savage,' Savage said. She held out her hand and Kendwick reached up and took it, his palm cold and dry. 'If you've finished your business with DCI Rollins then we may as well get going. It's a long journey.'

'I like the way you said that, Charlotte,' Kendwick said. He paused and held her gaze for several seconds before smiling. 'My business with them, rather than the other way round. Gets us off on the right foot. Gets me off, anyway.'

'Your bags?' Savage withdrew her hand and pointed at a nearby trolley laden with several cases and a rucksack. Kendwick nodded. 'Darius, would you?'

As Riley went across to the trolley, Savage thought about saying something to Rollins. Something about his behaviour being bang out of order. But she didn't want a confrontation in front of Kendwick and it was better he thought they all

28

sang from the same hymn sheet. Besides, Rollins was a rank above her.

'Been nice meeting you, Mr Rollins, Sergeant.' Kendwick grinned as he stood. 'We must do it again sometime, but not too soon, hey?'

'Remember what I said, Kendwick,' Rollins said. He put his arm out, blocking Kendwick's way. 'A single piece of evidence from the States and you'll be going back there. And when you do, they'll kill you.'

'Now, now, Kevin, that's not very nice.' Kendwick pushed the arm down. 'Besides, they don't kill people in California any more. The death penalty is out of fashion and they haven't carried out an execution since 2006. Something to do with the Eighth Amendment. Cruel and unusual punishment. That's irony for you, huh?'

'One of the girls was snatched from over the border in Arizona. They *do* still carry out executions.'

'Well, that might worry me if I was guilty, but we've just had a long conversation where I told you I'm innocent, so let's leave it be, shall we? No hard feelings.' Kendwick grinned again and then winked. 'Mate.'

As they walked away, Riley following with the trolley, Kendwick cocked his head towards Savage. She could smell mint on his breath as he spoke.

'He's jealous, Charlotte,' Kendwick whispered. 'And I don't blame him. On every count he's a loser. Compare LA to London; the NCA to the FBI; me to him. His fat, frumpy wife to the sweet California girls I've been with. He's a lot to be jealous about, don't you think?'

Savage tried not to smile, but the man did have a certain charisma and the way he'd dissed Rollins amused her. Still, she wasn't about to be taken in by Kendwick's charm because that's what made him dangerous. *If* he was dangerous.

Out front, Enders had pulled the car into the pickup area and Riley loaded the luggage into the boot, while Savage and Kendwick got in the rear. She wasn't exactly keen to spend several hours sitting next to somebody suspected of having killed multiple times, but she was the senior officer and she didn't expect Riley to do the dirty work for her.

'Cosy,' Kendwick said once they were all seated. 'Just the four of us on a little trip to the countryside.'

Enders huffed from behind the wheel. He had already made it clear that in his opinion the best option would be to drive to a quiet lane somewhere and put a bullet in the back of Kendwick's head. The DC flicked the indicator and pulled out into the traffic. Kendwick peered through the window.

'Grim. After California, at least.'

'Paradise over there was it, Mr Kendwick?' Savage said.

'Oh yes. Very much so.' He swivelled round to face Savage. 'Still, I'm very much looking forward to returning to Devon. My roots. Where the bones of my ancestors are buried. There's something about feeling connected to a place, don't you think? The US was exciting, vibrant, but I never felt truly at home there. It's a dangerous place too. Not like where we're heading. Cream teas. Watercolour pictures of little harbours. Dartmoor ponies. I bet you three don't have to do much more than hand out speeding tickets for tractors, do you?'

'I think you're over-romanticising.'

'Perhaps I am. But there's nothing wrong with a touch of romance, is there, Charlotte?'

Kendwick smiled at her, his teeth shining. For a moment, Savage saw the attraction some women might feel for the perfect specimen before her. Fit and good-looking, intelligent, humorous, successful in his career. This was a man whose persona could well fool the gullible, the easily led, the young . . . and they'd been young, hadn't they? The victims. Whether they'd been Kendwick's victims or the prey of another man, she didn't know.

Within minutes they'd escaped the confines of the airport and were heading west on the motorway. Kendwick turned back to the window and resumed his analysis of his long-lost homeland.

'Sad,' he said, gesturing out of the window. 'All these people living with this around them. Hemmed in. There's more space in America. At least where I was. More space to be yourself. I guess that's why I chose to come back to Devon rather than get a job up here in London. At least there's enough air to go around. A bit of wilderness to escape to. The sea. The moor. Doesn't compare with the Sierra National Forest, of course. That was a real wilderness, a dangerous wilderness. Get lost out there and nobody is ever going to find you. Makes Dartmoor look like your back garden.'

'I thought they did find them?'

'The bodies? Yes.' Kendwick nodded but continued to stare at the world rushing by. 'But it was like finding a needle in a haystack. Sheer chance.'

'I see.'

Now Kendwick did look back at Savage. 'And when they did find them, most were so badly chewed up by wild animals or so decayed that they didn't discover anything useful. No forensic evidence which could link the killer to the crime scenes.'

Savage took a deep breath. They had three hours or so but now was as good a time as any.

'Mr Kendwick, let's not play any more silly games. I don't know whether you did or didn't kill those girls. If you did then I'm with Rollins. I hope they find some evidence and extradite you. And not to California. Arizona would be my choice too, understand?'

'I'm hurt.' Kendwick made a sad face. Reached up with his hands and made his mouth droop like a clown's. 'We were getting along so nicely. Now you've ruined everything. Still, don't worry about it. You see, even if I *was* guilty, there's no way the nice legal system here would allow my extradition to the States. Not with execution on the cards. The European Convention on Human Rights wouldn't allow it. They don't bother with that sort of thing in America of course. Human rights. From the way you're talking, you might be a wee bit happier living over there.'

'I just want you to know where I'm coming from, Mr Kendwick. I can't abide deliberate cruelty and what happened to those girls was beyond cruel.'

'Like I told Rollins, I didn't kill them. Janey Horton, she set me up. What she did to me was way out of order, *beyond cruel*, if you want to put it that way. I'm the person whose human rights were violated.'

'Or not.' Enders. From up front. His hands clenching the wheel as he stared at the road ahead. 'If you did kill those girls, then kudos to the lady cop.'

Savage cursed. This wasn't the way she wanted to play things. The whole point of the journey was so they could have a quiet word with Kendwick, not get into some sort of slanging match.

'That's enough, Patrick. Concentrate on your driving.'

'Yes, ma'am.'

'If we could just start over, Mr Kendwick. Devon and—'

'Malcolm.' Kendwick smiled. Those teeth again. 'I've got a feeling we're going to be seeing quite a lot of one another so we might as well keep this friendly, don't you think?'

'OK, Malcolm,' Savage said. 'As I was saying, Devon and

Cornwall Police are agnostic on whether you committed those crimes in the US. However, we have a duty to protect those we serve. That duty extends to considering all the possibilities and putting plans into place to contend with every eventuality. To put it another way, should you even drop a piece of litter or park your car on a double yellow line, we'll be onto you.'

'Well, Charlotte, it's good of you to be honest with me. I like that. Honesty in a relationship. And I hope we're going to *have* a relationship.'

'Now, there's a way round this.' Savage ignored the way Kendwick was attempting to flirt with her. 'My boss has a proposal. If you consent to wearing an electronic tagging device then the need to keep an eye on you would vanish. You'd be able to go about your day-to-day life without scrutiny, without even a suspicion the police were harassing you. How would you feel about that?'

Kendwick laughed but then shook his head. 'I wouldn't feel good about it at all. It would be, how can I put this, a *fucking* imposition. What's more, by letting you tag me I'd be admitting there was something for you to be worried about. Highlighting my guilt. I don't think my legal team in the US would be very keen for me to do that, do you?'

Kendwick's mood had darkened. The laugh had been ironic and the smile which had followed quickly turned to a grimace. Now he glared at Savage, his pupils like pinheads, a tiny red vein in the sclera of his left eye pulsing fast in time with his heartbeat.

The jokes earlier about capital punishment, the joshing and word play over whether he'd killed the girls, hadn't touched him. This, though, had caused him to anger and, she realised, it wasn't to do with civil liberties or any legal niceties. It was because if Kendwick had to wear a tag the police would be able to track his every move. He'd be free to go about his daily life, but he wouldn't be free to do what he really wanted to do.

She held Kendwick's gaze for several seconds but then had to turn away and stare through the window at the traffic. His eyes had told her everything she needed to know. Malcolm Kendwick was one of the most dangerous men she'd ever had the misfortune of meeting.

Chapter Three

From Reading onward, Kendwick dozed. At some point, he jerked awake, disorientated, muttering a string of obscenities. He apologised. Jet lag, he explained, before slumping over and resting his head against the window.

In the front, Riley and Enders chatted in low whispers, but Savage found it impossible to follow the conversation enough to be able to join in. Instead, she tried to rest herself. An hour or so later, Kendwick woke and wanted to stop.

'A comfort break,' he said. 'I could do with something to drink too.'

A few miles farther along the motorway, just beyond Bristol, Enders took the slip road to Gordano services and parked up a little way from the main building.

'I'd forgotten how grim these places were,' Kendwick said, as he climbed out of the car. 'Piss-and-shit stops, overpriced confectionery and crap coffee, right?'

'The coffee's got marginally better, but everything else is just how you left it.'

'Let's hope the same applies back in Devon.' Kendwick smiled and then strolled off towards the building.

35

'Do you want me to go after him, ma'am?' Enders said. 'Check he doesn't get up to no good?'

'No. He's not under arrest. Let him go to the toilet in peace. If bodies start turning up in the next half-hour then we'll know who did it.'

Savage walked across to several picnic tables which sat on a patch of grass to one side of the car park. Riley remained to talk to Enders and then, after a moment or two, joined her.

'I've sent Patrick for some coffees,' Riley said. 'Reckon we could all do with a pick-me-up.'

'Thanks.' Savage moved to one of the tables and sat down. She nodded at Riley to sit too. It was the first time they'd been able to talk since they'd picked Kendwick up. 'What do you think of our passenger?'

'He's a cool one, for sure.' Riley gazed towards the main entrance of the service station. Kendwick had just pushed in through the doors and disappeared from view. 'All the joking and the double entendres. Would he really act like that if he'd killed those women?'

'I think his behaviour is very carefully calculated. It's a double bluff. Or even a double double bluff. He knows that we know that he knows that we know.' Savage paused. 'What about Kendwick as a man, as a person?'

'Tosser.' Riley smiled. 'But then us blokes are pretty shallow when judging each other.'

'What do you mean?'

'It's about the competition for a mate, isn't it? Kendwick's got all the attributes: good-looking, intelligent, talkative, well-off. Lesser mortals, such as myself and DC Enders, feel threatened.'

'Don't put yourself down, Darius.' Savage smiled back at Riley. 'Women would be better off with you than Kendwick.'

'They *would* be, yes, but that's not how the female mind works. Ask yourself why so many women end up with unsuitable characters? We see it every day at work, the scrotes with a cute girl in tow, ready to do the scum's bidding. There are plenty of nice guys out there, but a lot of women seem to be programmed to go for the arseholes.'

'Perhaps you're wrong about the number of nice guys. Perhaps there aren't enough to go round and the reality is that most blokes *are* arseholes.'

'Thanks.' Riley looked wounded. 'But back to Kendwick. He believes his charm will win out and he doesn't seem to care what we think.'

'Because he's home free.' Savage turned her head to where a soft-top BMW Z3 had slipped into a parking bay. Two young women climbed out. 'As long as he keeps his hands to himself, he's in no danger. He's already laughed in the face of the US justice system so they won't extradite him now, not without new evidence.'

'And *can* he keep his hands to himself?' Riley pointed discreetly at the women as they walked away. 'I mean, he's been inside for the past twelve months and now he's going to encounter temptation daily.'

'Recidivism is pretty much hard coded into people like Kendwick. If he *is* guilty, if he *is* a serial killer, then he's going to commit another murder. More than one if he gets the chance.'

'So we've got to stop him, is that Hardin's idea?'

'Probably. I think he planned this trip around some nebulous idea that everything would come good in the journey from Heathrow to Devon. He thinks I've got a handle on how men like Kendwick work.'

'You have, haven't you, ma'am?'

'Perhaps.' Savage nodded but didn't say anything more.

Hardin's trust in her was a last-ditch percentage play, the best card in a bad hand. The only option he had remaining. Picking Kendwick up and ferrying him back to Devon was more about Devon and Cornwall Police being seen to do something. Anything.

A few minutes later, Enders appeared with three cups of coffee stuck in a cardboard tray.

'You didn't get one for matey boy, then?' Riley said.

'No I fucking didn't,' Enders said. 'Besides, he's happy as Larry in there, playing the slot machines.'

They sat in silence for a few minutes, drinking their coffees. As Savage drained the last dregs from her paper cup, Kendwick emerged from the services, a small bottle of Coke in one hand. He paused at the entrance, glancing at an attractive woman as she walked past him, before strolling over.

'Made any money?' Riley said.

'Not a cent – or should I say penny.' Kendwick shrugged his shoulders. 'But that wasn't the point. I was watching other people play. Trying to understand the motivation behind their actions. I must say I don't get it.'

'What don't you get?'

'The attraction of gambling.' Kendwick took a sip from his bottle and turned his head back towards the service station. 'Why do something which has failure built in?'

Savage turned away as Kendwick began to expound his theory on human nature to Riley. People, he said, turned to fantasies rather than pursue reality. The lottery was a case in point. A one in God-knows-how-many-million chance but you hang your dreams on that. Kendwick said he didn't understand.

'It's the only hope some people have,' Riley said. 'Better that than nothing, surely?'

'Nonsense. Opium for the masses, isn't it? Fantasise about winning the lottery or becoming a YouTube sensation or appearing on some reality TV programme. They should try taking control of their lives instead of being pushed around by others. Make it real. Go out and get what you want. That's what I did.'

'Let's go,' Savage said, moving back to the car and opening the rear door. She'd had enough of Kendwick's fatuous moralising. 'We've still got at least an hour and a half left and I'd really like to get home in time for dinner.'

'Me too!' Kendwick beamed across at Savage. 'What's on offer?'

Savage didn't respond. Instead she ducked into the car. Moments later they were driving off and she settled back into her seat. Not too long now, she thought. They'd leave the motorway at Exeter and head up onto the moor. Chagford was a little town on the eastern edge. They'd see Kendwick into his house and then be done with him.

Stop-start traffic around Weston-super-Mare and an RTC which blocked the motorway just past Taunton saw them delayed by some ninety minutes, so it wasn't until after three o'clock that they took a winding road out onto the moor. As the countryside became wilder, Kendwick's interest was piqued. He stared out at the stone walls surrounding the little fields, at the distant tors standing guard over the landscape.

'Quaint, this,' he said.

'As DC Enders can tell you, the moor can be far from quaint in the wrong weather. There are areas of pure wilderness up there, right, Patrick?'

'Yes.' Enders gripped the steering wheel and stared ahead, apparently unwilling to elaborate further.

'I know the moor from my childhood and it's hardly a

wilderness.' Kendwick tapped the window. 'What is it, a hundred square miles, two? The Sierra National Forest is ten times the size and you've got Yosemite and Kings Canyon National Parks right next door. Real wild country, not this cream-tea countryside.'

'And that's where the killer took them, is it?' Savage said. 'Out in the wilds?'

'The girls?' Kendwick turned back from the window and met her gaze. He didn't blink. 'That's what they say. But to be honest, I've no idea, Charlotte. They found the bodies, but who can tell how they died or who killed them?'

Savage looked away. Kendwick's eyes were beguiling, but not in a good way. Serial killers were supposed to be sociopaths, unable to discern or empathise with other people, but Kendwick seemed to see right inside her. She sensed he might be able to unearth her vulnerabilities and use them against her. She couldn't allow that to happen.

They continued the journey in silence, eventually descending a twisty road and then climbing out of a valley and into the small town of Chagford. The place wasn't much more than a handful of roads meeting at a square. A few tourists shuffled along the streets, heading for the pubs and restaurants, but otherwise the place was quiet. Kendwick said something about stopping and having a late lunch or early dinner; his treat, he insisted.

'No,' Savage said. 'Not today.'

Kendwick nodded. 'Next time then?'

No one said anything until Enders spoke.

'Here,' he said, pulling into a parking space in front of a short terrace on the edge of town. 'And about bloody time too.'

Kendwick's house was the one on the end. A little two-up and two-down cottage with a long strip of back garden which bordered open fields. Beyond the fields, the moor rolled into the distance beneath a bank of dark cloud.

'Well,' Kendwick said. 'Despite what I said earlier, the view is certainly better than the one from the Fresno County Jail.'

They piled out of the car and Riley and Enders sprang the boot and retrieved Kendwick's luggage. Savage went to the front door with Kendwick. She pulled out a set of keys Hardin had given her and unlocked the door. Kendwick pushed it open and stepped in, crouching to avoid banging his head on the low beams. There was no hallway, the door opened straight into the living room. A narrow open staircase led up one side of the room, while to the back, an arch divided the living room from the kitchen area. Two rather tired armchairs and a sofa clustered round a fireplace. A pile of magazines sat on a low table in the centre of the room. Atop the magazines lay a chunky key fob, a local car rental company's name emblazoned over some paperwork beneath.

'Looks like your sister's thought of everything,' Savage said. 'Transport and a place to stay. You're lucky to have her to look out for you. She must be giving up a small fortune by letting you stay here.'

'It might surprise you to know I'm quite popular in some circles.' Kendwick strolled in. He stared down at the brown carpet. 'But I'll have to have words with sis about the state of the place.'

Behind her, Enders and Riley clumped the bags down just inside the front door. Riley went upstairs and a minute or so later came back down.

'Everything's fine,' he said. 'Two bedrooms and micro bathroom. Regular cosy.'

Kendwick wandered through to the kitchen and popped the fridge open.

'Sweet,' he said, reappearing with a bottle of white wine in one hand. 'If I can just find a corkscrew we can have a moving-in drink. You guys take a seat while I fetch some glasses.'

'I don't think so, Malcolm.' Savage tapped Riley on the shoulder and pointed outside. 'We've got better things to do. I can just about stomach being a taxi service, but I draw the line at socialising.'

'Shame.' Kendwick frowned and then cocked his head on one side. 'We'll meet again though, won't we? You and I?'

'I'm sure we will.' Savage followed Riley and Enders through the door. 'Try to be good, Mr Kendwick.'

'Oh, I intend to.' Kendwick grinned. 'Very good.'

He peered out of the tiny window and watched as they drove off. The black guy, the annoying Irish git and the woman. Yes, the woman. Kendwick considered her for a moment. She was . . . *interesting*. Too old though. Not really his type. Still, he wouldn't say no if he got the chance.

He turned to where his luggage stood in a heap. A flight bag, two Samsonite cases and a rucksack. He had a few books and some other oddments coming by freight but, aside from them, this was the sum of his ten years in the United States. Almost everything he valued was here.

What a waste. And all down to that bitch cop, Janey Horton. Kendwick shook his head. No good going over everything again. What was done was done.

He reached for a carrier bag which contained a litre of duty free rum. He still had most of the bottle of Coke he'd bought at the services so he took that and the rum into the kitchen, found a glass, and mixed himself a large drink.

Back in the living room he slumped down in one of

the armchairs and sipped from the glass. His eyes were drawn to a map of Devon which hung above the mantelpiece. He found himself shaking his head once more. Strange to be back here. Where he'd grown up. Where it had all started.

He'd been born in an anonymous suburb of Torquay to what, from a casual glance, must have seemed loving parents. In reality their relationship to him was always somewhat distant. Later in life, Kendwick put that down to him being an accident, a conclusion he drew from the fact that his siblings were over ten years older than him. He was an afterthought and the young Kendwick had got in the way of his parents' lifestyle. As he grew up, he often found himself offloaded onto various relatives as they went about their lives or took long holidays. Inevitably, when he asked, he was fobbed off with excuses: 'You can't ski well enough, darling.' 'It would be much too hot for you, Malc. You know how you hate the heat.' 'We'll be gone for four weeks and that would mean missing school. Best not, hey, love? Maybe next year.'

Kendwick compensated for his parents' behaviour by acting with a nonchalance intended to show an exterior face vastly different to the turmoil he felt within. He craved love, but didn't know how to ask for it. The various relatives he stayed with thought him grown-up for his age, but he was an emotional retard, the sociopathic tendencies misread for maturity. He never cried, never seemed to anger or throw tantrums like other children did.

Mostly, when his parents went off on their jaunts, he stayed with his uncle. His uncle lived on Dartmoor and Kendwick credited that fact as nurturing his love of wild spaces. Out on the moor you had to be self-reliant. Alone with nothing but the wind for company, your thoughts turned inward. He found when he was on the moor he became overly reflective, trying to find a reason for everything, trying to understand life and the cards he'd been dealt.

As Kendwick entered his teenage years, his parents began to realise their son wasn't like other boys. While adolescence had made his classmates go crazy, their bodies overladen with hormones, their minds stuffed with nonsense, Kendwick had passed the time more interested in chasing grades than chasing skirt. He didn't appear to care a thing for anyone. He went for long walks on his own, disappearing for hours at a time. Yet he never stayed out late, never went to parties, never got even slightly tipsy.

But then he began to adorn his bedroom with gothic imagery. Vampires and graveyards. Girls in black PVC dresses swooning in the moonlight, breasts full and white, tears of blood weeping from their eyes. Mist rising around some forsaken tor, another girl draped over the granite with her head arched back.

His parents shook their heads, but at least this new behaviour was nothing out of the ordinary. Secretly they were glad about the girls appearing on the walls of his bedroom. The girls showed he wasn't . . . wasn't . . . well, they showed he was *normal.*

However, even back then, Kendwick had known he was far, far from normal and had his parents bothered to pay a little attention, they might have been a good deal more concerned.

He took another sip of his drink and then contemplated the glass for a moment. He knocked back the rest in one gulp and then stood. Time to unpack his life from his bags. Time to think about what the future might hold.

* * *

'Thank fuck for that,' Enders said as he steered the car through the narrow streets of Chagford. 'Another minute in the company of Malcolm slimeball Kendwick and I'd have been committing murder myself. It's only a shame he managed to get out of the US.'

'You'd have liked him to face execution?' Riley said. 'With all the problems capital punishment brings?'

'Such as?'

'Miscarriages of justice for one. The fear of living on death row for years and years for another.'

'Fear?' Enders took his eyes off the road for several seconds and stared across at Riley. 'I don't think Kendwick bothered much about the fear his victims felt. He took them up into the mountains and did God-knows-what to them before killing them. If you want my view, a lethal injection would be letting him off lightly. I'd shave Kendwick's head, plug old Sparky in and send a good jolt of electricity through him.'

'Ma'am?' Riley half turned to look into the rear of the car. 'What's your opinion?'

'You don't want to know, Darius.' Savage stared out at the moorland now flashing past. 'My answer might offend your delicate London sensibilities. But I don't think what you said about miscarriage of justice applies to Kendwick. He killed those girls, I know he did.'

'You can't convict somebody on a hunch, ma'am. You need evidence.'

'And Janey Horton found that evidence.'

'As I understand US law, it wasn't admissible. First, part was extracted by torture, second, Horton didn't have probable cause to search Kendwick's car. The rape kit she found could never be introduced at a trial. The hairband discovered in his apartment was circumstantial, and again, problems

45

with probable cause to search. Anyway, aside from those issues, I don't believe the threat of the death penalty is a deterrent.'

Savage shook her head. She wasn't going to get into an argument with Riley. She liked him, but his views on criminal justice were way too liberal for her. The law wasn't something which should be inked down on a page leaving clauses which offered get-out-of-jail cards to the guilty. People had suffered at Kendwick's hands. Real people. Young women and their families. Lives had been changed, people emotionally scarred for life. If executing Kendwick could make things better for them in some small way then she was all for it. Deterrent or not.

'Passed a polygraph test too, didn't he?' Riley wasn't giving up. 'Too much doubt in my mind. There are no second chances with the death penalty.'

What Riley said about the lie detector test was factually true, but Savage wasn't convinced. Kendwick, as they had seen in the few hours they'd spent with him, was a manipulator. She wouldn't put it past him to have somehow managed to skew the results of the test.

The rest of the journey passed in near silence. When they arrived at the station Enders parked up and the three of them got out.

'Thanks, Darius, Patrick,' Savage said. 'Good work.'

'No problem, ma'am,' Enders said. 'Nice bit of overtime. See you tomorrow.'

Enders strolled off to his car leaving Savage with Riley. There was an uncomfortable silence for a moment.

'I don't disagree with you, ma'am,' Riley said. 'About Kendwick. He's a nasty piece of work and he may well have killed those women. However, the law says he's innocent. As police officers we have to respect that or else we're lost.'

'Are we?' Savage said. 'What about my daughter? We only got to the truth behind Clarissa's death by going outside the law.'

'That was different.'

'Really? Because it was personal?' Savage stared at Riley for a few moments. 'It was personal for Janey Horton too. If she hadn't done what she'd done to Kendwick, those girls would have lain up in the woods undiscovered. Kendwick would have gone on killing, gone on causing more misery.'

'I realise that but what she did was wrong.'

'Was it?' Savage turned to go to her car. 'Goodnight, Sergeant.'

'Charlotte?' Riley shouted after her. Savage turned back. 'Be careful, right?'

'Always, Darius, always.'

With that she walked across to her own car, aware Riley was standing and watching her go.

Savage drove home thinking about Riley's arguments. They didn't add up. He'd been willing to cross the line when he'd tracked down the lad who'd killed her daughter in a hit-and-run accident. He'd teamed up with a local gangster by the name of Kenny Fallon. The pair of them had gone out of their way to bring the name of the driver of the car to her attention, Fallon even supplying her with a gun to exact her revenge. Now though, Riley appeared to be on the side of Kendwick, even though it was obvious to Savage the man was guilty. Was Riley holding up his liberal credentials as a measure of what a nice guy he was? He should have known her well enough to realise that wouldn't wash. When it came to criminal justice, Savage didn't do liberal values. Certainly not when they related to men like Malcolm Kendwick.

She pulled into her driveway at a little after five. Jamie, Pete explained when she came in, was already in bed.

'I said you'd definitely be back before he went to sleep,' Pete said. He scratched his head. 'So, being logical, the little man decided to get in his jimjams straight after lunch to hasten your arrival. He's been tucked up in bed for the past hour.'

Savage went upstairs and popped her head round her son's bedroom door. Jamie was lying on the bed with his eyes open, staring at the ceiling. He turned his head towards Savage, an expression of delight spreading on his face.

'Mummy!' He leapt out of bed and scampered across to Savage, throwing his arms round her. She felt a rush of love as she knelt down and hugged her son, a feeling of guilt too; an empty void inside, as if missing a day and a half of his life was something which could never be filled. 'Did you catch any bad guys in London?'

'Not this time, darling,' Savage said. Jamie looked disappointed that there was no story to be had, so she told him about going to the VIP lounge at Heathrow and meeting officers from the NCA. Then she gave him another hug. 'Are you coming downstairs or are you going to stay up here for a bit?'

'Stay up here.' Jamie moved across the room to a low table where a host of Playmobil figures stood near a toy police car. An arrest was in progress, officers with guns drawn, two suspects already in handcuffs. 'These baddies need locking up.'

'OK, I'll call you when tea's ready.'

Downstairs she confessed her feelings of guilt to Pete. He was sanguine about the situation.

'You missed him, he missed you. Nothing wrong with that, is there?'

'No, I guess not.'

'Anyway, by tomorrow he'll have forgotten you've been away.' Pete gestured to the bar of chocolate and the copy of the *Beano* lying on the kitchen table. Savage had bought them on the journey up to London. 'And when he sees those he'll forgive you, no doubt. Not that he hasn't had enough chocolate today already, what with his Easter eggs and all.'

'They're not supposed to be bribes or compensation. Simply a gift.'

'And not the only gift you've brought us either, I see.'

'Hey?'

'The *Herald* have splashed news of your celebrity passenger all over their website. They're running an exclusive in the paper tomorrow. Malcolm Kendwick, Devon's most infamous son, returns. They're hinting at all sorts of things he might have done in America. I assume they've got legal advice but the story looks awfully close to libel to me.' Pete paused and then grinned. 'Oh, and there's even a photo of you and Kendwick at the airport and a small piece on your track record of catching serial killers.'

'Christ.'

'You didn't expect this? I thought the police were supposed to be media savvy these days. Old Conrad Hardin has surely gone on more than one PR training day. He should have made preparations for the public outcry.'

Savage sighed and then shrugged, too tired to continue the conversation. She went upstairs and took a long shower. Sitting in the back of the car for several hours with Kendwick had made her feel soiled. An uncomfortable crawling sensation itched across her skin. She stood under the jets of water and foamed her body with soap until she was sure every trace of Kendwick had gone. She couldn't cleanse her thoughts though and later, as she lay in bed beside Pete,

Kendwick's face kept creeping into her mind. The smile and his mint-fresh breath, those perfect teeth grinning at her. White like the bones of his victims which had lain scattered in the wilderness, bleaching under a hot Californian sun.

Chapter Four

He's driven out onto the moor so he can be alone in the darkness. Experience the isolation of the wild country. Perhaps find a solution to his problem.

The problem is that things are wrong. He thought the return would change things, make him see the issues in a different light. Starting over didn't mean having to go back to the way things were, did it? Surely it was possible to move on from the past?

He parks the car in the middle of nowhere and climbs out. He sets off along a stony track. The night excites him. He enjoys the coolness of the air, the peaty odour which emanates from the ancient bogs, the wind caressing his face. Nothing moving. Not another living human within miles.

Only the dead.

The dead, yes. They're not far away. A short walk along the track. The coolness. The peaty odour. The wind. Nothing moving. Not a soul. Nobody but the dead.

But the dead are the problem!

They won't keep quiet. They keep talking to him. Calling his name. He mutters to himself as he walks along, trying to drown out their voices.

The track is a grey thread curling into the distance as the route follows a contour line round the side of a hill and then *forges across a flat plain. He pads along, noting the bogs either side of the track, the smell of the marsh gas like decomposing flesh, the pools of water like mirrors, reflecting a sombre sky where the moon plays hide and seek with the clouds.*

In the distance a glow hugs the horizon almost as if the sun is about to rise. But the glow doesn't belong to the sun, the light comes from the city where people bustle back and forth living their insignificant lives. He thinks about the thousands of morons sitting in their living rooms, their eyes glued to a rectangular screen with flickering pixels, absorbing the drivel pumped out for them to lap up. Others are clustered in pubs and bars, talking rubbish to friends, to colleagues, to any fucking idiot who will listen. And then there are those who interest him. Not the morons stuck in front of their televisions. Not the wasters out on the piss. The others. The quiet ones. Demure and lying still in their beds. Hands by their sides, legs together, eyes tightly shut. Almost as if they were dead.

He knows he's not right in the head. Who walks the moorland after dark? Who stalks graveyards, delighting in the quietness of the stones, aroused by the presence of those who have passed beyond the physical? Nobody normal, that's for sure.

Fuck it!

He clenches his fists in anger for a moment but then relaxes. He's close now. Close to where he can get relief. Close to where they lie waiting for him. Where they've lain for all these years. He walks on and arrives at the gate. He pulls a key from his pocket and fits it into the padlock. Unlocks it and removes the heavy chain. He pushes the gate open and slips through. Shadows loom like welcoming friends. They're here. All around him. He steps up to where a silver lake glistens in the moonlight. He begins to undress, stripping off his clothes until he stands naked. He bends to the water and takes a handful. He splashes the cool liquid on his chest, the chill shocking him, exciting him. And then he thinks of the girls. His girls. His heart beats faster and his breath rushes in and out. Yes, he cries in the dark. Yes! Yes! Yes!

He stands there, spent. His breathing slows, his heart calms and now he is disgusted with himself. Disgusted it took such a fetish to turn him on. He shakes his head. What's done is done. He reaches for his clothes and dresses hurriedly. He tries to reconcile what has happened. What harm is there in it? None. Not this time. But tomorrow? Next week? Next month?

He plods down to the gate, goes through and refastens the chain. The harm is safely in his head, he thinks. His darkest thoughts nothing but swirls in his imagination. Soon, however, he knows the desire will build to a level where he can no longer be satiated by mere fantasy. He needs the exquisite feeling of flesh against his naked body. Flesh which is soft and cool and quite, quite dead.

Chapter Five

Back at work, Savage tried to forget about Malcolm Kendwick. Hardin had arranged for a twenty-four-seven surveillance on the man, but she wasn't involved. Other than that she was aware there'd been an incident in Chagford involving a reporter and a smashed camera and had seen a lurid head-line in one of the tabloids. Thankfully, in the week that followed, more pressing matters arose to distract her, including a woman who'd fallen from the eighth floor of a block of flats in Devonport. Suspicion was pointing to her boyfriend, 'a right scrote,' according to DC Enders who'd had dealings with the guy. Savage was reminded of her conversation with Riley about men being arseholes. They certainly weren't all arseholes but Plymouth seemed to have more than its fair share of them.

On Friday, five days after Kendwick had arrived in Devon, DSupt Hardin summoned Savage to his office. He told her he was axing the surveillance op, citing manpower and budgetary constraints.

'Nothing I can do about it, Charlotte,' he said. 'Besides, we can't keep watching him indefinitely. At least the bugger

54

will have got an idea of how serious we are about keeping tabs.'

'Yes, sir,' Savage said. 'But he's done nothing and gone nowhere, right?'

'Hmmm.' Hardin stared down at a log sheet detailing Kendwick's movements. 'Yesterday he went to the local shop, then to the pub for lunch, took a short walk, went back home, visited the pub again in the evening, went to bed. Not much of a life. He's got a rental car, but doesn't appear to have gone anywhere in it aside from a couple of jaunts on the moor.'

'If you ask me he's playing a game with us. He knows we're watching him.'

'Which was my intention. From now on he'll be looking over his shoulder, wondering if we're there.'

No, Savage thought. Kendwick was too canny for that. He'd be well aware the surveillance had stopped. He'd only let himself be followed so closely because he had nothing to lose. Now they were no longer keeping an eye on him he could come and go as he pleased.

'So that's it then? We're done with him?'

'Not quite.' Hardin picked up the log sheet and flicked the surface with a finger. 'I want you to pay Mr Kendwick a visit. Give him a bit of a talking to. Perhaps you can warn him off, maybe even scare him away. If he upped sticks and moved to another area it would be a weight off our backs.'

'And what am I supposed to say to him?' Savage sighed, exasperated. She'd spent five hours stuck in a car with Kendwick and wasn't sure what another hour's conversation would accomplish. 'Please bugger off?'

'I don't know, Charlotte. You're the one with the inter-personal skills. Be his friend. Tell him Devon's no place for him. If he doesn't buy that then make it clear we're going to catch up with him eventually. He'll get the message, I'm sure he will.'

Savage took an early lunch and then drove north from Plymouth. At Yelverton she headed up onto the moor, following the twisting road to the town of Princetown. A strong sun beamed down, flattening the landscape and obliterating the shadows. The tors stood a uniform grey, almost formless in the harsh light, their dark foreboding temporarily banished.

She drove across the moor and arrived at Kendwick's place in Chagford at a little after two o'clock. A knock on the front door of the cottage brought no response, so she moved to a window and peered in. She could see through the open plan living area to the kitchen where the back door stood open. She turned and walked along the street and went down a passage which led to the rear of the terrace. A path bisected the long, narrow gardens. Kendwick's was the one at the end and she found him lying in a teak reclining chair next to a small table. He wore a pair of shorts and a light shirt and a jug of something resembling Pimm's sat on the table beside a half-empty glass. He hadn't tied his hair up and his black mane cascaded across the back of the chair. Kendwick held a book in his hands. He closed the book as Savage approached.

'Charlotte!' Kendwick pushed himself up from the chair and stuck out his hand. 'How nice of you to visit!'

'Hello, Mr Kendwick,' Savage said. She shook hands, once again noticing how dry and cool the man's palm was. 'Just a courtesy visit.'

'Courtesy? Well that makes a nice change from the cops in the US. Manners are something which don't seem to have been invented over there. They're likely to pull a gun and cuff you just to tell you your stop light isn't working.' Kendwick nodded at the jug on the table. 'Can I get you a drink?'

Savage shook her head. 'Cut the false bonhomie, Mr Kendwick. I'm here to warn you that although we're stopping the surveillance you're not off the hook. One false move, one foot over the line, and we'll be onto you.'

'Not so much a courtesy visit then, more of a threatening one?'

'Stay on the straight and narrow and you've got nothing to worry about.'

'I assume it's the same for every citizen.' Kendwick eased himself back down into his chair and gestured at another recliner. He pulled a hairband from his pocket and tied up his hair. 'I'd hate to think I was being treated any differently.'

Savage moved over and sat down, perching on the edge of the seat. 'You've got history, Mr Kendwick.'

'Can we drop the "Mr Kendwick" tag please? We managed to be civil on the journey back from the airport. I'd like to think we can again.'

'Sure, no problem.'

'As to my history, that's a matter of conjecture. History isn't immutable, is it? Differing viewpoints tell differing stories. My story is I'm innocent of all the charges against me. I didn't kill anyone in the US. I'm pretty sure the US justice system sees it that way too, otherwise I'd still be over there.'

'So how do you explain your confession to Janey Horton?'

'It wasn't a confession.' Kendwick scowled at Savage. 'The bitch tortured me so I made stuff up to feed to her. If I hadn't she'd have killed me. The confession was pure fiction. I just blurted out the names of the girls I'd read about in the papers or seen on the news.'

'But your fiction happened to match fact. How come Horton was able to find a body from your directions?'

'The irony was the body wasn't her daughter.'

'True, but once officers searched the area they discovered the remains of the other missing girls, including those of Sara Horton.'

'It was luck. Just bad luck. If I'd mentioned a different river valley, a different forestry track, then she'd have found nothing.' Kendwick half smiled. 'Unless, of course, there are dozens of serial killers dumping bodies out in the wilderness.'

'And you expect me to believe that?'

'I expect you to believe the results of the polygraph test I took.' Kendwick pushed himself upright and sat leaning forward. 'Look, there was nothing found to link me to the body dump. What is it, Locard's Principle? The notion that every contact both takes and leaves traces behind? Well, there were no traces at the site, at my house, in my car or on me. I'm either made of Teflon or completely innocent.'

Savage stared at Kendwick, trying to keep a blank face. Body dump, Locard's Principle? Kendwick seemed all too knowledgeable about police terminology.

'What about the rape kit found in your car?'

'Rape kit? Listen to you! I leave a few things in a rucksack and the cops immediately label them as the tools of the trade of a serial killer. It was just stuff anyone might have in their possession.'

'Handcuffs?'

'Really, Charlotte. I bet half the couples you know have played around with a bit of bondage. I like to imagine you have.'

Savage ignored Kendwick's smirk. 'And the hair scrunchy found at your house? The one which belonged to Sara Horton. Strikes me that was a trace.'

'I picked it up while crossing the park. Have you never done that? I bet you have.' Kendwick cocked his head on one side. 'I bet your daughter has.'

'My daughter?' Savage felt a lurch in her stomach. How on earth did Kendwick know about her daughter? 'Leave her out of it.'

'Touchy.' Kendwick tutted. 'But I understand why. I've been doing some research on you on the internet. I thought if I knew you a little better I might be able to understand you a little more. So, I put your name into Google and all these news stories came up. A mother, wronged. A hit-and-run. A family tragedy. One of your twin daughters taken from you by a rogue driver. The irony that you, a cop, can't make the law work for you, can't get justice. Well, Charlotte, it happens the other way around too. Justice can easily become injustice. Which is why you should sympathise with my predicament.'

'I don't.' Savage stood. The interview was over. She'd delivered the message from Hardin and now it was time to go before the odious creature riled her. 'Remember what I said, we're watching.'

'Oh, I know you are. But I'm not going anywhere. No need.' Kendwick smiled again. He shifted his head and then craned his neck to peer over into the next-door garden. 'I've got everything I want right on my doorstep.'

Savage turned to look. The adjoining plot was neatly manicured. A large area of grass and, at the far end of the garden, a raised area of decking. Two expensive wicker loungers sat on the deck and lying on the loungers were two young women, sunning themselves in the unseasonal warmth. Twenties. Skimpy clothing. Blonde hair.

'That's why I'm out here. Mammary watch.' Kendwick grinned. He reached for his glass and sat back in the recliner.

'They're down from London for a couple of days. Quite friendly really. I'd told them I'd go for a meal with them later, show them the sights of Chagford, act the friendly local. Don't worry, I'm sure I'll be quite safe with them. They wouldn't dare hurt me, not with a choir of guardian police angels watching on.'

'Mr Kendwick, if anything—'

'You don't get it, do you?' Kendwick spat the words out, his mood changing in an instant. 'I'm innocent, so just fuck off and let me live my life. Now, get out of here before I call my solicitor and ask her to look into pursuing a harassment case against you and the force.'

'I'm off, but there's one thing.' Savage moved over to Kendwick and stood next to his chair. 'If you ever mention my daughter again, I'll . . .'

'You'll what?' Kendwick jerked his head. One of the girls from next door stood beside the hedge. She smiled at Kendwick, mouthed a 'sorry, later' and then walked off.

Savage waited until the young woman had disappeared inside the house and then she kicked the back of Kendwick's chair, knocking the prop free. Kendwick fell backward in a heap, his drink sloshing over his chest.

'I'll fucking kill you, that's what.'

With DI Savage gone, Kendwick went back inside the house to dry off and change his shirt. Savage's warning and sudden burst of anger had unsettled him, and staring at the girls next door was no longer fun.

Inside, he cleaned himself up and then poured himself another Pimm's. He went to the living room and lowered himself onto the sofa. He'd had a fair bit to drink and the alcohol was having a soporific effect. He sat back and tried to picture his neighbours, tried to imagine the pair of them sprawled naked in the garden. He sipped his drink, his free hand moving to his shorts, loosening the button. But then he shook his head. Nothing. He felt nothing.

He put the drink on a side table and lay back and closed his eyes. Memories swirled in his head. A dream of another garden, another time, a time when he *had* felt something. Felt something for someone. What was she? Seventeen, eighteen? He'd been younger, having turned fifteen a few weeks before. They'd been in the back garden, his parents out somewhere, Kendwick left behind as usual. The girl had been from across the street. Lithe, leggy, confident of what she wanted. Still, he'd scoffed when she'd suggested a game of hide and seek. Wasn't that for kids? 'Depends what you're seeking, doesn't it?' she'd replied with a coy smile. So he'd stood there, counting . . .

Ninety-seven, ninety-eight, ninety-nine, one hundred! Ready or not, here I come!

He whirls round, scanning the garden. Beginning to search. Over by the rose bushes? No! Standing straight behind the big old oak? No!! Hiding beneath the tarpaulin which covers the wood pile? No!!! Where on earth is she? He shakes his head and turns round once more. He spies the shed. Of course! He creeps over the lawn and clicks open the door. There she is!

Found you!

She doesn't move. Just lies there, her eyes closed but a smile gracing her lips, her pretty summer dress rucked up round her waist, her knickers round her ankles. He steps inside the shed and pulls the door shut. Darkness. A slant of golden light from the crack in the door running up her thigh. He breathes in. The air tastes dry and dusty, but there's a hint of something else too, something sweet and intoxicating. He slips one foot across the wooden floor, then another. Now he's standing over her. Marvelling at her stillness. He lowers himself to the floor of the shed and lies beside her. She doesn't move. He reaches out with his finger and traces a line on her thigh, following the shaft of light. His heart is beating ten to the dozen, his breathing coming in tiny little gulps. She, on the other hand, only betrays the fact she is alive with an almost imperceptible heave of her chest, her breasts swelling with each intake of air. She is passive but so very powerful. So utterly bewitching.

He pushes himself up and lies on top of her, trying to support himself with one hand while the other fumbles with his trousers. He doesn't know what he's doing, only knows that this was meant to be.

The girl's eyelids flutter for a second as he enters her and then she sighs, a long exhalation of air, the breath warm on his face. Then she is still again and he's the only one moving, his gasps now matching his rhythm, her face frozen but serene.

'Oh God!' he cries, as mere seconds later his body convulses. Now he falls on her in utter bliss and amazement, moaning in her ear, telling her that he loves her more than anything and will do so forever and ever and ever.

She says nothing and her eyes stay shut as he continues to whisper to her, to promise her his heart and soul. And then she blinks at a sound from outside.

Voices.

She pushes him off and stands, hurriedly pulling up her knickers and tidying her dress.

'Stay,' he pleads. 'Stay with me!'

She shakes her head, nothing in her eyes but contempt. She moves across the shed, flings the door open, and vanishes into the garden.

He turns to the door, pulls it shut and then slumps back down to the floor. The moment has gone and he wonders if anything can recapture the feeling he had as she lay there beneath him.

The next day he goes to the girl's house. Knocks on the door. Her mother answers. No, he can't come in. Her daughter doesn't want to see him. The mother raises her hand as if to shoo him away like a bothersome fly. He stares past her into the hallway where huge cardboard boxes sit in stacks. He can see a roll of carpet sticking from the door of the front room. The windows in the bay are bare, the curtains lying in neat folded piles. He gets it then. The family are moving. The girl is leaving. She tricked him.

Kendwick shook his head, pulling himself into the present and his current predicament. He reached for his glass and took a sip of his drink. The girl in the shed had engendered a terrible feeling of rejection, a feeling he'd known since he was a baby and she had reinforced.

'Bitch,' Kendwick said, not entirely sure if he was referring to the girl in the shed, the woman who'd smiled over the garden fence a few minutes ago or DI Savage. It didn't really matter. They were all the same. Sweetness and light and flashing a smile or a bare patch of skin so they could take control of his emotions. And then, when they'd got what they wanted, they simply walked away, leaving him lusting after something he couldn't have.

He'd learned to get the better of them by turning on the charm himself, but deep inside he couldn't kid himself. He always felt weak when he saw a woman he desired, weak because of the power she held over him, weak at the thought of what he might be able to do to her. If, of course, she'd let him.

And if she wouldn't let him?

Well, Malcolm Kendwick had ways of dealing with that.

Chapter Six

Combestone Tor, Dartmoor. Saturday 22nd April. 4.43 p.m.

The Smith family liked to get out in the wilds on a weekend. It was part of the reason why Nathan and Jane Smith had decided to move to Devon. Weekend life before Devon, or BD, as Nathan put it, had involved a trip to the local park or, if they were lucky, an outing on the South Downs. Then, years ago now, Nathan had won a prize in a magazine competition. A Valentine's weekend at the Gidleigh Park Hotel, on Dartmoor. The hotel was well out of their price range and the novelty of sleeping in a huge four-poster bed in a suite of rooms was wonderful. The place had a Michelin star and the food was, not surprisingly, out of this world. The break was only for two days, but the idea of a dirty weekend was fun and Nathan had imagined they would spend most of the time between the sheets. Jane had insisted on leaving the hotel, though. A stroll on the moor would burn off some of the calories and leave them re-energised and refreshed for the next bout of lovemaking.

Whatever, Nathan had thought. They'd been to Canada the previous year, South America the one before that. A walk on Dartmoor was hardly going to compare with Niagara Falls or Machu Picchu. And yet, when they'd ventured out into the cold February morning, the light had sparkled in an odd way. They'd driven up onto the moor where mist hung in the valleys as the sun brushed the tops of the tors. This wasn't like the South Downs at all. There was nothing manicured about the countryside here. As they parked the car and got out and clambered up the heaving granite mass of Haytor, Nathan felt something stir deep inside. And when they stood on top of the rocks holding hands, he turned to his wife, and without really thinking, he said he'd like to live here. Me too, Jane had replied.

Neither of them had thought much more about the conversation until they'd driven to a nearby town and looked in an estate agent's window. While for locals the prices might have seemed steep, for Nathan and Jane, who at the time lived in a nice Victorian semi-detached house in Guildford, nearly every property looked like an absolute steal.

After browsing the particulars for one idyllic place set in its own valley, Nathan's hand strayed down to Jane's stomach. He patted her.

'Be better for him, wouldn't it?' Only the week before they'd come on the trip, Jane had announced she was pregnant. Nathan had been thrilled.

'Or her,' Jane said.

That had been over ten years ago. They made the move within six months of that February, shortly before their daughter Abigail had been born. Luka, their son, followed a year and a half later and now they were well settled, the South-East all but forgotten.

Today, the family were on an expedition to bag a couple of tors they hadn't been to. The first, Combestone Tor, was slap bang up against a road, but Nathan had announced that driving to the tor was way too easy. They'd parked across the far side of the valley a good couple of miles away and walked over. Now, as they slogged up towards the tor, Luka was flagging.

'Come on,' Nathan said. 'Iron rations when we get to the top.'

Ever the clever one in the family, Abi piped up. 'I thought you said eat before you're hungry?'

'Stop before you're tired, wrap up before you're cold, eat before you're hungry.' Luka repeated the words like a mantra. 'Abi's right, Dad.'

'OK then.' Nathan stopped and reached into his pocket for a packet of glucose tablets. 'Time for go-faster sweets.'

'Yeah!' Luka said.

'And the first one to touch the rocks gets an extra biscuit.' Nathan handed out the sweets and smiled at his wife. 'On your marks, get set . . .'

Neither Abi nor Luka waited for the 'go'. Instead, they sprinted away from their parents, attacking the hill with an energy born from youth rather than experience. Nathan and Jane laughed and began to plod up the slope, knowing they'd catch up with their children before long.

'Great this,' Jane said. 'Precious moments, never to be repeated.'

'Bloody good job.' Nathan paused for a second and put his hands on his hips. 'I'm all out of puff.'

'There's a solution for that. We need to get out more often, get you fit.' Jane moved across to her husband and looped her arm round his waist. She pushed her fingers into the first sign of his middle-aged spread and then moved her hand down to Nathan's crotch and gave a little squeeze. 'There are other benefits to being fit too.'

'Stuff sex.' Nathan smiled. 'Right now I'd settle for a cup of tea and a scone with plenty of cream and jam.'

'Mum! Dad!' Abi's voice drifted down towards them.

Nathan turned his head to where his daughter stood atop the tor. She waved her arms. 'Hide and seek! Come and find us!'

With that she dropped out of sight, disappearing behind the huge hunk of granite.

'Shit. That's all we need.'

Nathan and Jane strolled the short distance to the rocks. Nathan suggested they should split up, Jane going to the right and him to the left. Once his wife had disappeared round the side of the tor, Nathan unhooked the rucksack from his back and dropped it to the floor. He opened the top flap, pulled out a bottle of squash and took several swigs of liquid. Then he packed the drink away, hoisted up the rucksack and set off again.

'Ready or not, here I come!'

Instead of circling the rocks, he headed straight to the tor and began to clamber up. He pulled himself onto a large boulder and then edged round between two more until he could climb up the rock his daughter had been on a couple of minutes before. He stood for a moment and then slowly turned on the spot. He saw his wife on the far side of the tor but there was no sign of the children. He jumped down and began to navigate between the granite columns. He thought about putting on a monster voice, but then reasoned against it. Luka, in particular, might panic and slip and hurt himself. Instead he repeated his shout of 'ready or not, here I come'.

He'd just squeezed into a narrow passage between two rocks when he heard something which made his blood curdle. A scream. Long, drawn-out and unmistakably belonging to his daughter.

'Abi!' Nathan yelled as he pushed through the gap and then, finding himself with more space, spun round trying to find the direction the scream had come from. 'I'm coming, Abi. Stay where you are.'

Nathan scrambled up and over a couple of smaller boulders, at the same time thanking God he'd packed the first-aid kit in his rucksack that morning. He just hoped his daughter hadn't hurt herself too badly.

The scream came again, this time accompanied by the voice of his son.

'Dad! Come quickly.'

Nathan hauled himself up a final piece of granite and saw, as he did so, that his son and daughter stood together on a large plateau of rock. Relief flooded over him as he realised that neither appeared to be injured. The relief quickly turned to anger.

'What are you doing?' he said. 'I've told you we don't joke about being hurt when we're on the moor. Fooling around's OK at home but when—'

'Dad!' Luka shouted again and pointed into a large crack between two boulders. 'Down there.'

For a moment Nathan felt a wash of horror as he wondered if it had been his wife who'd slipped and fallen. But then Jane appeared a few metres away. She moved across to the children and stared down at where Luka was pointing.

'My God!' Jane reached her arms out and turned Abi and Luka away.

'What is it?' Nathan took a couple of strides and jumped across to the plateau the three of them were standing on. He looked at his wife for an explanation. 'A sheep or something?'

Jane shook her head as she began to push the children down from the rock. 'We need to phone the police.'

'The police?' Nathan stepped forward to peer into the shadows. He squinted and tried to take in what he was seeing.

A hand with bright red fingernails, an arm leading to a bare shoulder and the round curve of a partially exposed breast, the skin pale and white. The rest of the woman's body was hidden from sight beneath an overhanging ledge and for a split second Nathan found himself craning his neck in an effort to see more. Then he changed his mind and hurriedly stepped away, following his wife and kids down off the rocks and at the same time pulling his phone from his pocket.

Early Saturday evening found Savage standing in the kitchen with a glass of white wine in one hand, a bottle in the other. Pete worked vegetables back and forth in a large wok on the cooker, steam billowing up into the extractor hood. For somebody who'd spent several years commanding a frigate and having all his meals prepared for him, he wasn't a bad cook. He reached out for the bottle of wine and took it from Savage, pouring a generous measure into the wok.

'Careful,' Savage said. 'You'll get the kids tipsy.'

'Good, might help Jamie sleep,' Pete said. 'He seems to spend most of the small hours in our bed these days.'

'Nightmares. It's common enough at his age.' Savage took a sip of her wine, thinking she could do with some sort of sedative too. Malcolm Kendwick had wormed his way into her dreams, his grinning face miraculously appearing as soon as she shut her eyes at night. 'He'll get over it.'

'Well, I hope—' Pete stopped mid-sentence as Savage's work mobile rang. He cocked his head and sighed. 'There goes another evening.'

By no means every call to her phone required immediate action, but Pete had an uncanny knack of guessing which did. Ten to seven on a Saturday evening, and it was a pretty good bet he was right. Savage moved over and picked the phone up from the kitchen table.

'DI Savage,' she said.

'It's DC Calter, ma'am,' the voice on the end of the line said. 'We've got a suspicious death on the moor. A young woman. From the sound of things it wasn't an accident.'

Savage blinked, seeing Kendwick's face fashion itself in the steam from the wok, mocking her for a second before dispersing. She listened as Calter explained the details and then hung up.

'A pound in the cop box then?' Pete said, referring to a piggy bank Jamie had plonked on the kitchen table one evening when Savage had been out. The fund, added to whenever Savage was called away, provided Jamie with crisps and sweets, a consolation – albeit a poor one – for the absence of his mother.

'I'm afraid so,' Savage said, nodding at her husband before knocking back her glass of wine and walking from the room.

The girl had been found at Combestone Tor, a lone set of rocks standing high above the steep-sided River Dart valley. Savage drove at speed along the A38 to Buckfastleigh and then turned off and negotiated the narrow lanes up onto the moor. Forty minutes after leaving home she was driving across the dam of the Avon reservoir and following a winding road which climbed towards the tor. As she neared the top, the last rays of sunlight were caressing the tip of the tor as the day took its leave. It was as if rocks were being devoured by a great black shadow, the warmth and brilliance of life being slowly extinguished. She knew photographers called this time of day the golden hour, a time when the light was warmer and redder. For police officers the term had a quite different meaning. The golden hour referred to the period immediately following the discovery of a crime. During this time information was available to the police in high volume and every effort had to be made to secure that information. Decisions made now would have consequences for the investigation later. Savage wondered about her own role and whether she would make the right choices.

The odd jumble of rocks which comprised the tor lay just a short walk from a gravel car park, but she could see that John Layton, their senior Crime Scene Investigator, was taking no chances. The road had been blocked off some two hundred metres from the tor where a couple of laybys provided parking for police vehicles. Hundreds of metres of blue and white tape lay pegged to the ground, the tape extending in a rough circle around the tor. Savage stopped the car and got out. DC Jane Calter was standing next to one of Layton's white vans flirting with a young-looking CSI. The CSI had pulled his mask away from his face, but was otherwise fully clad in a white protective suit. He laughed at something Calter said, the laugh curtailed as Savage walked across.

'Evening, ma'am,' DC Calter said, her strong South-West accent somehow at one with the rural surroundings. She nodded a greeting, her blonde bob curling round the edges of her face. Calter was late twenties but highly experienced. An old head on young shoulders. She gestured towards the tor where the rocks were now almost devoid of sunlight, the shadow line moving across the moor on the other side of the valley. 'Just waiting to be allowed up there. They're finger-tipping a route in and once they've done that we can go through.'

Savage nodded and then turned to the CSI. 'Anything for me?'

'A female,' the CSI said. 'Late teens or early twenties and she's in a sparkly dress. Not the kind of thing you'd be wearing up here. No ID or anything like that. No obvious signs of trauma, but she's wedged down in a deep crevice so we won't know much about cause of death until we get her out.' The CSI waved at a colleague a hundred metres away. 'Look, you can go over there now. Keep between the strips of tape.'

Savage thanked the CSI and she and Calter went to get kitted up. Ten minutes later and they ambled up between the two lines of tape towards the distinct clusters of rock, the tallest twice the height of a man. Over by one, several white-suited figures worked in a line, circumnavigating the rocks like a giant clock hand. At the tor, an aluminium ladder leaned against a pillar of granite. Savage's eyes followed the ladder upward to the top of the rock where another man stood surveying the view. Like the other CSIs he wore a white suit with bootlets and blue gloves. Unlike them he had a grubby Tilley hat perched on his head. As he turned his head he spotted Savage and raised a hand and tipped the hat.

'Charlotte!' John Layton's voice boomed out across the hillside. 'Come on over.'

Savage and Calter continued between the parallel tapes until they reached the ladder. Layton stood at the top looking down, his angular face silhouetted against the pale sky.

'I'm pretty sure they didn't come this way,' he said. 'So it's safe for you to come up. But be careful, hey?'

Savage moved to the ladder and began climbing. At the top Layton offered a hand, but she scowled at him and stepped onto the rock.

'I'm a woman, not a bloody invalid. What's got into you?'

'Sorry, I was only trying to help.'

'Well don't.' Savage looked past Layton to a tripod arrangement with a pulley and a rope. The tripod straddled a crack in the rocks. 'She's down there?'

'Self-evidently.'

Savage narrowed her gaze, trying to penetrate the gloom in the crack. Two metres or so down, a shelf of granite overhung a patch of bare earth. Sticking out from beneath the rock was a bare foot, mud and dirt on the sole, bright-red varnish on a toenail. Savage moved her head to try to see more. Sparkles came from a silver dress, another flash of light from something clutched in an outstretched fist.

'A nail file,' Layton said as Calter joined Savage at the crack. 'Only I don't think she was up here for a spot of manicuring.'

'Self-defence, ma'am,' Calter said. 'Which means this was no accident. And she's not exactly dressed for a day on the hills, is she? Not dressed for anything much, to be honest.'

'No.' Savage glanced back to the car park, just a stone's throw away. 'What about a lovers' tiff which got out of hand? They drove here for a smooch up on the rocks and something went wrong.'

'A smooch?' Calter smiled. 'You're showing your age, ma'am. I think people go in for more than smooching these days.'

Savage ignored Calter's jibe. 'This is surely too close to the road and too public a place to try and conceal a body.'

'Might have looked different in the dark.'

'True. But would anyone come here if they hadn't already visited?' Savage stood and turned to Layton. The crack was so narrow a full-grown man couldn't fit down. 'How are you going to get her out?'

'Barbara.' Layton pointed to where a petite woman in a white PPE suit was cresting the top of the ladder. 'She's small enough. The only question is, whether she's brave enough?'

It took the best part of half an hour to extract the body. DC Barbara Hooper was lowered into the gap and managed to attach a harness round the girl which enabled the body to be winched out. The process was painstaking, Layton keen not to cause unnecessary damage to the corpse. He signalled to Savage as the girl was carried down to ground level and laid on a body bag.

'She's not been here long,' Layton said as Savage came over. 'Twenty-four hours max.'

'Rigor mortis?' Savage said as she stared down at the girl's right hand where the nail file lay in a tight grip. A sparkly dress woven from silver thread had split down one side, the round of a breast partially exposed. Long blonde hair framed a face which wore bright red lipstick and heavy eyeshadow and eyeliner. The make-up looked odd on the now-sallow skin. The girl's right thigh had a graze down one side, rivulets of dried blood visible on the pale surface.

'Yes.' Layton gestured at the car park. 'But I was thinking more along the lines that this is a popular place, especially at the weekend. During the day, there'd have been witnesses. Which means she was dumped here when it was dark, most probably last night.'

'There's no sign of serious trauma,' Savage said. 'A few grazes on the arms and legs. That brown mark on her upper thigh.'

'Interesting.' Layton nodded as he knelt beside the girl. He pulled out a polygrip bag and a pair of tweezers and began to lift fragments of something from the skin. 'Red paint and rust,' he said, once he'd finished. 'As if she'd brushed against an old piece of metal at some point. The metal caused the graze and left these specks.'

'Where could they come from?'

'No idea.' Layton pushed himself up and turned to Savage. 'One other thing I noticed when I was, er, down there. She's not wearing any knickers. Do you think that's suspicious?'

As one, Layton and Savage turned to Calter.

'What are you looking at me like that for?' The DC blushed. 'I'm no expert.'

Savage rescued Calter. 'She could have taken them off, and I guess the most likely reason for that would be to have sex.' She peered down. Layton was correct about the lack of underwear; under the hem of the short dress, she could see the pubic area smooth and shaven, just a thin strip of hair above. 'Perhaps this is a simple sexual encounter which went wrong.'

'Dogging?' Calter said.

Savage looked across to the rock. 'An exciting place to do it. Up there. The dress suggests she'd been out somewhere, a club or a party. Could she have come here willingly with a lover?'

'Too cold for me, ma'am, but I get your drift.' Calter followed Savage's gaze. 'She climbed up onto the tor with her partner and then fell between the rocks. If the liaison was a risky one then whoever she was with may not have wanted to report the accident.'

'Sounds unlikely,' Layton said. 'They could have at least made an anonymous phone call to alert someone. Plus an accident doesn't explain why she's holding the nail file.'

'Ma'am?' Calter touched Savage on the arm and gestured for her to step away. She lowered her voice. 'Are you thinking what I'm thinking? The brief?'

'What brief?'

'The one from the FBI. Hardin circulated it amongst us junior detectives. More of an exercise than anything. Still, I remember reading that along with the human remains, the cops in the US found partially charred piles of clothing. Dresses, jeans, bras, shoes and socks. No knickers. The conclusion was the killer had taken the knickers away as some kind of trophy.'

Savage stopped a few metres from the body. She remembered scanning one of the FBI reports the night in the hotel. Tiredness had won over the reams of paper and hundreds of bullet points. She must have skipped over the section about the missing underwear. Now she turned back and looked at the girl and weighed the evidence. The victim had been dumped somewhere in the wilderness, had blonde hair just like the girls in the US, and was missing her underwear.

'Fuck,' she said. 'Malcolm bloody Kendwick.'

Chapter Seven

Combestone Tor, Dartmoor. Saturday 22nd April. 9.11 p.m.

In the gathering dusk, Savage walked away from the crime scene and over to one of the other sets of rocks. She clambered up to the top and checked her mobile. Yes, she had a decent signal. She called DSupt Hardin. He wasn't amused to be disturbed.

'I'm out, Charlotte,' he blustered into the phone. 'This had better be good.'

'There's a body on Dartmoor,' Savage said. 'Female, blonde and with missing knickers. Dumped.'

'OK, but can't you deal with this?' Hardin's voice came and went and Savage could hear the chink of glasses and the murmur of conversation in the background. 'I'm at the theatre, just about to take my seat after the interval. I don't want to miss the second half.'

Savage shook her head. Hardin plainly hadn't understood the connection.

'Malcolm Kendwick, sir. He's a definite for this. I repeat: the victim is female, blonde, she's not wearing knickers and she's been dumped in the wilderness.'

'*Kendwick?*' Hardin appeared to have cottoned on. 'Surely he wouldn't be so arrogant to kill within a few days of arriving back in the UK? Besides, he dumped the bodies where he thought they'd never be found. This one sounds entirely different.'

'Perhaps something's changed inside him,' Savage said. 'Serial killers aren't necessarily cold-blooded and rational. It could be the move from the US has triggered a need to do things differently. Or perhaps he simply craves the attention he's been receiving recently and wants more of it.'

'You mean we're responsible?'

'Us, the media, the police in the US. We're not to blame, of course not, but Kendwick has an ego and maybe this is a way for him to flatter himself.'

'Jesus, Charlotte, you want to arrest him? Tonight?'

'I want to bring him in for questioning, yes. The sooner the better.'

There was a long pause and then she heard Hardin's voice muffled and indistinct as if he had his hand over the phone. Eventually he spoke. 'OK, but by the book. Any sense we're harassing him and we'll be in all sorts of trouble.'

'I thought that's what you wanted, sir? To harass him.'

'I wanted to needle him. There's a subtle difference in approach, do you understand?'

'Yes, sir. I'll keep you informed.'

'You do that, DI Savage.'

Hardin hung up, leaving her staring across the Dart valley. The light had all but gone and to the east the moor spread like a dark, heaving morass. Here and there a few lights glowed from isolated farmsteads, but mostly there was a near-black nothingness which reached to the horizon. Above the skyline, a lone star hung in the north-east, twinkling against the grey background. Somewhere in that direction lay the town of Chagford, where Malcolm Kendwick would be snug in his little cottage.

Not for long, she thought.

Before she set off for Chagford, Savage called Inspector Nigel Frey and asked about the possibility of sending the Force Support Group to assist with the arrest. There'd be a short wait before they turned up, but she reasoned it would be worth hanging on for their arrival. Frey's officers would be armed and come equipped to cope with any eventuality. They'd be able to break down the front door and subdue Kendwick should that prove necessary.

'You think Kendwick's dangerous?' Calter asked as they drove away from Combestone Tor, the car's headlights piercing the darkness. 'I mean, he won't resist arrest, will he?'

'That's not the point. I don't think we'll have a problem but if we go in there with the FSG it will lay a marker down which tells him we're serious and are, in effect, as bad-ass as the guys over the pond.'

'I like your thinking.' Calter smiled. 'Rough him up a bit, hey?'

'You said that, not me.'

By the time they got to Chagford, a starry sky hung above the town's near-empty streets. They parked up a few doors from Kendwick's place, Savage noting the front-room light was on. A few minutes later her phone rang.

'We've got a possible on the girl, ma'am,' DC Enders said down the line from the station, his voice squawking for a moment as the signal broke up. 'Amy Glynn. Nineteen. She's from Plymouth and was out in town last night. Her parents reported her missing first thing this morning after realising she hadn't returned home. I'll email you a picture, but I can tell you she was blonde and wearing a silver dress.'

Savage hung up and then checked her mail. Enders was as good as his word and after a few seconds she had his email. Savage opened the accompanying image and passed the phone to Calter.

'That's her, ma'am. Her or her doppelganger.' Calter peered at the screen before handing the phone back. She shook her head. 'Poor kid. A few years ago I could have been her.'

'I can't see anyone getting the better of you, Jane. What's that sport you do? Jujitsu?'

'That and Taekwondo. A bit of Judo too. Mixed martial arts, everyone does it now. But that's beside the point. Why should women have to learn self-defence in order to feel safe? Still, if some fucker ever tried anything with me, I'd break their . . . well, you know, ma'am. Let's say they wouldn't be hurting anyone ever again.'

Their conversation was interrupted by lights sweeping the interior of their car. Savage turned to see the Force Support Group vehicle rolling up behind them, Inspector Nigel Frey in the front passenger seat. Savage got out of the car to meet him.

'Nigel,' Savage said, as Frey hopped down. 'Thanks for this.'

'Not a problem,' Frey said. 'Quite the opposite. I've been reading all about your Mr Kendwick in the papers. Be my pleasure.'

Savage could well imagine. Dressed in black fatigues and with a pistol holstered under his left arm, Frey resembled a life-size Action Man. His notion of policing wasn't finding lost children or catching speeding motorists, he liked to bash heads. If he wasn't bashing heads he preferred the waters of Plymouth Sound to the city's streets. A big police RIB was his plaything and he was often to be found zipping back and forth, buzzing yachts and other pleasure craft. Still, Savage had nothing against Frey since he'd saved her life on two occasions.

Frey made a hand signal back to the van and the side door slid open, four black-clad figures jumping out. Two of them held a big metal battering ram. A patrol car pulled past the FSG vehicle and edged along the street until it was well beyond Kendwick's place. Then the driver turned the car sideways in the road and both officers got out. A motorcyclist was coming towards them, but the officers waved at the rider to stop.

'OK, let's do this, Charlotte,' Frey said, setting off down the street with Savage trotting along beside him, trying to keep up.

They reached Kendwick's place and one of the FSG officers bent to the door and peered through the letterbox. He mouthed an 'all clear' and stepped aside as two more officers moved to the door with the battering ram. They took a practice swing and then brought the ram crashing down against the Yale lock. The door smashed open, bouncing back shut before another officer shouldered the door and moved inside.

'Armed police!' the officer shouted, his weapon raised. 'Stay where you are and don't move!'

The other officers ran into the house too, Savage behind them. Kendwick stood in the archway to the little kitchen, a tea towel in one hand and a mug in the other. The first officer braced himself, his finger caressing the trigger on the gun. A red laser dot flickered on Kendwick's chest.

'Face down on the floor! Now!'

Kendwick moved slowly but purposefully. He placed the tea towel and mug on a work surface and lowered himself to the floor. One of the other officers went over and yanked

Kendwick's arms behind his back. He clicked a pair of cuffs in place and then pulled the man up. Kendwick winced.

'Charlotte,' he said, talking past the huddle of officers and meeting Savage's eyes. 'I was just making a pot of tea. Fancy a cuppa?'

Savage pushed forward through the scrum. 'Malcolm Kendwick, I'm arresting you on suspicion of murder. You don't have to say anything, but if you do it might be used in evidence.'

'Say something? Of course I'm going to fucking say something! This is bang out of order. I've been back in my home country less than a week and already you're picking on me. I tell you what, this will be front-page news tomorrow and you lot will be in all sorts of trouble.'

'I don't think so, Malcolm,' Savage said. 'Nobody knows about this and to be honest I doubt if anyone much cares. You're yesterday's news.'

'That's where you're wrong.' Kendwick smirked and his eyes flicked up to the low beams above his head. As he did so, a female voice called out from upstairs.

'Hello? Can I come down?'

One of the officers wheeled round, his weapon trained on the stairs. 'Slowly!' he shouted. 'Keep your hands where I can see them.'

A figure emerged into view. High heels, legs encased in sheer nylon, a business-like skirt and jacket. The woman descended the stairs. She had blonde hair in a bouffant style, bright-red lips and plenty of make-up. The hair bounced with every step she took.

'Lower your weapon,' Savage said as she moved forward and waved the armed officer away. 'And you are?'

'Melissa Stapleton,' the woman said. The red lips parted in a smile. 'The *Daily Mail.*'

* * *

'The bloody *Mail*, Charlotte?' Hardin said as he paced the corridor outside the interview room at the custody centre. 'You don't think you could have gone one better, do you? Arranged for a live TV broadcast as well, one of those webcam live-streaming things perhaps? YouTube, Facecrap or some other bollocks?'

'I obviously didn't realise she was in there,' Savage said. 'Otherwise we wouldn't have gone in like we did.'

'Not "we", you.' Hardin jabbed a finger at her to emphasise his point. 'I specifically told you to go by the book, but instead you called up Nigel Frey and his band of thugs and went in there gung-ho, as if you were taking down the Krays. A battering ram and weapons? Jesus, there was absolutely no need to go storming in like that. I dread to think what the headlines will be in the morning. She heard everything, right?'

Savage nodded. Melissa Stapleton, the *Daily Mail*'s star feature reporter, had been powdering her nose in the bathroom as Frey's men had smashed open the door. Kendwick, it turned out, had signed a lucrative deal with the *Mail* to tell the story of his time in the US. Rough justice abroad. An innocent man facing the death penalty. The icing on the cake for Stapleton would be police harassment in the UK. A live TV crew or webcam wouldn't be necessary, her lurid prose would paint the picture just as well.

'I'm afraid so, sir.'

'Fuck!' Hardin whirled on his heels, looking for something to take his anger out on. He slammed his fist against a noticeboard and the impact caused a poster on domestic violence to peel away and slide to the floor. The irony was lost on Hardin and he turned again towards the interview room. 'And the only thing which could be worse than Stapleton's presence at Kendwick's house is that lawyer cow being in there with him now. There must be some kind of disease causing mass female delusion, no? How else to explain why two intelligent women would want to have anything to do with Malcolm Kendwick.'

Amanda Bradley was the 'lawyer cow' Hardin was talking about. Unfortunately, Stapleton knew how to pull the strings and as soon as Kendwick had been arrested the journalist had been on the phone to Bradley. She had, unsurprisingly, been only too keen to get involved. Savage had tangled many times with Bradley and knew she regarded her with contempt. The feeling was mutual.

'Sir, we are where we are,' Savage said. 'Kendwick is under suspicion of murder, if he's guilty it won't matter if he's got Wonder Woman in there with him.'

'Huh? Oh, I see. Well then, get in there. Do your stuff.'

A few minutes later, Savage entered the interview room with DC Calter. Kendwick sat at a table with Amanda Bradley alongside. Bradley was, despite the time of night, immaculately turned out in her best suit, the jacket open and several buttons of the shirt undone so as to reveal her ample cleavage. Like Melissa Stapleton, Bradley wore bright-red lipstick. Savage wondered if the colour was a warning. Certainly, the solicitor always meant business and more often than not came out on top.

Savage and Calter pulled out chairs and sat. Bradley bared her teeth, showing what Savage had always assumed were artificially sharpened canines. Kendwick laughed, seemingly in good humour, despite his predicament.

'I'm hurt, Charlotte,' Kendwick said. 'About this evening. You didn't have to come in there like that. You could have just knocked. I'd have made you a cup of something or maybe poured you a glass of wine. We could have got friendly. Still, I like strong women.' Kendwick turned to Bradley for a second and then glanced across at Calter and winked. 'Looks like I've got my hands full tonight. I'd better be a good boy, right?'

Savage ignored Kendwick and gestured at Calter. The DC explained the interview procedure and set up the recording equipment.

'Yeah, yeah.' Kendwick dismissed Calter with a wave. 'I've been through this all before in the States. Mind you, the police can be a bit rough over there. Especially the females.'

'Where were you yesterday evening, Malcolm?' Savage said. 'Specifically, from nine p.m. till three or four in the morning.'

'You found a body,' Kendwick said, ignoring the question. His right hand went behind his head and he began to twirl his ponytail round his forefinger. 'I know because Amanda told me. Shocking. I was obviously wrong about Devon. It's a dangerous world out there, even in sleepy cream-tea country. Better lock up your daughters.' Kendwick nodded and gave a little smirk. 'Especially your daughters, hey, Charlotte? Let them out of your sight for just one minute and they're gone. Puff.'

Unlike at Kendwick's place, this time Savage didn't rise to the bait. The interview was on camera after all. Once more she wondered how the hell Kendwick knew so much about her personal circumstances, knew, it appeared, about the death of her daughter, Clarissa. But then Bradley had probably filled Kendwick in on the details he hadn't been able to find on the web. She'd have delighted in telling him all about Savage's problems.

'Where were you yesterday evening, Malcolm?' Savage repeated the question, this time speaking slowly and emphasising every word.

'Look, I understand you're worried there's a serial killer

85

on the loose, but you needn't be concerned about me. The only young lass I've been near last night was the barmaid in the Globe Inn. She's a lovely girl, top-heavy where it counts, know what I mean? Beautiful smile, too. Trouble is, she's a brunette and, to coin a phrase, gentlemen prefer blondes.' Kendwick smiled again and then opened his mouth in mock shock. 'No! Don't tell me, this new girl, she *is* blonde?'

'Stop playing fucking games with us, Malcolm. It's a bit of a coincidence that a few days after you arrive in Devon a girl is abducted, murdered, and left on the moor. This isn't a joking matter, so just answer my question. Where were you?'

'I told you. I was in the pub to start with and then I shifted to a restaurant down the street. I had a leisurely meal and I think I tumbled in to my place around eleven-thirty. I was tucked up in bed and sleeping like a baby by twelve.'

'So you can't prove where you were after that?'

Kendwick shrugged. 'No, not unless a full transcript of my dreams might convince you. Then again, I think I might need to plead the Fifth Amendment before I let you into that little world. My dreams are, well, they're a little sordid.'

'Do you know the moor up near Combestone Tor?'

'No, but it sounds like my kind of place. Is that where the girl was found?'

Savage ignored Kendwick's question. 'You've never been there then?'

'Not that I can remember.' Kendwick shook his head. 'I guess I could have visited when I lived in Devon years ago.'

'But not since you've been back here?'

'No, definitely not.' Kendwick grinned and moistened his top lip with his tongue. 'Wild, is it? Remote? The sort of place you might hide something if you didn't want anybody to find it?'

Savage paused. Kendwick was either very good at bluffing or he really knew nothing about Combestone Tor's proximity to the road and popularity as a picnic spot. She turned to Calter.

'Mr Kendwick,' Calter said. 'You're aware we're searching your house?'

'Malcolm, please.' Kendwick leaned forward and lowered his voice to a whisper. 'I do so like to be on first-name terms with gorgeous women.'

'Ms Bradley?' Calter said, turning to the solicitor. 'You might like to inform your client that acting like a creepy little slug isn't going to do his case any good.'

'Cut the compliments, Malcolm,' Bradley said. 'They're wasted on these two anyway.'

'Suits me.' Kendwick shrugged. 'I'll save the tongue-work for the barmaid at the pub.'

Savage stared across the table at Kendwick, trying to work out the man. Surely he didn't believe in his own patter? Likely he was someone who got a thrill out of using his power to subjugate other people. The power could be simple physical force, or it could be psychological. Savage tapped Calter on the arm, encouraging her to go on.

'As I was saying,' Calter continued. 'We've got a team going through your house at the moment.'

'Well, they won't find much. I only arrived with a couple of bags and haven't had time to do much shopping yet. I need to get some pictures up, personalise the place, scatter a few little . . . knick . . . knick . . . knick . . . around the house. What's the word? Oh yes, knick-knacks.'

'You're on dangerous ground, Malcolm,' Savage said. 'Are you aware the killer in America took the girls' underwear as some kind of memento?'

'He didn't?' Kendwick feigned surprise and then half

87

turned to Bradley. 'Can we get this over and done with, Amanda? These two are making it up as they go along.'

'How long will the search take, DI Savage?' Bradley said. 'Because I assume that once you've finished and, provided you've found nothing, my client can go.'

'Mr Kendwick will be released when I've satisfied myself he played no part in the killing of this girl. So far your client has been rude and obstructive and we've made little progress. I suggest we conclude this session and you try to convince him of the seriousness of the situation. A night in custody will help. We'll resume in the morning.'

Savage pushed back her chair and stood as Calter officially suspended the interview. Once the recording equipment had been switched off Savage placed both her hands on the table and leaned across towards Kendwick.

'Look, you little piece of shit,' Savage said. 'There's a young girl lying dead in the morgue and a mother and father grieving for the loss of their daughter. Yet all you can do is make stupid jokes and fill every other sentence with mindless innuendo. We're going to start again tomorrow and I expect you to be more cooperative. Otherwise—'

'Otherwise what, Charlotte?' Kendwick said. 'You're going to tie me up and torture me?'

Savage turned away, hearing Kendwick chuckle behind her, thinking that torturing the man was exactly what she'd like to do.

She left Kendwick to sweat and headed back to Chagford to check on the progress of the search. It was well after midnight when she arrived, yet Layton's Volvo and a couple of white vans were parked kerbside in front of the terrace. Savage pulled on her white suit, gloves, bootlets and a hairnet. Then she stepped in through the front door.

'Nothing much yet, Charlotte,' Layton said as he spotted her. The CSI knelt next to the fireplace and was using a torch and a mirror at the end of a long pole to examine the chimney. 'Not that I know what we're looking for anyway.'

'Something,' Savage said. 'Anything.'

'Well, I don't think we're going to find trace evidence that the girl was here in the house. He wouldn't be so careless. Still, we've bagged a load of his clothing and footwear and the whole lot will be going to the lab for testing.'

'What about something to indicate he's been up near Combestone Tor?'

'Might be dirt on his shoes but I doubt we can isolate any residue to that specific location.' Layton pulled the mirror from the chimney and turned the torch off. 'Nothing up there.'

'Have you secured his vehicle?'

'Yes. Found the keys in the kitchen. The car's from a local rental company and is parked out the front. It's a brand-new Fiesta with only a few hundred miles on the clock. Clean as a whistle inside but we'll go over it anyway.'

'So you don't think the girl could have been in there?'

'Well, the car is so spotless then if she has we should find something.'

'Could he have rolled her in a plastic sheet or something like that?'

'Possible, but if he did and he's managed to dispose of the sheet then we've nothing, have we?'

Savage was about to say something when a female CSI came padding down the stairs. She had a laptop in her hands.

'Ma'am?' she said moving into the room and placing the laptop on the coffee table. 'I think you should see this.'

Savage went across as the woman lifted the laptop lid and woke the computer.

'There wasn't a password so I was able to get in,' the CSI explained. 'As far as I can tell the machine is brand-new. The box it came in was upstairs. Purchased from Amazon this week.'

'So what have you found?' Savage said as she watched the CSI bring up a browser window.

'There's almost nothing on here at all. Looks like Kendwick's been playing a few games and done a bit of web browsing. I went to his web history and the only incriminating site is this one.'

Savage watched as a website flashed up. Layton came across and peered over her shoulder. He tutted as the page loaded.

'Juicy Young Blondes,' he said, reading the site's title. 'I guess the question is, business or pleasure?'

'He bought a subscription a couple of days ago,' the CSI said. 'There's a membership email in his inbox.'

'It looks pretty tame,' Savage said. She'd seen plenty of hard-core pornography in her time as a cop and this was at the vanilla end of the spectrum. 'Perhaps he thinks we're keeping tabs on him and he wants to play it safe.'

'There's something else too, ma'am.' The CSI closed down the browser. She opened another window which showed Kendwick's files. There was only one folder and it was named 'Arresting Developments'. 'This.'

'Well?' Savage said. 'Open it.'

'Yes, ma'am.' The CSI clicked and the folder opened. Inside there were dozens of image files, each portrayed by a thumbnail. 'They're all blondes apart from one. Looks like he downloaded them from the website he joined.'

She clicked an image and up came a naked twenty-something female. The woman was leaning over the edge of the bed, her bum in the air, nothing left to the imagination.

The next picture was another blonde girl, this time in the shower, hot soapy lather streaming over her body. The CSI clicked again, and again, and again.

'I think I get the idea,' Savage said. 'You said they were all blondes apart from one. Show me.'

'Yes, ma'am, but . . .' A warm tinge appeared on the young CSI's face. 'I, um . . .'

'Come on, we're all adults. John and I have viewed material far worse than this.'

'Right you are, ma'am.' She scrolled to the bottom of the folder and clicked the last thumbnail. The image opened.

'Well.' Layton chuckled. 'Kendwick's certainly got a sense of humour.'

Now it was Savage's turn to blush. The picture showed a naked woman standing beside a set of vertical bars, legs apart, a smile on her face, a police cap on her head. In her right hand she held a large truncheon while a pair of handcuffs had been clicked round her left wrist and locked to one of the bars. However, what had caused Layton to laugh and Savage to blush was the colour of the woman's hair. It was red, the style and tone not a million miles from Savage's own.

Back outside, her face still glowing from the embarrassment, Savage stripped off her white suit and bootlets and shoved them in a plastic box to one side of the door. She strolled up the road to the Globe Inn, the pub Kendwick had said he'd been at early the previous evening. There was nothing but a dim glow from behind the bar, the place long since closed. That part of Kendwick's alibi would have to be checked out in the morning.

Returning to the terrace, she found DS Riley standing by the front door. He smiled as she approached.

'When did you get here?' Savage asked.

'Ages ago. Been walking round town, trying to get a feel for the place. All quiet now, everybody's in bed.' Riley paused and then smiled again. 'John Layton told me something about a laptop, ma'am? A distinctive picture?'

'A silly game Kendwick's playing. The whole thing with the image was specifically designed to annoy us. To annoy me.'

'Still,' Riley said, the smile now a cheeky grin. 'I'd like to see the picture.'

'You're not going to,' Savage snapped. 'Anyway, the woman's nothing like me.'

'So you say. John told me she's a dead ringer.'

'Nonsense. For one thing she's had a boob job.'

'Well, I guess there's only one way to find out.'

'DS Riley, you're to stop that right now.' Savage tried to stop smiling herself. Riley didn't often flirt with her but when he did she couldn't deny she felt a frisson of excitement. She tried to contain herself by stressing the seriousness of the situation. 'We're talking about a guy who's possibly killed half a dozen women. It's not funny.'

'Of course not, ma'am.' Riley glanced back towards the front door. 'Anything else in there?'

'No. I know he's not been in the house long, but it feels almost as if he knew this would happen. That he knew we'd be visiting. Aside from the laptop, the place is almost sterile.'

'Put yourself in his position. Innocent or not, he knows we're going to be keeping an eye on him. I can't say I blame him for being cautious. I can't even blame him for the joke with the redhead.'

'There was nothing jokey about it, Darius. The picture was a deliberate attempt to unsettle me.'

'And he has, hasn't he? Unsettled you.'

'Yes, he has.' Savage began to walk to her car but then turned back. 'I want you with me when we resume the interview tomorrow morning, Darius. Perhaps the presence of a bloke will curb some of his excesses.'

'A bloke?' Riley raised an eyebrow. 'Is that a compliment?'

'Possibly, but in the circumstances, probably not. Goodnight.'

Chapter Eight

*Charles Cross Police Station, Plymouth. Sunday 23rd April.
9.00 a.m.*

Savage was back at the custody suite at Charles Cross at nine
on Sunday morning. She needn't have bothered arriving so
early though, as they had to wait on Amanda Bradley. When
the solicitor breezed in at a little after ten, she was all smiles
for Savage, a heave of her chest for DS Riley. She nodded
with approval at the switch of interviewers and then apologised for her tardiness.

'Sorry, I had to return to the office for some papers. Then
a call came in.' Bradley smiled again and made a small
curtseying movement as if she was penitent and submissive.
Savage wasn't fooled. The solicitor had wasted their time
deliberately, knowing that the police could only detain a
suspect for an initial twenty-four hours. Bradley held up a
legal file and gestured to the interview room. 'Shall we?'

Kendwick was already seated at the table, exchanging
pleasantries with the custody officer sitting opposite him as
if they were old friends. The officer gave a grunt of embarrassment as Savage came over. He stood and left the room.

'Nice chap,' Kendwick said. He gave a conspiratorial wink
to Riley. 'He's got a few issues with his girlfriend, but I

offered my advice. I like to think I understand the female mind rather better than most men.'

Savage didn't dignify Kendwick's quip with a reply. Instead, she introduced Riley and set out the parameters of their second interview.

'We were at your place last night and this morning, Malcolm,' Savage said. 'The forensic team are still going over the house and if you've hidden anything there then you may as well come clean now.'

'Oh, I do hope they'll be careful.' Kendwick made a theatrical tutting sound. 'You see, the cottage belongs to my sister and she won't be amused if there's any damage.'

'Then it would make sense if you told us where to look.'

'To look for what? I've nothing *hidden* there. I dare say you found *everything of interest*.' Kendwick paused and then moistened his top lip. 'Well? Have you found anything?'

'Not yet.'

'Really?' Kendwick appeared disappointed. Then he cocked his head on one side and gave a little smile. 'Oh, Charlotte, you're playing with me. You *have* found something. I knew I should have put better security on that new laptop. And me a computer expert and everything. Now I'm embarrassed. What must you think of me? I can only say that those pictures were for my own personal enjoyment.'

Bradley glanced at Kendwick and tapped him on the arm. She raised her eyebrows. 'Do we need to discuss this in private, Malcolm?'

'Oh no. It appears Charlotte has discovered a few rather tame images I downloaded from the web. Naked women. Purely for masturbatory purposes, you understand? Harmless fantasies. What you might call light relief.' Kendwick spoke matter-of-factly, all the while keeping eye contact with Savage. She almost leaned back in repulsion, but stopped herself from showing any sign of weakness. Kendwick broke his eye contact and turned to Bradley. 'I suppose they are a little incriminating because they are all blondes. All except one, that is. If I remember she's a tasty redhead in somewhat revealing police attire. I guess she might look a little like DI Savage. What do you think, Detective Riley? A dead ringer? Of course there's the issue of matching collar and cuffs which I wouldn't know about. Perhaps you would?'

Savage tried to present a blank face as Kendwick turned back to her and began to laugh. Riley, sensing her unease, jumped in.

'Mr Kendwick,' he said. 'We're not playing around here. A young woman has been murdered and if you killed her I can assure you that you won't get away with it. If you didn't kill her then you're taking up valuable time which we could otherwise be using to track down the perpetrator.'

'OK, sorry.' Kendwick put his hands up. He gave another wink, this time at Savage, and then placed his hands back on the table, palms down as if he meant business. 'To coin a phrase, shoot.'

'Let's start again,' Savage said. 'Since you've been back in Devon have you been into Plymouth at all?'

'No. Next question.'

'Are you sure about that?'

'Yes, of course. If you knew anything about the good folk of Chagford, you'd be aware that they find the refined environs of Exeter far preferable to mixing with the plebs and lowlife of these parts.' Kendwick paused. 'Present company excepted, of course.'

Always the games, Savage thought. Any little chance to take a dig. Kendwick was aware of the rivalries between the two cities, the fact that Plymouth was far more important historically and far larger than Exeter and yet Exeter was the county town, widely considered the last place west of London where you could hold a civilised conversation.

'I take it, then, you've been into Exeter?'

'Yes. I needed some new clothes. I went in on Friday after you'd visited.' Kendwick leaned forward, eyes accusing. 'If you *remember*, while you were with me, one of my shirts got a little *stained*.'

Savage blanked Kendwick. 'And while you were there, did you do anything else?'

'Why, yes.' Kendwick leaned forward once more and looked from Savage to Riley to Bradley and then back to Savage again. He lowered his voice to a whisper. 'I looked at all the lovely women walking back and forth. *Exeter* women.'

Savage ignored Kendwick again and glanced down at her pad. She scribbled a note. If the victim was taken from Plymouth, would Kendwick have denied visiting? Surely he'd have concocted some sort of story to give himself a reason for being in the city. Otherwise, if they were able to pinpoint him somewhere – perhaps by CCTV or traffic camera snap of his car – his account would be compromised. And what was with this constant innuendo? Was it a bluff or a double bluff? Savage thought that Kendwick probably couldn't help it. Killer or not, he had adopted a persona which he couldn't cast off even if he was in danger of incriminating himself. She wondered if this was the way he'd behaved in America when he'd been in custody.

'Let's get back to Friday night,' Savage said. 'There's nobody to corroborate your story about, quote "sleeping like a baby by twelve". I put it to you, Malcolm, that you did go to the pub. However, once you were there, you found the experience quite uncomfortable. The bar was crowded with a number of young people, young girls. Maybe you did chat to the barmaid, but, like you said, she wasn't blonde. However, I bet some of the other girls were. You're not stupid though. You realised how risky it would be to carry out an attack on your home soil and in such a small place such as Chagford. You left the pub and went to a nearby restaurant, perhaps intending to try and calm yourself. It didn't work. When you'd finished your meal you were still aroused and, by now, desperate. You went home and then drove the hire car to Plymouth where you parked up and waited until a suitably drunk woman came along. You probably offered her a lift and she, making a mistake which would cost her her life, accepted. You drove her up to Dartmoor where you raped and murdered her.'

Kendwick stared at Savage, a blank expression on his face as if he hadn't heard a word she'd uttered.

'Mr Kendwick?' Riley. His voice laced with an undertone of anger. 'That's how it happened, isn't it?'

Kendwick sucked in air and then let out a long sigh. 'All right, you've got me. I lied about sleeping like a baby.'

Savage glanced at Riley. Was this another one of Kendwick's jokes? She looked back across the table. Bradley was fiddling with her papers. She'd obviously detected the change in the demeanour of her client. Kendwick swallowed and he raised one of his hands palm up. There was slight quivering before he dropped the hand to the table. Savage sensed the next words he said would be the truth.

'Go on,' Savage said quietly, not wanting to disturb the balance.

'OK.' Kendwick nodded. He turned to Bradley. 'Sorry for not telling you straight, Amanda.'

'I think this would be a good time to—' Bradley didn't get the chance to finish her sentence because Kendwick butted in, holding up his hand to silence the lawyer.

'No. Let me continue. All the stuff up until I left the restaurant is the truth, but at twelve o'clock I was far from sleeping like a baby. The truth is I was fucking a gorgeous woman senseless. I'd enticed her back to my house and taken her upstairs to my room. I stripped her off and pushed her back onto the bed and had her. Not once, either. Multiple times.' Kendwick looked pleased with himself, as if he deserved a medal. Savage felt like reaching across the table and smacking him one.

'You're admitting it?' she said. 'You're admitting abducting and raping this girl?'

'Girl?' Kendwick shook his head vigorously. 'Oh, I don't think she'd like being called a girl. As for abducting and raping, you've got that part completely wrong too. She was willing, more than willing.'

'Come now, Malcolm, she was drunk at best, comatose at worst.'

'Not at all. She was tipsy, the same as I was. She knew exactly what she was doing. In fact she was the one who initiated the sex.'

Savage shook her head, sickened by Kendwick's faux justification. Those who perpetrated sex crimes all too often blamed everyone but themselves for their actions. Kendwick, it appeared, was no different.

'That's not how it happened. Something went wrong, didn't it? Perhaps you weren't able to perform and that angered you. Perhaps she started screaming and you had to shut her up. Either way, she ended up dead and you had to dispose of the body.'

'I contest that. I *was* able to perform. As I told you, several times. Believe me, she was satisfied. Well satisfied.'

'So you say, Malcolm.' Savage tried to contain her anger and instead focus on obtaining the facts. She stared at

Kendwick. His right hand had gone to his ponytail, his finger twirling it round and round. She'd noticed the habit yesterday. Was it indicative of something? Nervousness? Guilt? 'Tell me what happened after the sex?'

'We both fell asleep. When I woke up in the morning, she'd gone.'

Savage nodded. Kendwick's tactic was clear now. Any time soon Layton would be calling through with forensic evidence from the bedroom. The girl's hair on the pillow, a spot of blood on the sheets, a piece of the girl's clothing which had slipped beneath the bed. Kendwick needed for the girl to have been at his place willingly and, more importantly, to have left alive.

'How convenient.'

'That's the truth.' Kendwick made another one of his shock expressions of horror, as if he was mortified that Savage didn't believe him. She felt a chill then, a sliver of doubt. Kendwick grinned. 'If you don't believe me, why don't we ask her?'

For a moment Savage wondered if Kendwick had lost the plot completely. Was he back at his body dump in the US? Walking amongst the dead and expecting them to respond as he whispered to them?

'What are you talking about?'

'Ask.' Kendwick smiled again, this time his mouth broad, his white teeth gleaming. 'Ask Melissa Stapleton. She's the woman I slept with. I was with her all night long. From when we went to the restaurant until she left in the morning. We met up again yesterday afternoon and she came round to my place to work on some notes. That's why she was there when you smashed down the door. Perhaps you can understand why I was so angry. I was in line for a repeat performance and you spoiled that.'

Savage's mouth dropped open, she was unable to conceal her surprise. Kendwick had well and truly skewered them.

'Sorry, Charlotte. I didn't kill the girl on Dartmoor. I didn't kill the girls in the US either.' Kendwick turned to Bradley. The lawyer was smiling too, high on the scent of victory. Kendwick looked back at Savage and Riley. 'And now, if you don't mind, I'd like to be released. I'm going to treat Amanda here to a slap-up lunch. Why, listening to me wittering on all morning, I think she deserves it, don't you?'

'Fuck, fuck, fuck!' Savage slammed her hand down onto the table. Kendwick and Bradley had gone, escorted by a custody officer to the front desk so Kendwick could be booked out. Holding him any longer was a pointless exercise. Riley stayed silent. 'How could I be so stupid? He was leading us a merry dance up the garden path and back.'

'He fooled me, ma'am,' Riley said. 'I thought the patter was all part of his personality.'

'Manipulation, that's what this is all about. He may not have killed the girl on Dartmoor, but believe me Malcolm Kendwick is a grade one sociopath. He has a need to be in control of whatever situation he finds himself in.' Savage waved her arm round, indicating the camera and the recording equipment. 'The interview setting is no different.'

'I don't see how we could have played it any other way.'

'He's the one who played us. He could have told us his alibi from the moment we arrested him. Stapleton was right there in the house, but he let us take him in, happy to spend a night in the cells just to heighten the tension.'

'But why?'

'Sometimes killers want to be involved with the police in a similar way arsonists enjoy seeing the fire brigade arrive at the scene of a fire they've set. Kendwick believes he's the

101

one in command, that he calls the shots and sets the agenda. That's why everything went so wrong for him in the States. When that cop had him tied to a chair and was torturing him he wasn't in control and there was no way he could play his game.'

'You're not suggesting we should adopt the same procedure?' Riley shook his head. 'It wouldn't have worked, ma'am. If this thing with Melissa Stapleton holds up then Kendwick's innocent. He couldn't have told us anything even if you'd pulled his fingernails out one by one.'

'Yeah, I know.' Savage scraped back her chair and stood. 'I guess that's what's making me angry. He may be innocent of killing the girl, but he's guilty of other things. You've seen him, he's dangerous. Mark my words, Darius, Malcolm Kendwick is going to cross our paths again.'

After completing the paperwork for the release of Kendwick, Savage left Riley to take care of the fallout from the collapse of the interview and went in search of Melissa Stapleton. A few calls revealed she was staying at the Three Crowns in Chagford and, after speaking briefly to Stapleton on the phone, Savage drove over there to verify Kendwick's alibi. She met the reporter up in her suite. A cosy lounge area had a sofa and a couple of armchairs, the day's newspapers spread across a low table, plump cushions on the sofa.

Stapleton was typing furiously on a laptop when Savage arrived. She'd already ordered a light lunch for both of them she said, if Savage didn't mind.

The lunch arrived a few minutes later and Savage didn't mind at all. Ham sandwiches, a plate of cheeses with an assortment of biscuits, a pot of mixed olives, a bowl of fancy salad. The whole thing presented impeccably.

'You must think me a bit of a slut,' Stapleton said, as she

poured sparkling water from a bottle to a glass. She handed the glass to Savage. 'A few hours in Devon and I'm jumping into bed with Malcolm Kendwick.'

'Your behaviour is perhaps a little bit more cosmopolitan than I'm used to,' Savage said, accepting the glass. 'But then you probably do things differently up in London.'

'Pah.' Stapleton reached for a sandwich. 'You're telling me people don't have rumpy pumpy down here in Devon? I don't believe it. The countryside is a hotbed of wife-swapping, husband-nabbing and swingers' parties.'

'Nothing wrong with sex,' Savage said, wondering where the journalist had got her take on rural life from. 'It's the sex with serial killers bit I don't get.'

'Malcolm's not a serial killer. Innocent until proven guilty the law says. And he hasn't been found guilty of anything.'

'I'd expect you to say that; after all, your paper's paying him handsomely for his story. Your competitors have taken a very different angle though.'

'That's just business.' Stapleton impaled a green olive with a cocktail stick. She held the olive between her teeth for a second before sucking it in and chewing. 'Sour grapes because they didn't get the plum.'

'So you don't think he did it then? Killed those girls in the US?'

'I'm agnostic leaning towards not. Do you really think I'd have slept with him if I thought he was such a monster? No, Kendwick's good-looking, witty, intelligent and successful. He doesn't need to go round kidnapping and raping.'

'That's what they said about Ted Bundy. I think you need to do a little bit more research into the reasons why serial killers do what they do. It's usually not about being some weirdo who can only get sex by force.'

'Go on then, enlighten me.'

For a moment Savage considered giving Stapleton a lecture on the vagaries of serial killers. About how it was the power rush which they were looking for. The subjugation of another human being, the feeling that they were in control. The thrill of hurting someone or something, the excitement of holding somebody's life in their hands, the God-like sensation when they snuffed the life out.

'The sex,' Savage said, deciding she wasn't going to do Stapleton's work for her. 'From one woman to another, what was it like?'

'Do you mean did he tie me to the bed and have me brutally from behind?' Stapleton speared another olive and then smiled. 'Well, he didn't. Actually he was rather sweet and gentle, almost boyish in his innocence. I can't say it was mind-blowing and he certainly behaved very differently from his outward persona.'

'What do you mean?'

Stapleton shrugged and made a flat smile. 'To be honest, I was somewhat disappointed he wasn't a little more forward. He didn't do enough to satisfy me. If I was writing for the movie or book review section of my paper I'd say two to two and a half stars. He was OK, but I've had better. Enough detail for you?'

'Plenty. I really only wanted to find out whether you did or didn't and I can see from your face that you did.'

'Oh, I see.' Stapleton shook her head. 'Clever. Perhaps you should be a journalist, you're really rather good.'

'Thanks. Where we move from a factual account to the realm of fiction is in Kendwick's version of your liaison. He said he was expecting a repeat performance. He also said you did it multiple times.'

'Men and their egos. They think they're great at sex and

the best drivers in the world, but one squirt and they're done, most of them. Malcolm was no different. To be honest, he was average at best and I certainly won't be looking to hop into bed with him again.'

'Right. Now I just need to establish the time your tryst took place.'

'Let me think, we went out for dinner and returned to his place sometime after eleven. We talked for a bit and then went upstairs. After the sex, I had a shower and returned to find he was fast asleep. That would be about one in the morning.'

'And before that you were with him all evening?'

'Not all evening. I arrived mid-afternoon Friday, checked in here and then went to meet him. I guess I turned up at his place at around four-thirty. I stayed until about seven and then returned to the hotel for an hour. We met up again at the Globe and then later went to the restaurant.'

'When did you leave his place?'

'First thing in the morning.' Stapleton lowered her voice to a whisper. 'It was rather embarrassing breezing up here having not used the room.'

'OK. So, just to be clear, were you together for the whole night?'

'Yes. He might have got up to go to the toilet at some point, but I'd have noticed if he'd slipped out for longer than a few minutes.'

'Are you sure?'

'Of course. I'm a light sleeper.' Stapleton smiled at Savage. 'And I guess, guilty or not, being beside Malcolm Kendwick all night didn't make for an entirely peaceful slumber.'

Savage reached for her glass and took a sip of water. Either Stapleton was lying or Kendwick didn't kill the girl on the moor. She looked across at the journalist. She'd turned her attention to her laptop and was busy typing something. She appeared confident in herself. She was at the top of the profession and was attractive and intelligent. Was it possible such a woman could be so stupid as to fall for Kendwick in the few hours they'd spent together? Was she now under his spell? Perhaps Kendwick *had* been brutal with Stapleton and perhaps she'd enjoyed the experience enough to lie for the monster. Savage shivered inside, not able to understand that sort of dynamic.

'Are we finished then?' Stapleton looked up from her laptop. 'Only I need to tidy this article up and file it.'

'Yes.' Savage stood and offered her hand. Stapleton reached up and shook it and Savage moved to go. Then she paused and turned back. 'Let's just say, for argument's sake, that Kendwick had killed the girl on the moor. How would you play it if you found out?'

'I'd get as much information from him as I could and then I'd tell you.'

'You wouldn't be worried about the story, the fact your paper has proclaimed him innocent?'

'No, not at all.' Stapleton smiled and then laughed. 'You've got a lot to learn about the newspaper industry. I'll let you into a secret. I talked about this with my editor before we signed Kendwick up. We had a meeting to analyse the risks involved. One scenario was that Kendwick *was* guilty of the murders in the US and that he carried on killing once he was back here in the UK. Do you want to know what my editor said?'

Savage nodded. 'Go on.'

'He said "It would be gold dust, Melissa. Just about the best thing that could happen."' Stapleton shrugged. 'So you see, either way I've got no reason to worry. It's a win-win situation for me and the newspaper. Now perhaps you understand why I slept with the man. It was simply too good an opportunity to pass up.'

Savage left Stapleton chuckling to herself and headed out of the hotel to find the weather had turned. A heavy April shower had filled the streets of Chagford with puddles and the pavements glistened in the rain. She stood in the porch and watched as a woman in her twenties scurried by, a flash of bare leg from the slit in a long coat.

She wondered if the serendipity Stapleton had talked of had smiled on Kendwick too. Something had come along which had been simply too good an opportunity to pass up.

Chapter Nine

He's angry. Very angry. She got away from him. She ran off and now she's dead. That wasn't what he wanted at all. He wanted her dead, yes, but not dead on a slab in a mortuary. Sliced up in some post-mortem. Head on a block of wood, guts on a metal tray, abused as if she was but a piece of meat. No, he wanted her dead in his arms and then dead on the ground in the darkness. Still and unmoving. His to touch and feel and love.

He shudders as an image of a pathologist performing an autopsy comes into his mind. He watched one on the internet once, appalled at the butchery which passed for science.

Butchery.

The girl last night had been a butcher. Or tried to be. He moves a hand down to his chest where she'd stabbed him with something sharp. Luckily, he'd half deflected the blow and his clothing had prevented anything more than a flesh wound. Still, the attack had left him reeling and she'd escaped. There'd been no chance of catching her in the dark, but she'd ended up dead anyway. He smiles at the irony and then frowns, thinking of her lying out on the moor, all lovely and pretty and waiting to be caressed. Stupid girl. Now the only touch would be from a scalpel and the bone saw which would trepan the top of her head and remove her silly little brain. If only she'd stayed with him she could have had some fun and then joined the others to rest in peace forever.

There's already quite a collection, he thinks. Out on the moor. In the wilderness. Quite an audience.

He salivates, thinking about doing it out there with the dead all around. The dead watching him fuck the next one. The next one joining the dead. The collection growing. More watchers. More excitement. More fun.

He frowns again, brought down to earth by reality and the continuing ache in his chest. After the girl had escaped, he'd gone to A&E. Sat with the plebs for three hours until a doctor had bothered to turn up and grace him with her presence. She hadn't liked the look of his chest, nor had she believed his story about slipping while using an electric drill. 'In the middle of the night?' she'd asked. He'd felt foolish for not thinking his little tale through. After she'd cleaned the wound and bandaged his chest she told him he needed to see his GP if the pain didn't subside after a day or two. Then, as he was leaving, she'd handed him a leaflet on knife crime.

The irony.

Never mind. There wouldn't be any irony next time. Nothing funny. Only a girl playing hide and seek in the wilderness. And the next time, he'd be the only one with a weapon and she'd be the one screaming in pain before she lay, still and unmoving and so beautifully dead.

Chapter Ten

Near Bovisand, Plymouth. Monday 24th April. 8.14 a.m.

'Do you enjoy them, Mum?'

'Huh?' Savage looked up from her bowl of cereal. Samantha was standing on the far side of the kitchen, brushing her hair, the red sheen accentuated by a beam of morning sun slanting in through the window. Her daughter had inherited Savage's colour while Jamie's hair was black like Pete's.

'Post-mortems.'

'How did you know?' Savage hadn't said anything to either Sam or Pete. She tried to keep her work life separate from her home life so as not to burden her children with any of the distressing details which every police officer came across on a daily basis.

'The mints.' Sam pointed at the tube of Polos on the table next to Savage's bag. 'You always pack them on a PM day.'

'They take away the smell.'

'Detective Superintendent Hardin told me a cooked breakfast works best.'

'*Hardin*? When?'

'On that take-your-child-to-work day last year. I asked him straight out.'

Savage laughed and then glanced round. Jamie had finished his breakfast and disappeared upstairs to play before school. 'Yes, he does say that, but I can't stomach it. Slimy eggs and bacon. All a bit visceral.'

'But do you enjoy them?'

'Enjoy is quite the wrong word, sweetheart. I hate them, I hate being there, hate watching. On the other hand, the PM is an important part of the process. At that stage the only thing we can do for the victim and their family is to find out how they died and use the information to catch the perpetrator. There's a certain satisfaction if the PM goes well and we find something to help in the enquiry.' Savage made a thin smile. 'But it's not enjoyment.'

'A bit like exams then,' Sam said with a grin. 'But with more blood.'

'Actually there's very little blood because the heart isn't pumping.' Savage took a spoonful of cereal. 'If you like, I can see what we can do for next year's take-your-child-to-work day. I'm sure Dr Nesbit would be happy to see you.'

'Yuk, no thanks! I think I'd prefer to go out with Dad on a frigate or something.'

'What frigate?' Pete had strolled into the room and caught the end of the conversation. 'The way the cuts are biting we'll be lucky to manage a three-metre RIB.' He tapped Samantha on the shoulder. 'Come on, or we'll be late.'

Sam pulled her rucksack from the floor as Pete went back into the hallway and shouted up to Jamie. She came around the table and leaned over and gave Savage a hug.

'Good luck, Mum. I hope you *do* find something.'

Savage nodded. 'Thanks, so do I.'

Half an hour later, Savage arrived at Derriford Hospital and made her way to the mortuary, mints at the ready. The parents of Amy Glynn had viewed the girl's body the previous day and confirmed her identity. Now, specialist officers were with them, trying to glean any information which might point to the person who'd abducted her. In most cases, a murder victim knew their killer; the myth of the dangerous predatory stranger was usually just that, a myth. So far, however, leads were thin on the ground. A jilted boyfriend had a cast iron alibi and an older relative who'd shown an unhealthy interest in the girl when she was younger, was being treated in the sex offender unit at Channings Wood, over near Newton Abbot.

The good news was that several of Amy's friends had come forward, and her whereabouts on Friday night was now known right up until the moment she'd left a house party in Durnford Street at exactly one forty-six a.m. A friend had taken a selfie with Amy as she'd bid her goodbyes, a timestamp in the top left corner marking the last moment anyone had seen her alive.

In the anteroom a hint of disinfectant hung in the air. The room smelled clean, but the chemical odour aroused an almost Pavlovian response from Savage, bringing with it the memory of grey organs piled on stainless steel trays. She tried not to retch, instead distracting herself by reading Melissa Stapleton's article in a copy of the *Mail* she'd bought in the hospital foyer. At first, the article seemed to be typical tabloid sensationalism, but as Savage read through, she realised Stapleton had peppered her writing with a number of salient points. The journalist was a shrewd operator, mostly coming down on the side of Kendwick, but also sowing a few seeds of doubt, enough to keep the readers titillated.

Savage looked up from the paper as the door to the anteroom banged open and a tall, thin man stooped his way through, arms articulating gestures in the air like some sort of robot creature, as he fought with the ties on a green robe.

Dr Andrew Nesbit, her favourite pathologist.

'Hello, Charlotte.' Nesbit smiled at Savage as he secured his scrubs over his tweed suit and then fiddled with a face mask, almost knocking off his half-round glasses in the process. 'Good to see you.'

'Andrew.' Savage put the paper down and held out her hand. 'It's been a while.'

'They keep on dying,' Nesbit said, taking her hand like a suitor from another age. 'But most don't meet such a grisly end as to require your presence.'

'Be thankful for that.'

'Oh I am, young lady, I am.' Nesbit turned and pointed back to his office. 'Now, sorry about the wait. You know my fellow pathologist, Dr Henry Wride? Well, as it happens he dropped down dead last week too. Turned out he had an undetected brain tumour the size of a large onion. As a consequence I've had to take on some of his paperwork because we're a little short-staffed.'

Nesbit's flat tone belied that there was anything much wrong. Dr Wride might well have been off work with a minor ailment or perhaps be taking a short golfing holiday. Savage had often thought that dealing with death on a daily basis and coming face-to-face with one's mortality might bring an acceptance of the situation. For herself, the horrors of the autopsy room did just the opposite.

She muttered some words of condolence as they walked into the dissection room together, wondering to herself whether Nesbit would have performed the post-mortem on his colleague, wielding the electric bone saw and cutting into the skull to find the tumour.

'Thank you, Charlotte, he was a dear friend and I shall miss him.' Nesbit paused, making a resigned face for a second, before brightening. 'Now, shall we?'

Amy Glynn lay on a stainless steel table, her head propped up by a block of metal. She still wore the sparkly silver dress and the material shimmered in the overhead lights. Her right hand was curled like a claw, but the nail file was gone.

'I've made a preliminary examination.' Nesbit waved his hands over the girl's body, as if he was a magician about to perform a miraculous trick. Unfortunately miracles didn't happen in Nesbit's profession. The girl wouldn't be levitating above the table nor, Savage thought sadly, would she be opening her eyes and sitting up. 'First, it doesn't look as if she was sexually assaulted.'

'No?' Savage was surprised.

'I took a swab and there's no sign of semen. There's no bruising of the sexual organs either internally or externally. Doesn't mean conclusively she wasn't raped, of course. The attacker may have worn a condom and the victim may not have consented but have been too fearful to struggle.'

'Right, so what killed her?'

'Well, John Layton noted there were no signs of major trauma and I agree. There are no broken bones, no marks of any kind on her neck, no blows to the head. Nor do I believe she was asphyxiated. That leaves drugs or poisoning or a natural death.'

'I see,' Savage said. 'And?'

'Toxicology samples were taken as soon as we got the body on Saturday evening.' Nesbit moved over to a side bench where he picked up a clipboard. 'The results show nothing more than a moderate amount of alcohol in the bloodstream. We'll be able to examine the stomach contents

114

once I've opened her up, but it doesn't look like she ingested anything untoward. There's also the possibility she had some underlying condition which could have caused her death.'

'You mean she had a heart attack or something like that?'

'Yes, but acute myocardial infarction is rare in somebody so young and there's nothing in her medical records to indicate that or any other condition.'

'I don't understand, Andrew.' Savage moved closer to the body and looked down at the girl once more. 'You seem to be excluding all possibilities.'

'Not at all. There's one obvious cause of death you're overlooking. One you and I have come across before.'

'Go on.'

'Think of where she was found and the state she was in. On the moor, with little clothing, up there under clear skies on a cool night.'

'Exposure?'

'Yes, hypothermia would be my hypothesis.'

Savage considered Nesbit's statement. The girl had been found between two large rocks. The initial assumption had been that she'd been dumped there with the intent to conceal the body. If Nesbit's guess was correct, then there was another possibility: the girl could have stumbled and fallen.

'There's no sign of major trauma, right?' Savage said. Nesbit nodded. 'What about bruises or grazes? I'm wondering if she could have slipped down between the rocks when she was still alive.'

'There are several small scratches on her arms.' Nesbit pointed at the girl. 'They haven't bled much, but there's enough blood to indicate they happened ante-mortem. If those scratches were made as she scraped against the rocks then yes, you could be correct. One other thing, look at the soles of her feet. They're dirty and cut up. It's as if she'd been walking around without shoes. There are numerous marks on her ankles and calves too. They could have been caused by the heather or bracken.'

'How's this for a theory, Andrew?' Savage moved away from the post-mortem table as Nesbit began to use a pair of scissors to cut away the dress. She strode across the room and turned. 'She was snatched from the streets of Plymouth and taken against her will to Dartmoor. Up there her assailant forces her to remove her underwear. He tries to assault her but she runs off. She comes across the tor and decides to hide in the rocks. While finding a hiding place she falls. The crack was narrow and once she's down inside, she can't extricate herself. The fact that she may have been drinking could have added to her difficulties. Unfortunately, the night is cold and she succumbs to exposure before anybody comes along the next morning.'

'That works for me, Charlotte.' Nesbit teased the dress away from beneath the body and placed it on a nearby trolley. Then he nodded to his assistant who'd been waiting patiently to one side of the room. 'Assuming, of course, we don't find any contra-indications when we open her up. Ready?'

Savage nodded but, as was her usual reaction at post-mortems, she turned away as the first cuts were made. She glanced back after a minute or so and instantly regretted it. Nesbit had peeled the girl's skin away from her chest and the mortuary assistant was beginning to cut through the ribcage with an electric saw. The person who was Amy Glynn was steadily being reduced to nothing more than skin and muscle and bone.

Kendwick rolled over in his bed, annoyed the light had woken him. He hadn't slept well. He guessed it was the knock on from spending a night in a police cell. The experience had taken him right back to his time in the States, banged up while the cops attempted to dig up any evidence they could to link him to the killings in the forest. And now, the pigs here in the UK were trying to find stuff too. He'd seen the news footage taken from a helicopter, the long swooping shots as the aircraft flew low over Combestone Tor. Other shots with a reporter standing at a police roadblock, the camera zooming over her shoulder to suck in a smudge of dark granite in the distance. Then the location footage had abruptly cut to a picture of him and the story had switched to his recent arrival in Devon. When asked whether the two things could be connected, the police had put out a 'no comment' statement.

Bollocks. Behind the scenes he knew they'd be working hard to find something to incriminate him. It was what police officers did. They didn't much care if they got the right suspect, a result was all that mattered.

He sat up in bed and stared towards the window. Last night there'd been several reporters camped outside in the street. Melissa Stapleton had dealt with the situation, promising a doorstep photo opportunity the next morning in exchange for them, in her words, 'buggering off'.

Then they'd spent the evening together working on a piece.

'All good this, Malcolm,' Stapleton had said. 'The more publicity, the more newspaper sales and, down the line, the more interest in your book.'

The problem was, Kendwick thought, 'down the line' seemed like a very long way off.

He got out of bed and went to the window. He pulled back the curtain a fraction. Aside from a young mum pushing a baby in a buggy, the street was empty. He breathed a sigh of relief. What Stapleton had said about sales may well have been correct, but all he could think of was the baying crowd who'd waited outside during the many court appearances he'd made in the States. They'd made it crystal clear the kind of justice they were after was akin to that from the Wild West and involved a tall tree and a good length of rope. He worried that the more the newspapers whipped up their readers, the more likely some good, honest UK citizens would decide to follow their American cousins and attempt to dish out some extrajudicial punishment.

Kendwick showered and dressed and then headed downstairs and made himself a cup of coffee. He took the coffee into the living room and slumped on the sofa. An empty bottle of wine and a couple of glasses sat on the small table. The remnants of last night's session with Stapleton. The 'session' hadn't unfortunately proceeded beyond a chat and notetaking. Kendwick had hinted they should repeat the events of Friday night, but Stapleton hadn't been interested.

'It was nice, Malcolm,' she'd said. 'But you're a little weird, know what I mean? I like to move around when I'm fucking someone. Get hot and sweaty. Feel as if there's some energy between us. All that lying still business. Not for me, I'm afraid.'

With that she'd packed away her laptop and left, promising to be back in the morning to deal with her journalist colleagues.

He'd felt the tension rise within him as she'd stood to go. He'd had to restrain himself from begging her to stay. From *forcing* her to stay. He'd clenched his fists, feeling his nails dig into his palms. Wondered about his hands round Melissa's neck. Squeezing the life from her until she was compliant. He'd managed to hide the anger with a smile.

Accepted the little peck on the cheek even as he'd felt himself become aroused.

Now, as he sipped the hot, black coffee, he thought about the way things were panning out. The way Melissa Stapleton had rejected him.

He took one more sip of his coffee and then threw the cup against the wall, the cup smashing, the liquid spreading over the surface in a huge, black stain.

Chapter Eleven

Combestone Tor, Dartmoor. Monday 24th April. 2.27 p.m.

After the PM, Savage picked up DC Calter from the station and they returned to Combestone Tor. Early-morning showers had drifted eastwards and the afternoon had turned out sunny and still. At the tor they found a solitary uniformed officer sitting in a patrol car.

'Ma'am.' The officer nodded a greeting as he got out of his vehicle to greet them. 'Any idea how much longer?'

'John's coming back up for a final look round later,' Savage said. 'Then we can release the scene.'

'To the ghouls.' The officer gestured over towards the far side of the tor where two people were approaching with their phones held out to their sides, recording video selfies of the murder scene. 'Bloody nightmare. I've had people doing that all day. Vultures, aren't they?'

Savage and Calter left the officer to deal with the sightseers and walked the short distance to the rocks. Layton had removed his ladder so they had to circle the tor until they found a place where they could scramble up. Once atop the rocks, Savage stood for a moment and then handed Calter a pair of binoculars she'd brought with her.

'What are we looking for, ma'am?' Calter said as she raised the binoculars to her eyes.

'I don't know, Jane. My guess is the girl ran across country to reach this spot. The question is, where did she run from?'

'Not the car park?'

'I don't think so. She had numerous scratches on her calves and the soles of her feet, likely caused by moving fast over rough terrain. Besides, if you were trying to escape from somebody, you'd want to put some distance between yourself and your attacker.' Savage turned back to the car park where the officer was remonstrating with the couple. 'Not a few dozen paces.'

As Calter continued to scan the landscape, Savage turned slowly through three hundred and sixty degrees. If the girl hadn't come from the car park then she must have approached from across the moor. She might not even have realised she was close to the few houses which comprised the hamlet of Hexworthy, a mile from the tor. In the early hours of the morning, there wouldn't have been any traffic and the hamlet lay in a little dip. Any outside lights would have been hidden from view. Savage's first circuit revealed nothing so she repeated the exercise, this time rotating even slower. As her eyes alighted on each feature, she paused and considered what she was seeing: a distant tor; a boggy area with a track running through it; a ridge with a valley carved like a bowl and a shimmer of blue water within; a tumbledown building; a stand of several tall pines; another tor; a small stream running down a hillside and passing through a succession of bogs.

'Nothing, Jane,' Savage said, shaking her head. 'At least nothing which jumps out at me. What do you think?'

'The same. She could have come from anywhere.' Calter

lowered the binoculars. 'If she came from over the horizon we'd be none the wiser.'

They stood there for a few more minutes and then Savage motioned for them to go. As she moved to the edge of the rocks and began to clamber down, something flashed in the sunlight.

'What's that?' Savage said. 'A couple of miles to the west. Over in the valley with the little lake.'

Calter lifted the binoculars again. 'I think it's a car, ma'am. Long abandoned by the look of it.'

'What colour is it?'

'It's . . . red.' Calter handed the binoculars to Savage. 'Just like the paint Layton found on the girl's thigh.'

They drove down from the tor, following a winding moorland road as it curled round above Hexworthy, eventually taking a left turn signposted as a dead end. A mile farther on, a turning circle marked the limit of the road, a five-bar gate blocking their way.

'I'll stop here.' Savage indicated a little grassy layby to one side of the lane. 'We'll have to walk the rest of the way.'

A rough track led away from the gate, weaving to and fro across the rugged landscape, but heading generally in the right direction.

'Wish we had Patrick and his trusty GPS here, ma'am,' Calter said as they got out of the car. 'For once.'

DC Enders considered himself something of an expert on hiking and the outdoors, although most of his self-styled 'expeditions' involved him and his family traipsing across Dartmoor in search of geocaches.

'I'm afraid it'll have to be old style,' Savage said, reaching into the glove compartment for a map. 'You know, paper?'

They set off along the track, a few minutes later rounding

a small hill. Within the slope of the hill lay a bowl-shaped depression a couple of hundred metres across. The little valley was filled with scrub and surrounded by a tall chain link fence. The track led up to a set of iron gates secured with a heavy chain and a chunky padlock. To one side of the gates, water slid down a concrete channel. The channel ran beneath the fence and angled up the right-hand side of the valley to a large bank of earth. Cut into the bank was a sluice gate with a set of large gears. Next to the sluice stood a small brick building. Savage pulled out the map and unfolded it.

'Some kind of reservoir,' Savage said. 'Probably feeds those houses in the hamlet.'

'Ma'am?' Calter stood by the chain link gates. 'In there.'

Savage moved across. A few paces inside the compound stood an old car, not red but blue. The windscreen had half gone, but what was left glinted in the sunlight.

'What is this place?' Savage said. 'A scrapyard?'

Calter pointed at a sign on the gate. 'Danger Deep Water. Keep Out.' Below the warning was an emergency contact number. Savage pulled out her phone, but saw there was no signal.

'This fence would be pretty useless at keeping people out,' Calter said. She moved to one side of the gate and tested the chain link. 'I reckon we could climb over. Shall we?'

Savage stood for a moment. Usually she would have no problem ignoring the rulebook. Anyway, they were investigating a crime.

'No,' she said. 'Let's go back to the hamlet and see if we can get some information.'

'That's not like you, ma'am.'

'I'm thinking of Malcolm Kendwick. What went on in the US. We don't have any stupid search rules which prevent us from taking a look, but if he's somehow mixed up in this then I don't want even the slightest hint of any impropriety.'

'You think he brought the girl here?'

'If we can find the red car you saw through the binoculars and the paint matches the residue on the girl's thigh, then *someone* brought her here.'

'But why here specifically?'

'That remains to be seen, but I can't see her having come along voluntarily, can you?'

'No.' Calter gave a little shiver. 'It seems unlikely.'

There was a moment of silence and then they turned and walked back down the track.

A few minutes later they reached the car, got in, and drove back to the junction. There were two small cottages close by and a larger farmhouse lying some distance off to the left. A track led down to the house, two concrete strips with water running between them. The track ran across a field and hairpinned back and forth until it came to a barn with an area of hardstanding. Various items of farm machinery lay scattered round the yard. A muck spreader, a huge reversible plough, a hay tedder. A pile of scrap metal sat in one corner, in another a heap of fence posts and coils of wire. Beyond the yard, the farmhouse sat in a twee garden.

'Well, the house is idyllic, if nothing else,' Calter said as they got out of the car. 'Apart from the fact a girl died not more than a mile from here.'

'Are you suggesting these people could be involved?'

'No, ma'am. Just pointing out the facts and quoting my ABC. Assume nothing. Believe nobody. Check everything.'

'Very good, Jane. I'm sure you'll pass your next set of exams with flying colours.'

They walked across to the garden gate and went up a narrow brick path to a wooden porch. The front entrance looked too pristine to be in use so they skirted round the edge of the farmhouse to the rear. Several sets of wellington boots hung upside down in a rack to the left of the back door. On the right, a large cowbell dangled from a wrought iron bracket. Savage reached up and rang the bell. The clanking sound echoed out across the farmyard and a few seconds later the door was opened by a slim woman in her fifties. A mass of greying hair sat piled atop her head, the whole lot secured with what looked like a pair of chopsticks.

'Hello,' the woman said, a half smile revealing high cheekbones. 'You've come about the puppies?'

'No,' Savage said, aware of Calter smirking beside her. She pulled out her warrant card. 'Police, Mrs . . . ?'

'Bridget. Bridget Chantry.' The woman's smile vanished. She shook her head. 'That poor girl. It must be about her, no? We had officers here Saturday evening asking questions. I'm afraid I couldn't give them anything useful.'

'Well, perhaps you can help me now. I'm trying to get access to the reservoir up the road. Would that be something to do with your farm?'

'Yes.' The woman nodded. 'But you'll need to see my husband about that. Won't you come in?'

She stood aside and ushered them in to a farmhouse kitchen. A large pine table sat in the middle of an expanse of red quarry tile flooring. Some kind of range stood over in an inglenook, but the range didn't appear to be in use since a number of framed family photographs stood on the black stove-paint surface. On the other side of the room, an area of worktop marked out a more modern kitchen. There was a smell of baking and Savage saw a saucepan on a halogen hob, water boiling in the pan, a glass bowl with melted chocolate floating in the water. The woman moved to the pan and prodded the chocolate with a wooden spoon.

'Nearly there.' She gestured to the table where a big man with a weathered face and little hair sat at one end. He stared down at an open newspaper. 'Graham, the police want to—'

'I heard.' Mr Chantry looked up and nodded. His face wore a scowl. 'What the fuck do you want to go nosing around in there for?'

'We believe the girl may have been in the vicinity on the night she died.'

'In the boneyard?' Chantry shook his head. 'Fool if she was.'

'The *boneyard*?' Savage cocked her head to indicate she didn't understand. 'Why do you call it that?'

'Ma'am?' Calter interrupted. 'The word has a double meaning, doesn't it? It's a term for a dumping ground for old vehicles as well as a graveyard.'

'The young lass is spot on,' Chantry said. 'You've seen pictures of 'em, right? In America? All those decommissioned fighter planes or bombers lined up in rows and parked in the desert. A boneyard. We've called it that round here since . . . well, since before I can remember. Years ago, back in my grandfather's day, the place was a quarry. With the stone all worked out it was good for nothing but a rubbish dump.'

'And it's always locked up?'

'Yes. It's dangerous in there. That's why I've got a fence round the whole area. Saves any legal action should some idiot slip into the water and drown. Only time I go in there is to clear the grids on the sluice a couple of times a year.'

'And the rest of it? The vehicles?'

'Worthless. They were dumped ages ago. The DPA have put a stop to the dumping now, even though it's my land.'

'DPA?'

'Dartmoor Park Authority. Bloody bureaucrats.'

'Why dump them there?'

'Where else? Better than leaving them to rot in the fields or by the side of the road. Must be twenty or thirty of them. Not all belonging to me, mind. Friends and neighbours. Used to be, if they had a wreck, then I'd let them tow the jalopy up there as a favour.'

'OK,' Savage said, thinking they had enough detail for now. 'Can we have access?'

'Sure,' Chantry replied without much enthusiasm. 'Bridget?'

Mrs Chantry turned and moved to the back door. She beckoned Savage and Calter to follow. Outside, but under the porch, a number of keys hung on a wooden board. Mrs Chantry reached out and selected one. 'Here you go. Pop it back when you've finished, OK?'

With that she turned and went back inside the house.

'Ma'am?' Calter said as they strolled back to the car. 'Are you thinking what I'm thinking?'

'That the key to the reservoir is all too accessible?' Savage glanced at the farmhouse. 'Yes.'

Back at the iron gates, Savage fitted the key into the padlock.

'Somebody could easily have taken the key,' she said, as the lock clicked open and she slipped the chain free. 'They could even have simply borrowed it and made a copy. If Chantry only checks the place a couple of times a year then he wouldn't have noticed if it was missing for a day or two.'

'Or it's Chantry, ma'am.' Calter made a mock shiver. 'I didn't like the man.'

'The law courts require something a little more substantive than your disapproval, Jane.'

'Pity. Would make the job a whole lot easier if we could get convictions based on my personal prejudices.'

Savage pushed one of the gates open and they stepped

in. A rough path led up a slope to the right, following the concrete sluice to the earth dam of the reservoir and the little brick building. Scrub crawled across the stony ground, trying to gain purchase in the thin soil. Here and there small trees, stunted by the lack of nutrients in the rocky spoil, had become gnarled and old without having grown taller than a couple of metres. A few animal tracks crisscrossed the area, but otherwise the terrain was almost impassable.

They tramped in, forging through a patch of brambles. They moved up the slope until they were level with the reservoir. The reservoir was nothing much more than a small lake, something like ten metres wide by three times that length. The small building next to the sluice looked to be an old pumphouse. The door was missing and an open window contained no glass. As they crested the rise and stood on one side of the dam though, the sight of what lay to the left of the reservoir was extraordinary: several cars, a couple of lorries sans trailers, two small tractors, an old bus, and, perhaps most remarkably of all, a two-seater light aircraft minus its wings. The bus sat half across the slope, the rear end jutting out into space as if it was auditioning for a part in *The Italian Job*.

Most of the vehicles had been there for a quarter of a century, Savage guessed, perhaps longer. The junk was spread out across an acre or more. She turned round, taking in each vehicle in turn, but now they were close to, she couldn't see the car they'd spotted from the other side of the valley.

'You go that way,' Savage said, indicating that Calter should head over to the other side of the reservoir. 'I'll skirt round to the left. Red, remember?'

Savage moved across the slope. To her right stood an old Ford Cortina. The chrome bumpers and door handles had long been pilfered, as had the wheels. A field of sparkling crystals covered the front seats – the remains of the windscreen. A small ash sapling grew in the left rear footwell and spiralled out through the passenger window. Across from the Cortina, a Transit van was in a far worse state. No wheels, no glass, no doors, no seats or interior fittings. The vehicle was simply a shell. A little farther on, Savage felt a pang of sorrow as she realised the next hulk was a classic MG similar to her own. The car was beyond restoration, the entire offside nothing more than a lace-like pattern of thin metal.

She moved on through the vehicles, following a trail which curved across the low scrub. While plenty of the old cars were rusty, none had the red colour she was looking for. She walked forward across a patch of bare ground where granite showed beneath a layer of sparse soil. She circuited a patch of brambles and came to another car. A red Marina van, the rear doors a mixture of flaking paint and rust. When she was a couple of steps away she stopped. A long silver thread hung from the jagged edge of one of the doors, rising and falling in the breeze.

'Calter!' Savage let out a call and then moved away from the vehicle. She pushed on through a mass of scrub she was sure hadn't been disturbed and circled up and to the right, avoiding any possibility of stepping on ground the girl might have crossed. She came out of the scrub and into another huddle of vehicles. She stepped forward, something cracking underfoot. She looked down, expecting to see a stick, but the thin, white object wasn't from a tree. It was a bone. Or rather, a number of bones.

For an instant Savage felt a chill. Several abandoned vehicles stood all round her. An old Massey Ferguson tractor had two headlights and a grille. The headlights stared at her like eyes while the grille appeared to widen in a manic smile. Across the way, the door on an ancient truck flung open as a gust of wind caught the superstructure. To the other side of the truck, an old Mini was almost skeletal in the way it had rusted to thin strips of metal. Something wasn't right about this place, she thought.

She shook herself. The bones probably belonged to a sheep. Savage stepped back, her foot again crunching on something in the undergrowth. She glanced down at the object which had fractured beneath her boot. Another bone. She stared down to where a section of spine lay trapped beneath the sole. She lifted her foot and the bone articulated like a snake. She whirled round, now seeing pieces of white everywhere.

'Ma'am?' Calter. Ducking into view from behind the truck. 'Oh fuck.'

Savage was about to say something when she realised the DC wasn't looking in her direction. Calter had turned her head to the Mini. She pointed and Savage followed in the direction of her finger.

Lying a step or so from the car, a long briar curled round something chalky. The bramble ran over a stone and then in one eye socket and out the other. The lower half of the jaw was missing, but the skull was unmistakably human.

Chapter Twelve

Near Hexworthy, Dartmoor. Monday 24th April. 4.32 p.m.

When they returned to the farmhouse to tell Graham Chantry of their morbid discovery, he appeared confused.

'Bones?' he said as he stood at the back door. 'In the *bone*yard? How's that then?'

'You tell me, Mr Chantry,' Savage said. 'It's your land, it's fenced off, and you've got the key to the gate.'

'I told you, I never go there except to check the reservoir.' He turned and looked back over his shoulder into the kitchen. 'Isn't that right, love? The reservoir. I never go there except to check?'

'No,' came a voice from behind Chantry. 'Never.'

'See?' Chantry turned back to Savage, seemingly convinced the confirmation from his wife would put an end to the matter. 'Now then, what are you going to do about it?'

'My colleague is reporting the find as we speak. Forensic officers will be here shortly, plus more detectives, the coroner and others too. A discovery of human remains is a serious business, Mr Chantry. I'm afraid there'll be some disruption.'

Some disruption was an understatement and within a couple of hours the once quiet scene at the reservoir had changed beyond all recognition. The police helicopter hovered high overhead, taking images to be used to help establish some sort of search pattern and to provide initial reference points. Half a dozen police officers and a team of search and rescue volunteers moved over the surrounding moorland beyond the reservoir plot. A group of CSIs had set up a large shelter just outside the perimeter of the fence and were shifting boxes from the lane to their temporary HQ, assisted by a couple of Land Rovers provided courtesy of the DPA. The coroner had also visited and Nesbit was due before too long.

Savage had walked back and forth from the end of the lane to the site a couple of times, trying to lend a hand with the coordination of the operation. So she was grateful when, on the third trip, a DPA vehicle pulled up alongside her. The passenger door clicked open and a man with a full beard leaned across from the driver's seat.

'Want a lift?' The man inside nodded down at the passenger seat. 'Save your feet, won't it?'

'Thanks.' Savage climbed up into the vehicle and offered her hand. 'DI Charlotte Savage.'

'Alan Russell,' the man said. 'I'm a DPA ranger. I must say I've seen nothing like this in all my time on the moor.'

'You've never come across dead bodies?'

'Oh yes, a couple. Walkers who've stumbled and frozen to death. Once a lone climber who dropped off a crag and splattered his brains all over the ground. Never bones though. At least not human ones.'

'You know the place, the boneyard?'

'Uh huh.' Russell nodded and then put the Land Rover in gear and eased up the clutch. He blinked as they began to move forward, big deep-set eyes surrounded by weathered skin. Wiry hairs made his beard appear like a giant pot scourer although, in contrast, the grey hair on his head was soft and bushy. He smiled through the beard as the vehicle bounced and jarred. His large hands grasped the wheel, the thumbs held out to prevent injury, his muscular arms fighting the shocks transmitted from the bumpy track. 'In fact I've been there recently to check the place. The DPA were worried material from the old cars could contaminate the watercourse and get into a leat which runs close by. It's the reason the dumping was stopped years ago. Now we run a yearly assessment to check everything's OK.'

'And you've just done that?'

'Yup. A couple of weeks ago.'

'And you didn't notice anything unusual?'

'No bones, if that's what you mean. But then there's been some torrential rain in the meantime. I guess some of the soil could have washed away. Of course I wasn't looking for bodies, just giving the site a quick visual and checking nothing else had been dumped. Not that Graham would do that, but others might.'

'And he's been cooperative, Graham Chantry?'

'Very. Never a hitch. I seem to remember when I told him he had to stop dumping stuff there he was a bit miffed, but he eventually accepted with good grace.'

'When was that?'

'Oh, must be at least a dozen years ago now.' Russell glanced at Savage before swinging the wheel to the right to avoid a large rock plumb centre of the track. 'You don't think . . . ?'

'At the moment we're simply gathering evidence. I'm sure there'll be many lines of enquiry.'

'I see.' Russell cocked his head. He'd plainly realised the level of police activity was unusual. 'So these bones don't belong to a hiker who got lost?'

'I don't really see how they could, but at this stage we've got to keep an open mind. We'll know more once we've finished our search.'

They lurched across the face of a steep slope before cresting a ridge. The moor lay spread out before them, miles of undulating terrain. The late-afternoon light washed everything with a warm, golden glow, the vista calm and serene. After another quarter of a mile Russell pulled off the track and swung the vehicle round on the heather so it was facing the way they'd come.

'Dartmoor Central,' Russell said. 'All change.'

'Thanks,' Savage said.

'No problem. You'll have to beg a ride back off one of your guys.' Russell gestured out the window to where a CSI officer was crouched down at the rear of a white van, peering beneath the vehicle. 'Assuming they're able.'

Savage got out, thanked Russell again, and walked over to the van.

'Ma'am.' The officer looked up. 'Busted the transaxle on a rock. John nearly came to grief too, but he got away with a bent bumper.'

Savage nodded and walked towards the iron gates, thinking that whoever was responsible for the bones would have had to bring the victims out to the boneyard in a 4x4, since both of the ordinary police vehicles had foundered on the rough track. Was that how Amy Glynn had got here? Or did she run to the boneyard from somewhere else and then move on to Combestone Tor?

She knew she was jumping to conclusions, thinking the Glynn case was linked even though the bones here were old. Still, they'd been in the open. Was it possible they could have got that way in just a few months?

At the gates, another CSI pointed down to a box containing PPE clothing. He held out an electronic log which Savage signed.

'Cwm Rust,' he said, grinning at her as she reached for a

protective suit. 'Nice spot to bring the kids for a picnic.'

Savage stared beyond the chain link fence. Remembered the section of human spine which had crunched and writhed beneath her feet. Said nothing.

Late on Monday afternoon, Kendwick strolled into the centre of Chagford. He took a circuitous route, stopping every now and then to glance round. Once he was sure nobody was following him, he made a beeline for the Post Office. He was forced to wait while those in front of him bought stamps, sent parcels, and chatted to the postmistress as if there was no one else behind them.

He smiled as he approached the window and bowed his head. Were they, by any chance, holding some mail for him? Post Restante? 'Kendwick,' he said when the postmistress asked his name. He pulled out his driving licence and pushed the identification under the glass division.

Five minutes later he was back in his front room with several letters and an A4 jiffy bag. He put the letters to one side and selected the jiffy bag. He laid the packet back down on the table and carefully peeled open the flap, noting that his hands were shaking as he did so. He reached in and pulled out the items one by one.

His gaze flicked to the window for a moment. Sending the packet to himself had been risky. More than risky, actually. Almost suicidal, as if he had a death wish. The fact he'd done so showed the importance he attached to the contents. He needed them close. They were all he had to remind him of his time in the US. Tonight, he'd secrete them somewhere on the moor.

He sighed and lay back in the armchair, one hand loosening the button on his jeans, his eyes closing, his mind casting back into the past for something to arouse him.

He wasn't surprised when, once again, nothing he thought of stimulated him. Even visualising Melissa Stapleton didn't work, despite the sex they'd had. In fact, when Kendwick had been with Melissa, he'd had to close his eyes and put himself in a very different place. She'd stripped off in front of him and he'd felt nothing. His outward demeanour projected a red-blooded male, but ever since he'd been a young child he'd known his urges were quite different from his peers. Growing up, for a long time he'd labelled himself as asexual. As a teenager he'd just not been interested in girls or boys, either as friends or as objects of desire. Until the incident with the girl in the shed, the only person who'd caused any sort of spark had been his Aunty Orla.

He remembered his aunt feeding him Turkish Delight from a tin. 'Our little secret,' she'd said, clutching him to her bosom as she dished out the sweets. 'For good boys only, yes?'

He hadn't felt like a good boy, not with the strange sensation in his stomach and the tingle of excitement spreading to below his waist. But the tingle had never grown to anything more. Many boys of his age moving into puberty would have had fantasies about their stern and scolding aunt, fantasies which were quite healthy and normal. Not so Kendwick. He felt nothing beyond the vague butterflies in his stomach. Stronger urges wouldn't come until he encountered the girl in the shed. And a year after that momentous day, poor Aunt Orla had dropped dead from a brain aneurysm.

His aunt was one of two sisters and three brothers, one of those brothers being Kendwick's father. The family's roots lay in Ireland and Orla was staunchly Catholic. The arrangements after her death were traditional, right down to the open coffin.

That was the first time he'd seen a dead body. He'd journeyed with his parents to his aunt's place in a sleepy village near Bristol. A sweaty crush of friends and relatives stood in the hallway and front parlour, pressing close, muttering condolences and drinking the free alcohol. As quickly as possible, Kendwick had hurried out to the garden to escape the nauseating claustrophobia. One of his uncles, not related to Orla by blood, but on his mother's side of the family, had come across as he stood alone next to a rose bush. His uncle had reached up and pulled down a stalk with a yellow flower at its tip.

'Smell this, lad. Sweet, hey?'

A sniff and a nod of the head. The rose did smell sweet, but sickly too.

'You want to see her?' His uncle bent low and whispered conspiratorially. He gave a wink. 'Come on, she's alone now.'

His uncle was younger than most of the other adult relatives, perhaps in his mid-thirties, and Kendwick, although less than half his age, felt an affinity to the man. His uncle had something about him, a glint in his eye, a hint of impropriety. The rest of Kendwick's extended family – the other uncles and aunts and grandmother this and great grandfather that – seemed stuffy and from a far-off generation. The most fun he'd had had been on the moor with his uncle. Out in the low cloud and the rain or forging through deep snow in the depths of winter. The atmosphere in the front room was close, a heavy vapour in the air. The thick carpet hushed their shoes as they moved across to the casket, the room now deserted as the guests sought out more food and drink. Kendwick stared down into the coffin where his aunt lay. She was a big woman, all plump and round, her eyes closed but her face bearing a wry smile as if the last laugh was on her.

'So serene, hey?' His uncle smiled. 'Serene and beautiful.'

'Yes, beautiful.' The answer came without a thought, Kendwick mesmerised.

'You know what the name Orla means?' His uncle looked back from the coffin as Kendwick shook his head. 'Golden princess. And that's what she is, a princess.'

'A princess.' Kendwick parroted the words.

'Do you want to kiss her?' His uncle winked once more. 'I do.'

Then he turned back and bent to her face, his lips brushing hers. There was a silence in the room as he straightened and licked his lips.

'Like a rose,' he said. 'Now it's your turn.'

His uncle moved aside and guided Kendwick forwards. Orla's smile appeared to grow a little as he leaned across and touched her lips. He was in awe of her stillness, the way she lay there so peaceful and unmoving and yet still containing the spirit she had in life. It was hard not to compare the way she was with the girl he'd lost his virginity to in the dark closeness of the shed in the garden.

'Lovely, hey?' his uncle said. 'Now off you go and not a word.'

Kendwick jerked awake, back in the present, back in his own front room, rather than that of his aunt's. He was aware his right hand had slipped inside his trousers. He quickly pulled it out, frightened at the way his heart was beating with excitement.

Savage spent several minutes struggling into the protective suit. Finally, she adjusted her hair net, pulled up the hood and put on a pair of gloves. She turned to the CSI at the gate. He hadn't spoken since he'd delivered his ill-received joke.

'Where's John Layton?' she said.

'Here.'

Savage swung to her left. Twenty metres away Layton stood beside a huge tractor tyre. He wore a white suit and he held a long, thin bone fast in a blue-latex-gloved hand.

'They're everywhere, Charlotte, just about any place you care to look.'

'John,' Savage said. 'Am I good to come in?'

'Sure.' Layton indicated several areas pegged out with crime scene tape. 'Just keep out of the places we've got finds.'

Savage turned round, confused. There were several cordoned-off patches scattered across the valley. Higher up the slope she spotted two of Layton's CSIs standing and peering down into a plastic crate. More tape surrounded them.

Layton followed Savage's gaze. 'One of the skulls,' he said.

'*One?*'

'We've got two so far. But from the number of bones I'm thinking there'll be more. Several more.'

'You're kidding me?' Savage scanned the valley. This was a spooky place even without the bones. The fact there could be two or more people who'd met their deaths and ended up here only made it worse. 'Does Hardin know?'

'A little.' Layton smirked. 'But I thought I'd leave the full details to you.'

'Thanks, John. Love you too. He'll have kittens when I tell him.'

Savage wondered how the DSupt would take the news. He'd try to figure out a way of breaking the story to the media gently, of course, only how the hell did you put any kind of a gloss on the fact a killer had been dumping bodies on Dartmoor? Inevitably questions would be asked about how this had been allowed to happen. How the victims had gone missing without anybody noticing. Then there was the

Kendwick effect. The media would be wanting to link these killings to Kendwick's appearance in Devon. Never mind that the remains were likely years old, they'd want to work up the angle, somehow make the story seem relevant and contemporary.

'Hardin will find a way to cope. Probably by shouting at the rest of us.' Layton stepped round the tractor tyre and placed the bone carefully in a plastic box. For a moment he stared down at its contents. Then he looked up. 'I'll give you a tour.'

'You think they've been here a while?' Savage asked as they walked up the slope. She stared at the old Ford Cortina. She tried to judge the rusting heap's age by the state of decay. Likely the car had been in position for a decade or two at least. Had the bones arrived before the cars, during the period they were being dumped, or after? She put the question to Layton.

'Hard to say until we've run some tests. From the state of the bones we've found so far, I'd say we're looking at ten years minimum.'

'And were the bodies buried or just left?'

'From what I've seen I think the latter is more likely.'

'Interesting.' Savage didn't elaborate, but she knew Layton would be thinking along the same lines as her. The novice killer might imagine that burying a body was the easiest way to dispose of the evidence. However, leaving the corpse in the open could often be advantageous. Within a week or so maggots would be hard at work consuming every portion of flesh. At the same time other animals, such as badgers or foxes, would turn up and attempt to drag pieces away. After a month's exposure to the elements, the skeleton would begin to separate. Now, any manner of animals could assist in scattering the bones over a large area. Of course the bones could still be discovered, but now they might be mistaken for a sheep or a cow. In addition, the cause of death would be very hard to establish.

There was one further point which Savage didn't think Layton would have thought of. Certain serial killers liked to return to their victims' bodies long after they were dead. They could find sexual satisfaction with the corpse even if it had been dismembered and only bones remained. If a body was buried in the ground, the killer had nothing to return to. Savage kept that gruesome and disturbing notion to herself.

'So, John or Jane Doe number one,' Layton said as they reached the two CSIs. The CSIs stood inside a taped-off area about five metres square. Savage could see several bones lying on the surface or partially buried beneath loose soil and stones. A skull lay in a large plastic box. The CSIs were photographing the bones and then tagging them and placing them in shallow trays.

'Any clothing?' Savage addressed the question to one of the CSIs.

'No, ma'am, not a sign.'

'None anywhere,' Layton said. He gestured across to another area of tape near the back of the old Mini. 'Over here there's something interesting, though.' They walked across until they reached the tape. More bones lay in a haphazard spread. Layton reached over the tape and down into a plastic box. He pulled out a little petri dish. 'Look.'

Savage stared at the dish. Inside, nestled on a piece of cotton wool, was a ring. The band was flat and wide with a plain zigzag pattern on it.

'It's going to be hard to track down the owner,' Savage said. She turned the dish this way and that, thinking something wasn't quite right about the ring. It just didn't look like a piece of jewellery someone would wear on their finger. 'Unless . . .'

'Unless the ring was found amid a collection of bones from a foot.'

'A toe ring, right.' It took a pretty stupid killer to leave an obvious aid to identification, such as a ring, at a crime scene. However, a ring worn on a toe might easily be overlooked. And a missing persons report compiled by somebody intimate with the misper wouldn't fail to mention the piece of jewellery, distinctive possibly only by the fact it was worn on a toe.

Savage handed the petri dish back to Layton and turned away. She ran her eyes back and forth across the strange little valley which hung above the steep slope leading down to the track. The place had been a magnet which had drawn the killer back here at least twice. Was it simply because the place was a good dump site or did the cars have something to do with it as well?

'The ring's where our luck runs out, I'm afraid,' Layton said. 'Nothing else to go on so far.'

'We'll have dental records.'

'Of course, but they're only useful when we've got a misper we can match them to.'

'DNA?'

'Yes, but it could well be poor quality. The bones have been exposed. Bleached by the sun, rained on, frozen, chewed by animals.' Layton reached into the plastic box again and removed a small bone. 'Look at the structure. Dozens of holes and very brittle.'

'How come nothing's been found before?' Savage said. 'We're in the middle of nowhere, but anyone seeing these vehicles would be drawn to them. If you were walking past you'd investigate, if only because you were curious. I'm sure some people would be tempted to climb over the fence.'

'But the place is such a huge tangle of nettles and brambles and small trees.' Layton waved an arm around. 'It's so overgrown that I guess nobody bothered to do much more than skirt the perimeter.'

Layton was probably right, Savage thought. And, although there were a number of interesting industrial sites on Dartmoor to do with mining and quarrying, this wasn't one of them. Nobody would come upon the boneyard except by accident. Nobody, that was, aside from the killer and Graham Chantry. Assuming they weren't one and the same.

'How long until you've finished?'

Layton bit his lip and then moved his head back and forth and scanned the valley as if making some sort of guesstimate. 'I'd say a couple of days to be sure we've found everything here. Mind you, if we're talking about stretching the search to the surrounding moor then I hope Hardin's got deep pockets. It would take months and, to be honest, where the fuck do we draw the line?'

They walked back down towards the entrance, Layton spelling out to Savage the additional resources they needed. The list was exhaustive.

'Right at the top is some better transportation,' Layton said as they reached the gates. He pointed to where his Volvo sat half off the track, the front bumper hanging loose. 'No way am I coming out here in my car again.'

Chapter Thirteen

Crownhill Police Station, Plymouth. Monday 24th April.
8.53 p.m.

As the sun dipped low over the western horizon, Savage headed back to the station. She found Hardin in his office standing beside a huge map of Devon and Cornwall. He gazed at the map as she told him the full extent of the finds at the boneyard.

'Who's in the frame for this, Charlotte?' Hardin pointed to a section of the map devoid of roads. 'Who's been killing these people and dumping them on Dartmoor?'

'Malcolm Kendwick.' Savage said the name almost without thinking of the consequences. She'd pondered whether Kendwick could be involved on the drive back over the moor and, although the idea was simply a theory, she thought she could back it up with facts. 'I'd like to work on the possibility he's mixed up in this.'

'*Kendwick?*' Hardin wheeled round from the board. 'Have you lost your mind? He might have been born and brought up in Devon, but he lived all of his adult life well away from here. He went to university in Manchester and then dropped out and founded a tech start-up in Birmingham. After that he went to California. There's no evidence to suggest he killed anyone before he went to America.'

Savage nodded. She had to applaud Hardin's knowledge. He'd obviously brushed up on Kendwick's biography.

'Well, sir, there is now. And if the bones turn out to be a decade or more old then the timings fit.'

'But Kendwick didn't live in the area, he'd have had to have travelled here.'

'And what's wrong with that? As I understand it, some of his extended family live in Devon. It's not beyond the bounds of possibility he could have visited them.'

'You're clutching at straws.' Hardin turned from the board and went across and sat down behind his desk. 'Kendwick's a pain in the butt, but can you imagine the uproar if we put this forward? The media will have a feeding frenzy and it won't just be Kendwick they'll come for. There'll be questions asked of us too.'

'That will happen anyway.' Savage paused for a moment. 'Sir, do you remember that psychologist guy, the Candle Cake Killer? He went to America too. While he was gone the killings stopped. He returned and he picked up right where he left off. We got it very, very wrong with him and I wouldn't want to make the same mistake again.'

'I'll bear that in mind, DI Savage.' Hardin picked up a sheaf of papers and ruffled through until he found the sheet he was looking for. 'Graham Chantry. According to the information I have, he shot two pedigree dogs a few weeks ago. Apparently he was within his rights as they were worrying his stock, but he was abusive to the owner. She made a complaint and the local bobby and an RSPCA inspector paid Chantry a visit. Not much they could do, but they gave him a warning.'

'And that makes him a serial killer?'

'It's part of his backstory. I thought you liked that sort of stuff. A suspect's narrative.'

'I do and Kendwick's *narrative* is far more compelling. He's got a—'

'Don't get flippant, DI Savage.' Hardin paused and then glanced back down at his desk. 'Now, so far Layton's confirmed there are at least three victims. I don't need to tell you that the first thing to do is identify them. Until then we're shooting in the dark.'

'We've found a ring which Layton believes one of the victims may have worn on a toe.'

'*A toe*?' Hardin's face creased as if he couldn't imagine why anybody would wear a piece of jewellery on their feet. 'Is that a sex worker thing or the badge of a swinger perhaps? Like an ankle chain?'

'I don't think so, but it could prove useful in linking the body with a missing person.'

'Right.' Hardin rearranged the papers once more and squared them on the desk in front of him. 'Back to Kendwick for a moment. He's in the clear with the Amy Glynn case so I want him left alone. To question him on anything other than a solid lead would be dangerously close to harassment. Amanda Bradley would be all over us. However, the person who abducted Amy could, I suppose, have been involved in these scrapyard killings. Let's be clear though, that person wasn't Malcolm Kendwick. Understand?'

Savage bit her lip and nodded. 'Can I at least check up on what he was up to before he went to the States? See whether he might have come down to Devon visiting relatives? If I draw a blank then at least we've eliminated him from our enquiries.'

Hardin rolled his eyes. He placed his hands together and then separated them and slapped them down on the table. 'Look, to be candid with you, I've had the Chief Constable on the phone earlier. She's been imploring me to "think

Kendwick" too, but I've been resisting. You see, this is all about political pressure and passing the buck. If I go after Kendwick and it turns out he's not guilty then I'm the one who carries the can. The CC doesn't care about that though. All she's worried about is pleasing her political masters and mistresses. The problem is at the end of the day I'm the one who is operationally liable. I need to justify my actions in the policy book. A hunch isn't good enough.'

'Research, sir, that's all I'm suggesting.'

'You don't give up, do you?' Hardin sighed and then smiled. 'OK, but I don't want you hassling Kendwick in any way. He's a clever one. Devious.'

'Sir, the way you talk it sounds as if you *do* think he's guilty.'

'Based on the evidence I've seen from the States, he probably is responsible for the killings over there.' Hardin turned his head back to the map on the wall. 'However, now Kendwick's here in wee little Devon there's fuck all we can do about it, OK?'

Savage nodded. 'Yes, sir,' she said.

After talking to Hardin, Savage headed down to the crime suite where she found Gareth Collier, the office manager, hard at work with all the administrative tasks involved in setting up a new investigation.

'Operation *Warrener*,' he said. His right hand roamed over his close-shaved head as he contemplated one of the whiteboards, a marker pen held in the other. 'Now an order of magnitude more important than the Amy Glynn case. Unless they're connected.'

'The boneyard?'

'Yes, of course.' The roving hand again, this time scratching the back of his neck. 'It's the usual conundrum we face in situations like this: do we lump the crimes under the same investigation or run them as separate but parallel cases? The choice we make has implications. Only at the moment I'm not sure what the fuck those are.'

'I'd say it's highly likely the rust and paint from the red Marina van will match with the samples lifted from the girl's thigh, and the silver thread I found almost certainly came from her dress. All of which means she was definitely there.'

'Sure, but that doesn't mean zilch if her presence was simply a coincidence and the bones are from a crime committed by a different killer at a different time.'

'I find it hard to believe they're unrelated.'

'You're probably right.' Collier turned and looked at Savage. 'That being so, I don't think it's a coincidence Mr Chantry owns the place. I think we need to start with him.'

'He told us he knew nothing. Denied the bones had anything to do with him. He claimed he only went to the place to check the reservoir and that only happened twice a year.'

'He'd hardly admit it, would he?' Collier jabbed the marker pen at the board. 'Look, the boneyard is a perfect place for Chantry to dump bodies. On his own land and behind a high fence. No prying eyes.'

'I'd say the opposite. Why incriminate yourself when there's the whole of Dartmoor to hand?'

'Because he wants to go back there time and again.'

'I did think that. These type of killers often want to revisit their victims, to relive the experience for sexual satisfaction.'

'Well then.' Collier smiled. Savage could tell there was something else. He reached for a piece of paper and handed the sheet to her. 'There's also another thing to consider.'

Savage glanced down at the paper. It appeared to be a surveillance log of some kind. Times and dates of vehicle movements. Vehicle registrations. Street names.

'What's this?'

'Your Mr Chantry's been playing away from home. His car has been spotted on fifteen occasions. Milbay. Stonehouse. You know, pay as you go.'

'Kerb crawling?'

'Just so. He's even been sent a warning letter. Although these particular details are recent, there's also a caution on file from years ago.'

'Paying for sex doesn't make you a killer. If it did we'd have to arrest a good proportion of the male population.'

'Again, you're correct, but his actions add a nuance to his character, don't they? Perhaps he's got over whatever caused him to kill by visiting prostitutes. They're an outlet for his sexual deviancy now. A release for the pressure valve.'

Savage sighed, thinking about Hardin and his ideas about Chantry's *narrative*. 'That doesn't happen. Killers rarely stop once they've started. Anyway, your theory would put him out of the frame for the death of the girl.'

'Maybe Mr Chantry is the exception to the rule. He stopped for a while but something made him start up again.' Collier reached for another sheet of paper. Various lines of questioning had been set out on the sheet along with details of Chantry's kerb crawling activities. 'Why don't you go and ask him?'

Chapter Fourteen

Now he's not just angry, he's really angry. First the girl gets away and then there are people at the boneyard. Not just any old people. These people are police types. Uniforms, detectives, forensic officers. Earlier, there'd been a helicopter flying overhead. Buzzing like some hideous giant insect intent on sucking blood.

He stands next to his vehicle in the darkness, half leaning against the open door so he can hold his binoculars steady in his shaking hands. The police are a mile away, across the other side of the valley, the boneyard glowing white in the illumination from their lights. If they could see him they might be suspicious. Then again, perhaps he's just another rubbernecker with a ghoulish interest in the macabre. Perhaps he's a reporter. Perhaps he's a fucking stargazer. He is, in fact, none of those things. If the police drove past they'd probably nod a greeting, little more. They certainly wouldn't be arresting him and taking him in because he doesn't look like a nutter from the outside. But on the inside, he's crazed up like nobody can guess.

The boneyard is history now. Gone. He can't go there ever again. He peers through the binoculars, seeing the image shake as his anger boils over. Never again. He doesn't like the sound of that, but he repeats the words in his head just to check the situation is as bad as it seems: *Never again.*

Fuck it!

He puts the binoculars down on the bonnet and slumps against the front wing. Problems, he thinks. Big problems.

He picks up the binoculars and gets into the vehicle. Sits there in the gloom. He was so looking forward to taking the new girl to the boneyard. Visiting her every day. It had been years since the last one. But there won't be any new ones there now. Not with the police swarming across the ground like ants. Picking over the remains of his girls and taking them away in plastic boxes.

He thumps the steering wheel. How dare they! He'll show them. For every girl they've stolen from him, he'll take another one right back.

He reaches for the ignition. There's a lot of work to do. A lot of girls to replace. Best get moving. Best get going. Best get . . . hunting!

Chapter Fifteen

Crownhill Police Station, Plymouth. Tuesday 25th April. 10.00 a.m.

On Tuesday morning Savage went to the initial Operation *Warrener* briefing. For now, the Amy Glynn incident was being kept separate, although Chantry was a possible suspect in both cases. John Layton was first up and he detailed the forensic finds so far and explained about the logistical difficulties involved with securing the site, preserving the evidence, and recovering the remains. Layton handed out a summary sheet to everyone and then he made his apologies and was away, back to the moor to continue his work. Next to speak was Gareth Collier. He outlined the investigative strategy and the resources needed. The case was unusual, he said. The victims were unknown and they had very little to go on as regarded identification.

'How's that then?' Hardin leaned across the table, displeased. 'Are you telling me several people can be murdered on our patch and yet nobody comes forward to report them missing?'

'The murders aren't recent, sir. We could be talking years ago. Perhaps as many as fifteen or twenty. That's so last century.'

Collier grinned, pleased with his joke. Several other officers laughed. Hardin just glowered and silenced the room with a sweeping stare.

'I don't bloody care if it was this century, last century or the fucking one before that. When someone goes missing, a loved one notices. Usually they report it to us.'

'Usually they do and often we can use that information to identify a body. Not in all cases though.' Collier glanced down at a sheet of paper. 'According to the figures, there are over six hundred unidentified bodies remaining on record for England and Wales, some twenty of those belong to us. If identification was that easy, we'd have cleared those cases up.'

'Well, easy or hard, we're going to clear *these* ones up.' Hardin half opened his mouth and stuck his tongue over his bottom lip in his characteristic fashion. 'Aren't we?'

An hour later the *Warrener* meeting was done. Savage grabbed DC Calter from the crime suite and they headed for Dartmoor to interview Graham Chantry.

'It's not just murder we can get this killer for, ma'am,' Calter said as they sped along the dual carriageway. 'There's the greenhouse gases too. How many miles have you done driving back and forth between Kendwick's place, the station, Combestone Tor and the boneyard?'

'Too many,' Savage said. 'We're probably spending more on petrol than crime prevention.'

'There you go then.'

When they arrived at Hexworthy, they found Chantry all too keen to speak to them. Sitting in the kitchen with a big mug of tea, his wife once more at the cooker, he was blurting out a story before Savage and Calter had even sat down.

'Hang on a moment, Mr Chantry,' Savage said. 'Let us get our notepads out, OK?'

Chantry nodded enthusiastically and Savage wondered at the state of the man. He seemed nervous and she'd seen the same kind of response from suspects who wanted to get their side of the story in first. He leaned forward, the steam from his tea rising to his face. Once Savage had sat down at the table, she told Chantry to continue.

'I seen him,' Chantry blurted out. 'The killer. He was up to something last night.'

'Wait a moment,' Savage said, holding up her hand. 'Start from the beginning.'

'I was out on the moor after dark. Wandering around. Hunting. Hunting the bastard who killed that girl.'

'*Hunting*?'

'Yes. And I almost caught him, didn't I? Lucky for him I didn't get close enough or else I'd have had a pop at him with my shotgun.'

'Mr Chantry, you can't go roaming the moor at night with your gun.'

'Oh, but I can. I've got a licence for shooting vermin and that's what the bloke is, right? Vermin.'

'OK, let's leave discussions about legality aside. Carry on.'

Chantry nodded. He explained he'd been driving around the area in the small hours, more in hope than in expectation of actually finding anyone. On his way home he'd seen a figure on the skyline, silhouetted against the moonlit sky.

'He was walking on a track near Laughter Tor. That's just north of here on the Two Bridges to Dartmeet road. Funny time for a stroll, I thought, so I switch off my lights, drive closer and park up. I get out and follow him along the track. After a while, I lost him in the dark, but when I got near the tor I saw him again. This guy was standing on the horizon staring across the moor to the south. He was looking at the boneyard. It was a couple of miles away, but you could

154

plainly see the lights you lot had put up. Anyway, he was, well . . .' Chantry looked across at his wife and then back at Savage and Calter. 'He had his trousers round his ankles, see. Moving his hand. You know.'

'Are you telling me he was masturbating?'

'That's the one. Right out there in the open. No shame.'

'And you watched?'

'Yeah, but not like that.' Chantry screwed up his face. 'Not like I was enjoying it. I'm not some pervert. He's the weirdo, not me.'

Savage nodded, thinking that remained to be seen. 'What happened then?'

'Well, he yanked his trousers up. I raised my gun to let off a shot but he disappeared behind the rocks. I searched round for a few minutes and then I saw the lights of a car back on the main road. The bugger must have circled the tor and got past me. By the time I'd legged it back to my Land Rover, he'd long gone.'

'Thank God for that. Just think of the consequences if you'd shot an innocent person.'

'But they weren't innocent, were they? About as far from it as you can get.'

'Whether they were or not, catching the killer is a job for the police, Mr Chantry.' Savage decided to change tack. She didn't want to get into an argument while he was being co-operative. 'Can you give a description of the person you saw?'

'Not really. I only saw him against the night sky.'

'And you couldn't identify the vehicle?'

'Nope, too far away.'

'Was the man tall, short, fat, thin?'

Savage looked at Chantry as he shrugged and then hunched forward. Was he telling the truth or was the whole thing some kind of fabrication?

155

'Mr Chantry, do you often drive about on the moor at night with your shotgun?'

'No,' Chantry said. He took a swig from his mug of tea as his wife brought a plate across to him. A couple of rashers of bacon lay sandwiched between two doorstops of white bread. Chantry stared down at the sandwich where red sauce oozed out. 'It was the girl, wasn't it? The thought of somebody up there doing another one.'

'What about those dogs you shot?'

'That was in the daytime, not at night. Besides, they were worrying sheep.'

'I was just wondering whether you'd seen anything else odd recently when you've been out at night.'

'No.' Chantry picked up his sandwich and took a bite. Spoke through a mouthful of food. 'Not other than the bloke.'

'Do you think he had a connection to the boneyard? Do you think whoever dumped those bodies had a connection? I reckon the person must know the area, possibly be a local. Do you know anyone local who might be involved? They'd need to have access to the reservoir. Be able to unlock the gates. Go there at any time without suspicion.'

'No.' Chantry put down his sandwich and reached for his mug once more. He was about to take a sip when he cottoned on to Savage's line of questioning. He clumped the mug down on the table, tea splashing out. 'You're fucking joking! I've got nothing to do with this. I didn't have a problem with you looking round the place and now I'm telling you about this weird bloke. How do you explain that?'

'It's called being canny, Mr Chantry. We've only got your word about this man. It could be that you want us to go on a wild goose chase.'

'NO!' Chantry repeated his denial, this time shouting.

156

'I'm happily married, not some pervert. Why do you think I'd rape and murder young women?'

'Nobody's said anything about rape nor the bodies at the boneyard being female.'

'Stands to reason they're female. And there was the girl in the rocks. Besides, these nutters always go for women.'

'Do they?' Savage stopped again and held Chantry's gaze. 'That's interesting, because you've got a bit of a problem with women too, haven't you?' Savage pulled out the piece of paper Collier had given her. 'Your car has been spotted multiple times in the red light area of Plymouth. You've even been sent a written warning letter.'

'Graham, is this true?' Mrs Chantry's voice was barely louder than a whisper, but Savage could detect the nuances within it. The accusation about prostitutes hadn't come as a complete surprise.

'No, of course not.'

'But the letter . . . ?' Mrs Chantry looked across at Savage. 'The police, they don't lie about this sort of stuff, do they?'

'No, we don't,' Savage said.

'Tell me the truth, love. Better out than in.'

'That's the fucking problem, isn't it, woman?' A wry smile came over Chantry's face. 'It's all out and no in. What's a man to do when his wife's kept her legs shut for the past twenty years?'

The smile on Chantry's face vanished and he stared down at his mug of tea. Mrs Chantry had gone red, but Savage wasn't sure whether it was from embarrassment or anger. Perhaps it was both. Mrs Chantry put the cup she was drying down on the drainer and hung the tea towel on a peg.

'I'll leave you with the police officers, Graham,' she said. 'Some things are better discussed in private.'

Mrs Chantry slipped across the kitchen and disappeared

down a hallway, her footsteps accentuating the silence she was leaving behind. Savage waited for a few moments until she heard a door click shut. Then she turned to Chantry.

'So you admit it, Mr Chantry?' Savage said. 'You've been visiting prostitutes in Plymouth.'

'Yes.' Chantry nodded. 'Once or twice.'

'It's been more than that. Your car was spotted over a dozen times in six months.'

'You wouldn't understand, love.' Chantry shook his head. 'You're a woman and women have different urges. Anyway, it's not as if I've done anything illegal.'

'Kerb crawling *is* illegal, but let's concentrate on the boneyard. There's nothing you want to tell us, is there?'

'No there isn't.'

'Are you sure?'

'Of course I'm fucking sure.'

'Where were you on Friday evening?'

'Here. All night.'

'And your wife can verify you didn't go out?'

'We've separate bedrooms, so after about eleven, no.'

'Convenient.' Savage paused and let the silence build for a minute. 'Look, Graham, we're going to identify the remains and if any turn out to belong to prostitutes then it's going to look pretty bad for you.'

'I've no more idea who those poor women are than you have.'

'OK.' Savage pushed back her chair and stood. 'DC Calter will take a more detailed statement about the man you saw, while I have a talk with your wife. After that I suggest you might want to have a word with her yourself.'

DS Riley was pleased to be assigned to the *Warrener* case, not so pleased that his part appeared to be desk based and involved painstaking searches on the National Police Computer. Trying to identify the remains was obviously important, but he'd become used to getting out and knocking on doors, doing face-to-face interviews and gathering the evidence at first hand. Now, stuck staring at a screen full of text, he felt removed from what was happening on the ground.

Riley was London-born, of distant Caribbean descent. He'd transferred from the Met to Devon and Cornwall Police after a drugs case in the city had turned rather spicy. He'd been undercover, his identity blown, some major league criminals not impressed with the sudden emergence of his alter ego. Relocation had been the only option. He'd been expecting his new job to be somewhat quieter, but the West Country had, so far, proved every bit as dangerous and exciting as the capital. He sighed and scrolled down through the information on the monitor, thinking a little excitement wouldn't go amiss right now.

He'd spent the morning following several different leads, each connected to a misper who'd vanished between five and twenty-five years ago. Three of the mispers had, in fact, turned up, a fourth was suspected of having emigrated and the fifth was dead. Riley shook his head as he logged off from his machine and headed for lunch. If people at least bothered to tell the police when a missing person case was closed, it would save thousands of hours of time.

Back in front of the computer after a cheese sandwich and a pot of plain yoghurt, Riley continued the trawl through the results. He'd now moved on to using keywords to do with the toe ring. Countrywide, there were dozens of hits. He went through them one by one, checking when and where they went missing and reading the descriptions of all those who'd never turned up. Within a few minutes he'd found a possible match.

'Jennifer Kassel.' Riley said the name aloud, as if to articulate it would somehow lend the misper substance.

Kassel came from a village on the north side of Dartmoor and had gone missing way back in 2001. Riley stared at the picture of the young woman on his screen. Blonde, blue-eyed, a girl next door type but no less attractive for that. In the accompanying notes he saw she'd owned a distinctive zigzag patterned ring which, according to her mother, she wore on a toe. He read on, feeling the familiar sense of excitement he always got when pieces of the investigative puzzle began to fall into place.

After he'd digested the information, he pushed back his chair and went across to Collier. He gave the office manager the name.

'Looks good,' Collier said as he listened. 'I'll pass it to one of the civilian researchers to run some further checks.'

Ten minutes later, Riley was back at his computer having treated himself to a celebratory cup of coffee. Collier strolled across and Riley looked up. The office manager had a glum expression plastered across his face.

'Kassel's a no go, I'm afraid,' Collier said. 'She was found dead in a squat in Exeter a few months after she went missing. Cause of death specified as a heroin overdose. You'll need to delete her from your list.'

'Fuck.' Riley shook his head as Collier walked off. Detective work consisted of something akin to walking around a maze. Every turn appeared to lead to a dead end but you had to keep going no matter how many cul-de-sacs you encountered. With patience, eventually you might find what seemed a dead end in fact contained a hidden path which led out of the maze.

A *dead* end . . .

Riley cast his mind back to the mispers he'd been tracking

in the morning. One of those had turned out to be a wrong turn, literally, because the girl had been deceased. For some reason the misper file hadn't been updated.

He looked at the details again for Jennifer Kassel. Then he did a search for news stories concerning her. A plethora of results came up, mainly from small provincial newspapers in Devon. Riley clicked through to several, reading the girl's biography. Kassel had come from a middle-class family and they'd been devastated at what had happened to her. The funeral service and burial had been held at Exbourne, a village some ten miles north of Dartmoor. Dozens of the girl's friends had attended, music from the Beatles, Oasis and All Saints among the tracks played to the grief-stricken congregation.

Riley stared at the screen, trying to reconcile the fact the ring had been found at the boneyard. If the ring was Jennifer Kassel's, which seemed likely since she was from the area, then there were several possibilities here. One, the girl had given the ring to somebody else, or perhaps somebody had stolen it from her. Maybe even as she lay dead in the squat. That could suggest working up action points around investigating Kassel's acquaintances in Exeter. Another possibility was the mother had retained the ring after her daughter's death, but passed it on or mislaid it. In either case the ring had somehow ended up with the unidentified victim on the moor. There was a third possibility, however, one which was more off-the-wall as well as being unsavoury and disturbing. However, the more he thought about it, the more logical the notion became.

'Shit,' Riley said to himself, realising he was going to have to go with his hunch. He selected a couple of the articles and sent them to the printer. He collected the printouts and went over to where to DC Enders sat bug-eyed in front of a screen.

'From John Layton,' Enders said, blinking and pointing at a set of photographs of the teeth in one of the skulls. 'According to Layton this bridgework is distinctive and very expensive. He reckons we should make a countrywide appeal to dentists.'

'Good idea,' Riley said, waving the newspaper articles in front of Enders. 'But I've got something else to show you. This might be a flight of fancy from my disturbed mind but I think it's worth exploring.' He explained to Enders about the possible implications, about how the ring could have been taken by a second individual and it was this person whose remains had been found on the moor.

'But the way you're saying it, sir, you're convinced the ring wasn't given away, right? So what's the other possibility?'

'Have you heard of Ed Gein?'

'Is he the killer who inspired *Psycho*?'

'Yes, other stuff as well. Know any more?'

'No, sir, not really. I'm not much up on serial killers. You should ask DI Savage.'

'Gein was a murderer, but that's not really what he was famous for. The police found body parts belonging to numerous people at his isolated farmstead, but in fact he only committed two murders.'

'How come?'

'Work it out, Patrick.' Riley placed the newspaper print-outs down on the desk. He pointed at the picture of Jennifer Kassel's funeral. 'It's all there.'

'Right.' Enders scanned the picture and read the article. He looked up. Riley wasn't sure whether to feel sorry for him that he hadn't managed to come to the same conclusion as he had, or be relieved the young DC didn't have quite the same sick mind. 'Sorry, sir, I don't get it.'

'I'm pretty sure the toe ring wasn't stolen from Jennifer

Kassel. It went with her into her grave, the one in the grave-yard of the church in the picture.'

'But that doesn't make any sense. How could . . .' The expression on Enders' face at once changed to one of sheer horror. 'You're saying . . . ?'

'Yes.' Riley almost smiled. Enders' sensibilities prevented the DC from vocalising what he now knew. To save him from embarrassment, Riley finished the sentence himself. 'It's quite possible none of the victims at the boneyard were murdered. For sure Jennifer Kassel wasn't. Her body was exhumed from the grave at Exbourne church and taken to the moor where our suspect did God-knows-what with the corpse.'

'Necrophilia,' Enders said, finally getting the word out. 'Unbelievable.'

'Unbelievable but very real. In one sense it's a relief to discover the boneyard is not a dump site for a serial killer. On the other hand, you can imagine the way the media will go with this.'

'Well, at least Kendwick's out of the picture. DI Savage was like a dog worrying a . . .' Enders tried not to smirk. 'You know what I mean, sir.'

'Yes, I do.' Riley smiled at Enders. 'But let's try and think of a better analogy, shall we?'

Inevitably, Kendwick held his uncle responsible for his failure with women. The awkwardness he felt when confronted with a living, breathing human body was down to him. Melissa Stapleton had brought up the issue and made him feel embarrassed and angry.

You're a little weird, Malcolm. I like to move around when I'm fucking someone.

Of course, the girl in the shed deserved a share of the blame too, but a good portion had to go to his uncle.

163

It had been the night of the day he'd visited Aunt Orla's house. He was staying with his father and mother at the other end of the village, guests of one of Aunt Orla's friends. The funeral proper was the next day and then they'd be driving back to Devon. He'd been put in a tiny box room where there was not much more than a bed. A Velux window slanted across the ceiling a few inches from his head, the stars arcing through the dark sky as he tried to get to sleep. He'd thought of God and of time passing and of Aunt Orla. Almost unconsciously, his hands had moved beneath the covers.

Later, he heard his parents come upstairs and go to bed. He waited and watched the stars move and the hands on the bedside clock sweep round until midnight had come and gone. Then he pushed back the covers and rose from the bed, finding his clothes and dressing quickly but silently. He sneaked from his room and headed downstairs. He unlocked the back door and went out into the night. The village was quiet as he made his way to Aunt Orla's place.

As he walked, a cat screeched in the night as if possessed by the devil. Was the sound a warning or an encouragement? He didn't know. He went down a small cut which led to the rear of his aunt's house. A tall gate stood in his way. He opened the gate and stepped through to the garden. Just to the right of the gate stood a little summerhouse where he remembered once lying prone on the floor in the sun while Aunt Orla worked nearby, her dress translucent, the shape of her full figure visible through the shimmering material.

He shivered and turned to the house. He moved to the back door and tried the handle, surprised the door was unlocked. He pushed the door open and slipped into the darkness of the kitchen. Another memory. Aunt Orla feeding him those sweets. Calling him a good boy and crushing him tight to her bosom. The flicker of arousal.

He slid his feet across the kitchen floor, drawn inevitably to the front of the house where Aunt Orla was waiting. In the hallway a scent hung in the air. Syrupy, sticky, intoxicating. He inhaled deeply. Once. Twice. His head swam with a strange sort of ecstasy.

He crept down the hallway, his feet silent on the thick carpet. The door to the living room was cracked open a few inches, a vertical bar of soft yellow. A low light had been left on and he was glad of that. But as he moved closer, there was a sound. A cough or a gasp. Somebody was in there with his aunt. Then Kendwick remembered. Tradition held that someone should remain with the deceased at all times to watch over them and protect them from evil. He breathed a sigh of relief, no longer nervous, thankful holiness could win over perversion. He would enter the room and sit with the person and pray for forgiveness, banish the vile thoughts from his mind. He stepped forward and put his face to the gap, pushed the door, and leaned in.

The coffin stood on two trestles, but Aunt Orla wasn't inside. Her clothes sat in a neat pile at one end. A formal dress, black tights, bra and knickers. Aunt Orla herself lay on the floor, naked, her legs spread. His uncle sat on the floor to the side, his trousers round his ankles, his head hung low. He was breathing heavily, sucking in great gulps of air. Then he looked up, his eyes alighting on the figure in the doorway.

'Why, it's you, you little tyke!' But his uncle didn't seem angry. He was euphoric, a smile spreading across his face and then unadulterated laughter. 'The golden princess, Malcolm, our secret, hey?'

Kendwick nodded. There wasn't anything to say, but something unseen passed between them.

'Good lad.' His uncle pushed himself onto his knees and then stood. He struggled with his trousers, pulling them up and fastening the belt. He glanced down at Aunt Orla. There was a triangle of pubic hair beneath a curving belly. White thighs full and soft. Heavy breasts which sagged to each side. To Kendwick, she looked absolutely beautiful. His uncle inclined his head towards the doorway. 'Now it's your turn. If you'd like.'

'Yes.' The word slipped out as a whisper, barely audible, as if nobody else needed to hear it but Kendwick and his uncle. And Aunt Orla of course. 'I'd like that very much.'

Chapter Sixteen

Near Hexworthy, Dartmoor. Tuesday 25th April. 11.58 a.m.

Savage found Mrs Chantry out in the back garden, stooping over a raised bed. Neat rows of leeks ran along on one side, whilst on the other a lattice of canes held rapidly burgeoning runners. Mrs Chantry bent to extract tiny thistles from between the rows.

'Weeds,' she said. 'If you don't keep an eye on them they choke off the vegetables. No vegetables means nothing for the table. Did you know you can harvest leeks near all year round? Something tasty for the winter. Assuming the pests don't get them.'

'Right,' Savage said, moving across. 'Mrs Chantry? Inside, I got the feeling you weren't entirely surprised when I raised the subject of Graham and prostitution.'

Mrs Chantry looked up, but appeared not to have heard Savage's question.

'Years ago, you stored produce and ate seasonally,' she said. 'You were satisfied with what you had. Thankful to be able to eat at all. Nowadays you can just go to the supermarket. You're spoilt for choice and can buy whatever you fancy.'

Savage nodded, wondering if the extended metaphor was deliberate. 'And that's what Graham did?'

'Seems so, doesn't it?' Mrs Chantry shook her head. She stared at Savage, running her eyes up and down her from tip to toe. 'I'm no great looker, not like you, but I'm his wife. What's wrong with me?'

'Nothing, nothing at all.' Savage smiled. 'How long do you think this has been going on?'

'I couldn't say. I guess it might be a good few years.' Mrs Chantry turned from Savage and bent to the raised bed again. She plucked another weed and held the plant in her hands for a moment before tossing it onto the path. 'He promised to love and cherish me, instead he's spending our money on whores.'

'Does Mr Chantry often go out at night, perhaps come home late?'

'Not often, no. Once every couple of months. Been happening a bit more recently though. I thought it was something to do with the dogs. Graham and Alan have been off hunting for strays. They've been causing havoc with the pregnant ewes.'

'Alan?'

'Alan Russell. He lives over near Widecombe. He works for the Dartmoor Park Authority.'

'Oh yes, I've met him.' Savage remembered the bearded ranger who'd given her a lift to the boneyard.

'Alan and Graham are pals, have been for years. They sometimes go drinking in Plymouth. Only now I'm wondering if drinking was all they were up to.'

'Is Mr Russell married?'

'He was. Beryl. Nice woman. They split up a few years ago.'

'Did she ever mention her relationship with her husband, perhaps raise suspicions with you?'

'No. That's just the point. When the boys went into Plymouth we used to meet up. Discuss TV and that sort of thing. Have a few drinks ourselves. I remember telling her I was happy Graham and Alan were together, that they'd stop each other getting into mischief.'

'But if he's a mate of Graham's, might he not cover for him? If they went into town together, then Alan could provide an alibi for Graham.'

'An alibi?' Mrs Chantry cocked her head. 'We're not talking a crime here, are we? You're not suggesting Graham could have had anything to do with the bodies in the bone-yard?'

'What do you think?'

'Graham?' Mrs Chantry looked truly shocked. 'Oh no. He abhors violence of any sort.'

'I see.' Savage wondered if the woman had forgotten about Chantry's slaughter of two pedigree dogs only a few weeks back. 'And was he going out at night years ago?'

'Graham's always popping out at night, but that's something you get used to when you're a farmer's wife. You might have a difficult calving, there might be foxes or dogs – like recently. There's lambing time, not to mention any orphans, although I'll often feed them. Then, in the summer there's plenty of work to be done and Graham will take advantage of the long evenings and work the fields until late.'

'I understand.' Savage paused and stared down at the growing pile of weeds. 'So this issue with the prostitutes, it's possible it could have been going on for a while?'

'When I was younger?'

'Yes.'

'But I was . . .' Mrs Chantry's face coloured. 'I mean we . . .'

'Do you have children?' Savage said, thinking of the pictures on the range in the kitchen.

'Yes.' The woman brightened. 'A boy and a girl. They've

both done well for themselves. Martin's at university and Liz is training to be a doctor. As you can imagine, it was a lot of work with the farm and all. There never seemed to be enough hours in the day to do everything.'

No, Savage thought. It had been the same with her family. Children took up a good part of your life and time for relationships often went out the window. Frustrated with the lack of attention from his wife, had Graham Chantry begun seeking comfort elsewhere? More pertinently to the investigation, had he begun to indulge in activities which had led him, inexorably, to murder?

'You think he was cheating on me all along? From the very beginning?' In the silence, Mrs Chantry had cottoned on. Her face sank, the attractive roundness of her cheeks all of a sudden gone, the skin now sagging and showing her age. She bent and began to pick up the weeds, dropping them into a nearby bucket. 'The bastard,' she said.

Riley knocked on DSupt Hardin's office door with some trepidation. He was sure the information he'd discovered about Jennifer Kassel wouldn't go down well.

So it proved.

'You're telling me somebody went to a graveyard, dug up this poor girl's body, and then took the corpse to Dartmoor where they had sex with it?' Hardin stared at Riley, something like disgust in his eyes, almost as if Riley was directly responsible. 'No, I won't have it. Not on my patch, not on my watch. The boneyard case is weird enough already without this.'

'Sir, it's not a question of what you wish might or might not to have happened. This is the most likely scenario given the evidence.'

'Can you imagine the press?' Hardin was shaking his head,

plainly already visualising the headlines. Playing the media game was something the DSupt enjoyed, but only when he was in control. When the media set the agenda he was likely to blow his top or attempt to clout a nearby journalist. 'We need to sit on this. At least until you have more proof.'

'That's why I'm here, sir. I've contacted Jennifer's mother. She confirmed her daughter was buried with the ring. Apparently it was her favourite piece of jewellery. I didn't mention anything else, merely that we were trying to eliminate some evidence from an enquiry.'

'Well, thank God you didn't. Can you imagine the distress?'

'Yes, sir, but we need to go further. The only way to know for sure is to request an exhumation. To dig up the coffin and see if Jennifer Kassel is inside.'

'Request an ex . . . oh shit. Please tell me you're joking, sergeant?'

'The bones have been in the open and are in poor condition. Layton is hopeful that we can get some kind of DNA match but told me the result may be partial. Kassel's dental records have been destroyed so there's no hope there. We also don't know exactly which bones belong together so we don't know which belong to Jennifer. If that wasn't bad enough, we haven't, unfortunately, found all the skulls. Exhumation is the only way to prove my theory.'

'Christ.' Hardin tapped his fingers on the desk and then pushed back his chair and stood. He moved to the map of Devon and Cornwall. 'What's going on here, Darius? At the boneyard? DI Savage suspects Kendwick is mixed up in the whole thing. If he is, does that mean he's some kind of nutter with a dead person fetish?'

'Necrophile is the word, sir.'

'But Kendwick?'

'I'm just following the evidential trail. Jennifer Kassel's death was from misadventure, she had a funeral and was interred and yet it's possible her remains are up on Dartmoor. She died well before Kendwick went to the States, when, in fact, he was sixteen and still living in the area. That could link him in.'

'Are you saying he was roaming graveyards when he was a teenager?' Hardin turned from the map.

'I've no idea. As I understand it, Charlotte is following up on his history. However, until we test my theory we won't know what happened to the girl's body.'

'OK.' Hardin moved back to the desk. 'How do we proceed?'

'John Layton's ready to go. He'll set the wheels in motion. Apparently we need approval from the Diocese and of course we also need to inform Jennifer Kassel's family.'

'Well,' Hardin said, a grimace spreading across his face. 'I can tell you that's going to be your job.'

After interviewing Mrs Chantry, Savage strolled away from the farm and back up the lane. The farm was roughly equidistant from the boneyard and Combestone Tor and she wanted to stand at a point where she could see all three. There was such a thing as geographical profiling, where nodes on a map became patterns which could point to suspects, but she was more interested in her gut feelings.

At the top of the lane she stopped and looked at each in turn: Combestone Tor, popular with tourists and locals, not much to it aside from a heap of dark rocks where the girl had met her death; the boneyard, a dumping ground for old wrecks, a reservoir which fed the hamlet, the resting place of several as yet unidentified individuals; the farm, where Mr Chantry lived and all was not as it seemed. She was trying to string the threads together when she heard Chantry's Land Rover start up. The vehicle skidded round in the yard and then set off up the track towards her. Chantry sat hunched over the wheel, staring forward, oblivious to Savage, and she had to step to the side as the Land Rover roared past.

Her thoughts disturbed, Savage went back down the track. As she reached the farmyard, Calter came round the side of a barn. The DC was red-faced and appeared to be in some distress.

'Are you OK, Jane?' Savage said as Calter walked across.

'Yeah, just about.' Calter stopped and looked back at the farmhouse. She sniffed and reached up and wiped moisture from her eyes. 'I've not got much good to say about Graham Chantry. For a start, he's a serial liar. He couldn't get his stories straight about when he might have picked up prostitutes. He got completely mixed up with the dates and insisted the whole thing had only started recently. I kept it to myself that we knew about the earlier caution.'

'Right, but there's more. Something's upset you.'

'I'll show you, ma'am.'

Calter turned and Savage followed. As she did she explained about her conversation with Mrs Chantry.

'So you see, it could have been going on for years.'

Calter nodded, but didn't appear to be paying much attention.

'I came out of the farmhouse and didn't know where you were. I thought you might have gone for a wander round the buildings.' Calter gestured towards the barn and a nearby pigsty. The sty looked ancient, the roof missing a few slates. Calter began to walk across. 'So I came over here. That's when I saw them.'

'What?'

'There.' Calter pointed at the entrance to the sty. 'Take a look.'

Savage stepped to the sty. A wooden door had been latched closed, a piece of baler twine holding it fast. She unhooked the twine and pushed the door open.

On the floor of the sty were four little bodies. Black and white and lying in a neat line. A smear of blood ran across the concrete floor to the brick which had been used to crush their skulls.

'Shit,' Savage said.

'The puppies Mrs Chantry mentioned when we first came here, ma'am.' Calter stood beside Savage, but faced away from the sty, not wanting to look. 'He's murdered the puppies.'

Savage bent and touched one of the pups. 'He's just done this. They're still warm.'

'I'd about finished interviewing Mr Chantry when his wife came in. He left and I talked to the wife for a few minutes. He must have done it then.'

They returned to their car and sat for a few minutes, debating what action to take. Calter was all for reporting Chantry to the RSPCA, but Savage argued they wouldn't be interested.

'It's farming,' she said. 'Perhaps nobody wanted the puppies so Chantry killed them. I've heard of it happening before, although I think usually they'd be drowned.'

'Yes, but he did it out of anger, ma'am.'

'You're right and the way he killed them suggests he is, despite his wife's claims, prone to violence.'

'So we *should* contact the RSPCA and let them deal with it.'

'Ordinarily yes, but in this case, no. Look, Chantry could well be our main suspect for both the girl at Combestone and the remains at the boneyard. Right now I'd prefer if he didn't know we found the puppies. It gives us something to use against him in the future.'

'I get that, ma'am, but we can't let him off the hook.'

'If he's guilty in either the Amy Glynn case or the boneyard case then he's going to be getting his deserts. A fine or a suspended sentence for killing the puppies will be irrelevant.'

Calter sighed. 'OK. So what now?'

'There's a DPA ranger – one of the people who helped ferry Layton's stuff to the boneyard. It turns out he's a friend of Chantry's. I think we should speak to him and see if he can shed any light on what Chantry may have been up to.'

Mrs Chantry had given Savage Alan Russell's number, but when Savage called, the ranger explained he was over on the northern side of the moor. Since he wouldn't return home until late, she arranged an interview for early the next day.

They drove back to the station in near silence. Calter sat slumped in her seat, still bristling with anger. Given the opportunity, Savage was pretty sure the DC would have confronted Chantry face to face. Luckily for Chantry's physical health, that hadn't happened.

Up in the crime suite, Savage found Collier, Riley and Layton standing at the whiteboards.

'Charlotte,' Collier said, beckoning her over. 'Developments in the *Warrener* case. Major developments.'

Savage walked across. Riley's shrug of his shoulders suggested the news wasn't good.

'Go on, Gareth,' Savage said. 'Don't keep me in suspense.'

'John first.' Collier waved a hand at Layton. 'Bit of a bombshell.'

'We've found three more sets of remains,' Layton said. 'There could be one additional set, but we're not sure yet. We'll know when we get all the bones back to the lab.'

'Six in total?' Savage looked at Layton open-mouthed. 'Fuck.'

Collier nodded sagely as Layton went on to say he thought they were nearing the end. If the office manager was worried by the growing complexity of the case, of the possibility there'd been an historic serial killer at work in Devon, he didn't show it.

'The bone find per grid square ratio has dropped close to zero,' Layton said. 'As we work our way nearer to the top of the hill there's very little to be found. Likely the remains have migrated down the hillside over time. I'm pretty confident six will be the final number.'

'Unbelievable.' Savage struggled for the words. She'd worked on investigations with multiple killings, but this was right up there with the most infamous cases in British criminal history. So why was Collier acting so sanguine? 'There's something you lot aren't telling me.'

'Yes, ma'am.' Riley cleared his throat. 'It doesn't look as if this is a murder investigation any longer.'

'What are you talking about? Six bodies dumped on the moor, the bones scattered, some weirdo fulfilling his fetishist desires amongst the old cars? Of course it's a murder investigation.'

'No, ma'am.' Riley pointed to the whiteboard where Collier had stuck up a couple of newspaper articles. 'We've got a positive identification on one of the sets of remains and a possible on another. Both died before they were taken to the moor.'

'So? It's a body dump. He killed them somewhere else.'

Riley tapped one of the articles. 'I mean they died but weren't murdered. Jennifer Kassel here succumbed to a heroin overdose in a squat in Exeter. There was a post-mortem, an inquest, a burial at a twee little countryside church north of the moor. Her friends attended the funeral. Tunes from the nineties were played. Oasis—'

'I don't . . .' Savage stared at the whiteboard. 'Oh shit.'

'We're thinking Ed Gein.'

'You mean grave robbery and necrophilia?'

'Yes.'

'John?' Savage turned to Layton. 'What's your opinion?'

'Nothing I've found rules it out. There are certainly no injuries apparent from the bones. No skull fractures, for instance. Unfortunately the dental records for Jennifer Kassel have been destroyed. We're going for DNA from all the bones but Riley has already approached Hardin with another option to test his theory.'

'Exhumation,' Savage said, turning to Riley. She let out a whistle. 'Did he go for it?'

'To say he wasn't keen is an understatement,' Riley said. 'But he agreed in the end. We're stressing the urgency of the situation to the relevant authorities and I'm hopeful we can get it done this week.'

'What about the relatives?'

'In hand. I'm taking Luke Farrell with me to break the news to the parents this afternoon.'

Savage nodded. Farrell was a family liaison officer, well used to dealing with sensitive and difficult situations. 'Good luck to you both,' she said.

Chapter Seventeen

Mutley Plain, Plymouth. Wednesday 26th April. 8.35 a.m.

First thing Wednesday and Savage drove into Plymouth to pick Calter up from her place. The DC squinted against the strong sun as she opened her front door in response to Savage's beep of the horn. She stumbled down the path and got into the car.

'You didn't go out last night?' Savage said.

'I did,' Calter said. 'With Milo. He's that new CSI on Layton's team and he was very definitely worth it. His attention to detail is quite astonishing.'

'He didn't wear gloves and use a fingerprint brush, did he?'

'Not quite, but I did wonder if he was working to a search grid. Nothing went untouched.' A smile grew on Calter's face, but as she settled back in her seat the expression faded. 'Life's for living, although I might try doing without alcohol for a few weeks. I'm not looking forward to those twisty Dartmoor roads on the way to Alan Russell's place.'

'You can open the window. The fresh air will do you good.'

Calter nodded, but didn't look convinced. She sat with her head bent to one side and the window half down, as they drove through Plymouth and then along the dual carriageway east. The DC napped until Savage took the slip road a little way beyond Ashburton, and headed up onto the moor.

'That's better, ma'am,' Calter said, perking up as they climbed away from the town, the lanes winding through a patchwork of little fields. 'Cobwebs blown away. Brain back in gear.'

'Right then, have you heard the latest as regards the boneyard?' Calter shook her head so Savage went on to explain about Riley's theory. 'If Chantry did abduct Amy Glynn then it's possible he's moved on from necrophilia. On the other hand, he might be involved in one crime but not the other.'

'And Malcolm Kendwick?'

'I've been told to forget him by Hardin. There's nothing to link him with the boneyard and he's got a credible alibi for the Amy Glynn abduction.'

'You believe Melissa Stapleton?'

'I think so. She doesn't seem the type of woman to fall under Kendwick's spell. However, if she was a little out with her timings, perhaps slept more soundly than she told me, then Kendwick may have had time to drive into Plymouth and take Amy to the moor. Once she'd escaped from him, he'd have realised the whole endeavour was pointless and returned to Chagford. Stapleton didn't notice his absence. If she had, he could have explained it away.'

'It's a long shot. He'd have put in a whole load of miles in his car. An hour into Plymouth, an hour back to the moor. Then there's the time when he was prowling for a girl and the time up on the moor.'

'That's why I'm nearly done with him.'

'*Nearly*?' Calter turned from the window and grinned. 'I thought Hardin told you to forget Kendwick? You're not a great role model, ma'am. Disobeying a direct order from your superior.'

'Nonsense. His sister lives over in Cornwall. I intend to pay her a courtesy visit to see if I can offer any support for her poor, blighted brother.'

'All part of the service, hey? Your caring neighbourhood police officer?'

'The only deception is who exactly I care about and it's certainly not Kendwick.'

'You think she'll be of any help?'

'Probably not, but I'd like to get the lowdown on Kendwick's activities before he left for the US. Specifically his life in Devon.'

'We're back to him and the boneyard again.'

'Yes.' Savage said nothing for a minute or so. They encountered a tractor and trailer coming the other way and had to reverse to let it pass. 'I'm not convinced Riley's theory explains everything which went on there. If it doesn't—'

'Malcolm Kendwick might?'

'Exactly.'

A little while later they passed through the chocolate-box village of Widecombe-in-the-Moor, took a tiny lane off to the left and, after half a mile, turned down a track which led to a twee little farmstead. Unlike Chantry's place, Alan Russell's yard was neat and tidy. To the right of the house sat a stone barn, hanging baskets adorning the walls, vivid flowers cascading down. The house itself had freshly painted windows, the door a crystal ice white.

Russell was over at the back of his Land Rover, pulling a length of chain from the rear. As they got out of the car, Russell turned, blinking into the strong sun.

For a moment he stared at them, one hand scratching his beard as if in puzzlement, but then he recognised Savage and raised a hand.

'Hello, good to see you again,' he said, smiling. He

gestured at the pile of chain on the ground. 'Just checking everything's in order after having to haul you guys out from the boneyard. By the way, my rate's gone up if you're needing another pull.'

'No tow required this time, Mr Russell,' Savage said. She walked across the yard and shook hands with Russell. 'Just a couple of matters to clear up.'

'Would you like tea?' Russell nodded at the house. 'Or shall we talk outside?'

'Outside would be fine.' Savage turned as Russell indicated a strip of green to one side of the yard. A garden bench sat next to a duck pond where several brightly coloured water-fowl paddled in the shallows. 'Lovely.'

'My passion, this place.' Russell walked with Savage and Calter across to the pond. As he did so, he explained about his property. It was, he said, a hobby farm, no more. 'You've seen Graham Chantry's spread? That's what a proper farm is like. All that mess. See, he hasn't got time to clear it up. Not like me.'

'It's very pretty.'

'I like to keep things looking good.'

They reached the bench and Russell and Savage sat down. Calter stood over near the pond. A couple of ducks swam over to see if she had any food.

'How well do you know Graham Chantry, Mr Russell?' Savage said. 'Would you say you're close friends?'

'Yes. We've known each other for years. Why, is he in some kind of trouble?'

'Do you go drinking with him in Plymouth?'

'Occasionally.' Russell looked across to where Calter stood. The detective was making notes. 'Can I ask what this is about?'

'Were you aware that Chantry visits prostitutes?'

181

'Yes.' Russell shook his head, his face pained. 'I mean, no.'

'Yes or no?'

'Yes. Look, I've been in town with him when he's wanted to go and pick up a girl. I get the impression it's something he does on a regular basis. That's not for me, though. Whenever he's suggested it I've always told him I'm not interested. I was happily married for years and after my wife left I promised myself I wouldn't stoop to that.' Russell smiled. 'To be honest, I prefer to spend my money on other things. This place, holidays abroad, my hobbies and interests.'

'So while you're aware of what he's been up to, you've never been with a prostitute yourself?'

'No.' Russell made a little shake of his head and then swallowed. He bit his lip and then gazed at the duck pond. 'I told you, I'm not interested.'

'Has Graham ever told you about his experiences? What he gets up to, perhaps what he likes?'

Russell turned back to Savage. 'No, of course not. That might be a girl thing, but blokes don't go into those kind of details.'

'So he never said anything about his sexual preferences? Mentioned he likes particular types of women? Particular fetishes?'

'Fetishes? You mean leather and whips and that kind of stuff?'

'Perhaps. Perhaps other things.'

'No. I'm not into that and I certainly wouldn't want to hear about it from Graham.'

'What do you know about the boneyard's history?'

'Not a lot. Just that the place was used by locals for dumping cars. If anyone had a vehicle they needed to get rid of, Graham would always offer to take it.'

'Don't you think that was a bit strange?'

'No, not really.' Russell gestured at his cottage. 'People help each other out, don't they? Graham helped with my extension. Provided a load of stone one year. In return I mucked in with his haymaking. Anyway, the car dumping's stopped now. Partly down to me, I'm afraid. The DPA couldn't allow it any more. Some scientist bod became worried about pollution into a nearby watercourse.'

'And Graham never talked about the place apart from the car dumping? For instance, he never said he took prostitutes there or anything?'

'Are you crazy? Why would he do that?'

'The place might have meant something to him. The cars.'

'Listen, love, you city types might get off on those kinds of things, but out here we're a bit more straightforward.'

'I guess you've been there a few times on DPA business. Ever seen anything suspicious?'

'I've been a lot of places on DPA business and apart from the occasional couple having sex at Haytor I can't say I've ever come across anything weird. Not old cars and stuff.'

'Can you think of anyone else associated with the area?'

'No. Graham keeps the place under lock and key. He's worried about the reservoir. Kids falling in, for instance.' Russell turned his head and glanced back at his Land Rover. 'Surely Graham's not involved with anything so perverted?'

'At the moment we're still gathering evidence. I'm investigating the girl in the rocks too.'

'Poor lass. A terrible business. What was she doing up there?'

'That's what I'm trying to find out.'

'But Graham couldn't have been involved in that either.'

'Why not?'

Russell shook his head. 'I don't know, to be honest.'

'Aside from the incidents with the prostitutes, is there anything else you can think of, anything odd?'

'I wouldn't want to say.'

'Mr Russell, we're talking about the abduction and death of a young woman and the discovery of the remains of several people at the boneyard.'

'Look, Graham can lose his rag sometimes. Like he did recently with the dog owner and her two Labradors. He didn't have to shoot those dogs, but he did. I've seen him smash things too. We were working on a fence together and he banged his thumb with a hammer. He went ballistic, took the hammer to a nearby footpath sign and clouted it so hard the sign broke in half. Of course he was angry about the path being there in the first place, but there was no excuse for it.'

Savage tried to coax some more from Russell, but he clammed up. Chantry was a friend, he said. As bad as his temper sometimes was, he couldn't imagine him killing anyone.

'OK.' Savage reached into her pocket, pulled out a business card and handed it to Russell. 'If you think of anything else to do with Graham Chantry or the boneyard, please give me a call. Oh, and one more thing. Do you know of Malcolm Kendwick?'

Russell reached up and scratched the top of his head. 'He's that bloke in the papers, isn't he? Just moved to Chagford?'

'Chantry wouldn't have come across him, would he? Perhaps years ago when Mr Kendwick lived in Devon?'

'I can't see how or why to be honest. Not Graham.'

Savage stood, but Russell remained seated. She thanked him and then she and Calter walked across the grass and back to their car.

'What do you think?' Savage said.

'I don't know,' Calter said. 'He didn't seem much interested in helping.'

'No.' Savage turned to get into the car. As she did so she saw Russell stand and move to the edge of the pond. He tilted his head back for a moment and then jerked it forward, spitting a great globule of saliva out onto the water. A duck swam across and gave an experimental peck at the resulting bubble and then shook its beak in disgust. 'Not interested at all.'

Back at Crownhill, Savage attended the afternoon briefing. John Layton was in full flow, presenting his final analysis of the boneyard finds.

'Six bodies in all,' Layton said. 'Although we've only discovered three complete skulls and a partial. The missing remains could be anywhere on Dartmoor, either moved by animals or possibly the perpetrator kept them for some nefarious purpose.'

'What purpose?' Hardin said. 'To use as garden ornaments or a doorstop?'

'Charlotte?' Layton gestured at Savage. 'Perhaps you could explain.'

'Sure,' Savage said, cursing inwardly that Layton had dumped her in it. 'Probably to prolong the relationship with the deceased. It's not unknown for a killer, or in this case not the killer but the necrophile, to have oral sex with a decapitated head, even with a skull. Irrumatio rather than fellatio since, self-evidently, there's only one active participant.'

'My God!' Hardin's face scowled in disgust. 'DI Savage, please tell me I didn't hear you correctly? That this is something from some B-grade horror movie? This whole necrophilia thing is quite bad enough without your morbid embellishments.'

'They're not embellishments, sir. There's ample evidence, including confessions, to suggest this has happened on a number of occasions. And not just in America.'

'Stop.' Hardin shook his head, held up his hand and turned away from Savage as if he'd heard quite enough. He muttered something under his breath and then lifted a hand and ran a finger across his forehead. 'The only good news is so far the media haven't cottoned on to the extent of what's going on.'

Collier coughed. 'Er, I'm afraid they have, sir. There was a helicopter buzzing the site yesterday. This is the result.' He unfolded a copy of the *Herald* and showed it to the room. A front-page picture showed a series of aerial shots and a graphic explained the search grid. 'They're saying the extensive nature of the search is evidence of a large-scale investigation.'

'Fuck.' Hardin stared at the newspaper for a moment and then looked back to his notepad. 'Can *anyone* give me some good news on either the *Warrener* case or the Amy Glynn girl?'

'Graham Chantry's on our radar for the Glynn attack,' Savage said. 'And owning the boneyard must put him in the frame for that too. As far as we can tell, he's been a regular kerb crawler on his visits to Plymouth.'

'There's no evidence this girl was involved in prostitution, is there?'

'Well, it wouldn't be the first time a student has turned tricks to earn her way through college, but no, I don't think Amy Glynn was standing on the corner looking for trade. However, after she left the party on Durnford Street she could have walked through an area frequented by prostitutes, so it's possible Chantry mistook her for a sex worker and that led to her downfall.'

'And the boneyard?'

'Nothing substantial. Chantry is an unpleasant man though. DC Calter found some puppies he'd killed and we already know about those dogs he shot on his land. In addition, Alan Russell, the DPA worker who's been helping us on the moor, told me a story of Chantry smashing up something using a hammer. Apparently he just lost it.'

'You're thinking cranial damage to the skulls?' John Layton leaned forward, interested. 'Unfortunately there were no such fractures on any of the remains we've found so far. No broken bones which could have been caused by a hammer.'

'It's tangential, but I thought I'd raise it.'

'Well,' Hardin said, 'why don't we bring him in?'

'We don't have any substantive evidence, sir.' Savage looked to Layton. 'At least nothing on the forensic front, correct, John?'

'Sadly, Charlotte's right.' Layton tapped a sheet of paper on the table in front of him. 'And remember Amy Glynn wasn't murdered. Unfortunately for us that means there are very few clues on her body. She wasn't raped and although the nail file suggests she put up some kind of fight, we couldn't recover any useable material from it. In addition, she was wearing a dress which was smooth and shiny. The nature of the surface precluded potential fibre evidence. The other problem is, Chantry has a legitimate reason for being at the boneyard. He even admitted he'd visited recently to check the sluice on the reservoir. We know Amy was there from the silver thread we discovered, but should we find anything to put Chantry in the same spot, it's rendered worthless by his statement.'

'Devious bastard,' Hardin said. 'Getting his excuse in early.'

'Exactly.' Layton sat back in his chair and folded his arms.

'Charlotte?' Hardin grimaced. 'Suggestions?'

'We continue to work on the last movements of Amy,'

Savage said. 'Start from there. If we can place Chantry in Plymouth, then we have something to go on. Witnesses, cameras, that sort of thing. He denied being in town on the night she went missing, but his alibi is weak.'

'And that's it?' Hardin didn't seem impressed. He looked round the room and then glanced down at his pad for some kind of inspiration. When he looked up he shook his head again. 'Bollocks,' he said.

Chapter Eighteen

Central Plymouth. Thursday 27th April. 3.02 a.m.

Riley rose at three a.m. He dressed quietly and made his way to the kitchen. Breakfast consisted of a slice of toast and a glass of orange juice, but the toast he left half uneaten, his appetite almost non-existent.

He'd been to many post-mortems and seen bodies in various states of decay and mutilation. This though, was different. There was something about digging up a grave that, even though he wasn't religious, he found deeply unsettling. As he cleared away his breakfast things, he shook his head. He was being selfish. The parents of Jennifer Kassel were the ones who'd been caused the most anguish. Breaking the news to them had been difficult and he'd been glad of the support of Luke Farrell, the family liaison officer, who'd accompanied him to their home. To have lost their daughter was bad enough, but years later to be told someone might have desecrated her grave and abused her body was just plain cruel.

Half an hour later, Riley parked up outside Hardin's bungalow. A curtain in the living-room window twitched and then Hardin was stepping out the front door, pulling it closed, and shuffling down the path to the street. He clicked open the car door and climbed in.

'Morning, Darius.' He stared out at the clear sky where stars still twinkled. 'If you can call it that.'

The journey to the graveyard was conducted in near silence, both of them too tired to want to indulge in anything but the most trivial conversation. They passed through the town of Tavistock without seeing a single person and then skirted the northern edge of the moor. As they neared Exbourne there was a hint of light in the east, but by the time they arrived at the church, clouds had darkened the sky again and a light drizzle floated in the air. Parked along the verge by the churchyard wall were several other vehicles: Layton's Volvo, a coroner's van, a liveried patrol car with two officers sitting snug inside, and a gleaming white Fiat 500 which, judging by the sticker on the rear window, belonged to the local vicar. According to the sticker, God's love conquered everything. Considering the circumstances, Riley thought the statement to be somewhat inaccurate.

They climbed out of the car into the damp pre-dawn and stood beside the gate to the church. The drizzle swirled on a soft breeze, wetting Riley's face. Hardin nodded across to the far side of the graveyard where a large white forensic tent stood in the darkness. A light source from within burned a halo of concentric rings on one side of the tent until a shadow slid across, obliterating the rings.

'Let's get this over with,' Hardin said as he pulled on his coat. He made to open the gate to the churchyard and then paused. 'Half of me hopes you're wrong about this, DS Riley. On the other hand if you *are* wrong then we're going to find the girl, aren't we? Over fifteen years she's been down there.' Hardin shook his head and then pushed the gate open and traipsed in.

They walked amongst the graves, zigzagging between the stones until they reached the tent. The entrance flap had been tied back and Hardin ducked his head and entered. Inside there was barely room to move. John Layton and a CSI stood over to one side. The local coroner was at one end and the sexton and the vicar at the other. Two grave-diggers stood along the remaining wall. A slab of granite lay on the ground near the vicar, gold lettering glittering in the light from several sets of battery-operated halogens which festooned back and forth across the roof of the tent.

Layton introduced Hardin and Riley to the others. The coroner, a man by the name of Rupert Edggerton, eased back and forth on his toes and heels, plainly nervous. The vicar was quite the opposite and he nodded across and said 'good morning' in a cheery voice. The sexton and the grave-diggers were keen to be about their business. The gravediggers were probably paid by the job, Riley thought. Get this over with quickly and they'd be home for breakfast.

As one of them raised a spade, the vicar held up a hand. He wanted to say a few words first, he insisted. Everyone bowed their heads and then the vicar spoke for a minute or so, most of what he said consisting of meaningless platitudes. After the speech there was silence for a moment before the vicar nodded. The gravediggers looked across to the coroner and he nodded too. Then they began to dig.

Soon the spoil heap of soil began to rise in a mound alongside the grave as the hole got deeper. The conversation was muted, as meaningless as the vicar's words. An obser-vation about the weather. A comment on the roadworks taking place on the A30. A short diatribe from the vicar on the travails of minor counties cricket.

Within half an hour the gravediggers were shoulder deep in the hole. Talk now focused on the technical issues. They were close now, one of the diggers said. Another foot or so.

Ten minutes later a distinctive thud echoed out as one of

the spades struck the top of the coffin. Soon the earth and rocks had been cleared away and a tarnished hunk of wood revealed itself. The coroner beckoned the gravediggers from the grave and they clambered up a small stepladder which the sexton had placed at one end. For the moment their work was complete. Riley turned to see that John Layton had disappeared, but a second later he stepped through the tent entrance now fully clothed in a PPE suit and equipped with a filtration mask for good measure. He climbed down the ladder and knelt. His assistant handed him a toolbox and he selected a screwdriver, a chisel and a hammer. Riley looked across at Hardin. The DSupt was nodding to himself, almost as if he was weighing the options so that neither result would surprise him.

'Here we go,' Layton said, his voice muffled. He put the tools to one side and ran his fingers round the edges of the coffin lid. 'You might want to step back until I see what we've got in here.'

The coroner reacted instantly, almost stumbling into the tent's side. Riley, Hardin, the vicar and the others moved away but with a little more dignity. Now, Riley could no longer see anything but the top of Layton's head and his back as he arched over in the hole, working the lid free. There was a creak which could have come straight from the sound effects department of a horror movie and then Layton was muttering something to himself.

'Well, well, well.' Layton stood upright in the hole. He pulled the mask away from his face and smiled. 'You'd better take a look.'

There was a delayed reaction as if nobody wanted to see. Riley took the initiative and stepped forward. He peered down into the hole. The CSI at the graveside had a torch and he flicked the switch on and aimed the beam down. The light shone on some silky material which had fallen away from the lid of the coffin, for a moment the sparkle disorientating Riley. But then the beam shifted and the CSI played the light round the interior of the coffin where there was nothing but a few small stones and a scattering of soil.

Aunt Orla went into the ground on the first day of May, in the year 2001. Kendwick didn't see his uncle again for a couple of months, the occasion a wedding of a distant cousin. The ceremony took place in a tiny church in a small village near the north Devon coast, the party afterwards in the local hall.

Kendwick stood on his own in a corner of the hall where he munched on a cucumber sandwich and drank tea with five sugars from a plastic cup. He watched a pretty bridesmaid laugh and dance, her dress flying up as she spun round. A glimpse of thigh, a flash of underwear. He thought of the girl in the shed.

He spotted his uncle over at the far side of the hall, circulating clockwise, moving inexorably round the room. Kendwick froze, forgetting about the bridesmaid, instead staring at the floor. A pair of black brogues slid into his field of view.

'Hi there.' His uncle tapped Kendwick on the shoulder. He indicated the open door and the veranda. Beyond the veranda, a man sat on a chattering ride-on mower, gliding across a cricket pitch. 'Shall we?'

Outside, his uncle guided him towards a table. Kendwick sat in a chair with his uncle opposite. Two pints of lager stood on the table, the liquid glowing amber in the sunlight. Beside the drinks lay a number of local newspapers.

'For me?' Kendwick said. His uncle nodded. Kendwick reached for the beer and then remembered his manners. 'Thank you.'

'I figured if you're old enough to . . .' His uncle's huge hands closed round his own glass. He raised the glass to his lips and took a gulp. 'Well, you get my drift?'

There was an uncomfortable silence. His uncle's eyes followed the mower back and forth across the field. As the mower got nearer the rattle of the blades got louder. Soon the music and laughter floating from the hall was drowned out.

'Aunt Orla.' His uncle craned his head. The spire of the church where the wedding had taken place was visible in the distance. 'Gone.'

Kendwick took a sip of his lager. Shivered as the cool liquid ran down his throat. He was afraid of what his uncle might say, might suggest. 'You don't want to . . . ?'

'No.' His uncle reached for the newspapers. The *North Devon Gazette*. The *Tavistock Times*. The *Okehampton Bugle*. He took the *Gazette* and opened it out. Folded the paper back on itself and handed it to Kendwick. 'But there are others.'

Kendwick stared down at the classifieds. Dogs for sale. Miscellaneous items. Services. His uncle's fat finger moved across the page to the far side. Death Notices. Three down, a pencil line circled some text. Tabitha McVeigh. Service at Saint Bartholomew's. Interment.

'You might have seen the headline,' his uncle said. 'The lass was nineteen. She went swimming with her friends in a quarry. Got cramp and drowned. I've seen her picture. Pretty as a peach. Still is, I should imagine.'

Kendwick had a vision of the bridesmaid, no longer spinning but instead lying still on the floor, the dress rucked up, her knickers removed. He blinked as another paper slid across the table towards him. Another column of notices. Another announcement circled in pencil.

'Simone Bell. Forty-five. She died of a heart attack. She

was local to Tavistock, Simone. She worked in Tesco. Good looker. Big knockers.'

Finally, the *Bugle*. This time Kendwick put his hand out and the newspaper ruffled up against it. 'I think I understand,' he said.

'Do you?'

'Yes. You want to dig them up.'

His uncle nodded. 'Dig them up and take them somewhere. Somewhere quiet with no chance of being disturbed. Nobody would ever know. Nobody would be harmed. We could have as much fun as we wanted. I've thought about it before, many times, never done it. Be much easier with the two of us.'

'And they'd be loved?'

'They'd be *cherished*. That's more than love, isn't it?'

Cherished. Kendwick liked the sound of the word. The syllables slipped over his lips and he thought of Aunt Orla all round and soft and lying on the floor with her legs spread wide.

'And we'd do it at night?'

'At night, of course.' His uncle gestured at the newspapers. 'Those are just examples. We'd choose country churches. Graveyards with no neighbours. Pull them from the ground a few hours after they've been buried and no one will be any the wiser. There's an endless supply and we can have the pick of the crop. They're always willing and ready and, to be honest, what harm can it do?'

What harm can it do? Kendwick repeated the words in his head as he reached for his glass of lager and supped down the last dregs, already feeling a little dizzy. A warmth was spreading within him, though whether from the drink or from the delicious sense that a whole new world was about to open up in front of him, he didn't know.

His uncle reached for the empty glass. 'Want another?'

Kendwick looked at his uncle. The man had a soft voice but a commanding one. Kendwick trusted him. He'd never seen him in a temper, never heard him say a bad word about anyone. For that matter, he'd never heard anyone say a bad word about his uncle. Yet the man was about to lead him down a one-way path.

What harm can it do?

None to the victims, Kendwick thought. And as his uncle had said, nobody would ever know. But there would still be scars. They'd be hidden, but they'd still be there. Carved into Kendwick's very soul. For the path his uncle was suggesting led to only one place. And that place was hell.

'Malcolm?' His uncle had lowered his voice to a soft whisper. 'The drink?'

'Yes please,' Kendwick said.

Once the initial shock had subsided, Riley and Hardin left the others in the tent. Layton and his assistant were examining the coffin for evidence, while the coroner, the vicar and the sexton were deciding what to do next.

'Unpleasant this, Darius,' Hardin said as they walked back to the car. Dawn had arrived and the pale daylight revealed the worry on the DSupt's face. The proof there had been a necrophile at work was more disturbing to Hardin than the activities of a serial killer. Murder was something he could fathom, even if he had trouble understanding the motives. Necrophilia was so far removed from his everyday experience that he could do little more than shake his head and turn to Riley for advice. 'You think the others are the same? All of them?'

'It would explain why we're having trouble identifying them,' Riley said. 'Grave robbing is, in a sense, the perfect victimless crime. Assuming the perpetrator isn't discovered in the act, there's nobody to tell on him, no visible crime to report. There's no insurance pay out, no wasted police time, no harm done to anyone.'

'No harm done? Don't talk stupid, man.' Hardin stopped at the churchyard gate and turned back to face the church. 'What about the family?'

'They'd never have known. Just like the others won't know until we tell them.'

'But there's the . . . the . . .' Hardin shook his head again. 'The *act*. What he . . . *does*. It's abhorrent, demeaning. To the victim as well as what it does to society.'

'I'm not sure I follow you, sir. There's a dead body. Nothing the necrophile can do to the corpse is any worse than cremation or dissection on Dr Andrew Nesbit's post-mortem table. He might have sex with the corpse, he might masturbate over it, he might remove body parts to keep for later. Judging from what we found at the boneyard, he almost certainly returned many times to be with the remains.'

'Bloody crazy nutter.'

'Almost by definition. He's probably even disgusted with himself, he knows he's mad. The trouble is he can't help it. He craves those dead bodies, he wants to be close to them, to cuddle them, to have sex with them.'

'What's wrong with a bloody life-size doll?'

'Just that, sir. It's a doll. It was never living, doesn't feel the same, doesn't smell the same.'

'Oh Christ, I really don't need to hear any more.' Hardin turned his head and stared at Riley. 'I sometimes worry about you detectives at the coalface. Wouldn't you prefer a change of scene? Perhaps a spell dealing with fraud cases or maybe take a break and get out on the roads. You're a decent driver. I could see you as a traffic cop.'

'No thanks, sir. Those guys really do get to see some grisly scenes.'

'Well, yes, I guess you're right.' They walked through the gate and reached the car. 'The poor girl's family, they're victims now. And the others, too. We'll need to track them down and tell them.'

'Now we know what we are dealing with I don't think it will be too difficult. They'd probably be better off not knowing though.'

'Yes.' Hardin opened the door of the car and ducked down and got in. Riley got in the driver's side and slammed the door. He started the car. Hardin shook his head for the umpteenth time. 'They'd be a *lot* better off not knowing.'

Chapter Nineteen

Mid-morning, Savage set off to visit Kendwick's sister. She lived over in Cornwall on the edge of Bodmin Moor, so Savage crossed the river Tamar via the bridge and headed west. The names on the road signs she passed as she drove were as strange and unfamiliar as the countryside: Doublebois, St Neot, Warleggan. Her satnav took her most of the way, but for the last couple of miles she had to resort to a map and the directions she'd been given by the sister. Eventually, she took a lane leading across a piece of unfenced moorland. The lane dropped down from the moor to a lush wooded valley where fields with white-painted post and rail fences suggested somebody with a passion for horses and the money to own them. At a set of gates, the lane turned to gravel and then ran up to a large house with huge leaded windows and mock turrets. To one side, a coach house had been converted to a garage while at the rear Savage could see a sand school, a stable block and a covered yard. In the school a girl sat on a large horse. The horse trotted diagonally in a jerky fashion, hooves kicking sand as they snatched up and down.

As Savage pulled the car round to a set of grandiose steps at the front of the house, a woman, who'd been leaning against the fence surrounding the school, turned and came striding across.

Savage got out of the car, showed her identification, and introduced herself.

'I'm Aline,' the woman said as she inspected the warrant card. 'Aline Rogers. Kendwick was my maiden name.'

She smiled and Savage saw the family resemblance in the shape of the mouth. The woman's smile though was warm and had none of the veiled menace of her brother. Forty-something with strong features and high cheekbones, she was slim and well-dressed in casual country wear. Well-kept too, Savage thought, taking in the surroundings.

'We spoke on the phone,' Savage said. 'It's about Malcolm.'

'Of course, shall we?' Aline motioned towards the sand school, where the rider was dismounting and leading the horse away. 'That's my daughter. Horses are my hobby, but they're Olivia's profession.'

Savage nodded as Aline went on to explain her daughter was a three-day eventer. Last autumn she'd come third at Burghley and her dream was to ride at the Olympics in 2020.

'We're off to Badminton next week,' Aline said. 'Fingers crossed she can do well there too. It's an expensive business though. Money like water.'

'Forgive me for saying so, but it looks like you can afford it,' Savage said.

'Yes.' Aline leaned on the paddock rail and watched her daughter lead the horse round to the stables. 'Luckily I can.'

'Can we talk about your brother? I have a few questions about his life before he moved to the US.'

'I don't understand. All the charges against him were

dropped. He's innocent. Surely you should accept that. Besides, you can't very well investigate crimes which took place in another country, can you?'

'This isn't about what happened in America. I'm just looking for some background information to eliminate Malcolm from an historical case.'

Aline turned back to Savage. 'You're not here about the girl on the moor then? The one who was found the other day? Some of the newspapers are hinting Malcolm could be involved.'

'No. Your brother has an alibi. He's in the clear.'

'The press seem to think otherwise.'

'Well, as far as the police are concerned he's innocent.' Savage tried to appear honest even though she was lying. 'That's all I can say.'

'OK. Go ahead.'

'Your parents lived in Torquay, right?'

Aline nodded. 'Yes. Until Malcolm flew the nest. After he went to uni they moved to Spain. Said they were fed up with the weather here. It might be unseasonally warm in the winters, but we never get hot summers and they wanted to live in a drier climate.'

'And by then you'd left home too?'

'Yes, I'm a decade older than Malcolm and my sister, Margery, has a few years on me. Malcolm was – how shall I say? – an afterthought.'

'An accident?'

'I guess so.' Aline gazed across at the stables. Olivia Rogers was wheeling a barrow round the side of the building. 'I love my children. I don't feel they interfere with my life. However, I think my parents resented Malcolm's appearance just at the time when they were beginning to get their lives back.'

'But you weren't around when he was a child?'

'No, I wasn't. I'd been packed off to boarding school, which I hated. Malcolm didn't go himself, but he was always being farmed round. My parents would go off somewhere and expect various relatives to look after him. They'd sweeten the deal with a few hundred pounds. In the summer holidays he'd often be left in Devon while they went on some European tour.'

'Was he ever left with you? After all, you'd have been in your twenties when he was a teenager.'

'Yes, he did sometimes come and stay with me, but I lived in London until after Olivia was born. By the time we moved back to the West Country, Malc was living up north.'

'And did he visit then?'

'A couple of times. We aren't that close.'

'What about other relatives? Do you think he came back to see them once he'd left the area?'

'He might have, I don't really know.'

'But there are some living in Devon?'

'Yes. A couple of cousins, an uncle. And our grandmother of course. She's in her nineties though.'

'Talking of your grandmother, you let Malcolm have the place in Chagford, even though you say you're not close.'

'I guess I feel a little guilty and he's family, isn't he? Poor Malc got a rough deal from my parents. After the trouble in the US I thought he needed a helping hand.'

'But he's well off, isn't he?'

'He spent a lot of money on lawyers in the States, but yes, I guess he is.'

'So?'

'Well, it wasn't the financial arrangements. I felt it would be good for Malc to be wanted. He sounded so low when I spoke to him. Not only had there been the arrest and all that followed, he'd also been rejected. There was a girl he got engaged to over there a year or two after he arrived. The wedding was all planned, the future bright. I was glad for him because he sounded so happy at the time. Then she just called it off out of the blue. Malcolm was devastated. I don't think he ever got over it. He certainly never talked to me about any other relationships. I don't think he wanted to take the risk he'd be dumped again.'

'Was there anyone before he went to the States?'

'Not that I can recall. Of course we lived miles apart, but he never mentioned anyone. The way my parents treated him made it hard for him to form friendships. I'm sure he had casual girlfriends, but nobody permanent.'

'No one down here he visited?'

'I wouldn't know.'

'And when did you last see Malcolm?'

'It was a number of years ago. We spoke on the phone loads when he was in prison in the US though. Now he's back home I hope I'll be seeing more of him.'

'Thanks for your time.' Savage pulled out a business card and handed it to Aline. 'If you could email me the contact details of any relatives who live in Devon and Cornwall that would be great.'

'That's it? Malcolm's in the clear?'

'Investigations are ongoing, but you've been very helpful.'

Aline moved from the fence and began to walk with Savage back to the house. 'Malcolm's misunderstood, Inspector. That's his problem. He's very clever and I think that makes him a little arrogant at times. I know one thing, he wouldn't hurt a fly.'

Savage nodded as they approached her car. She thanked Aline Rogers once more and got in. As she pulled away, she glanced in the mirror. Aline stood staring towards the sand school as if she was deep in thought, as if Savage's visit had unsettled her. Although the woman's information had been short on specifics, Savage thought she'd got a better handle on Kendwick. He had a problem relating to the opposite sex, a problem borne out of rejection as a kid and in later life. His outward demeanour suggested somebody confident and assured, but beneath the surface lay a different Malcolm Kendwick, one Savage was sure the phrase 'he wouldn't hurt a fly' could never apply to.

Back at Crownhill mid-morning, Riley had the dubious honour of informing Collier of their discovery.

'So?' Collier said, as Riley stumbled bleary-eyed into the crime suite. 'What have we got?'

'Nothing,' Riley said. 'The grave was empty.'

'Now tell me the bad news.' Collier shook his head. The office manager knew what was coming. 'The status of the investigation.'

'Obviously the team's going to be cut back. Hardin said there's no other option. We've got the Amy Glynn case to focus on. Now we've established the boneyard is in all probability no longer a dumping ground for a serial killer, the DSupt's brought the axe down.'

'How many have I got?'

'Two.' Riley glanced across the room to where Enders was collating a bunch of misper files. 'Me and him.'

'Could have been worse, I suppose.' Collier stared at Enders. 'But not much.'

Riley nodded and then discussed with Collier the best way to proceed. They at least had a list of people to work with. No longer thousands of mispers scattered countrywide, now their search was confined to females who'd died in the last twenty or so years and been buried within Devon. Burials were rarer as opposed to cremations and they could likely discount a great many graves because of their location. There would still be thousands and there was no way of knowing whether their necrophiliac had ventured farther afield, but Collier was content with the parameters.

'We work this lot through and see what we come up with,' he said, staring at a number six on his whiteboard, the figure ringed several times in red marker pen. 'At least it's doable. Even if we are left with a skeleton crew.'

Riley laughed at Collier's bad joke and returned to his desk. 'Doable' the office manager had said. Possibly. With some effort they might well be able to identify the remains and locate the empty graves. Finding the perpetrator of crimes which had been committed a decade or longer ago was going to be much more difficult. Of course, they could get a lucky break. Perhaps the other bodies came from the same area as Jennifer Kassel, even the same graveyard. Perhaps there'd been a common funeral firm involved or a registrar who'd be able to weed out suitable corpses. Short of that, the task was nigh on impossible unless they discovered evidence which might implicate Graham Chantry in some way.

By the afternoon, Riley was flagging. He wondered whether he should call it a day. He'd been up since three, officially on duty since four. He decided instead to grab something else to eat and give it another hour or so. He wanted to work up some action points to go through with Collier before he quit. A few minutes later, back in the crime suite after a Danish pastry and a coffee, Riley found DC Enders in an agitated mood. As Riley entered the room he stood and came scurrying across.

'Sir?' Enders waved a sheaf of printouts in the air. 'I've got something you need to see.'

Riley nodded as Enders came over and laid several photographs on his desk.

'Here are the six sets of bones.' Enders arranged the six pictures in a row. Riley could see each picture contained varying numbers of bones, a common theme being a skull, or partial skull, at the top, although that was missing from two of the images. Enders slid one of the pictures away. 'Say, for argument's sake, that this one on the right is Jennifer Kassel. Once we get the DNA sorted she'll be out of the frame.'

'OK,' Riley said.

'So we've got five remaining. All recorded dead, we suppose. Meaning we need to go through death records to match possibles with the skeletons.'

'Yes, I'm following you so far. What's your point?'

'This one is the skull with the fancy dental work.' Enders pointed to the picture on the far left side. 'Well, dental and medical records are destroyed ten years after death which means the search we instigated – you know the one where we wrote to dentists? – that's irrelevant now.'

'Looks like it.'

'Only it isn't.' The DC grinned at Riley. 'See, we've got a result. A dentist in Barnstaple contacted us to let us know that he's pretty sure he was responsible for the work. Although it was a while ago he remembers the patient. In fact, she's still on the practice records although he hasn't seen her for years.'

'Well, he wouldn't, would he? Not if she's dead.'

'That's just it, Darius! I ran the woman's name through the register of births and deaths and she's not dead. In fact, when I checked her name on the PNC she came up as a missing person. Can you see what I'm getting at?'

206

Enders produced another piece of paper and passed it across to Riley. The woman's name and details were printed on the paper. Melany Lodwell. She'd been twenty-three when she went missing in 2007, a checkout assistant from Bideford. A year before, she'd been involved in a serious car accident which had required extensive dental treatment. The misper report suggested the scars were not only physical, but mental too. The woman had given up her job after the accident and hadn't returned to work. She'd been depressed and her doctor had recommended psychiatric treatment. Whatever treatment had been laid on was too late because Lodwell had gone missing just before Christmas in the year following her accident.

Enders waited while Riley read the report and then spoke again. 'But now she's not missing, is she? We've found her.'

'But . . .' Riley scanned the details again, the realisation beginning to hit him. He looked back across to where Collier was wiping a load of pen scribbles from the whiteboard, the boneyard case now just an unpleasant sideshow to the main event: the abduction and death of Amy Glynn.

'There's only one conclusion to draw, sir.' Enders was grinning like an idiot. 'It's obvious.'

Riley had it then, but being of a generous nature he let the DC have his moment of glory. 'Go on, Patrick. Tell me.'

'Our necrophile got bored of waiting for another corpse, so he went out and started from scratch. Melany Lodwell wasn't taken from a coffin because she was never registered as dead. So, if she was never registered as dead and we've found her body on the moor, then the only conclusion is . . . ?'

Enders cocked his head on one side, his face beaming with delight. Plainly he *wanted* Riley to spell it out, just to emphasise how clever he'd been.

'She was murdered,' Riley said.

On her return to the station, Savage bumped into DS Riley in the corridor outside the crime suite. He had some news for her. She listened as he explained the yo-yoing of the *Warrener* investigation back and forth between unlawful killing and necrophilia.

'So you see,' he said after he'd revealed the evidence about Melany Lodwell. 'This might be a murder investigation after all.'

Savage told Riley about her visit to see Aline Rogers, Kendwick's sister. 'Kendwick could well have been present in Devon at the time of the grave robbing. In fact, he left for the US shortly after you say Lodwell went missing.'

'Could just be a coincidence. He was living away from here, wasn't he?'

'He may have visited. I wonder if he killed Melany and that was a catalyst to get out of the country.'

'I'm on my way to see the DSupt. Want to come?'

'Not really.' Savage smiled. 'But I guess I'd better tag along.'

Hardin took the news badly. He prowled back and forth behind his desk, every now and then glancing at the map of Devon on the wall.

'Do you know where I've been for the past hour?' he said as he reached the office window and did an about-face to start another march across the room. 'I'll tell you. I've been at a press conference where I had the unenviable task of explaining that we've downgraded the *Warrener* investigation from a multiple murder enquiry to one which merely involves necrophilia and grave robbery.'

'I'm sorry, sir.' Savage shrugged. 'I should have been there to back you up.'

'You?' Hardin wagged his finger. 'Not a chance. A woman talking about men having sex with dead bodies? The press would've wanted a photograph of you all pretty and lush so they could fashion some ridiculous headline around it.'

Hardin was back at the window again, staring down into the car park. Savage smiled to herself, finding it hard to believe the DSupt had just used the word 'lush' to describe her.

'They're down there, packing up.' Hardin tapped the glass. 'What the bloody hell am I supposed to do? Shout out the window that it's about face and we're back to dealing with a serial killer? About farce more like. We'll be a laughing stock.'

'I'm not sure we *are* dealing with a serial killer, sir,' Riley said. 'Until we identify the other sets of remains we can't know. If they turn out to be people who have died then no, but if they're missing persons, then yes.'

'Bloody hell, make your mind up.' Hardin finally pulled out his chair and slumped down. He was cross, but Savage could see he understood the situation. 'But this last one, she's a definite, right?'

'Looks that way.' Riley showed Hardin the evidence Enders had discovered. 'The dental records confirm the skull belongs to the woman, but her death has never been registered. All we have is a missing person report.'

'Which means we've got a murderer who moved from digging up dead bodies to killing people. How come?'

'Perhaps the dead bodies dried up,' Savage said, immediately regretting her unfortunate choice of phrase. Hardin scowled at her. 'Perhaps he found it more convenient, or the girl's death was an accident. Whatever, after she was dead he proceeded to dispose of her body in the boneyard.'

'But there are no more bodies, at least not at the boneyard, have I got that right?' Hardin looked hopefully at Savage. 'They're all a decade or more old according to John Layton. Either he stopped, he went somewhere else, he was imprisoned, or he died.'

'Yes. However, I doubt he stopped. Having descended into such depravity, it's unlikely he could rescue himself. He almost certainly carried on either grave robbing or killing or both.'

'Shit.' A grim smile formed on Hardin's lips. 'But not on our patch, hey?'

Savage had had a few minutes to draw her own conclusions. She began to articulate them to Hardin.

'I think the bodies he obtained from the graves satisfied him for a time, but something caused him to begin killing. Perhaps that first murder shocked him and he was able to take a respite. However, some while after, he resumed his activities. He left Devon, thankfully removing the problem from us but transplanting the horror to somewhere else.'

'You're back to Malcolm Kendwick again.' Hardin's face flushed. 'I thought I told you to forget him?'

'Sir, this latest revelation about Melany Lodwell fixes the date pretty accurately. If I'm not mistaken, Kendwick left for the States just a couple of months after she went missing. The killing could have been the spur to emigrate. The offer to buy his company came in and he took it.'

'But, as I said before, Kendwick didn't live in Devon at the time.'

'He visited regularly.'

'How do you know?'

'His sister told me.'

'*What*?' Hardin paused and he allowed his mouth to half open before cocking his head on one side. 'You've been to see her? I specifically told you not to get involved.'

'I needed to—'

'You've seen this?' Hardin pointed down to a printout on his desk. 'John Layton's report on the forensics gathered from Kendwick's place?'

'Yes.' Savage had glanced at the report before she'd set off to interview Aline Rogers. At best the results were inconclusive, at worst the lack of any evidence from Kendwick's house, clothing and car made it extremely unlikely he'd had anything to do with the death of Amy Glynn.

'The man's innocent. In the clear. Off our radar. Understand?'

'Sir, Kendwick's childhood was spent away from his parents. They rejected him. He often stayed with grandparents, uncles and aunts. The confusion he must have felt, the ambivalence towards his parents, is classic stimulus which can result in—'

'Serial killing and necrophilia? No, DI Savage. You've been reading too many FBI casebooks and watching too many shlock documentaries on some obscure TV channel.' Hardin got up and placed his hands flat on the table. He stared across at her. 'Now, I'll discuss the boneyard case with DS Riley alone. Meanwhile, get back to work and find whoever abducted Amy Glynn. I want suspects, I want arrests, I want some action. Understand?'

'I was only—'

'Enough!' Hardin turned and walked back to the window. 'And DI Savage? Unless Malcolm Kendwick turns up down there in the car park with a bloody decapitated head on a fucking pointed stick, you're to leave him alone, OK?'

Savage nodded as she stood, unable to bring herself to

utter a 'yes, sir' as that would almost certainly be a lie. She went out into the corridor and pulled the door shut, fuming as she walked off.

Chapter Twenty

*My goodness he needs it soon, he thinks. The thing with the
student had gone wrong. Very wrong. After she escaped he'd
been desperate. Still, he hadn't panicked. He'd contained
himself. Hadn't gone off on some mad killing spree. Oh no.
He'd thought about the mistakes he'd made. Laughed at the
way the police went about their business. Missing the chance
to catch him. So, all in all, although it had been a bad day,
he could consign the event to history with two words: never
mind.*

Never mind!

*Now he's out on the moor again. Night has fallen and
everything is quiet. A soft wind blows across the heather, a
scent on the breeze, a scent he can taste on his tongue. He's a
hunter now. A beast after his prey. Until he's satiated there
can be no stopping him. He nods to himself. The moor might
seem an unlikely place to find what he's looking for. Better,
surely, the bright lights and dark alleyways of the city? Usually,
yes, but tonight is different, tonight he knows he's going to be
successful in his search. He's seen the flickering lights. Heard
the high-pitched squeals. They're out there on the moor.*

Tonight, they've come to him.

*The heather is bouncy beneath his feet as he floats across
the ground. He knows the moor like his own front room. Better.*

He can navigate in the dark, in the mist, in the snow. The wilderness holds no fears. He has an unerring sense of direction, an internal compass. He knows every little dip, every ridge, every clump of rocks. The night-time horizon is a jagged black line which he matches with patterns in his head. Tors stand against the inky sky, their shapes as distinctive as if they wore an illuminated sign spelling out their names.

He cuts across a ravine, skipping down a small boulder field and then clambering up the other side. He hasn't come the same way as they have, hasn't followed the trail. He doesn't need to.

When he saw them park their car, he knew where they were heading. The flat plateau next to the water, the spot so popular with wild campers. The stream is like a magnet, the bubbling sound as the waterfalls tumble over rock akin to the call of a Siren as the merry tune draws them in.

He can hear it now. A sparkling cascade of notes interspersed with their voices. He works his way along the ravine, following the ragged progress of the brook as it splashes a silver path in the night.

There. An orange glow from a light within a tent. A crackle from a fire, sparks ascending into the darkness. Round the fire dark shadows, young faces occasionally lit by a flicker of flame. Now there's a hiss as another can is opened. He sniffs the air, recognising a familiar scent. Cannabis, yes, but something else sweet as well.

The smell of female.

Giggles ring out and echo off the sides of the ravine. Girls having fun. Laughing. Exchanging stories. He smiles, wishing he was close enough to hear the substance of their tales. They are sexual, no doubt.

Hiss. Another can. Chink, the sound of bottles against glasses. Wine in one. Something stronger in another. All good, he thinks

214

as he moves ever closer until he finds a spot not twenty paces from where they sit. A rock provides cover, a clump of bracken a suitable screen to peer through. He eases his legs straight so as not to get cramp. He has a long wait ahead, but he licks his lips in anticipation of the fun to come and leans forward to stare.

Oh my! Up close they're so beautiful! His breath quickens and his heart races, even though he knows he must be patient. He counts them. Four. One is called Tash, another Kimmy. The other two names he misses, but it matters not. He doesn't care about their names or their personalities. He's more interested in other things. Physical things. And anyway, they won't be talking, much. In fact, if everything works out, they won't be talking at all.

Chapter Twenty-One

Savage woke from a dream about a graveyard. There'd been open graves, zombies rising from within, the sound of a church bell tolling her final moments as the undead horde emerged and surrounded her.

She blinked in the dark, pushed the duvet away, and then reached for her phone to silence the trill.

'Charlotte,' she said, propping herself up on one arm. 'This had better be important.'

'It is, ma'am.'

Savage shook her head as she recognised Riley's voice. 'Go on.'

'The worst situation imaginable. One dead, one critically injured, two others hurt.'

'Who, Darius?' Savage pulled the phone away from her ear long enough to note the time. Four a.m. 'Where?'

'A group of young women camping on Dartmoor, not far from Princetown. They've been attacked in their tent. One girl bludgeoned to death, a second with serious head injuries. It sounds like something out of a horror movie.'

'Bloody hell.' Savage sat up, the remnants of sleep gone. Beside her in the bed, Pete stirred and then rolled over,

216

pulling the duvet over his head. 'Presumably response have already secured the scene?'

'Yes. The pathologist is on his way and Layton's preparing a team. Meanwhile there's a manhunt going on. Nigel Frey is currently airborne in the helicopter with a number of his officers.'

Savage shook her head as she tried to assimilate all the information and think in logical steps. 'Are you at the station?'

'Yes, ma'am.'

'I'll be there as quick as I can.'

As good as her word, Savage arrived at Crownhill twenty-five minutes later. The car park, usually empty at this early hour, was half full as the station went into overdrive. Riley stood by a pool car talking to DSupt Hardin. Savage got out of her own car and moved alongside.

'Bloody nightmare,' Hardin said. 'What did they think they were doing camping on the moor while this nutter was out there prowling?'

Savage said nothing but thought the DSupt's comments harsh. It was hardly the victims' fault. If anything the blame lay with the police for not apprehending the monster.

'Charlotte?' Hardin turned to Savage. 'I'm organising the mobile incident room and other resources. We're throwing everything at this.'

'Where are the survivors?' Savage said.

'The injured girl and the other two have been taken to Derriford. I'm still waiting for their statements. Meantime, I want you up on the moor when Dr Nesbit gets there. Get the lie of the land, see if we can relate anything to the existing cases.'

Hardin turned and wheeled away, allowing no time for

217

discussion. Savage gestured at the car and she and Riley got in.

The journey to their destination would usually have taken some twenty-five minutes; they managed it in fifteen, roaring up the moorland road from Yelverton and pulling over in a layby at a little after five in the morning. A couple of miles away to the north-west, a vague glow marked Princetown, but close to there was nothing but wilderness. They climbed from the car and went over to a police four-wheel-drive vehicle which was acting as a checkpoint. Nearby, two of Layton's CSIs, torches in hands, worked their way round a smart yellow Mini parked in a layby. Both of the tyres on the offside were flat, the rims of the wheels resting on the gravel. Savage walked across.

'The girls' car,' one of the CSIs said. He looked up from where he was kneeling and smiled. Savage recognised him as Milo, DC Calter's latest conquest. 'All four tyres have been slashed. Presumably to stop them making a getaway.'

'But they managed to phone for help?' Savage moved away from the car, noting the footprints in the soft muddy verge.

'Yeah. You can imagine the shock when the paramedics turned up.' Milo stood and gestured across the road to where a glow stick hung on a pole. 'They had to calm the girls and go down to the scene. Horrific by all accounts.'

Savage nodded and beckoned Riley. The DS had already exchanged his shoes for walking boots. Savage cursed. She had a pair of boots in the back of her own car, but that was at the station.

They set off along a path which zigzagged down the slope towards the valley bottom. Every fifty paces, a pole had been stuck in the ground, a green glow stick hanging on each. The markers were fast becoming superfluous as the sky

218

brightened in the east. Even so, Savage took care with her footing. A slip here and she could twist her ankle.

The path flattened out and entered a small grassy area with a brook bisecting the plateau. At one end, the water rushed away in a narrow channel. Beyond the channel, the stream had forged a route downhill and carved out a ravine. Boulders stood either side as the water cascaded in a series of waterfalls, each leading to a small pool. On the far side of the plateau, an orange tent was a jumble of poles and ripped material. John Layton stood nearby next to a stack of plastic stepping plates, fiddling with a set of battery-operated floodlights. He turned at the sound of their approach.

'Round the edge,' he said, pointing to the top end of the grass patch. 'And then down the stepping plates.'

Savage nodded. 'Is she still in there?'

'Yes.' Layton turned back to the tent. 'I'm about to cut away the side wall, but I want to wait until Nesbit gets here.'

'Anything useful?'

'The murder weapon is over there.' Layton turned and pointed to one side of the stream where a large branch lay half in the water. 'It's a log from the fire. The killer smashed the side of the tent, guessing where they lay. Then, in the commotion, he tried to drag one of the girls out. By the looks of things he started to set off down the ravine with her, but the others managed to stop him. There's a specialist dog and handler coming. Hopefully they'll have a chance of picking something up.'

Savage sighed inwardly. Because the attack had happened in the middle of the night, getting all the resources they needed – people and equipment – was necessarily taking time. The problem was every hour of delay meant the trail was growing colder.

'And Inspector Frey?'

'He came in by 'copter a while ago. He went down the ravine with three of his men.' Layton shook his head and raised his hands, turning the palms skyward. 'Like something out of one of those special forces books, only the one he's in is called *Bravo Too Stupid*.'

Savage half laughed. The situation was dire, but Layton could still add a dollop of humour. It was the only way to get through times like these and the thought of Frey, no doubt fully clad in black and with boot polish on his face, creeping down the ravine, was highly amusing.

'I guess the killer's well away from here by now.' Savage took in the steep sides and rocky nature of the valley. 'Probably came out at the bottom. Darius, what do you think?'

'That'd be Burrator Reservoir,' Riley said. 'I know the area from the illegal diesel operation I was on with DI Maynard. The killer could have parked a car down there and worked his way up the ravine until he came across the tent.'

'Not by luck, surely?'

'He probably saw them as they were leaving the road. Their backpacks and equipment would have told him they were rough camping. If he knew the area then I bet he guessed they were headed for here. He simply had to drive round to Burrator and come up from there. Tricky in the dark, though.'

'So he's familiar with Dartmoor then, meaning we're talking Chantry again or even Kendwick.'

'Or DC Enders or any one of the thousands of people who use the moor on a regular basis.'

Before Savage could ask Riley to elaborate, a figure clambered up beside the waterfall. He wore black fatigues, a balaclava and had a Heckler and Koch slung over one shoulder. He raised a hand and for one split second, Savage thought

220

the man would sail, Ninja style, into the air and perform some sort of balletic martial arts manoeuvre. Instead the hand waved and then moved to pull up the balaclava.

'Charlotte.' Nigel Frey moved round the waterfall and joined Savage. 'We've found his ER.'

'ER?'

'Escape route. The way he went out.'

'DS Riley was saying. Burrator?'

'No.' Frey turned and pointed back at the left side of the ravine where the shadows were starting to dwindle with the coming of the dawn. 'He climbed out of the valley about a mile down. One of my lads spotted some footprints where he crossed the stream. We followed his trail up the side of the ravine. At the top there was a track and signs of vehicular activity. Plenty of tyre prints in the peat up there. We need to get that bloody dog here.'

'Can they follow a car?'

'Sometimes, yes, so it's worth a try. My lads have secured the area so we're good to go.'

Savage nodded, trying to stop herself smiling. Frey sounded like he had just taken out a bunch of terrorists and was due a Distinguished Service Medal and the gratitude of the nation. She almost asked Frey exactly what he'd secured the area against. Was it a flock of sheep or a herd of Dartmoor ponies?

A few minutes later, any attempt at humour would have been misplaced. Dr Andrew Nesbit had arrived and after a cursory inspection of the tent, he allowed Layton to cut away the fabric to reveal the horror within. The tent seemed to be filled with a jumble of sleeping bags and clothing, a red slick of blood spread over everything inside. The dead girl lay half out of her bag, her hands cupped round her face in what must have been a vain attempt to stop the attack.

'My God,' Nesbit said, as he knelt. 'The force of the blow was considerable.'

Savage moved a little to the side to see what the pathologist was talking about. She regretted her action. Nesbit had gently pulled one of the girl's hands away from the face. The entire right side of the skull had been smashed in, shards of white bone mixed with a pulp of brain and flesh and hair and blood. For the first time in her police career, Savage felt bile rise in her throat and realised she was going to be sick. She stepped away from the scene and moved quickly to the side of the plateau where she vomited into a clump of heather.

By the time dawn arrived, the body in the tent had gone, strapped to a rigid gurney and carried from the campsite by several mountain rescue volunteers. Nigel Frey reappeared, admitting the trail had gone cold and that he was calling his men in.

'Dog was no bloody good and the helicopter has had to return to base.' Frey shook his head. He stared at the remains of the tent where Layton and another CSI were working. 'Whoever did this is long gone.'

Savage went back to the road and found Riley standing next to their car. She pointed to the horizon and then opened the car door.

'Let's go.'

'Where?'

'Chagford.'

'Kendwick didn't do this, did he? Not his style. None of the girls in the US were bludgeoned to death. The whole thing seems too random, too manic for him.'

'He's lost it, Darius. Entered some frenzied state where he can't help himself.' Savage sat in the passenger seat and

222

pulled the door shut. She wound the window down. 'Come on.'

For a second Riley didn't move, but then he shrugged and shifted round to the driver's side of the car. He got in and started up.

'Your call, ma'am.' Riley paused, his hand on the gearstick. 'Have you informed the DSupt?'

'No. Operationally it's down to me. Kendwick's a suspect. We bring him in. Simple as that.'

'I like your gumption.' Riley put the car in gear and pulled away. 'But I'm not sure I want to be there when Hardin finds out.'

'If Kendwick's guilty, I'll get a medal.'

'And if not?'

Savage said nothing. Kendwick *was* guilty, she knew it. They were missing something, true, but in the end he was mixed up in the boneyard, with the death of Amy Glynn, and with the attack on the campers. They just had to prove it.

Half an hour later they cruised into Chagford and parked up alongside the terrace of cottages. A light shone from the downstairs window at Kendwick's place. They got out of the car and Savage walked across to peer in the window, but the curtains were still drawn and the crack where they met in the middle revealed nothing more than a strip of carpet.

She went back to the front door and rapped hard using the brass knocker. Nothing. She knocked again and then bent to the letterbox, flipped up the flap and shouted through.

'Malcolm! Open up!'

Riley stepped forward. 'Shall I, ma'am?' He lowered his shoulder and nodded at the front door.

At that moment a sound came from behind the door, a bolt drawn back with a scrape, a latch unlocked with a click.

'Why, Charlotte, what a nice surprise!' Kendwick stood

there half naked, a towel round his waist, his long black hair glistening with moisture. 'Forgive my appearance, but I was in the shower. Care to join me?'

'Where have you been this morning, Malcolm?' Savage pushed past Kendwick and went inside. A cereal bowl sat on the coffee table, a copy of yesterday's *Daily Mail* alongside. There was a distinct smell of stale curry in the air. 'I'd like you to account for last night too.'

'No!' Kendwick's mouth dropped open as he did his stage expression of horror. 'Another crime. How awful. What is it this time? Shoplifting? A burglary? Don't tell me . . . it's . . . it's . . . it's a girl! My, my, the shock. If only Melissa was still here, but she's decamped to London.' Kendwick gestured at the newspaper. 'Some celeb has been caught with his hands in another celeb's knickers. Apparently tittle tattle is of more interest to her readers than I am. Still, another murder can only be good news for the sales of the book. Might even entice her down here again.'

Savage ignored Kendwick and beckoned Riley in. 'Check upstairs, especially the shower. If the water's still running, turn it off.'

'Good of you to think of my utility bills or is it the environment?' Kendwick closed the door behind Riley. He waved an arm in the direction of the stairs. 'Be my guest.'

Riley climbed the stairs while Savage walked through to the kitchen. She stopped in the centre of the room and listened. A faint electrical whirr came from a unit to the left of the sink. She stepped forward and pulled open a cupboard door to reveal a washing machine. Sud-filled water sloshed back and forth inside the machine. She reached out and turned the rotary dial to off.

'Laundry day, is it?' Savage said. 'The first thing you do when you get up is put a wash on?'

'So?' Kendwick shrugged. He appeared unperturbed. 'I bunged a load of dirty clothes in a few minutes ago. More than dirty, to be honest. Filthy and mud splattered.' Kendwick nodded towards the kitchen door. In the patio area out the back Savage could see a mountain bike propped against the fence. Clods of mud hung on the frame. 'Went out on the moor yesterday evening. Nothing illegal in a late-night ride, is there?'

Even as he spoke Kendwick had a smirk on his face. He couldn't help the innuendo, the silly schoolboy smutty humour. *Late-night ride* was a double entendre designed to irk Savage. She could respond or ignore the comment. She chose to ignore it and went back into the living area.

'Where?'

'Oh, a moderate ten K jaunt around the neighbourhood. Up hill and down dale. Can't remember the exact route.'

'Nothing here, ma'am,' Riley said as he came back down the stairs.

'Well, what were you expecting?' Kendwick spread his arms wide. His towel hung loosely, just one end tucked in. It looked like it might fall from his body at any moment, an event Savage realised he'd enjoy. 'A body in the bedroom, Jeffrey Dahmer style? Another shoved in the bath tub. And why not take a peek in my fridge? Chances are alongside the remains of my takeaway you'll find a severed head. Then you'll have me, what is it – bang to rights?'

'You appear to know a lot about serial killers, Mr Kendwick,' Savage said. 'Is your interest professional or do you just get off on reading about their activities?'

'I could ask the same about you, Charlotte. I rather suspect that under your school ma'amish disapproval you're secretly attracted to men who kill. Many people are. You know, while I was being held in the States I received stacks of fan mail from women. Blue does not adequately describe the contents of some of the letters. What they wanted me to do to them was, quite simply, unspeakable.'

'Well, I hope for their sake they didn't give you their addresses.'

'Oh, but they did. A couple even offered me a place to stay, should I need it.' Kendwick cocked his head on one side. 'And these women, Charlotte, they were like you, not deluded, not mad, but intelligent and attractive.'

'Shut up, Malcolm. Go upstairs and get changed. We're taking you in.'

'I'm disappointed in you, Charlotte. Very disappointed. We could have been friends, perhaps more, but now you've gone too far. I'm not going to forget the way you've behaved and I'm afraid I won't be able to forgive you either.'

'Save it. DS Riley, take Mr Kendwick upstairs. If he resists, then cuff him and arrest him.'

'Yes, ma'am.' Riley held out a hand and gestured at the stairs. 'Mr Kendwick?'

'Sure,' Kendwick said, moving to obey Riley but looking back at Savage. 'But you're making a very, very big mistake.'

At the custody centre in Plymouth, they went through the rigmarole of booking Kendwick in once again. An interview room was arranged and Amanda Bradley contacted. By the time Bradley had turned up and consulted with her client, it was nearly midday. Savage and Riley had been twiddling their thumbs for several hours and now Savage was keen to get down to business.

In the interview room, Kendwick and Bradley sat on one side of the table, two plastic cups of coffee in front of them. Kendwick was wide awake, his eyes darting back and forth.

Bradley scowled. As Savage and Riley came in she reached for her cup and took a sip.

'This had better be good, DI Savage,' Bradley said. She made a face at the cup. 'Because the coffee isn't and neither is my mood.'

'Oh, it's good, Amanda,' Kendwick said before Savage had a chance to answer. The jokey bonhomie he'd displayed when they'd first entered his house was gone. He glared across the room and then made a deliberate show of spitting on the floor. 'The bitch wants to get me for murder again. She just can't let it rest.'

Savage talked directly to Bradley. 'We want to question your client about an incident which took place in the early hours of this morning. A young woman was killed and another is in a serious condition in hospital.'

'It wasn't me, because I don't bloody leave any of them alive, do I?' Kendwick said. 'I fuck them and kill them and then discard them in the wilderness. Or haven't you read the newspapers?'

'Malcolm, calm down.' Bradley placed a hand on Kendwick's arm. 'I'll deal with this. You'll be out of here before you know it.'

'And then I'll make her bloody pay.' Kendwick leaned forward. 'You're going to wish you never started this game, Charlotte, you'll see.'

Alongside Savage, Riley shook his head. 'Watch it, Mr Kendwick. You're threatening a police officer.' Riley turned to Bradley. 'Do your job and advise your client of the seriousness of the offence.'

'I think Malcolm means he's going to make a complaint. I believe he has every right to do so and I fully expect DI Savage to be reprimanded. This is an ongoing campaign of harassment, nothing less.'

Riley had by now turned on the recording equipment and he informed Kendwick of his rights and then they began the formal questioning.

'Mr Kendwick.' Savage leaned forward a little, her voice steady. 'A group of young women campers were attacked on Dartmoor very early this morning, sometime after midnight. Do you deny having anything to do with it?'

'Deny it?' Kendwick smiled. 'Oh no. I reckon I might as well come clean now and admit everything. If you'd like to write out a statement of what I got up to, I'll be only too pleased to sign it. Next stop, a court case in which I promise to plead guilty to every crime you charge me with. The judge, no doubt, will recommend I serve at least thirty years.'

'Do you deny attacking the girls?'

'Mailbags. Hidden shivs on the landings. Being raped in the showers. Twenty-three-hour lockup. Crap food.' Kendwick leaned forward. He held his hand to his mouth and made a stage whisper. 'But d'you know what? I can take it. Every shiv to the face, every cock up my arse. The boredom, the suffering. You see, I'm strong whereas you're weak.'

Savage tried to ignore Kendwick and instead repeated the question. 'Do you deny attacking the girls?'

'Weak because you're overprotective of the ones you love. You could never do a spell inside because you'd miss playing happy families at your place in Bovisand. Miss your husband, your son, your beautiful daughter.'

'Malcolm.' Bradley placed a hand on Kendwick's wrist. 'That's enough.'

'Samantha, isn't it?' Kendwick shrugged free from Bradley's grip, his hand moving to his ponytail. 'A young girl ripening into a woman.'

'I told you before not to mention my daughter,' Savage said, feeling the anger building within her. 'Let's get back to—'

'But I can't help it, Charlotte. You know I like teenagers.'

'I'm warning you.'

'Lush, I'll bet. Pretty in a dress.' Kendwick's finger twirled at his hair, winding it faster and faster. 'I wonder what she looks like with no knickers on. My, I'm getting all hard thinking about what I could—'

Savage launched herself across the table, one hand grasping for Kendwick's hair, the other swinging a punch which glanced off the side of his cheek. Riley jumped up and grabbed her arm, pulling her back across the table. Savage fell back into her chair with a crash.

'My, my, my,' Kendwick said. 'Temper, temper, temper.'

'DI Savage,' Bradley said, smiling. 'You just landed yourself in one heap of trouble.'

'Calm down.' Riley released Savage and held his hands up. 'Your client wound up DI Savage. Let's just forget about this and start again.'

'Oh no.' Bradley pursed her bright-red lips and then showed her teeth once more. She gestured at the video camera where a little red LED flashed on and off. 'I don't think we can forget about it. In fact I suggest we suspend this interview immediately. I also recommend that unless you have some firm evidence linking my client with the incident on the moor you release him.'

Savage pushed back her chair. Kendwick flinched but she just turned and walked to the door.

In the corridor outside, Riley stood shaking his head.

'For God's sake, Charlotte,' he said. 'What the fuck were you thinking?'

'Sorry.' Savage stared at the floor. 'When he threatened me, I could deal with that. When he brought up my daughter and intimated he knew where we lived . . .'

'Yes, but—'

'He's a monster, Darius. You know he is.'

'I'm sorry, ma'am, I don't. He's a sly bastard, nasty, but we need evidence if we're going to take this any further.'

'I'll get evidence, you'll see.'

'I don't think so, ma'am.' Riley made a slight movement with his head. Savage turned to see DSupt Hardin charging down the corridor, face like a beetroot, spittle flying from his mouth as he roared her name.

Chapter Twenty-Two

Riley turned up at the station on Saturday morning to find
Hardin had drafted in a dozen extra officers to work on the
Dartmoor cases. As yet, he explained at the morning briefing,
there wasn't enough to connect the Amy Glynn death with
the attack on the girls. Nor could either crime categorically
be linked with the boneyard finds.

'But we assume nothing, believe nobody . . .'

Riley leaned back in his chair. Hardin was off on one,
quoting procedure as if all officers had to do was start at
one end of the textbook and work their way through to the
end. As the last page was turned, by some arcane magic, the
perpetrator would be revealed, presumably by the posi-
tioning of rain clouds somewhere above the moor. Falling
back on procedure was, Riley guessed, a sign of panic. It
rarely worked. At times like these you needed to follow a
hunch or rely on your gut instinct or intuition. Unfortunately
the officer best placed to use intuition, *female* intuition, had
been suspended.

What the hell was DI Savage thinking? It was one thing
to swing a punch while arresting a suspect in the heat of

the moment. Nobody would argue with that. Quite another to do so in the presence of a lawyer and under the ever-watchful gaze of a video camera.

'DS Riley?' Hardin glared from the far end of the table. 'Your thoughts on the matter?'

The question took Riley by surprise. He cast a glance round the table for some sort of clue as to what the hell Hardin had been talking about. John Layton was casually reading his notes. A couple of junior detectives whispered to each other. Only Nigel Frey seemed alert.

'I think we need a proactive arrest strategy,' Riley said. He gestured in Frey's direction. 'A control room and commander. Surveillance, roadblocks, that sort of thing. Treat this as if it's a crime in action.'

Hardin nodded intently, while Frey smiled. Riley had plainly lucked out with his guess.

'Bit late though, isn't it?' Hardin said. 'Stable door and all that?'

'Whoever he is, he's out there, sir. Prevention might now be the only option. Plus, if we flood the area with officers we could get lucky.'

The discussion continued with Frey outlining action points and Hardin, now enthusiastic about Riley's suggestion, barking out assignments. Riley, hoping to be part of the new strategy, leaned forward once more. He was disappointed. Nothing came his way and at the end of the meeting he was reduced to asking Gareth Collier for something to do.

'Tasha Galper,' Collier said. 'One of the girls in the tent. She's back home after a night in hospital, so she's yours.'

'Couldn't I—'

'No.' Collier turned to where Frey was holding court. His Force Support Group number two was beside him, hanging on every word. There was talk of automatic weapons, helicopters, perimeter containment, lethal force. 'Proactive is all very well, but I prefer slowly, slowly, catchy, monkey. Right?'

Savage woke with a splitting headache. As she squinted against the morning light she remembered the bottle of red she'd helped Pete consume the previous night. No, that was wrong, she hadn't so much helped as led the way.

She sat up in bed and looked at the time on her phone: 9.08 a.m. Shit. The before-dawn start of the previous day and the late-night drinking had left her exhausted.

She remained still for a moment, listening. The house was silent. Pete must have taken the kids off somewhere. All of a sudden she felt guilty and a little ashamed at her self-indulgence. Still, there'd been a good reason for it.

Hardin had arrived at the custody centre already angry with Savage for arresting Kendwick without his permission. He'd then sat in a side room and watched the live video feed of the interview, his anger turning to rage as Savage had lashed out at Kendwick. Things had got worse when Amanda Bradley emerged from the interview room to tell the DSupt to his face that she'd be making a formal complaint. As Kendwick was led out of the interview room and Bradley sauntered away, Hardin had exploded. Savage was a loose cannon, he said. A liability which he couldn't afford to have on such an important case.

The end result, which Savage had seen coming as soon as she'd let go of Kendwick and slumped down in her chair, was she was suspended pending further investigation into the assault.

As Bradley and Kendwick had reached the end of the corridor, they'd turned as one. Bradley wore a wide smile and was laughing openly. Kendwick just stood for a moment and then made his hand into a knife shape and drew it across his throat. Unfortunately, both Riley and Hardin had their backs to the pair.

The DSupt had continued to berate her, but all she could do was to respond with lame excuses. It was left to Riley to make her case, telling Hardin that Kendwick had been trying to rile her. However, despite his efforts, Hardin couldn't be won round.

Savage pushed herself off the bed and groped her way across to the en suite where she splashed cold water on her face, trying not to look herself in the eye. She was cross, not primarily because of what she'd done to Kendwick, more for the reason that she was now off the case and impotent. Kendwick, on the other hand, was free to do as he pleased.

She took a shower and as she washed she pondered Kendwick's threats. Was that what they were? Did the fact he knew where she lived, knew about her private life, point to a man trying to play games with her psyche or someone who was a real danger to her and her family?

Savage dried herself and got dressed, realising she couldn't afford to take the risk. She went downstairs, filled the kettle and heaped coffee into the cafetiére. A note from Pete sat on the kitchen table, the message explaining he'd taken the kids out on the boat for the day and wouldn't be back until the evening. The last line caused her to swallow hard, tears filling her eyes.

We all love you LOADS. See you later. Pete, Sam and Jamie. XXX.

She huffed out a breath and shook herself. Kendwick was right, her family was everything to her, but the feelings she felt for them didn't represent weakness. Quite the opposite. And not only did Samantha, Jamie and Pete mean everything to her, she'd do *anything* to protect them too.

She poured the hot water into the cafetiére and then went out into the garden. She crossed the patio and walked onto the sunlit lawn. At the bottom of the garden, a grassy path curled beneath an arbour of willow and then ran along the rear fence. She walked along the path until she came to a gate secured with a bolt and padlock. The padlock wasn't designed to keep people out, it was there to prevent Jamie from opening the gate and wandering beyond the garden. Savage bent over and undid the lock. The gate swung open and she went through to the clifftop path.

The ground underfoot was rough, the path a mixture of grass and rock and earth. This wasn't a public right-of-way, just a route which the family used. Savage moved slowly. A few metres to her right, a sheer drop plummeted to the sea below. She walked on until a large gorse bush appeared ahead. Just before the bush the path divided, the left-hand branch continuing along the clifftop, the right-hand branch easing downward across a steep patch of scrub. She took the right-hand path and followed the zigzags back and forth until she arrived at the tiny pebble beach below.

The stones rumbled down at the tideline as the waves ebbed and flowed. She walked a little way across the beach until she came to an old concrete groyne. She scrambled up onto the groyne and moved to the rear side where another hunk of concrete sat. She put her hand into a large crack and delved inside until she found what she was looking for. She pulled the package out. An ice cream tub. She placed the tub on the concrete and levered off the lid. Inside, several plastic bags were wrapped round something heavy. She removed the bags to reveal a small hand towel caked with oil. She unrolled the towel.

There. A handgun. Alongside the gun, a loaded clip of bullets. Let Kendwick do his worst, she thought. If he came visiting, she'd be ready to protect her family. Whatever it took.

A police officer stood guard outside the front door of the house on Woodford Avenue in Plympton. He nodded as Riley and Calter came up the front steps to the semi-detached property.

'All right?' Riley said.

'Yes. Quiet as the proverbial out here. Nothing to report.' The officer jerked his thumb at the front door. 'Different story in there. From the sound of things, she's taking it badly. A right racket earlier.'

'Hardly surprising, is it?' Riley glared at the officer. 'Your best mate killed and another friend in hospital. Not to mention you're a living witness to a psycho's crimes.'

'There is that, I suppose.'

Riley shouldered past the officer and pressed the bell push. Seconds later a woman opened the door. Long dark hair in curls, make-up applied in a hurry, dark bags under her eyes. She half smiled as Riley introduced himself and Calter.

'I'm Kathy, Tasha's mother, come in.'

Minutes later, Riley and Calter were seated on a sofa, Kathy Galper somewhere out the back making tea. Tasha, she had assured them, would be down shortly. The tea came with biscuits, and as they drank it a clock on a sideboard ticked over an uncomfortable silence. Kathy left and Riley heard voices raised. Somebody came down the stairs, feet heavy, and then the door pushed open. A young woman, nineteen or twenty, stood at the threshold. Dark hair the colour of her mother's lay in tangled strands. Her face was tearstained.

'Tasha.' Riley stood and offered his hand. He introduced Calter and then gestured at an armchair. 'It's good of you

236

to talk to us. I can understand how upsetting this must be.'

Tasha mumbled something and then went across and sat down. She stared into the space between Riley and Calter, not wanting to meet either's gaze.

Riley glanced down at his notes. 'We've got the statement you made at the scene. It's helpful, but what we're looking for from you now is something which might help us track down the attacker.' In fact, the statement was far from helpful. The girl, quite understandably, had been almost incoherent, her words not much more than a tirade of grief. 'Can you tell us where you were before you drove to the campsite and why you decided on that particular spot?'

'We were in the pub,' Tasha said. She stopped, as if that was enough information. Then realising Riley was waiting she sighed and continued. 'The Plume of Feathers in Princetown. We had a meal there. Saved bothering to cook up anything at the campsite. After the meal and a few drinks we drove to the camping spot.'

'And why did you choose the place?'

'Vicky . . .' Tasha swallowed and then closed her eyes, her fists clenching. 'Vicky . . .'

'It's OK,' Calter this time, taking over from Riley and speaking with a soft voice. 'There's no rush.'

Tasha opened her eyes and wiped away fresh tears. Composed herself. 'Vicky had been there before. We were originally going to camp at a different spot over near the river Dart, but as we parked up we saw a couple of police cars and a DPA vehicle close by, so we changed our plans. By rights we shouldn't have been camping at either spot, there are certain areas you can and can't wild camp, but we wanted to be beside a stream and not too far from the car.'

'So you changed your plans?'

'Yes. Vics suggested this other place so we turned round and went there.'

'Were you aware of anyone in the pub paying you undue attention? For instance, staring or perhaps getting up to leave at the same time as you did?'

'Not that I recall.'

'Nobody followed you when you drove off?'

'It would be hard to tell. That road down to Yelverton is pretty busy. I guess it's possible.'

Calter glanced across at Riley. He nodded. It was time to get to the business end of the interview.

'So you got to the campsite at about eightish?' Riley said.

'A bit later. Vic got lost and the rest of us were too pissed to help.'

'What happened then?'

'Well, we got the stuff out of the car and carried it to the campsite. Vic and I went back for a second trip to get some bottles of water. It was well dark by then, but we managed to pitch the tent and then set about collecting some wood for a fire. There was a place where stones had been put in a circle so we made the fire there. Then we opened some beers and a bottle of wine and sat around drinking.'

'And nobody came past?'

'No. The site is set down in a dip, invisible from the road. I'm not sure if we would have noticed anyway.'

Riley paused. The campsite might well have been invisible, but the car was back on the main Princetown to Yelverton road. Somebody who'd spotted the girls before would easily eyeball the bright-yellow Mini.

'What time did you call it a night?'

'We finished the wine and then . . .' Tasha stopped and

looked at Calter, as if the female detective would offer more encouragement than Riley. 'We . . .'

'It's OK, Tasha,' Calter said. 'We know you smoked a few joints. That's of no concern to us.'

A brief smile flicked across Tasha's face. 'We rolled up a couple of spliffs and passed them round. After we'd smoked them we got ready for bed, brushed our teeth, that kind of thing.'

'This would be . . . ?' Calter shrugged.

'It was after midnight, I know that. Once in the tent, we talked for a while and then fell asleep.' Tasha swallowed. She shook her head. 'The next thing I knew Kimmy was screaming and the whole tent seemed to be collapsing in on us. Then everybody was shouting and I realised we were being attacked. Somebody was smashing something against the tent. They just kept doing it over and over again even though we were yelling and Kimmy was crying. Why would they do that?'

'I don't know,' Calter said. 'What happened then?'

'Three of us – that was myself, Kimmy and Jaq – scrambled out of the tent. Standing to one side was this man. It was dark, so I can't describe his face, but he held a huge log which he'd been using to batter the tent. He tried to grab Kimmy, but Jaq picked up one of the rocks from near the fire. She lobbed the rock at the man. In the dark I don't think he saw it coming and it hit him on the head and knocked him down. Then he got up and ran off, just like that. I don't think he thought we'd fight back. To be honest, if it hadn't been for Jaq, he'd have killed us all.'

Riley nodded and let the silence build for a moment. 'And then you called the police?'

'Yes, I did. Meanwhile, Kimmy found a torch and went back inside the tent to check on Vicky. She's a nurse, so

239

when she came out and said the situation was serious we knew it was really bad.'

'OK.' Riley peered down at his notes. There was something in a statement from one of the other girls taken at the scene he was interested in. He wanted some corroboration. 'We're nearly finished. When the man was attacking the tent, did he say anything?'

'Yes.' Tasha's face blanked, as if once more she couldn't understand what had happened or why. 'As we struggled to get out of the tent, he kept on smashing the log down over and over. All the time he was yelling the same thing repeatedly.'

Riley waited, but the girl shook her head. She needed to be prompted. 'What did he say?'

'He kept shouting it again and again.' Tasha cracked and tears began to flow down her cheeks. 'Be still, be still, be still.'

The gun had come from Kenny Fallon, a local gangster. Fallon, for reasons Savage was highly suspicious of, had helped her find the person who'd killed Samantha's twin, Clarissa. The gun had been for her to exact revenge, but she hadn't needed the weapon, since the lad she'd thought was responsible had turned out to be innocent. Still, she hadn't wanted to dispose of the gun and at the time hiding it had seemed the best option.

Savage took the package and climbed back up to the house. Once inside, she placed it on the kitchen table. Pete wouldn't be home until much later, time enough for her to give the gun a once over and secrete the weapon somewhere she could reach in a hurry.

She was wiping the metal clip down with several pieces of kitchen roll when her mobile rang. She rammed the phone under her chin as she rubbed her oily fingers on the tissue.

'Hello,' she said, trying to pull another sheet from the roll.

'Charlotte? Is that Charlotte Savage, the British cop?' The voice drawled in Savage's ear, a heavy American twang evident. 'It's Janey Horton.'

'Janey . . . ?'

'Officer Janey Horton. From California.'

'*California*?' Savage shook her head, having trouble understanding. 'Do you mean . . . ?'

'Yes. I'm Sara Horton's mom. Malcolm Kendwick killed my daughter. Other girls too. And now he's doing it again, isn't he? Only this time it's in England and you guys haven't got a fucking clue what's going on.'

'Janey, it's good to talk to you, but you must know I can't share those details with you.' Savage shook her head, realising she was becoming defensive. Horton had lost her daughter in tragic circumstances. Savage, of all people, should be more sympathetic. 'Sorry, I'm being rude. How are you doing? Are you OK?'

'Of course I'm not fucking OK! Kendwick's free to do what the hell he likes, to ruin lives and bring tragedy to families. We can't let that happen. We've got to stop him.'

'*We*?'

'Yes, we. You and I, Charlotte. No one else is going to do it, no one else has the guts. Kendwick is as wily as a fox and however many dogs the cops send after him, he'll always find a way to evade capture.'

'Look, Janey, we're doing all we can over here. We just don't have any evidence that Mr Kendwick is responsible at the moment.'

'Not responsible? You're not looking right, girl. Of course

241

he's fucking responsible. If you don't have the evidence then we've got to get it, haven't we?'

'There's a full team of officers working on the case.' Savage didn't mention the team no longer included her. 'It's only a matter of time before we catch the perpetrator.'

'Time is what we don't have. Kendwick's killed again, hasn't he? Do you want more deaths on your conscience?'

Savage sighed. She understood what Horton was trying to do. She wanted to get involved so she didn't have to feel so powerless. Savage could relate to that since it was exactly how she now felt.

'Perhaps you could provide some insight into Kendwick's character. Maybe send me any material you have on him. It could be useful. When I've had a chance to look at it we can speak again.'

'Don't fob me off, Charlotte. You know that's not what I want.' There was a crackle and a moment of silence. 'Look, this girl on the moor. Amy Glynn. I'll tell you something we never released to the public, something to prove it was Kendwick who killed her.'

'Go on.'

'The killer made her run across country because he likes to chase them. When you found her, a piece of her clothing was missing. Kendwick had taken her panties as a trophy.'

'You're right, but we know about the underwear. It was in the FBI report. Something about how you found the burnt remains of clothing such as bras and shoes, but never any knickers. The theory was he was collecting them.'

'Correct. We never found the underwear, he must have hidden them somewhere.'

'It's not enough, Janey. We can't convict somebody because . . .' Savage stopped, all of a sudden realising what Horton had said a moment ago was important. She moved across to a chair and sat down. 'Hang on, what did you say about telling me something? Your exact words?'

'Charlotte?' There was a pause from Horton's end too. 'I said, I'll tell you something we never released to the public, something—'

'You never told anyone, not even Kendwick or his lawyers?'

'No. We didn't get to the disclosure stage.'

'Shit.' All of a sudden a cold chill swept over Savage. 'Janey, when we questioned Kendwick he made a joke about unpacking knick-knacks. He said the word in such a way as to make us think he was going to say knickers. He then admitted he knew the attacker in the US took the girls' panties as souvenirs. Yesterday he made a lewd comment about my daughter. He specifically mentioned her underwear.'

'But he could only know that if he *was* the attacker. I told you it was Kendwick, now do you believe me?'

'Yes, I do.'

'OK, we need to meet face-to-face to discuss this.'

'I'm afraid that's quite out of the question. Devon and Cornwall Police's budget doesn't stretch to transatlantic flights. Perhaps we could do a Skype call or something?'

'Fuck Skype. And you needn't worry about the budget, everything's sorted.'

'What do you mean "sorted"?'

'I'm coming to you.'

'Now, Janey, you can't go making a journey like that. You're not even in the police any longer. Plus, I've been suspended from duty too, nothing would be official.'

'I'm not too bothered about official. The system I was a part of failed my daughter. These days I prefer to go it alone.'

'Nevertheless, I don't think coming all the way over from the States is a good idea.'

243

'Too late, Charlotte. I'm already here. My plane landed at Heathrow an hour ago. I'll be in Plymouth early afternoon. Any chance you could pick me up from the railway station?'

Chapter Twenty-Three

Plymouth Railway Station. Saturday 29th April. 2.35 p.m.

At a little after two-thirty, Savage parked her classic MG in a short-term drop-off bay at the railway station and walked into the ticket hall. It wasn't hard to spot Janey Horton amongst the crowd. She was a bottle blonde with shoulder-length hair, a straight-cut fringe above dark eyebrows and eyelashes heavy with mascara, purple eyeshadow on the lids. Red lipstick accentuated a full mouth and matched Horton's glossy fingernails. A tight white T-shirt stretched over full breasts and Savage noted several tattoos on the woman's bare arms. Combat trousers and stout boots completed the look. She was probably late thirties, but dressed as if she was seventeen. A large rucksack slumped against her knees, one of the straps bearing a label with the letters 'LHR'.

'Charlotte!' Horton hollered as Savage went over. Savage held out her hand, but Horton spread her arms wide and as Savage approached she embraced her. 'It's so good to meet you!'

People turned their heads as they skittered round the two women.

'And you, Janey,' Savage said, as she extricated herself from the bear hug. 'You really didn't need to come—'

245

'The fuck I did!' Horton bent for her rucksack and hefted it onto her shoulder. 'No chance I'm going to let Kendwick get away with any more of his bullshit.'

Savage led the way out of the station and across to her MG.

'Cute.' Horton admired the gleaming vehicle. 'Don't tell me this is a British squad car?'

'No, she's all mine.'

'Cool.'

Savage helped Horton put the rucksack behind the seats and they got into the car. Savage started up and pulled out of the station slip road.

'Shit,' Horton said. 'For a moment there I forgot you guys drive on the wrong side of the road.'

'Where are you staying, Janey?' Savage realised she should have asked before they left the station.

'No idea.' Horton pulled out her phone and peered at the screen. 'Got something called a Premier Inn here. Sounds like a slice of Little Old England. Any good?'

'Well, it's definitely not an inn and the premier bit depends on your point of view and your budget. Still, I stayed at one recently and it was fine.'

Savage headed into town and negotiated the city centre traffic. A few minutes later she turned onto Sutton Road and pulled up in front of the Premier Inn.

'Nice place,' Horton said, apparently without irony. 'And right next to a dinky little harbour too. How far to your pad, I can catch a cab, right?'

'Not really, we're out in the country.'

Horton opened the car door and got out. 'Can you wait while I check it out?'

'Of course,' Savage said.

Horton strode across the car park and disappeared into

246

the reception area. A minute or so later, she reappeared. She trotted across to the car.

'No room at the inn. Apparently there's some kind of Christian conference on and everywhere is fully booked.' She glanced up at the sky for a second. 'D'ya think he's trying to tell me something?'

'Could be.' Savage laughed and then paused. She looked across as the American climbed back into the car. Horton was a woman not just from across the tracks, but from another world. Still, there was something about her which appealed, something in her eyes which Savage recognised. She didn't much believe in fate or anything and yet here was Horton, turning up the day after Savage's suspension, ready to go after Kendwick. 'Look, Janey, I've been thinking, it's a bit rash of me, but why don't you come and stay at our house? We've got an annexe and you're welcome to use the place.'

'Well, Charlotte! That's real sweet. Southern hospitality just when I wasn't expecting it. I accept.' For a moment Horton looked wistfully at a fishing boat tied up to the quayside behind the hotel. 'And I can check out the tourist spots later, right?'

Savage exited the hotel car park and headed out of the city. As she drove, Horton sat beside her chatting away, telling her all about her flight and how she'd decided on the spur of the moment to come over here when she'd read about the death of Amy Glynn. When they took the coast road and passed Jennycliff, Plymouth Sound a shimmering blue expanse on their right, Horton reached out and touched Savage on the arm.

'Hell, this is great,' Horton said. 'I knew we were going to get along, Charlotte. We've got things we've shared, haven't we? Loss for one. My daughter was older than yours but I don't suppose it was any better or worse. Just the same.'

'How did you . . . ?'

'The internet. I saw a picture of you and Kendwick on your local newspaper's website. You were picking him up from the airport. Alongside, there was an article about how you'd caught a bunch of killers. Looked like you were my type of cop, so I did some more research and discovered we'd got a lot in common.'

'Clarissa was just a little girl,' Savage said. 'And she was killed in a hit-and-run, not murdered like Sara. I can hardly begin to believe what you've gone through.'

'Yeah, well, it's been a journey, I can tell you. Reckon I'm close to the finish though.' Horton took her eyes off the view for a moment and looked at Savage again. 'Any more news on Kendwick?'

Savage explained recent events concerning the women camping on Dartmoor, how she'd arrested Kendwick and how her reaction to his taunts had led to her suspension.

'What about evidence?'

'Nothing so far. He's got an alibi for the night the first girl went missing, nothing for the attack on the campers though.'

'This alibi wouldn't happen to involve another woman, would it?'

Savage took her eyes off the road long enough to give Horton a glance. 'Yes. How did you know?'

'Just a feeling. Kendwick is a charmer. Some women – that's you and me, Charlotte – can see right through him. Others fall for the intelligence and humour and good looks. They don't see past all the superficial crap into his soul. If they could they would run away screaming.'

'So you don't think we should believe his alibi?'

'Believe it? I'd take it and ram it up his ass.'

Savage laughed. 'Unfortunately that's not standard procedure in the UK.'

'Nor where I come from, more's the pity.'

'Is that why you resorted to some out-of-hours work?'

'You know about that, then?'

'Yes.'

'I'm not proud of what I did, but then again I ain't shedding no tears either. I don't know if it's the same with you, Charlotte, but sometimes you get a sixth sense about a suspect. You just know he's the perp. That's how it was with Malcolm Kendwick. I *knew* he'd killed my daughter and the other girls. The only thing was I couldn't prove it.'

'So . . .' Savage glanced at Horton for a moment before concentrating on the twisting road again. 'You tortured him.'

'Let's just say I helped him to tell the truth.'

'And that led you to find the remains of the girls?'

'Some of them, yes. He left them in the mountains. It took me hours to get up there and then two days of searching to find anything. I did though, eventually.' Horton looked across at Savage before continuing. 'Trouble was I fucked up badly. I should have tipped off my colleagues instead of going there myself. Everything I found out from Kendwick was inadmissible. That's how he got to walk free. That's how he got to end up on your doorstep. And I'm real sorry for that.'

'Not your fault. I always say, it's the criminals who commit the crimes. They're the ones who are accountable.'

'You're right there.'

'The question is, how do we hold Kendwick accountable?'

'We'll find a way, Charlotte. He's guilty. The stuff I told you about the missing underwear proves that. Nobody but the killer could have known we didn't find any panties with the remains. Kendwick joked to you about it, but the last laugh will be on him.'

Savage slowed the car as they approached her house,

indicated and pulled into the driveway. She killed the engine and then turned to Horton.

'I hope so,' she said.

The first time had been the worst. His uncle had contacted him a few weeks after they'd met at the wedding. Be ready Tuesday night, he'd said. Twelve o'clock outside your place. Dress warm.

Kendwick had crept from his room sometime just before midnight. He'd padded down the stairs, gone through to the kitchen and out the back door. Earlier, he'd hidden a bag of clothes in the garden shed and now he went to retrieve them. A few minutes later he was walking to the end of the street where his uncle sat in his car.

'All right?' his uncle said as Kendwick got in. 'Good to go?'

'Yes.' Kendwick stared ahead, not wanting to meet his uncle's gaze. He didn't want to give away the fact he was having second thoughts. Aunty Orla was one thing, this was quite another. 'Where are we going?'

'Exbourne. Other side of the moor near Okehampton.' His uncle pointed across at the dashboard. A newspaper lay tucked under the windscreen. 'Check it out, there's a torch in the glove compartment.'

Kendwick reached for the paper. It had been folded back on itself, already on the correct page. He opened the glove compartment and found a small torch. He turned it on and shone the light on the paper.

Death Notices.

The heading stood bold at the top of the page.

Death . . .

He sucked in a breath, tasting the odour of Aunt Orla's lounge, at the same time realising that they weren't going to anyone's front room. He scanned down the page to where an oval of red felt-pen ringed an entry.

Jennifer Kassel, aged twenty-three. Died unexpectedly. Now with the angels. Burial at St Mary Blessed Virgin, Exbourne on 24th July, 11 a.m. Family flowers only. Donations to Christian Aid.

'How did she die?'

'Not sure. Local radio says tragic circumstances.' His uncle chuckled. 'When they said her age, I knew I needed to find out more.'

Kendwick waited as his uncle stayed silent. 'And did you?' Kendwick said.

'Yes, I did. I went up there today.'

'You went to the funeral?'

'I didn't actually mingle with the crowd, but I watched from a distance. I saw the gravediggers fill the hole in and, once everyone had gone, I walked across to the grave.' His uncle turned and the lights from an oncoming car illuminated his face as he winked. 'Ground's nice and soft. Digging her up is going to be easy.'

Kendwick stared down at the newspaper again.

Jennifer Kassel, aged twenty-three . . .

Was she blonde or brunette? Was she stick-thin or as nicely plump as Aunt Orla had been? Would she *feel* as good as Aunt Orla? He shivered, both frightened and excited. He closed his eyes, trying to imagine the next few hours. Dozed. Sometime later he woke from a deep sleep, his uncle's hand on his shoulder, gently rocking.

'We're here. Exbourne.'

Kendwick stared through the windscreen. Trees loomed dark against the starry sky. A church tower rose above the tallest of the trees, mini spires at each corner pointing to heaven. He looked around. They were parked on a narrow lane. The church stood isolated in large grounds, although an orange glow from a village streetlight seeped into the sky off to their right. His uncle explained there were houses all round, but that the grave lay a fair distance from any of them and was shielded from view by the church itself.

They got out and unloaded some equipment from the boot of the car. Two shovels, a crowbar, a trenching spade, a regular spade and a toolbox. His uncle had a couple of lanterns with clever little hoods which swung down and produced a gentle glow of dim light. He clicked one on and showed Kendwick how it worked.

'Now then, lad,' he said, his voice quiet but serious. 'Get your bearings. If anybody should come we make a dash for the car and get out of here. We forget about the tools, we forget about the girl, we just run, OK?'

'Yes.'

'Good. Now, as they say in the movie, let's go to work.'

They'd parked next to a low boundary wall and it was easy enough for Kendwick to climb over. His uncle passed the tools across, climbed the wall himself and then led the way, weaving among the slabs of granite, stopping every now and then to check they were alone. But of course, they were. Apart from the dead.

Jennifer Kassel's grave lay in an adjoining area, carved out of the corner of a field. His uncle explained this was for new burials, the graveyard round the church having been filled many years ago. A path cut through the grass, stones on either side.

'She's the final one on the left,' his uncle said. 'Here.'

Kendwick stopped. They'd gone beyond the last stone, but a long, low mound of earth suggested his uncle was right. Kendwick helped his uncle unfold a large square tarpaulin. They'd shovel the earth onto that, his uncle said.

It would be easier to put the spoil back when they'd finished. Then they began to dig.

The top layer of soil broke apart easily, the loose earth spattering on the tarpaulin. Soon, a decent mound had formed as the hole began to get deeper. Within thirty minutes, they had to take it in turns standing in the hole and by the hour mark his uncle was up to his shoulders, one of the lanterns at his feet shining as he scraped the last of the soil away to reveal the lid of the coffin.

'Toolbox.' His uncle put his hands up and Kendwick carried the heavy box across to him. 'Tricky bit, this,' he said. 'Getting the lid off.'

Kendwick stared down to where the wash of light from the lantern shone on the casket. His uncle was sweeping soil from the lid. He was almost reverent in his actions, as if there was something inside the coffin which was sacred, precious. Once he'd cleared the soil away, he set to work with a pair of pliers and a screwdriver, huffing to himself every so often as he struggled to remove the fixings.

Then it was done. His uncle passed the toolbox up to Kendwick and, standing astride the coffin, he bent and lifted the lid.

'There she is,' his uncle said. Kendwick edged forward and peered down. His uncle picked up the lantern and played the light on the girl. She was the most beautiful thing Kendwick had ever seen. 'Help me get her out.'

His uncle bent and lifted the girl under her arms, pulling her up so she appeared to be standing next to him in the grave. He pushed her against the side of the hole and gestured for Kendwick to hold her as he climbed out.

Kendwick knelt at the graveside. He reached down and wrapped his arms round the girl, feeling the smoothness of the white gown she was wearing, the cold softness of her breasts. All of a sudden he felt giddy, as if he would pitch forward and fall into the hole with the girl. Then the two of them would lie together at the bottom. He wouldn't care if that's what happened. He wouldn't care if his uncle shovelled earth on top of them and they had to lie down there forever.

'Come on then!' His uncle knelt beside him and together they hauled the young woman from the grave. They carried her a little way and laid her down on the grass. 'Now we put the lid back in place, fill the hole in, tidy up, and get the heck out of here.'

By the time they'd finished up and carried the body to the car, another forty minutes had gone by, the church clock striking half-past three. The girl went on the back seat, slightly curled and hidden under a blanket for the journey back. It was close to five o'clock by the time they had her laid out on a big old oak table in his uncle's shed. They worked in silence as they cut off her clothes, revealing an ice white skin.

Once she was naked, they stood next to the table admiring her. The woman had small breasts but full hips. A triangle of pubic hair concealed the delights between her legs. Her eyes remained shut, but her lips, Kendwick was sure, had formed into a smile, as if she was keenly awaiting a lover's touch.

'You've been a good lad, Malc,' his uncle said, moving across to the door. 'A good worker. Because of that, I'm going to let you go first. I'll go inside and take a nap. Come and wake me when you've finished.'

'But . . .'

Too late, his uncle had gone, and Kendwick was left alone with the body.

* * *

254

Riley stood in the crime suite listening to Gareth Collier waffle on about the investigation. The office manager was well-meaning, but Riley had other things on his mind. How, for one, he was going to rescue Savage from the mess she'd got herself into. If, by some miracle, Kendwick turned out to be responsible for the attack on the girls, then she'd probably get off with a warning. If he was innocent, then she was stuffed and at best she'd be demoted. At worst, her police career would be over.

Collier said something about widening the parameters in the Amy Glynn case and Riley nodded, still only half listening. The problem was, Kendwick had toyed with them from the start. Ever since they'd picked him up at Heathrow, he'd wound them up. Riley was sure Kendwick's behaviour was intentional, a way for him to double-bluff them, to trick them into doing just what Savage herself had done. Her actions had opened clear blue water between Kendwick and the investigation. They now needed real and verifiable evidence before they could go anywhere near him.

'Graham Chantry,' Collier said. He tapped the white-board. 'Back in the frame in my mind.'

Sure, Riley thought. Back in the frame only because no other fucker was. 'Right.'

'Chantry knows the moor well. You said the girls' first choice for a camping spot was over near the Dart river, not a million miles from his farm. He also told DI Savage he often went out at night. So, here's my theory: he sees the girls turn up at the Dart. Thinks, hmmm, they're nice. Later, he's driving round on the moor and comes across the Mini. He realises they're camping nearby so he parks up his vehicle and goes off in search of them. Finding them is easy. He waits until they retire to their tent and attacks them. They fight back, so he runs off. Inspector Frey says he found the

255

point where the attacker climbed out of the ravine. The tyre tracks there belong to a 4x4, possibly a Land Rover. Bingo!'

'Are we going to pull him in?'

'Well, that's where we have a problem.' Collier itched his chin. 'Hardin told me he doesn't want any more mistakes. This time he wants the evidence to be incontrovertible.'

'So we sit on our hands until he strikes again?'

'Not quite.' Collier smiled. 'Remember Operation *Cowbell*? All that surveillance you did on those farmers buying illegal red diesel?'

'Oh fuck, you're joking?'

'No. You'll lead a small team to keep a 24/7 watch on Graham Chantry, but there'll be a number of armed Force Support Group members on stand-by in case things turn nasty. We begin this evening.' Collier's smile turned into a grin. 'And, since you were so keen to get out from behind your desk, you'll be pleased to hear that you and DC Enders have got the first shift.'

Chapter Twenty-Four

Near Bovisand, Plymouth. Saturday 29th April. 3.40 p.m.

The annexe sat to one side of the house, an afterthought stuck on without much care or attention to detail. For several years, the little studio flat had been home to Stefan, a male au pair from Sweden who was also a semi-professional sailor. He'd helped Savage look after the kids, a near-impossible task for a working policewoman to do on her own. Now Pete was at home most of the time, Stefan had said his goodbyes.

Savage showed Horton where everything was and then left her to freshen up. A few minutes later, the American came striding out of the house. She breezed over to where Savage was sitting at a table on the deck enjoying the sun. For a moment she stared out at the incredible view over the Sound, letting out an appreciative whistle. Then she turned to Savage.

'So, honey, let's do it, shall we?' she said. She handed Savage a tablet.

'What's this?' Savage said, reaching up and adjusting the parasol to provide a little shade.

'Just about everything I know about the fucker. News stories, pictures, maps, crime reports, lab reports, autopsies.'

'Kendwick's confession?'

'Yeah, that too.' Horton cocked her head on one side. 'You wanna see it?'

'I'll get some coffee first. Then you can show me the other stuff. After that, maybe.'

They started with the crime reports. Missing persons later turned into murder victims by Horton's grisly discovery out in the wilderness. Stephanie Capillo, Amber Sullivan, Chrissy Morales and Jessie Turner. And, of course, Sara Horton. By the time Horton had found the first body, the cause of death was impossible to establish, although blood discovered nearby suggested that she may have been stabbed. The remnants of several dresses had been recovered from near the dump site and were quickly matched to the missing girls. One by one, police located the other bodies. DNA evidence confirmed their identities.

'He can't have thought they would ever be found, surely?' Savage said. 'Way out there in the National Park.'

'Wanna hear my hypothesis?' Horton said. Savage nodded. Horton flicked her fingers over the tablet and brought up a map with a satellite view. 'The bodies were here, right? The nearest access to any vehicle is a mile away. There's a loggers' track which you can get a 4x4 down.'

'And Kendwick had a 4x4?'

'No.' Horton shook her head. 'That was one of the things his lawyers brought up. However, we know he hired one on a couple of occasions. Unfortunately the dates didn't match the days when any of the girls went missing. I'm pretty sure he rented vehicles at other times though. Probably from backstreet dealers using cash. Much safer than using his own vehicle.'

'OK. Your theory?'

'So, Kendwick drives to this point where there's a dead

end. From the look of the track hardly anyone goes there. There's no view and it's not particularly scenic. The terrain is pretty rough for hunting too. Hunting animals, that is.' Horton's finger moved back to the map. 'So Kendwick brings them here. He gets his captive out of the car and tells her to remove her shoes and run. She heads down into the wood. Meanwhile, Kendwick burns the shoes and any other clothing aside from the girl's dress and her knickers. The latter he keeps as a trophy. We found evidence of scorched leather and melted plastic soles from several different pairs of shoes alongside the track.'

'And the girls were always wearing dresses?'

'Yes. What was left of them – scraps mostly – were found at the dump site.' Horton continued: 'Anyway, once the girl is in the wood, she'd have come across a gully. It's pretty impossible not to be drawn to follow it. The natural instinct when running is to take the easiest path, especially barefoot. He gives her a head start, a minute, five minutes, ten minutes, fuck knows how long. Then he comes after them.'

'He hunts them down, that's what you're saying?'

'Yup.'

'How do you know?'

'There's the dump site.' Horton pointed to a clearing amongst the trees. 'Around a mile from where I reckon he parked his car. The gully leads straight down. It gets wider as it descends, but the sides get steeper. Once in it there's no getting out.'

'He could have just walked them there.'

'Uh-huh, he could. But what about the shoes? By forcing them to remove their footwear it makes the task of getting the victims to the dump site much harder. No, in my mind he chases them. He makes them go barefoot because he wants them vulnerable and he doesn't want them to be able

259

to run too fast. If he'd wanted to simply walk them there under his guard, he'd have let them keep their shoes on.'

'There's another track leading to the clearing.' Savage stared at the map where a thin line bisected the dark green of the trees. 'He could have come along that one.'

'Years ago, perhaps. But look a little farther away. There, see? The track ends. A large section was swept away in a landslip in the early nineties. Before then cars could be driven right to the dump site. In fact they were. The place was a regular boneyard.'

'A *what*?'

'A boneyard. Sorry, that's a US expression. It means—'

'I know what it means. It's a dumping ground for vehicles.'

'What's up, Charlotte? You look like I just laid something real heavy on you.'

'You did.' Savage gestured down at the tablet. 'Have you got pictures of the dump site?'

'Sure.' Once more Horton bent to the tablet. She brought up a series of thumbnails and then magnified them one by one. Rusty cars overshadowed by huge, towering trees. A truck half submerged in a froth of white water as a stream tumbled over it. Three pickups stacked one atop the other like some kind of weird modern art installation. 'Reckon there must be a hundred vehicles down there all told. Everything from eighties Jap imports right back to cars that look like they rolled off Mr Ford's production line sometime in the thirties. The odd thing, aside from the cars, were the paths running everywhere. Some had been cut through the grass. Regular little trails. I reckon Kendwick got off on scampering round the place amongst the remains of the girls.'

'Shit, Janey, this is incredible.' Savage pushed back her chair. 'Come on, you need to see something.'

* * *

They took the MG and headed along the A38 to Ashburton. After they'd turned off for Dartmoor, the sun vanished behind a bank of cloud and drizzle started to mist the windscreen. Savage pulled over to fit the hood on the car.

'Don't they have a button for that nowadays?' Horton said. 'They seem to have one for pretty much everything else. Not that all those buttons have made the world a better place. The opposite, I reckon.'

'You could be right, Janey,' Savage said as she clicked the last couple of poppers in place. 'But that's why I keep the car, despite the fact she's rusting to pieces.'

'Happens to all of us in time.'

Savage got back in and they drove off, Horton admiring the scenery as they sped across the winding roads of the moor.

'I can understand why Kendwick moved back here,' she said. 'It's not the Sierra National Forest, but the landscape's wild enough.'

'There are areas on the moor miles from any road.'

'And that's where we're going?'

'I've kept quiet so far. You'll just have to wait a while longer.'

By the time they reached Hexworthy, the drizzle had stopped. Low cloud hung in the troughs of the valleys, but the ridges and tors were clear. Horton had borrowed a pair of Savage's wellingtons, while Savage put on walking boots. They set off along the track towards the reservoir, all the time Horton asking what they were going to see. Once again, Savage told her to be patient.

Horton shrugged and they walked on along the rocky track until they came to the shallow rise which led to the hanging valley. Horton raised an eyebrow as she spotted the first rusty car sitting on the slope inside the fencing.

'I'm getting an inkling, Charlotte.'

Savage said nothing as they walked closer. Part of the fence had been cut away by Layton and streams of crime scene tape flapped across the gap. Savage lifted the tape and then walked through and began to climb the hill to the reservoir. Near the top Savage paused.

'Close your eyes, and no peeking.'

'OK, but I sure hope this isn't some trick. I open my eyes and Malcolm Kendwick is there. Turns out he's your secret lover or something.'

'Not funny.' Savage took Horton by the arm and guided her the next few steps. She stopped at the top of the slope. 'OK, now open your eyes.'

Horton did so, turning her head from left to right and back again. 'Fuck me.'

'We found the skeletal remains of six people in this valley. Several we believe came from graves. They were already dead. However, one victim was definitely a missing person. Our theory is that a necrophiliac changed his preferences and became a murderer. The missing person vanished in 2007.'

'No shit, Charlotte, you kidding me?'

'Not at all.'

'Two thousand and seven was the year Kendwick arrived in the US.'

'Exactly.'

Horton began to walk in amongst the vehicles. 'This place gives me the creeps. There are no trees but the set-up is just like the dump site in California. Look at these paths. They remind me of the trails cut in the grass at the boneyard back home.'

'I thought they were made by animals.'

'*An* animal. A human animal.'

'There are fewer vehicles than your American boneyard though.'

'Hell, Charlotte, that's just the way it is.' Horton turned and grinned. 'Everything's just bigger and better at home. Unfortunately that also includes the A-holes.'

They continued to stroll amongst the rusting hulks. Every now and then Savage pointed out where they'd found human remains. When they reached the spot near the Mini where Calter had spotted the first skull, they stopped.

'He got a taste for killing here,' Savage said. 'I don't know what pushed him to go beyond robbing graves, but something did. When he moved to America, he found it all too easy to carry on. As you said, everything is bigger and better, and that includes the wilderness. Out in the National Park, his body dump had almost zero chance of being discovered.'

'Yeah, he could do whatever he fucking wanted to them. Alive or dead.' Horton stepped away from Savage and spat into a bush as if she was trying to remove a foul taste from her mouth. 'The question is, what do we do now? I take it you found no evidence to link Kendwick with this place?'

'None. He was away for ten years. Forensically there was nothing.'

'So we're stuck with what he's been up to recently. What he might be going to do.' Horton moved across to the rusting Mini and put a finger to the car's roof. She dislodged a flake of metal. 'What are the chances of getting your boss to run another surveillance op? To watch this place perhaps?'

'He won't wear it. He doesn't have the budget or the inclination. Hardin is worried about Kendwick but he's more worried about the media and Kendwick's solicitor.'

'In that case it's down to us, Charlotte. You and me. Right?'

Savage nodded without much enthusiasm and they began to head back to the car. As they walked, they tried to come up with some sort of plan. Had they had access to police resources, Savage would have expanded the investigation round Kendwick, delving further into his history and tracking down friends and relations so as to try and build a picture of the man. Without such help, they were left floundering.

'We watch him, Charlotte,' Horton said. 'Just as I did back in the US. Things are happening so fast he's bound to be unsettled. If we can keep an eye on him, at least for some of the time, the chances are he'll do something to give himself away.'

'You think?' Savage glanced at Horton. The American seemed buoyant and confident. Savage wasn't convinced. So far Kendwick had played a game and every round had gone to him. She thought back to the soft porn he'd had on his computer, the interview in which he'd led them a merry dance until revealing Melissa Stapleton as an alibi, the way he'd goaded Savage about Samantha until she'd cracked and lost it.

'Yes, I do think.' Horton moved across the track and linked arms with Savage as they walked. 'He's smart, but us dames, we're a whole lot smarter, you'll see.'

They returned to Bovisand where Horton offered to prepare dinner. While she did so, Savage gathered together the things they needed for a surveillance operation: a plentiful supply of snacks, a couple of torches, waterproofs for them both, and several other items she thought might come in useful. Finally, she went upstairs and retrieved the oily package she'd placed at the back of her wardrobe. She brought the package downstairs and laid it on the kitchen table.

Horton looked up from cracking eggs into a mixing bowl as the towel the gun was wrapped in made a muffled thud. 'Huh?'

'This,' Savage said, unwrapping the towel. 'Just in case.'

264

'Shit, Charlotte.' Horton cracked another egg into the bowl and came over. 'I thought you had strict gun control in this country. Plus I didn't think British cops were armed.'

'We do and they're not. This is illegal. We should try not to fire it unless we have to. If I'm caught with a gun in my possession then my career is over and I'll be going to prison.'

'Welcome to the club. You do something right and they crap all over you. It's called law enforcement, but sometimes it seems as if there are no laws and no enforcement.'

Horton returned to the worktop and began to beat the eggs. Savage checked over the gun once more.

After they'd eaten, Horton dozed on the sofa in the living room while Savage packed their stuff into a rucksack. Then she went to her room and lay on her bed and thought about Malcolm Kendwick. About how they would handle him. She heard Pete and the kids come in a little while later and went downstairs to find them in the hallway.

'What's this?' Pete said, gesturing into the living room where Horton lay conked out on the sofa. 'A scene from *Sleeping Beauty* or is it *Goldilocks and the Three Bears*?'

'Her name is Janey Horton,' Savage said. 'She's just arrived from the US. I guess the jet lag finally caught up with her.'

'The US?' Pete cocked his head. 'She's not that cop who—'

'She is and she's our guest.' Savage looked across at Jamie and Samantha. 'So, kids, go upstairs and Daddy will bring you some snacks. Janey needs to sleep a little longer.'

A little longer was an underestimate. Three hours later and Horton was still unconscious. Savage gently roused her and helped her across to the annexe.

'Thanks, Charlotte. I'm all tired out. Been a long day. Guess we'll have to postpone our little trip to see Kendwick. We'll start over tomorrow, right?'

Savage said they would and then bid her goodnight.

Back in the house, Pete was still all questions. Savage tried to answer truthfully, but in the end she had to embellish the facts.

'Janey's here to help the police with some profiling,' she said. 'I offered to put her up because we'd been in contact before.'

'Even though you're suspended?' Pete shook his head, plainly not believing the story. 'Doesn't make sense, love. Why can't she stay at a hotel?'

'Budget cuts. Anyway, the good news is I get to remain involved in the investigation as Janey's chaperone.'

'I thought you were permanently off work until the thing with Kendwick is sorted?'

'Doesn't include paperwork. And that's what this is. Taking notes, that sort of thing.'

'Right.' Pete moved to the fridge and pulled out a bottle of lager. 'Still, seems strange. Don't you—'

'Shall I cook something for you?'

'What?' Pete opened the beer and took a mouthful. 'Oh, yes. Great.'

Further discussion was avoided, because Samantha came into the room, all bouncy and smiley on account of a text she'd just received. Her boyfriend had undumped her, she said. This was the best day ever. Life couldn't get any better.

'That's wonderful, sweetheart.' Savage cast a sideways glance at her husband. Pete rolled his eyes. 'But take things slowly this time, hey?'

Samantha scowled, her mood changing in an instant. 'That's the trouble with you two. Any chance I get at happiness, you're down on it like a ton.'

'I didn't mean—' Too late. Sam turned and ran from the room, her footsteps thudding up the stairs.

'One emotional woman, I can deal with,' Pete said. He

266

shook his head and then took a long draught of his beer. 'But two under the same roof . . . ?'

'You won't *be* under the same roof if you're not careful.'

Pete laughed and then took another sip of his beer. 'Janey, she's highly strung too, right? Must have been to go after Kendwick like that. Tie him up and all.'

'What do you expect? He killed her daughter.'

'Allegedly. If there'd been any real evidence, Kendwick would still be in the US.'

'Well, that's why Janey's here.' Savage pulled a frying pan from a cupboard and moved to the stove. She poured some oil into the pan. 'To act as a consultant and make sure we don't make the same mistakes.'

'I can't see the British police torturing anyone, can you?'

'No,' Savage said, watching the oil begin to bubble and thinking all of a sudden about pouring the hot fat over Kendwick. 'Of course not.'

Chapter Twenty-Five

Near Bovisand, Plymouth. Sunday 30th April. 8.41 a.m.

Horton breezed into the kitchen on Sunday morning, refreshed from her marathon sleep. Savage gave her breakfast, after which Horton mucked in with family life; she guided Sam through some homework and helped Jamie get ready for a birthday party he was going to. There was a present to wrap and a card to write.

Later, as Jamie stood on the front step ready to head off for the party, he gave Savage a kiss and whispered in her ear.

'I like Janey, Mummy,' he said. 'She's kind.'

With that, he was gone, scampering across to Pete and the waiting car and waving like mad once he was seated. Horton stood alongside Savage and waved back.

'I miss that,' Horton said. 'The mom thing.'

'You're young enough to do it all again,' Savage said.

'In body, maybe.' Horton reached up and tapped her forehead. 'But not up here. Up here I'm all done in. I ain't ever going to recover from what happened and I sure as hell don't want to have another child and risk messing up like I did before.'

'You weren't responsible.'

'No, I wasn't *responsible*, that was the problem. I let my baby slip away from me when I should have held her close. To be honest, I had Sara when I was way too young. I was just seventeen. Through my twenties and thirties I was too busy with my own life, too selfish. My daughter would still be alive if I'd been a better mother, if I'd spent more time with her.'

'Janey, Kendwick's to blame, not you.'

'Don't worry, he's on the rap sheet too. Numero uno. But I'm an accessory before the fact. Aiding and abetting. Second on the list.'

With that, Horton turned and went back inside the house. Savage stood on the porch for a moment, thinking about the invisible scars that crime left; invisible but indelible. She'd seen even something as seemingly insignificant as a bag snatch or a minor theft cause stress and anxiety long after the event. More serious crimes, such as murder, rape and assault, were life sentences for the victims and their families. Not for the first occasion, Savage felt depressed and angry that the perpetrators escaped justice or got off with punishments which most decent folk thought were way too lenient.

That wasn't going to happen this time, she thought.

An hour later, Horton's mood had brightened and she was keen to be off in search of Kendwick.

'We'll go this afternoon,' Savage said. 'I just need to break the news to Pete that he's dealing with the kids tonight and tomorrow morning.'

Back from his taxi duties, her husband was accepting of the situation. Having been an absent parent for many of the years he'd been in the Navy, he could hardly complain if Savage was away for a night.

They left Plymouth at four and drove north in the MG. They arrived in Chagford as the town was beginning to empty of shoppers and fill with tourists looking for somewhere to eat. People wandered the streets in the late-afternoon sun, the buildings washed with a warm glow. Savage drove through the town and parked up beyond Kendwick's place. His hire car sat half on the pavement a couple of doors up from his cottage. Unless he'd gone off on foot, he was in. That was confirmed at around seven-thirty when the front door of the cottage opened and Kendwick strolled out. Horton's hand was on the door handle, but Savage tapped her on the shoulder.

'Steady, Janey,' she said.

'It's seeing him again.' Horton scowled through the window as Kendwick disappeared down the street. 'Makes my blood boil he's all free and easy like this.'

'Stay here,' Savage said. She got out and walked down the road, following Kendwick at a distance. At the end of the street he ducked in through the open door of the Globe Inn. She went past and wandered round for a few minutes before returning and taking a cursory glance through the open door of the pub. Kendwick was on the far side of the lounge, a newspaper and a pint of beer on the table in front of him. Savage returned to the car.

'It's going to be a waiting game,' Savage said. She reached over to the back seat and grabbed the bag of snacks, opened a packet of tortilla chips, and handed them to Horton. 'Ninety-nine per cent boredom and one per cent terror, isn't that what they say about police work? Or is that war?'

'Same difference.' Horton accepted the tortillas and pulled a couple out. 'Especially when you think of the body count with Kendwick.'

Savage nodded. She found something to eat for herself.

'I don't get your legal system, Janey,' she said. 'How could Kendwick get off when the evidence was there in plain sight? How could such evidence be inadmissible? Seems like something's wrong when he can walk away scot free.'

'I don't get the fucking system either.' Horton munched on her food. 'But I can tell you he's not getting away scot free. Not while I've got a single breath left in my body.'

Horton's words raised a silence between them. Her anger was palpable. Savage wondered what would happen should they have to confront Kendwick. There was a real chance the American would lose it.

The silence didn't last long and soon they were chatting again. Mostly about Savage's family, about Horton's life in the States, anything but Malcolm Kendwick. Every half hour Savage walked back to the pub to check on Kendwick and each time she found him either sitting at the table or leaning against the bar.

Later, the air began to chill. The light slipped from the sky and the surrounding moorland lost its brown green hue and turned to grey. A nearby tor darkened and was soon black against pink clouds. Janey dozed some more as the clock on the dashboard moved on. Nine, nine-thirty, ten, ten-thirty.

'What the fuck's he up to?' Horton said, waking as Savage returned to the car after checking on Kendwick once again.

'I can imagine,' Savage said. 'He's got a silver tongue, what we call the gift of the gab. He'll be chatting to the barmaid, conversing with locals, impressing them with his intelligence and knowledge.'

'He's eyeing up what's on offer more like. Sniffing out his prey the way he cottoned on to those girls who went camping.'

Savage shivered at the thought but before she had time

to say anything she saw somebody moving in the shadows at the far end of the road.

'It's him!' she said, sinking low in her seat as the figure looked in their direction. 'Get down!'

Kendwick walked along the street. Before he got to his house, he stopped at his car. He opened the door and got in. The headlights came on and he pulled out and drove towards them. He went past without a glance in their direction. Savage started her car, quickly turned in the road, and followed.

'I told you,' Horton said, leaning forward with her hands on the dash. 'I fucking told you!'

Savage gripped the wheel. Although she was focusing on the road ahead, all she could think of was the rucksack on the back seat and the heavy piece of metal stuffed in the side pocket. If lives were in danger, would she be able to use the gun, thus ending her police career and possibly putting herself in prison?

No question about it.

On leaving Chagford, Kendwick took a succession of tiny lanes until he reached the main road where he turned right for Two Bridges. He coasted along at a steady forty miles an hour, seemingly in no rush. At Two Bridges he took a sharp left towards Dartmeet.

'The boneyard,' Savage said. 'It's over the ridge to the south.'

They followed until after a couple of miles, Kendwick indicated and swerved off the road into a little layby on the left. Savage coasted on past until she rounded a bend. Horton looked back over her shoulder.

'We're clear,' she said. 'Stop here.'

Savage pulled over onto a grassy verge and waited as a pair of headlights came up from behind. The car went by and she saw it wasn't Kendwick. She killed the lights and turned off the engine. Another car drove past. Still not Kendwick.

'Laughter Tor,' Savage said, pointing through the windscreen. 'The local farmer said he saw somebody up there looking across at the boneyard one night. I wasn't sure I believed him at the time, but it looks like he was right.'

'Well, we'd better go and see what Kendwick's up to, honey.' Horton had already clicked open the door and now she got out. 'And bring your – well, y'know . . .'

Savage retrieved the rucksack and got out. She clunked the door shut and the interior light dimmed, leaving them in darkness. All about them the moor was a formless mass of near black. They walked back along the road until they came to Kendwick's car. In the distance they could see a tiny beam of light flickering back and forth as somebody with a torch headed away from the road along a rough track.

They followed Kendwick for half a mile until he struck off onto the moorland and began climbing towards a mass of rocks standing above the track. For a moment they lost sight of him, but then they saw the light from the torch, the beam dancing across the heather.

They began to make their way up the hill to the tor, stumbling as they forged cross country. After ten minutes, they reached the first of the rocks. As they moved silently among the hunks of granite, a glimmer of light played on the rocks perhaps twenty-five metres away. The light seemed to be moving off in the opposite direction, so they crept forward. They rounded a large boulder with a flat top and then both stopped dead.

Kendwick knelt in a crevice between two pillars. He was delving into the crack with his right arm, straining to reach something. Then he pulled back and sat on his haunches, playing the torchlight over something he'd retrieved from the crack. He placed the torch on the ground and the beam picked out a small container. Savage heard Kendwick chuckle as he opened the box. Then he reached out and switched the torch off. With the light extinguished, he disappeared from view, his body hidden in the dark shadows of the stones.

'The gun!' Horton whispered and Savage removed the rucksack and opened the side pocket. The weapon slipped into Savage's hand.

They both remained still. In the darkness Kendwick groaned and Savage thought she heard a rhythmical movement. The groaning increased and then Kendwick let out a cry.

Savage strained to see but Kendwick was still in shadow. Then he switched the torch on again. He shone the torch in the crack in the rock and replaced the box within. He stood, dusted himself down, and then moved off. The torchlight jerked this way and that as he made his way back down toward the track.

'Jesus, the dirty fucker,' Horton said. 'He just masturbated over something he had in the box.'

They stood and watched as Kendwick carried on along the track. Within a few minutes he'd reached his vehicle. The headlights came on and then he was driving off, heading back the way he'd come.

'In the rucksack,' Savage said. 'Grab the torch.'

Horton reached into the pack and pulled out a flashlight. They walked forward to where Kendwick had been kneeling. Horton shone the light down on the ground.

There. A few globules of white in among the grasses. Kendwick's semen.

Savage shivered with disgust. Horton raised the torch and shone the beam in the direction of the crack in the rock. The light made little impression. The crack went back and then turned to the right. They both moved closer and Savage delved in with her arm, her fingers feeling along the surface of the stone until they touched something plastic. The box was right at the limit of her reach but she was able to scrabble it a little towards her and then pull the container out.

She stepped back away from where Kendwick had been standing and moved across to a large, flat rock. She placed the plastic container on the rock and Horton shone the torch down. It was a sandwich box with four click down flaps on the lid. For a moment Savage cursed the fact she didn't have any gloves with her but then realised that given the situation, it made little difference. She flipped up the flaps holding the lid. She lifted the lid away and Horton swept the light over the box. Red and white and black. Silk and nylon and cotton.

'Here.' Horton had a pen in one hand. She used the pen to gently tease one of the items from the box. A pair of red knickers, lacy at the edges. 'Fuck.'

Savage stared down at the label. The brand was unknown to her but she could see the sizing information was in Imperial measurements only. There was some washing advice too, the word 'color' standing out. There was also a contact number: 1-800-WALMART.

'My God,' Savage said, as Horton laid the knickers down on the rock and used the pen to hook out several other pairs. 'These are from . . .'

'My daughter and the other victims.' Horton lowered the torch, the underwear vanishing in the darkness. Horton spoke again, her voice angry and wavering. 'There's your evidence, Charlotte.'

Horton was right, no doubt about it. The underwear in Kendwick's secret stash hadn't come from women in the UK. No, somehow he'd managed to import his little collection from the US. Five victims, five pairs.

'Shit,' Savage said, feeling numb. She pulled out her phone and flashed off a number of snaps of the box and its hiding place. 'If we don't put the box back, then he'll know we're onto him. On the other hand, we can't risk losing the evidence so we'd probably better take it.'

'He'll know soon enough anyway, Charlotte. Malcolm Kendwick is a cold-blooded lust killer and we've got to stop him.' Horton flashed the torch onto the rock, picking out the dull metal of the gun. 'Whatever it takes.'

Riley sat in the passenger seat of one of the pool Focus cars. DC Enders leaned forward, resting his elbows on the steering wheel as he peered through the windscreen.

'Waste of bloody time,' Enders said. 'Just like last night. Doesn't look like Chantry's going anywhere.'

Riley glanced at the dashboard clock. It was after midnight and so far there'd been no sign of Chantry making a move. The previous night they'd done the same shift – eight until four – leaving as the faintest hint of dawn had brushed the eastern horizon. They'd parked in a layby high above the farm and had a decent view across the valley and down into the farmyard. Chantry's Land Rover sat plum centre in a pool of white cast from a security light high on the side of one of the farm buildings. Soon after they'd arrived, Mrs Chantry had appeared and gone over to a chicken pen where she'd shooed the birds from their run into a small house. Then she'd retrieved something from the boot of her car – a little Toyota Yaris parked in an open fronted byre – and headed back to the house. Later, Mr Chantry had ambled out for a cigarette. He'd leaned against the Land Rover for a few minutes and then returned inside. The tableaux had been repeated tonight. The Chantrys were nothing if not creatures of habit.

'We're on until four again,' Riley said, his words eliciting a groan from Enders. 'But I think you're probably right. Chantry will soon be tucked up in bed, cuddling up to his missus. Which, to be honest, is just where I'd like to be.'

'With Mrs Chantry? She's an attractive woman for her age, I'll give you that.'

'No, you idiot.' Riley laughed. 'In my *own* bed with *my* girlfriend.'

'There we go.' Enders tapped the windscreen. A downstairs window lost its cosy glow as a light went off. The DC eased back in his seat and closed his eyes. 'Wake me up at four.'

'I'll wake you in half an hour, mate.' Riley clicked the door of the car open and stepped out. The air had chilled and a cool moorland breeze glided over his face. He stared down into the valley. Was Chantry really the man who'd attacked the girls in the tent? If so, would he risk another hunting trip so soon after the failure of the last one? On the other hand, perhaps the very fact he'd been thwarted would make him hungry for action.

Riley pushed the door shut and strolled up the lane a few paces. The floodlight glowed from the corner of one of the barns, but otherwise there was no light pollution of any kind. He turned his eyes to the sky where thousands of stars shone with a brilliance he'd rarely seen before. For a moment he felt utterly insignificant. Those stars had wheeled across the heavens for aeons and they would continue to do so long after he was gone. He looked back at the farmyard. Chantry was nothing in the grand scheme of things, whether he was guilty or not almost irrelevant. If he was guilty, then he wasn't the first man to satisfy his crazed lust by killing and he certainly wouldn't be the last.

Far in the distance, a set of headlights climbed the horizon. Riley watched them until they disappeared and then turned and strolled back to the car. He was about to open the door when he caught the sound of something on the wind. An engine. He peered back at the farm. The circle of light in the farmyard was empty, the Land Rover gone. He focused on the track where in the gloom a shadow rumbled up towards them. Chantry was trying to pull a fast one by driving off without turning on the vehicle's lights. Riley yanked open the door to the Focus.

'Patrick, wake up,' he said as he climbed in. 'Chantry's away.'

'Huh?' Enders lurched into consciousness and moved his head from side to side as if he wasn't sure where he was. He reached for the ignition. 'Right.'

'Come on!' Riley glared at Enders. The DC really had been asleep and was taking valuable time to come round. Eventually he started the car, but when he flicked the head-lights on Riley berated him. 'Off! Turn them off!'

'Sorry,' Enders said, as he pulled out of the layby. 'I wasn't thinking.'

By this time, Chantry had reached the top of the track. He turned right and set off down the lane, keeping the Land Rover in the centre of the road.

'If anyone comes the other way, it's curtains,' Riley said.

Enders grunted something as he leaned forward, his nose almost against the windscreen. 'Might be curtains long before that, I can't see a thing.'

'Do your best.' Riley reached for the handheld radio. He called in their location and direction of travel to the support team. Then he pulled out his phone. He opened a satnav app and tried to follow the squiggles on the screen to see where Chantry might be going. What did he hope to find at this time of night?

Chantry headed for the main road and struck off for Two Bridges and Princetown. Now he switched his headlights on and Riley indicated to Enders he should do the same.

'But stay back, right?' Riley held his hand up. 'Leave plenty of distance so he doesn't know he's being followed.'

Enders turned the lights on and then relaxed. Following Chantry was a whole lot easier now since they only had to keep an eye on the red taillights as they floated in the near distance.

'Plymouth?' Enders said as Chantry continued towards Princetown. 'Possibly for some on street action?'

'Could be,' Riley said. 'But we're going to pass the place the girls were attacked. He might be returning to the scene.'

'Sick bastard.'

A mile later Chantry confounded them both. The brake lights came on and he turned right down a small lane.

'Shit,' Enders said. 'What now?'

'Follow him, but sidelights only.' Riley made another radio call as Enders swung the Focus across the road. Chantry had kept his headlights on and the beams swung back and forth as the lane hairpinned right and left, climbing a small rise. Then, all of a sudden, the lights were jerking up and down, as if the vehicle was riding a switchback.

'What the hell?' Enders slammed the brakes on. 'He's left the road, sir.'

Riley peered through the windscreen. The tarmac lane ran out, the surface changing to mud and rubble. 'Get after him!'

'I'll try, but I wouldn't hold out much hope.'

The Focus bounced as Enders crept the car forward, its front wheels riding up onto the track. A hundred metres farther on, Chantry's Land Rover was tackling the terrain with ease.

'He's getting away. Shit!'

The car bumped along, lurching from side to side.

'It's no good,' Enders said. 'Without the headlights I can't see anything.'

'Go on then, put them on.' It was do or die, Riley thought. They had nothing to lose.

As Enders flicked the lights on, Riley knew they'd had it. The track was like the surface of Mars. Rocks the size of footballs peppered the route ahead. He grasped the side of his seat as Enders swerved to avoid one rock, but in doing so rolled right over another. The steering wheel broke free from the DC's hands and the car careered left.

'Hold on,' Enders said, as he tried to grapple with the wheel.

Riley stuck his legs out, to brace himself for the inevitable as they left the track and slid gracefully off to the side. A large boulder loomed in the lights and the car hit the rock square on with a crunch. Steam hissed from under the bonnet.

'Fuck,' Riley said, jerking against the seat belt.

'Sorry.' Enders banged the steering wheel. 'Nothing I could do.'

Riley undid his seat belt and pushed open the door. He got out and stared into the distance. The Land Rover had vanished over the brow of the hill, but for a few seconds the beams from the headlights swept a stand of trees on a nearby ridge. Then they were gone.

Nina Staddon waved to her friend, LJ, that everything was OK. The night had been a slow one, the streets of the

Stonehouse area of Plymouth eerily quiet. A drizzle had kept the punters away and this guy was only the third of the evening. Given the time, he'd be the last. Nina would be glad to get home with money in her pocket. To tiptoe into her daughter's room and wish her goodnight. She was the only reason Nina did this. Put up with the crap. With the danger.

'Text you later,' she shouted out to LJ as she opened the passenger door of the vehicle and climbed in. Pulled it shut. Looked across at the punter. He was all right, she supposed. Older but clean. That's all that mattered. They were all wankers really. She'd never got used to sex with strangers, never would. It was just a job, a way to earn some money. She smiled as the man clunked the gear lever forward. 'Hello, my name is Layla, what's yours?'

Layla? What crap. She used the pseudonym because she didn't want to hear some slimeball uttering her real name as he dumped his load in a rubber inside her. Layla, on the other hand, didn't give a toss. She did what the punters wanted and took the money. Later, Layla gave the money to Nina, but mostly the memories stayed with Layla. Mostly.

The man muttered something she didn't hear as they pulled away, but that didn't matter. They were all the same. Some gentle, some rough, some apologetic, some chatty. The chatty ones were the worst, she found. Like she gave a fuck?

'Take the next right and then right again, love.' Nina pointed through the windscreen. 'Nice and quiet down there. We won't be disturbed.'

'Good,' the man said as he flicked the indicator. 'Especially the quiet bit. I like quiet very much. Quiet and still. I don't like anyone interfering. I like to take my time.'

God, she thought, she hoped he wouldn't take long. Not that most of them did. If it was oral or a hand job she could

281

usually have them coming within a minute or so. If they wanted full sex then the nauseating process usually took longer, but not much. This one had asked her how much a blowjob was, so, allowing for a little chat to warm him up, she reckoned she could be back with her friend in fifteen minutes.

They pulled up in the deep shadow of a large warehouse. A little way down the street a yellow streetlamp cast a reassuring glow. At the end of the road there were more lights, some sort of distribution depot open twenty-four hours a day. A man was stationed in a little box next to the gates to the depot.

'Can we get in the back?' The man pointed to the rear bench seats.

He had a point. There wasn't much room in the front. In the back she could move about and work more easily. Nina smiled. Sixty seconds. Maybe a little longer.

'Sure,' Nina said. Once they'd relocated to the rear she coaxed the money from him. 'You give me something and then I give you something in return, right?' The shy ones and the first timers were embarrassed about the exchange of cash. This way it made it easier. As the man handed over the money, she tried to work him out. He seemed nervous, but there was something about him which told her this wasn't the first time he'd paid for sex. She slipped the money into a little zip-up pocket on her skirt and then shifted over towards the client. 'All right, honey, let's loosen you up a bit, hey?'

The man nodded and reached for his trousers. 'Can you help me?'

'Love to.' Nina moved her hands across and helped with the belt buckle. 'Now, what sort of surprise have you got hidden for me down here?'

'This one,' the man whispered as he pushed down on the back of her head.

'Hold on, tiger. I haven't got your cock out yet.' Nina cursed, hoping the punter wasn't going to be difficult. Then she felt something cold slip round her neck. She instinctively recoiled but the man held her down. There was a click, hard steel against her throat as something locked in place. Then came a rattle of a chain and she found herself dragged by the neck down to the floor, her face coming up against a huge block of iron. 'What the fuck!'

There was a further rattling of the chain and then the man clambered over into the front. He sat in the driver's seat and started the engine.

'Let me go!' Nina let rip a scream, but she was face down on the floor. She flailed her arms and legs around, but couldn't reach anything. 'You fucking bastard!'

'Shut up!' the man said. 'The more you shout the more I pull on this.'

Nina heard a rattle of chain again and then was aware of the ring of metal closing on her neck. The fucker had rigged some kind of contraption which held her down against the floor. When she struggled, he yanked the whole thing tighter.

The vehicle moved away and turned in the road. Forward a little, backward and then forward again, accelerating with a spin of wheels. She screamed again, realising they would soon be passing the corner where she'd stood with her mate. This was her last chance.

'Heeelllppp!'

'I told you to keep quiet, didn't I?'

The voice from the front rang in her ears as the constriction round her throat tightened again. She put her hands up and grabbed at the ring, trying to gulp in air, all the time

283

kicking out with her feet in an effort to smash something.

'You may as well stop struggling. No one's going to hear you.' The man said. He laughed. 'Especially not where we're going.'

Chapter Twenty-Six

The girl's running and he's chasing. Down the hill, through the forest. He can hear her breath coming in little high-pitched squeals, hear too, her feet padding in the dirt. Strange though how he makes no sound. He appears to glide across the terrain as if he is some kind of spectral being floating after the soul he must possess.

Then, all of a sudden, he stops. She's vanished into thin air. He turns, staring in all directions, but seeing only the trunks of the sequoia trees vaulting into the sky. And then he spots her, darting out from behind a gnarled stump. Game over, he thinks as he begins to chase her again. This time he ends it quickly, catching up with her and knocking her to the ground. She's lying there in her ripped dress, unconscious and still. He smacks his lips together in delight and then lowers himself onto her, ready to enjoy everything on offer. But then a shadow passes across the ground and he looks up. There's a woman in a grubby T-shirt, a tattoo on her arm, blonde hair with black roots. She's got a gun and the gun is pointing straight at his head.

Now the world is spinning. The woman's hair has changed from blonde to red but she still has the gun. Her finger caresses the trigger. Then comes a shot and another and another. Bang! Bang! Bang! The grey world turns to black and he's shouting and screaming, somehow alive even though three bullets have passed right between his eyes.

Which was when the dream ended and Kendwick woke up.

He stared into the darkness and then rolled over and groped for his phone. Two a.m. He'd only been asleep for an hour or so. He lay back on the bed and stared up at the ceiling, not quite sure if the patterns he was seeing were in the swirls in the Artex or in the recesses of his mind.

Janey Horton. Charlotte Savage.

He'd been enjoying his dream until they came along. He reached up and touched his forehead. There was no hole, of course there wasn't, but the sensation felt very real. Was the dream a warning or an omen? Perhaps the images conveyed a message. Certainly Horton and Savage were each one-of-a-kind, although outwardly very different. Horton was trailer trash, all tattoos and foul language, bright-red made-up lips and a bad attitude. Savage was educated, hardly wore a touch of make-up, didn't thrust her tits out the way Horton did. And yet there was something about Savage which reminded him of Horton. Bitch wasn't the word; bitches could be controlled, subjugated. A quick slap and they behaved just like their canine counterparts, slinking away or rolling over to accept a collar and lead.

Savage and Horton weren't like that. Rile them and something powerful rose from deep inside. Kendwick had always tried to avoid women possessed of such an inner strength. Now though, Savage was on his trail in the same way Horton had been. Only this time he'd done nothing wrong. He sensed that wouldn't stop her.

He pushed himself up from the bed. He wouldn't be able to sleep now, not for a while. He groaned and then slipped from under the duvet and climbed out. He stood there, naked, as the air cooled the sweat on his skin. Then he heard a voice. A whisper from somewhere downstairs. Somebody calling.

'*Malcolm!*'

Next came a tap, tap, tap. The clatter of the big door knocker. That's what had woken him, he thought. Three bangs, three taps. Not the dream. The gunshots had been the sound of somebody at the front door.

He moved across the room to retrieve his dressing gown. He slipped it on and knotted the cord.

'*Malcolm . . . Malcolm . . . Malcolm . . .*' The voice came again, hissing in the dark and snaking up the stairs. '*Malcolm. Let me in!*'

He moved out onto the landing and peered over the banisters. He could see a rectangle of glowing light in the centre of the front door. Somebody was holding open the letterbox, the wash of a nearby streetlight flooding in through the slot.

'*Malcolm!*'

He descended the stairs slowly. When he was halfway down the flap on the letterbox clanked shut. At the foot of the stairs he moved to the door and put his eye to the spyhole. A circular view of the street filled his vision. A line of cars made yellow-grey from the streetlight. Nothing else. Nobody out there who could have . . .

Click.

He spun as he heard the noise from the kitchen. The back door latching open.

'*Mal . . . colm . . ., Mal . . . colm . . .*' A *voice* from the kitchen. A *person* in the kitchen.

Kendwick walked quickly across from the front door to the fireplace. He reached for the fire irons hanging on a stand, selecting the heavy poker. Then he moved towards the kitchen.

'*Malcolm. Come on now. We've got work to do.*'

He stood still for a moment. A bulky male figure loomed against the kitchen window, his back to Kendwick, one of his hands working the tap on the sink. Water gushed out and into a glass. He turned, the glass in his hand.

Kendwick reached for the light switch and flicked it down. 'Malcolm!' The figure stood there.

'What the hell do you want?' Kendwick held up the poker and stepped forward. Then he stopped. Over by the door someone lay in a heap of limbs. Thigh boots, short skirt, ample boobs cascading out of a skimpy top. 'Oh fuck, no!'

'What I *want* is a bloody *drink.*' The figure raised the glass and took a gulp of water. 'Thirsty work this girly business, isn't it?'

She's upstairs now. Tied to Kendwick's bed. Her ankles are bound together, rope leading from them to the footboard. A knot fastens the rope to the frame. Her arms are secured with separate cords, one to each side of the headboard. The ropes aren't really necessary because the girl is unconscious. Paralytic would be a better word, because he plied her with drink as she lay in the back of the vehicle. Perhaps plied is the wrong word too. Forced more like.

He had to drag her upstairs himself, because Kendwick went crazy. Not just a little upset, but completely mental. Still, he seems to have calmed down somewhat now. He's sitting on the floor over in the corner of the bedroom. True, he's pulled his knees right up to his chin and is staring out with a vacant expression, but at least he's no longer shouting. To be honest, Kendwick's been a disappointment. He doesn't seem keen on the plans for the girl. Not keen at all.

Never mind.

He dismisses Kendwick from his thoughts and goes to work. He's brought a couple of things with him. Medical things.

They're sitting on the bedside table. A precision electric drill and a syringe with a big needle. OK, so the drill is one he bought in a model shop and the syringe and needle came from a printer cartridge refill kit, but he reckons they'll do the job.

'Been an effort this, Malcolm,' he says, looking at Kendwick. 'First the one I picked up in Plymouth. A student. Pissed out of her head she was, but when I got her to the boneyard the little bitch tried to stab me. She fled clean away. Got her knickers though. Back home if you want them.'

'No, I don't want them.' Kendwick whispers from behind his knees. 'I don't want any of this.'

'Suit yourself.' He's cross with Kendwick. Cross with his attitude. It's as if they've no history together, as if the lad is trying to play the innocent party. He continues with his story. 'Then there were those lasses on the moor. Easy pickings, I thought, but they fought back too. Never managed to get even one of them.'

'That was you?'

'Who else d'ya think it bloody was?' He shakes his head, thinking his nephew has grown soft. 'Finally, I tried Plymouth again. Found this tasty number. Fifty quid but I got my money back. Should have gone for a prossy from the start.'

'You should have quit.' Kendwick spits the words out, raises his head and gestures at the woman on the bed. 'Don't you get it? The police are all over this. Anything happens and they're round here checking up on me. They've searched my house and I've been arrested twice. One of their officers even assaulted me, the bitch. I made a flippant comment about her teenage daughter and she went ballistic.'

'Are you talking about the redhead?' He licks his lips and grins at Kendwick. 'Tasty bit o' mutton from what I've seen. Not lamb though. A bit old for you. Still, sounds as if the daughter might do in her place, no?'

'She's onto me, understand? She knows.'

'She knows nothing, lad.' He taps his forehead. 'She's not one of those fucking psychics, is she?'

'She's a detective. That's what they do. Detect things.'

'Well, we'll just have to stop her detecting things.'

'No way, she's dangerous. We steer clear.'

'We?' He holds up one hand, thumb raised. 'That's more like it, Malcolm. The two of us together. Like the old days.'

'Forget it, I've had enough of your fucking demented ideas.' Kendwick grimaces and turns his head away. 'I want to be left alone.'

'Nonsense, if you wanted to be left alone then why did you come back to Devon, hey?' He lets the silence hang for a moment and then changes tone, trying to sound confident, trying to win Kendwick round. 'Now then, don't you worry, my boy. You'll soon get back into the swing of things. And this one will be easy. A few minutes work and then we'll have exactly the girl we need. The perfect girl. She won't hardly move, she won't run, she'll lie still, she'll stay with us and we can do whatever we want. If I do say so myself, my idea is genius.'

'And if it doesn't work,' Kendwick whispers from behind his knees. 'If the experiment goes wrong?'

He told Kendwick it was an experiment earlier and now he's regretting the term. Realises the word implies something with a dubious outcome.

Never mind.

'It won't go wrong,' he says. 'And this way we get to keep her. She'll be both dead and alive all at the same time. You'll see. I've been thinking about this for ages. All the time you were shut in that prison in America. Me stuck here with no fun to be had. I thought about what we'd do when you got back. How we couldn't just carry one like before. Not here. Not in Devon. That's where I got the idea we'd kind of have to do things a bit different. And now, we're sorted, right?'

He looks at Kendwick but the boy doesn't move. So be it. He rubs his hands together and crosses the room to the bed. Time to get started. He reaches out and picks up the drill. It's cordless and sits neatly in the palm of his hand. He presses the little button on the side of the drill and the motor whirrs into action, the sound reminiscent of the noise heard in a dental surgery. He puts the drill down and picks up the syringe. He turns the syringe so the needle points to the ceiling and then squeezes the plunger a little. He doesn't really know why you need to do that but he's seen them do the same thing on television. On Casualty. He guesses the programme must conduct rigorous research, so it seems a good idea to follow their example. A tiny squirt of liquid pumps from the end of the needle. He blinks, not wanting to get any in his eye.

'Sodium hypochlorite,' he says to Kendwick, simply because the words sound so good and it makes him feel as if he's a real doctor. Still, they wouldn't be injecting the stuff into any patients on Casualty. Sodium hypochlorite is better known as household bleach. 'Tesco Value, but I think it should do the trick.'

He places the syringe back down on the table and takes up the drill once more. This is it, the moment of truth. He holds out the drill in front of him, noting that his hand is shaking. He's not sure if it's from nervousness or excitement or fear. Perhaps it's a little of each.

'Here we go, Malcolm, here we go!' He leans across the bed. The girl has blonde hair. The yellow strands cascade down across her face and he needs to reach up with his left hand and sweep the hair away from her forehead. 'There, there,' he says, even though she can't hear his voice because she's completely blotto. 'Everything's going to be fine. Everything's going to be perfect. Absolutely bloody perfect.'

Then he presses the button on the drill and lowers the bit towards the girl's head.

'Oh Christ no,' Kendwick groans from the corner of the room. 'Oh fucking Christ no!'

Kendwick sat in the corner and stared across at the bed. The girl lay on her back, the ropes now loose. To all intents and purposes she was free to go. But she didn't move.

Her eyelids fluttered open and closed. Her pupils gazed upward, black pinpricks seeing nothing. In the centre of her forehead his uncle had stuck a small plaster. The plaster covered the eighth of an inch hole which had been drilled in her head. His uncle had filled the printer syringe with bleach and injected the contents directly into the girl's skull.

'Zombification,' his uncle had muttered as he'd worked. 'No more graves, no more killing. She'll be just as we like 'em.'

After he'd finished, he'd untied the ropes and left Kendwick alone with the girl. Kendwick had heard water running in the bathroom, his uncle singing as he took a shower. And then he was back. Standing there with a towel round his waist, a disgusting bulge in the towel.

'Come on, Malcolm, help me get her clothes off.'

Kendwick had refused to move. He'd simply watched as his uncle pulled off the girl's skirt and top. Removed her bra and knickers. Watched as his uncle had dropped the towel from round his waist.

And then, done within a couple of minutes, his uncle had rolled off the bed and left. Not just left the room, but left the house. Gone. As if he'd just popped round to return a borrowed book.

Kendwick continued to sit in the corner and contemplate the girl. His uncle had flipped. Lost the plot. The student at Combestone Tor, the camping party, and now the girl on the bed. The killing was one thing, but this was quite another. And yet, wasn't this what Kendwick wanted? Wasn't the girl, as his uncle had said, quite perfect? She was still, she was compliant, she was as unmoving as anyone could be without being dead. They could have her over and over.

He shook his head and clenched his fists, fighting the horrors in his head. He thought, somehow, he'd escaped this. The twelve months behind bars had been like going cold turkey. Back in the UK, he'd flirted with DI Savage and played along with the police's notion of what he was like. He'd acted up, partly to confuse them and partly because he'd enjoyed it. There'd also been the matter of the book and newspaper rights. They were paying for a monster, not a nice guy. Still, he'd never intended to go back to his old ways. The night with Melissa Stapleton had proved he could have some kind of normal relationship with a woman. Only she'd rejected him, hadn't she?

. . . a little weird . . . not for me, I'm afraid.

Cow.

Kendwick pushed himself up and moved over to the bed. The girl *was* very beautiful. Full breasts hanging slightly down to each side. A little old for his taste, but she had long, firm legs and a lovely face. And, aside from the gentle rise and fall of her chest, she was perfectly still.

He put one hand out in front of him, holding the palm above the girl's body. His fingers quivered with fear. This was like the first time. The time in the shed. Like the time with Jennifer Kassel in his uncle's barn too.

'Oh God, no,' Kendwick said. 'No, no, no. Please help me. Dear God, somebody please help me.'

All his bravado had gone. His pithy one-liners, his way of casually dismissing worries, wouldn't work here when he was alone with only his personal demons for company. In his heart he knew resisting was hopeless. To be honest, he'd known from the moment he'd arrived in the UK and been free from the reach of the US justice system. His uncle was right: he could have gone anywhere in the country, but he'd chosen to return to Devon, to the place it had all started. Now his descent into hell was beginning all over again. Lust had taken over from reason and there was nothing he could do about it.

He swallowed and for a second considered rushing to the window and smashing his way through, falling to the ground exactly as he'd thought about falling from the aircraft on the return flight from the States. Then he shook his head and let his hand fall down onto the girl's stomach where his fingers began to trace lines and his mind started to run wild.

Chapter Twenty-Seven

Crownhill Police Station. Monday 1st May. 8.25 a.m.

Despite not crawling into bed until after four a.m., Riley was in the crime suite early Monday morning. Out on the moor, he'd summoned a car to pick him and Enders up and roused the relief team. The team had raced to Chantry's place and later reported that Chantry had returned to the farm at fifty-one minutes past three. He'd been absent for nearly four hours. Where he'd been and what he'd been up to was a mystery until Collier came over to Riley later in the morning.

'Here.' Collier handed Riley a sheet of paper. 'This misper report just came in. The woman went off with a client and never came back.'

'A sex worker?' Riley took the sheet, his interest piqued.

'Yes.' Collier held up his hands. 'Nina Staddon, known as Layla to her punters. Now, sex workers aren't the most reliable at the best of times. Runaways, drug users, but this is different. The woman has a young child. She leaves the little one with her own mother while she works. She's not on drugs, no domestic issues, nothing to suggest she would go off.'

'Where?'

'Back of the ferry terminal. A PCSO, friendly with some of the girls who work the streets down there, took a call from a concerned friend. Nina turned a trick in the early hours and hasn't been seen since.'

Riley nodded. He didn't want to get too excited. 'How many female mispers were on the overnights?'

'Three.' Collier jabbed a finger down at the sheet. 'I know, we can't go assuming everyone is a victim of a serial killer, but Chantry has a penchant for prostitutes.'

'So angered by his failure on the moor, he comes into the Stonehouse area of the city and takes the easy option?'

'Yup. And remember Amy Glynn? She went missing from near there. Chantry could have mistaken her for a pro.' Collier pointed at the sheet of paper again. 'Aside from that there's a couple more things.'

'Go on.'

'One, Nina had a phone on her. There's been a preliminary check of the area where she was picked up from and there's no sign of it.'

'Right.' Riley tried to contain his excitement. As long as the phone hadn't been switched off they could get its rough position. In the city, with many mobile masts to triangulate from, the position could be accurate to within a few metres. Out on the moor the accuracy was likely to be a good deal worse. Still, this could be the breakthrough they'd been waiting for. 'And two?'

'Nina's friend has identified the vehicle which picked up Nina. Or at least the make.'

Riley nodded, but once more stayed calm. They needed more than just the make. 'Did she get the registration?'

'No, but it hardly matters.' Collier smiled. 'You see the vehicle was a Land Rover Defender.'

In the end, they'd decided to take the plastic sandwich box containing the knickers, reasoning the evidence was far too valuable to risk losing. On the drive home they'd argued what to do. Horton was for confronting Kendwick with the knickers. He'd react violently, she said. When he did, they could kill him in self-defence. The knickers would prove beyond doubt he was guilty and there would be little fuss. Savage had to remind Horton the UK was somewhat different to the US and there'd be plenty of fuss. Once they got home, they talked some more. A bottle of wine came and went and by the time Savage poured the dregs into their glasses they'd got no further.

The next morning, after Pete had left to take the kids to school, Savage put on a pair of latex gloves and tipped the contents of the plastic box onto a newspaper on the kitchen table. Horton came into the kitchen, fresh from showering.

'Do you recognise any of these?' Savage said, as she spread the knickers apart.

'No,' Horton said. 'But then I wouldn't. Sara was nineteen. She bought her own clothes. I suppose there might be . . .'

'DNA?' Savage filled in the word as she continued to sort the underwear and then looked up. Horton had tears in her eyes.

'Sorry, I guess it brings it home. The knickers. Talk of my baby's DNA.'

'No need to be sorry. This isn't your fault, remember? It's Kendwick's.' Savage moved round the table and put her arm round the American woman. 'And if there is DNA belonging to your daughter or the others then that'll be part of the evidence which can be used to extradite him back to the States.'

'So what should we do?'

'At some point we'll need to return the box to its original hiding place and then tip off John Layton, our senior CSI, to the location.'

'But not until we're sure?'

'Exactly.' Savage began to put the underwear back in the box. She clicked the lid shut. 'On their own I don't think the knickers are enough.'

'You're right.' Horton put her hand to her head. She stifled a yawn. 'I could really do with some coffee. Last night.'

Savage laughed. 'I know what you mean. We never should have opened that bottle.'

'Never say never, Charlotte.' All of a sudden Horton looked rather wistful. 'These days I live for the moment and fuck what anybody else thinks.'

Savage nodded and then stared across the room and out the window. The sunlight was harsh but clean, the waters of Plymouth Sound already dotted with white sails.

'Come on,' Savage said. 'Let's go out and buy some food for a late breakfast. Fresh coffee and croissants. Bagels, if you prefer.'

'In that toy car of yours again? Cool!'

Five minutes later they were heading up the hill away from Savage's house, Horton turning her head to the left and admiring the view.

'You sure got a nice place here. Can't quite believe why my ancestors ever left. I guess they were chasing something, a dream. But then ain't we all?'

They reached the T-junction at the end of the lane and Savage stopped and checked for traffic. She looked across at Horton and realised she felt an affinity for this strange woman with her bad language, tattoos and very different political outlook. No, Savage thought, not just an affinity, more affection, perhaps even something approaching love.

'Hit the gas, sweetheart,' Horton said, gesturing through the windscreen at the empty road. 'We're good to go.'

'Sure.' Savage released the clutch and pressed the accelerator hard down. The rear wheels squealed and the car spun out onto the main road.

'Rock 'n' roll. This little beauty can really move, can't it?'

'Yes.' Savage nodded as they swept down the curving coast road towards Plymstock. 'When she wants to.'

'She? Hah! I get it. Like you, yes? And I thought Brits were all laced up tighter than a showgirl in a cheap leather corset.'

'We are, but we like to loosen up now and then. Underneath I guess we're not that much different.'

'You reckon?' Horton appeared to consider Savage's proposition for a moment. 'You ever been deer hunting? You know, with a bow out in the wilderness, stalking a sixteen pointer for hours until you get a clean shot and then taking the beast down with a single arrow.'

'Never.'

'Ever been in a catfight with another woman, scrapping in the dirt with her because she's taken a dislike to you for some goddamn unknown reason?'

'Nope.'

'When was the last time you went out to a bar and picked a guy up, took him home, fucked him senseless and then kicked him out in the small hours so you could get a good night's sleep?'

'Not recently.' Savage laughed. 'But I reckon my DC, Jane, is a fully paid-up member of that club. Can she stand in for me?'

'Well, sure she can honey, but you get my drift?'

'I meant on a more basic level, what people are like deep down inside.'

'You're not talking about other people, you're talking about us, what happened to our daughters, yeah?'

'I'm talking about what's right and wrong. The things

which matter. Most people care about the same things in life.'

Horton nodded and fell silent until, a few minutes later, Savage pulled into the supermarket car park.

'Most people care, Charlotte,' she said, reaching out and touching Savage on the arm. 'But not all. Not Malcolm Kendwick.'

Savage switched the ignition off, turned to Horton, and gave her a resigned smile. 'No, not him.'

Unlike DI Savage, Riley made sure he obtained Hardin's permission to call in Nigel Frey and the Force Support Group. With Graham Chantry having a licence for two shotguns, the permission was forthcoming with no argument and only a word or two of advice from the DSupt.

'Let's try to avoid a scene, shall we?' had been Hardin's parting words as Riley headed off for the moor.

Unfortunately, a 'scene' was what developed soon after the FSG van and two ARVs swept into the farmyard. Chantry spotted them arriving and barricaded himself in a barn along with one of his shotguns.

Riley tried to act as an impromptu negotiator from behind one of the police cars as Frey's men flanked out and looked for alternative ways into the barn.

'Mr Chantry,' Riley said. 'You need to put down your weapon and come on out. We can discuss this.'

'Discuss what?' Chantry's voice floated from behind the wooden slats of the barn. 'I've done nothing wrong. I killed a couple of dogs that were worrying my sheep, but that was legal.'

'This isn't about the dogs. This is about a prostitute who went missing last night.'

'I've given all that up. The missus insisted.'

'We followed you, Mr Chantry. After midnight. You went for a drive cross country in an attempt to lose us.'

'So what? Driving's not against the law, last time I looked. Anyway, I was searching for the girl killer. I've got my suspicions and wanted to check up on something. Afterwards I came back here.'

'If that's true, then you've nothing to worry about. You can tell me your suspicions while our forensic guys take a look in your Land Rover. They'll be able to ascertain if the missing girl's been in there.'

'They'll not go anywhere near it. That's my vehicle and you're on my land. Get out of here before I do something I might regret.'

'Mr Chantry. We—'

Riley didn't finish his sentence. The barrel from Chantry's shotgun slid through a crack in the barn door and a shot rang out, a hail of pellets spattering against the side of the police car. Riley ducked down beside Frey.

'We can take him,' Frey said. He nodded at Riley and then made a hand gesture off to the right. A black-clad figure crawled forward behind a low stone wall. 'There's a side door. Five minutes while I get my lads in position and then we fire a flash-bang in through the front. Meanwhile, two of my men enter through the side and it's all over.'

'Not yet,' Riley said. 'We've only been here a few minutes. I want to give Chantry some time to calm down.'

'What about the girl? She could be in danger.'

'There's no sign of her.'

'Then she's probably already dead.' Frey's face was a picture of bleakness. 'We might as well end this now.'

'Fuck.' Riley eased himself off his haunches and sat against the patrol car. He peered round the front wing at the nearby stone byre. The previous day, Mrs Chantry's Toyota had been parked inside, now the bay stood empty. Riley explained to Frey. 'The wife, she's out somewhere. We need to contact her. She might be able to soft talk some sense into him.'

'She could be anywhere.' Frey raised his arms and looked heavenward. 'We can't afford to wait. Not if there's even a slim chance Nina Staddon might still be alive.'

Riley sighed. Frey was being magnanimous. He was the senior officer, but Chantry was Riley's suspect. Still, Frey would make a decision soon and, a few minutes after he did so, Chantry would be dead. Riley shook his head and stared up the long farm track. He could see DC Calter by the gate to the lane. There were several police vehicles up there and a cluster of officers stood chatting. Calter was talking to a man with a full beard. He wore green fatigues, but he wasn't one of Frey's officers.

A little while later a message from Calter was passed to Riley. The man, it appeared, was a close friend of Chantry's. He knew the farmer well and was offering to speak to him.

'Nigel?' Riley tapped Frey on the shoulder and pointed up the road. 'Can we get that guy down here?'

Frey turned his head. 'Sure, who is he?'

'Chantry's last hope.'

They continued the rest of the journey in silence and a few minutes later Savage swung into an empty bay at the Plymstock Morrison's. They went inside and purchased fresh bread, croissants, bagels and coffee and then they were heading back up the road to Bovisand.

'Kendwick's got to be sorted,' Horton said. 'You know that. A man like him can't stop. There might be a hiatus, but the urge will keep coming back. He'll kill again and again and again until he's put away or dead.'

'You'd like the latter.'

'If we had the evidence and if the system was functioning properly I'd prefer he came back to the US to face justice.'

'You mean the death penalty?'

'Yeah, I do. Only thing the law's fucked up right now. California hasn't executed anyone for a decade, yet we've got serial killers on death row who are responsible for dozens of murders. I can't see the situation changing anytime soon. And anyway, even with new evidence, there's no chance your government would allow extradition unless the DP is off the agenda.'

'Kendwick told me. In fact he made a joke about it.'

'I bet he did.' Horton shook her head. 'So you see, Charlotte, we've got to stop him. Whatever it takes.'

'Do you think there's any chance the knickers provide enough new evidence for an extradition and a new trial?'

'Do you?'

'Bearing in mind the identity of the two ex-cops who found them, probably not. He'll say we planted them, that you brought them over from the States in an attempt to frame him.'

'Well. There you go.'

Once more there was silence until they swept into Savage's drive and pulled up in front of the house.

'Let's forget about Kendwick for a while,' Savage said as they got out. 'We can sit on the deck and have breakfast and then afterwards see if we can come up with some sort of plan.'

'Sure thing.' Horton smiled. 'I like you, Charlotte. I like your place, your kids, your husband. Hey, talk of the devil!'

Pete came out of the front door brandishing a mobile in his right hand. 'Where the hell have you been?'

'The shops.' Savage held up the bags. 'For breakfast. Why are you home from work?'

'You forgot your phone, you fucking idiot, you—'

'Hang on, partner.' Horton had moved round the side of the car. She puffed herself up and raised a fist. 'You don't speak to my friend like that.'

'Wait.' Savage held up her hand. She could see something was very wrong. Pete rarely got angry and when he did he was never vicious or abusive. 'What is it?'

'Samantha,' Pete said, a look of utter shock on his face. 'I've just had one of those automated calls from the school asking why she wasn't at registration.'

'But you dropped her off?'

'Yes. At the top of the road. The usual place.'

'Are you sure there hasn't been some mistake?'

'Yes, I'm sure. There's a text on your mobile.' Pete moved across to Savage. He held out Savage's phone. 'It's from Sam's number, but not from her.'

'What do you mean not from her?' Savage felt a chill creep up her back. 'Show me!'

'Look.' Pete tilted the screen towards Savage. He pointed to the message.

Stay away from the moor or your daughter will die.

'No,' Savage said in a whisper, aware of Horton beside her, a hand grasping her arm. 'No, it can't be him.'

'It is, Charlotte,' Horton said 'It has to be him.'

'Who?' Pete said. 'For God's sake will one of you tell me what's going on?'

'Kendwick.' Savage stood still, feeling the chill leave her body and a blood red rage sweep over her. 'Malcolm Kendwick has our daughter.'

Chapter Twenty-Eight

Near Bovisand, Plymouth. Monday 1st May. 10.17 a.m.

Inside the house there was confusion for a few minutes until they'd run through everything again. Savage tried Samantha's phone several times, but it went through to voicemail. Then she called the school to double check her daughter was absent. It was exactly as Pete had feared, Samantha hadn't attended registration. Savage cursed herself. She should have paid more attention to what her daughter had been up to. She'd known her family was in danger, that's why she'd retrieved the gun from the beach.

'Well?' Pete said. 'Aren't you going to phone the station and get things moving? An incident room, search teams, officers to apprehend Kendwick?'

'No.' Savage cast a glance across at Horton. She could see Horton was thinking along the same lines. 'Kendwick's playing some sort of game. He might well have Samantha, but if he was going to harm her he'd have already done it and there's no way he would be leading us on like this.'

Horton nodded. 'I agree. Kendwick wouldn't telegraph what he was up to without a specific reason. He wants Charlotte to come after him.'

'So we just do nothing?' Pete shook his head. 'For God's

sake, Charlotte, think! If this was one of your cases it would be getting the full spectrum of resources. You'd have all sorts of avenues of investigation open and you'd be wrapping the family up in cotton wool while overtime was cancelled and dozens of officers began a search for the missing child.'

'Exactly.' Savage moved across to Pete. 'If I report this then from now on in it won't be me making the decisions. Somebody else will be looking after Samantha's interests, not me, not us. We'll have people swarming over the house, a bug on the telephone, armed officers in the driveway. We won't be able to do anything and Samantha's future will be out of our hands.'

'She's right,' Horton said. 'And I should know, I've got experience.'

'But that was the States,' Pete said. 'Things are different here. The police take missing children very seriously, don't they, love?'

'Of course we do,' Savage said. 'But there's a difference between the police taking things seriously and *me* taking things seriously. A very big difference. For my sanity, *our* sanity, I've got to handle this myself.'

'Christ.' Pete shook his head. 'This could go wrong. Very wrong.'

'Yes, but that could happen whichever way we play it.'

'So, what do we do?'

'You go and pick Jamie up from school. Make some excuse as to why he needs to come home early, but I want to know he's safe. Meanwhile, Janey and I will find Kendwick. If he's got Sam, then we'll bargain with him. Whatever he wants we'll give him, as long as we get her back.'

'Suppose he doesn't admit to anything? Suppose he doesn't tell you the truth? He could simply deny everything.'

Savage cast a sideways glance at Horton. 'Then we'll just have to make him talk, won't we?'

'Make him . . . ?' Pete followed Savage's gaze. He knew enough about the background to the case in the US to work out what she was thinking. 'For God's sake, Charlotte, don't do anything stupid.'

'I'm not going to do anything stupid. I'm simply going to do whatever it takes to get our daughter back. You're not going to argue with that, are you?'

Pete said nothing for a few moments before speaking in a whisper. 'No, I'm not.'

Alan Russell shuffled into position behind the squad car and then crouched beside Riley. Frey had taken the man on a circuitous route across a couple of fields and into the farmyard, the way in either out of range of Chantry's weapons or behind hard cover. The DPA ranger listened as Riley explained the situation. Frey crouched beside them with his weapon at the ready.

'And he did this?' Russell said, scratching his beard as if he couldn't contemplate such a thing. 'Attacked those women on the moor and killed the girl at Combestone Tor?'

'He's a suspect. There's enough circumstantial evidence to connect him with both incidents. There's also a prostitute missing from Plymouth.'

'DI Savage talked to me about Graham. I told her I'd been into Plymouth with him, but never to pick up whor . . . sorry, prostitutes.'

'I want you to try and reason with him. Explain that he needs to give himself up for the sake of his wife and family. There's no way he can escape. I'm hoping a friendly voice might bring him round.'

'OK, what do I do?'

Riley crawled to the front bumper again. 'Sit here, but for God's sake don't stick your head round the edge of the car.'

'Sure.' Russell manoeuvred himself into position and then took a deep breath. 'Graham? It's Alan. Alan Russell.'

There was a pause before Chantry answered. '*Alan?* Is that really you?'

'Aye, mate. Seems to me like you've got yourself into a bit of a pickle. Worse than that time your muck spreader came off the back of the tractor and tipped up beside old Mrs Wilkinson's garden. The flood of shit toppled all those precious gnomes of hers, didn't it? A right knocking over nightmare, if I remember. Strewth, the hours we spent clearing the mess from her lawn.'

There was nothing for a few moments and then Chantry answered. 'This is a different order of crap and you bloody know it.'

'Never mind.' Russell paused and bit his lip, as if thinking of what to say next. 'Look, Graham, you can still do the right thing. You just need to put down your gun and come on out. No good can come of this. Somebody's going to get hurt and most likely that'll be you.'

'I'm not talking to you. I'm not talking to anyone.'

Russell glanced back at Riley. Riley encouraged him to continue.

'They've got evidence, Graham. The game's up. Come out and face the music or else they're going to kill you.'

'They can fucking try. I won't be taken alive.'

'Think of Bridget. How's she going to cope without you? She'll have to sell the farm and leave behind everything you've both worked for.'

Riley put his hand on Russell's shoulder. 'Good. Leave it at that for a moment. Let your words sink in.'

'I'm afraid I didn't help much,' Russell said as he slumped down against the squad car. He shook his head and looked at Riley. 'It pains me to tell you, but you should know Graham's got a violent temper. He won't give himself up. I think you'll have to shoot him.'

'Let's see,' Riley said.

There was silence from the barn for a minute or two and then a clank of a bolt. The barn door swung open, Chantry standing there.

'Bloody hell.' Riley stared across as Chantry walked forward. He had the muzzle of the shotgun under his chin, his left hand holding the barrel in place while his right hand was farther down the weapon, his thumb curled round the trigger. Riley waved at Russell. 'Get on the ground and stay there.'

'Easy, Graham,' Frey said, as he moved upwards and swung his Heckler and Koch over the roof of the police car. 'Put the gun down.'

'You fuckers are the cause of all this,' Chantry shouted. 'Coming here and messing everything up. Well, I won't let you take me alive.'

Riley glanced round the edge of the car as Chantry staggered forward. His reach was only just long enough to enable him to point the gun at himself, but there was no doubt if he pulled the trigger, the blast would take most of his head away. That would be bad, but Chantry was now halfway across the yard and the angle between him and the car was narrowing. In a few seconds he could swing the gun down and take aim at Riley and Russell.

'Stop there, Mr Chantry!' This time, Frey shouted. His finger tightened on the trigger of his weapon, his head lowering to the sight. 'Don't come any closer!'

Then Frey made a tiny nod of his head and, as if by the

magic of his gaze alone, Chantry suddenly threw the shotgun down, his arms flailing and his knees buckling. He fell forward and collapsed in the dirt, a pair of thin wires leading from the small of his back to the corner of the barn where an officer stood holding a Taser. Chantry spasmed as the officer pulled the trigger again and another jolt of electricity surged down the wires.

Frey ran around the car and moved to Chantry. He stood over him, his weapon pointing down, as two other officers ran forward. They wrenched Chantry's arms behind him and one snapped on a pair of cuffs.

'Stay there,' Riley said to Russell, and then pushed himself up from the ground and walked across to Chantry. He stared down. Chantry was breathing hard, spittle on his lips. Riley gave the man a few seconds to calm down and then knelt. 'Where's the girl, Mr Chantry? Where's the prostitute you kidnapped?'

'There is no girl,' Chantry said between breaths. 'I told you, I'm innocent.'

Riley stood and turned. Calter was coming down the track with several other officers.

'Search the barns,' Riley said. 'Search the house and the land. Search every-fucking-where.'

Before they left for Kendwick's place, Savage made a phone call to John Layton requesting an urgent cell site analysis on Samantha's phone. Usually, Savage could tell roughly where her daughter was, because the family used a locator app to keep in touch. However, somebody had either disabled the app or turned the phone off because the last location shown in the history was close to the school gates earlier that morning. She gave Layton the mobile number without telling him who it belonged to. Layton said he'd get right on it, with only a casual aside to remind her that, as she was suspended, this was unofficial and if anyone asked, he'd never spoken to her.

'Oh, and Charlotte?' Layton said. 'DS Riley asked for a cell site survey this morning too. This wouldn't be connected, would it?'

'On who?'

'A missing prostitute. I haven't got the results back yet, but Riley and Nigel Frey have gone off to arrest Graham Chantry.'

'Chantry?'

'Yup. A Land Rover was involved in abducting the woman apparently. What with Chantry's night-time excursions, he's right in the frame.'

Savage thanked Layton and tried to get her head round the information. Was it possible Chantry was involved *with* Kendwick? Or were there two separate incidents?

With the call made, they set off, Savage opting to take the family's battered Galaxy, rather than the little MG. First, the Galaxy was less noticeable, second, there was more room. Hopefully, they'd be bringing Samantha back with them. If not, then Kendwick could be the one taking a ride. On the way they discussed what to do.

'He'll know we're coming,' Savage said. 'He'll have this all planned out so we mustn't fall for any of his traps.'

'Sure.' Horton nodded but then tapped the glove compartment door where Savage had hidden the gun. 'But he won't know about what's in there, will he?'

'No, so we confront him and see what he says. If he doesn't come clean then we'll move on to the second part of the plan.'

'The second part?'

'We'll pretend to arrest him, put him in the car and get

away from Chagford so we've got time to think about what to do next.'

'Jeez, Charlotte. I like your thinking.'

The journey over to Kendwick's place took forty-five minutes and when they arrived in the little town it was late morning. Savage swung the car round to the back of the terrace where a track ran down the far end of the long gardens. Some of the residents parked their cars there and it looked like a place where the rubbish bins were put out for collection. She inched the car along the track.

'He's in,' Horton said. 'The back door's open.'

'Right.' Savage stopped the car and turned off the engine. She checked her phone, hoping to see she'd missed an incoming call or message from Pete. There was nothing from him but there was a text from Layton.

Negative on cell analysis. No signal last 3 hours.

Savage felt her heart miss a beat. She stuffed the phone away, reached across to the rear seat, and pulled a small bag into the front. She peered into the bag: gaffer tape, a hessian sack with a drawstring, a large knife, several hanks of rope and a pair of handcuffs. She showed the contents to Horton and then pointed at the glove compartment.

'That'll do,' Horton said approvingly as she retrieved the gun. 'For starters.'

'Let's go then.'

They climbed out of the car and walked across to the garden gate. A bolt secured the gate, and Savage reached over and slid it across. The gate swung open and they walked up the path to the house. The next-door property – the holiday house the two women Kendwick had ogled had been staying at – appeared empty. Beyond that, sounds of a radio came from next-door-but-one, the occupier hopefully oblivious to their presence.

At the back door they stopped and Savage peeked into

the kitchen. She stepped into the room, Horton close behind, the gun held low but steady.

Savage gestured at the arch which led to the living room and they both tiptoed through. The living room seemed dark after the brightness of outside but a light washed down the stairs from above.

'Up,' Savage whispered.

She moved round to the stairs and began to climb. Halfway up a floorboard groaned in protest. She froze and listened.

Nothing.

She carried on, aware of Horton stepping over the loose floorboard behind her. At the top, they stopped on the landing. A bathroom door gaped wide and to the left, the faint sounds of a radio on low floated from the rear bedroom. A news channel. Savage slid one foot after another across the floor until she reached the bedroom door. She looked in through the hinge. Kendwick lay on the bed in a foetal position, his knees up by his chest. He wore a hooded top, the hood pulled over his head, his arms curled round his face. He appeared to be asleep.

'Come on.' Savage mouthed the words and they both slipped into the bedroom. The radio stood on a chest of drawers. Savage reached over and turned it off.

'Huh?' Kendwick mumbled and then uncurled himself in an instant. 'What the fuck!'

'Hello, Malcolm,' Horton said, raising the gun. 'Bet you didn't think you'd be seeing me again.'

'Woah!' Kendwick pushed himself up. He pulled down his hood and turned from Savage to Horton. 'What is this?'

'Officer Horton is here on secondment,' Savage said. 'Now stay on the bed. Janey won't hesitate to shoot you if you don't do exactly as we say, so roll over on your front.'

'Look, Charlotte. I don't know what this is about, but—'

'DO IT!' Savage shouted and in response Horton waved the gun.

'OK.' Kendwick held up his hands in surrender and then lay down and turned on his front.

'Lie still.' Savage moved forward and pulled out the cuffs from the bag. She dropped the bag on the floor and then clicked the cuffs in place. 'Now roll back over and sit up.'

Kendwick struggled round and wriggled himself upright. 'OK, so you're arresting me again even though I haven't done anything. You're just wasting everybody's time.'

'Where's my daughter?'

'*What*?'

'My daughter. You've taken her. I want to know where she is.'

'Really, Charlotte, you know me better than that. We're friends, aren't we? Why on earth would I kidnap your daughter?'

'I don't know. But then I don't understand why somebody would take five young women into the wilderness and rape and kill them.'

'Nor me.' Kendwick smiled as if he was about to make some quip, but then he sobered. He didn't look in a mood for jokes. 'Because, as I keep telling you, I didn't *kill* anyone.'

'I don't believe you, Malcolm.' Savage stepped forward and slapped Kendwick across the face. 'This isn't a game. Where's my fucking daughter?'

Kendwick fell backwards. 'Ouch, that hurt.'

'It's going to hurt some more unless you're honest with me.'

'I'm taking the Fifth. Right to remain silent. All that stuff. I'm not saying anything until I've spoken to Amanda Bradley.'

'Fine.' Savage glanced over at Horton. Kendwick didn't

appear to have cottoned on to the fact that their visit wasn't official. 'Janey, watch him while I check the other bedroom. Then we'll take him in.'

Horton nodded as Savage turned and went out onto the landing. To the left, was the bathroom. To the right the spare room. She stepped across the landing and pushed the door. Drab curtains hung drawn across the window, the room dark with shadow. Savage peered in. A figure lay on the bed.

'Samantha?' she said, as she reached for the switch on the wall. 'Is that—'

Light flooded the room. Savage moved forward. Not a girl, not Samantha. A woman. She lay in the centre of the bed, clothed in a skimpy dress. The girl at first appeared to be sleeping, but as Savage walked across, she opened her eyes and blinked. She made no attempt to move and simply stared up towards the ceiling.

'Hello?' Savage reached the bed and waved her hand in front of the girl's face. She was oblivious, high on drugs or something.

Savage glanced across at the bedside table where a plastic carrier bag sat neatly folded, a clothes hanger on top. Under the hanger lay a credit card receipt. She bent and read the purchase details. The shop was a Chagford fashion store and the item had been bought just a couple of hours ago. The credit card used for the purchase was Kendwick's. Then Savage spotted something else on the table, half hidden by the bag: a small cordless drill and, next to the drill, a syringe with an improbably thick needle.

She turned back to the girl. A wisp of hair half covered a sticking plaster in the centre of her forehead. Savage leaned across and stroked the girl's cheek. Then she turned and went back to Kendwick's room.

'He's got a girl in there,' Savage said. 'All drugged up. God knows what he's being doing to her. Go and see.'

Horton handed Savage the gun and popped out of the room, returning seconds later.

'The fucker.'

'I'm calling an ambulance.' Savage handed the gun back to Horton and then pulled out her phone. 'We'll leave before they get here.'

As Savage made the phone call, Horton waved the gun and Kendwick shifted himself off the bed and walked from the room. The three of them descended the stairs and Horton pushed Kendwick through to the kitchen and out the back door. They stood on the patio for a few moments while Savage completed the call and then they walked along the path to the gate and the rear of the car.

'You're making a mistake,' Kendwick said. 'This isn't what you think. I had nothing to do with kidnapping the girl in there and I don't know where your daughter is.'

Savage ignored him and sprung the rear hatch. Horton turned Kendwick away so he was facing back towards the house. Then Savage reached into her bag and pulled out the hessian sack. She threw it over Kendwick's head and tightened the drawstring.

'What the fuck!' Kendwick screamed and tried to stagger away but Horton smashed the pistol into the sack. Savage grabbed him by the shoulders and pushed him backwards so he fell into the boot. Then she slammed the lid shut.

'So,' Horton said. 'What now?'

'We need to find somewhere quiet.' Savage pulled her phone out again. She flicked through her contacts until she came to the entry she wanted. 'And I know just the man to help us out.'

Savage tapped the phone and a few seconds later her call was answered by a gruff voice.

'Charlotte,' the man said. 'Been a long time.'

'I need a favour, Kenny,' Savage said. 'A big favour.'

Chapter Twenty-Nine

Near Hexworthy, Dartmoor. Monday 1st May. 11.14 a.m.

It took Chantry a while to recover from the effects of the Taser. He sat slumped in the back of a squad car, still groggy but all the while denying he had anything to do with the disappearance of Nina Staddon. Riley crouched on his haunches by the open door, trying to keep up the pressure. If the girl was on his property, they'd find her, he told Chantry. No use delaying the inevitable.

'I know Nina,' Chantry said. 'Her working name's Layla. Seen her a few times. She's a nice girl. Why the heck should I want to kidnap her?'

'Because she wouldn't play along with your fantasies, she wouldn't come to the boneyard. So last night you abducted her and killed her.'

'What the heck are you talking about? I told you, I was driving round looking for the killer. If I'd have found Layla, I'd have told you.' Chantry stared blankly. 'Anyway, why on earth would I want to take a lass up to the boneyard in the first place? Especially now, after what you lot found.'

'Because it gets you off, Mr Chantry. The bones. Dead

people. You prefer sex that way. That's why you dug up female corpses and took them there.'

'Are you bloody crazy?' Chantry cocked his head. 'Look, I don't want to bring the colour of your skin into this, but you lot have got some fucking perverted ideas. Voodoo. Witch doctors. That sort of thing. Shagging dead bodies must be right up your street, hey mate?'

Riley was taken aback by the racism, but tried not to show his reaction. 'The girl, Mr Chantry. One last time. Where is she?'

'I don't. Fucking. Know. Get it?' Chantry turned back and stared forward. 'And now I'm keeping schtum until I get to speak to a lawyer.'

Riley stood and looked over to where Frey was rounding the corner of the barn. Frey held out his hands, palms up. Nothing. Not a dickie bird.

'Shit.' Riley slammed the door of the car shut and signalled to the officers inside to go. As the car pulled away, Calter ran over. 'Jane. Anything?'

'We've found her,' Calter said. 'Somebody called an ambulance and the control centre tipped us off.'

'Where?'

'Chagford, sir. Malcolm Kendwick's place.'

They arrived at the terrace of cottages to find the ambulance parked in the middle of the road outside Kendwick's house. Calter stopped their car behind the vehicle and Riley jumped out and sprinted in through the open door. Nina Staddon was being carried down the stairs. She'd been strapped to a spinal board and the two paramedics contoured themselves as they tried to manoeuvre the stretcher down the narrow stairway and out the front door. As they exited the house, Riley held up his hand. He gazed down at the girl. She blinked once and smiled at him, but the expression was vacant, as if she was in another place.

'She's not right,' one of the paramedics said. He pointed at the top of the girl's head and a great swathe of bandage which held a large compress in place. 'Not surprising since the nutter drilled a hole in her skull.'

Riley stepped back and allowed the paramedics through. He followed them as they walked over to the ambulance and slid the girl into the back. Then he turned and went into the house.

Inside he found DC Enders slumped in an armchair, his head in his hands.

'Patrick?' Riley said. 'Are you OK?'

'No I'm fucking not.' Enders looked up. His face had the same blank expression as the girl. 'Did you hear what Kendwick did? We should've topped him when we had the chance. How could anyone do such a thing?'

Riley didn't have an answer. 'How did you get here so soon?'

'I was over at the boneyard with Layton, sir. We set off as soon as we had the cell data on Nina's phone.' Enders flicked his eyes to the ceiling. 'Layton's upstairs. You should go and take a look up there. Might change some of those woolly liberal ideas of yours.'

Riley nodded and then patted Enders on the back.

He found Layton in the spare bedroom. The CSI stood at the head of the bed. When he saw Riley, he held up a polygrip bag with a syringe inside. He nodded at the bedside table where a miniature electric drill sat in its plastic case.

'Looks like Kendwick injected bleach into the girl's frontal lobe.' Layton shook his head. 'Beats me what the fucker was up to.'

'He wanted to create a zombie,' Riley said. 'Something that was dead but alive. A natural progression from the murder and necrophilia.'

'There's nothing natural about it.'

'I only meant this sort of thing has been seen before. Kendwick wanted to have somebody who he could control, who was compliant. A dead body is like that, but there are obvious issues with keeping a corpse for any length of time.'

'What's got into you?' Layton stared across at Riley. 'You're beginning to sound like DI Savage. As if you understand these lunatics.'

'Don't worry, understanding doesn't imply empathy.' Riley pointed at the bed. 'Has she been here since last night?'

'Looks like it.' Layton began to examine the bed. 'No sign of urine on the sheets, but he could have taken her to the bathroom. From what I saw, she was exactly as you said. In some sort of state between conscious and unconscious. She might have done his bidding.'

'Christ.' Riley leaned against the doorjamb, all of a sudden feeling weak. 'He joked about it, you know? He specifically mentioned a body in the bedroom, namechecked Jeffrey Dahmer. He must have known what he was going to do.'

'Talking about serial killers, where's Charlotte?' Layton lowered his voice. 'She's still investigating, you know? She wanted me to do a location search on a mobile number, only the thing was turned off several hours ago.'

'Whose?'

'She didn't say at the time, but when I got the data back I could see the phone was registered to her daughter.'

'Samantha?' Riley looked at the bed again, working the possibilities. 'Shit. Charlotte's been here, I know it. She must have seen the girl, and phoned it in. I reckon she's on Kendwick's trail.'

'Are you saying Kendwick's done something to DI Savage's daughter?'

'He threatened to when we were questioning him. That's why Charlotte smacked him one.'

'Fuck. She's in all sorts of trouble and I'm not far behind.'

'I'm going to speak to the neighbours. Somebody must have seen something.'

Five minutes later Riley had discovered that the next-door property was a holiday rental, nobody in. Beyond, at the next-but-one cottage, an elderly man answered Riley's knock and stared quizzically at his warrant card.

'I guessed something was up,' the man said. 'The ambulance and all you lot. Quite a stir.'

'I'd like to ask you a few questions, Mr . . . ?'

'Langton. George Langton.' Langton stared past Riley as two CSIs, fully suited up, walked down the street and disappeared inside Kendwick's place. 'Problems with Mr Kendwick are there?'

'Do you know him?'

'No, I don't. I eyeballed him in the pub the other night. Read about him in the papers. That's about the extent of it. Never spoke to him.'

'Can you remember when you last saw him?'

'Earlier today. Late morning.'

'And what was Mr Kendwick doing?'

'He was talking to one of you lot. That woman. The lass who's been in the papers. Red hair.'

'DI Savage?'

'That would be her, yes. Kendwick was talking to her.'

'When you say talking, what do you mean?'

'Well, not so much talking as shouting. Looked like your

322

policewoman was arresting him or summat. Took Kendwick out the back and loaded him into a car. Only I didn't see that, just saw them drive off.'

'Are you sure?'

'Yes. Kendwick, the redhead and this other woman. Blonde hair, a couple of nice tattoos on her right arm. She didn't look like police to be honest, but she had a gun.'

Fuck, Riley thought. What was Savage up to? And who was the strange woman with her? Riley thanked Langton and then went back to Kendwick's place in search of Enders.

'Any good, sir?' Enders said. The DC was standing in the kitchen. 'Any sign of him?'

'No,' Riley said, trying to appear deflated even though his pulse was racing. 'Nobody's seen anything.'

'Well, he hasn't gone far.' Enders held up a plastic bag. He waved the bag at Riley. Inside were a set of car keys. 'Not without his motor.'

Potholes riddled the track, great puddles of water splashing as Savage bumped the car along the rough surface. To the right of the track, a forest of mature pine blocked the view to the south, while to the left the rolling countryside of the South Hams stretched for mile after mile until Dartmoor rose in a brown hump far in the distance. After a few minutes, they came to a small concrete apron standing before a set of iron gates. Chain link fencing surrounded a grassy knoll, the whole area about an acre in size. At first sight the place looked as if it was an old water tank, with the steep, grass slopes leading up to a plateau where several pipes poked above the surface. However, at one end brick buttresses held back the earth and led to a set of large metal doors.

'What is this place, Charlotte?' Horton said. 'Looks like some sort of bunker from World War Two.'

'Not the Second World War, the Cold War. Kenny Fallon owns it. He was intending to create some sort of house here, but as he told me, it sometimes comes in useful for other purposes.'

'And you can trust him?'

'About as much as anyone, yes.' Savage wasn't about to tell Horton the full story concerning her relationship with Kenny Fallon, but what she'd said was true. Fallon wasn't really a friend, but they had an understanding. He was an old-school crook with a vicious streak, but there was a line he wouldn't cross. When Savage had called him up, seeking somewhere they could take Kendwick, Fallon had been only too pleased to help. He'd texted Savage directions to the bunker and the code to a combination lock which secured the place.

She stopped the car and nodded at the gates. 'Would you?'

Horton got out of the car and went over to the gates. A chain held a hefty padlock and Horton rotated the combination wheels and unlocked it. She pushed the gates open and Savage drove through. Horton closed the gates behind the car.

Inside the compound, the concrete apron ran round the bunker. Savage eased the car forward and turned the corner so the vehicle wouldn't be visible from the track. She got out and went round to the rear of the car. Horton joined her as she sprung the catch.

Inside Kendwick was curled in a defensive ball. The sack over his head had shifted somewhat but was still in place and his hands were still cuffed behind his back. Savage and Horton manhandled Kendwick until he slid out of the boot and rolled to the floor. A muffled cry came from within the hood and then a stream of expletives. They pulled Kendwick to his feet and guided him round to the front of the bunker.

There was another padlock with the same combination and once Horton had unlocked it, she pushed the big green doors open.

Savage reached for a light switch and old-fashioned fluorescent tubes sprang into life. The interior of the bunker looked something like a cross between a hospital and an office building. A corridor ran away from them, numerous doors in the walls, little name plates on each door.

'This way, I think.' Savage gestured into the heart of the bunker. 'There's a lower level which is supposed to be able to survive a nuclear blast. Kenny told me it's soundproof down there.'

Horton grinned. 'Methinks your Kenny's done this before.'

Savage didn't smile back. She didn't want to dwell on what had gone on in the subterranean chamber.

At the end of the corridor, a stairwell dropped away to the right, stairs marching downwards in a rectangular pattern. Savage stood and peered into the centre. The stairs went down at least four or five levels.

They eased Kendwick forward so he could feel the steps. He began to protest, but Horton told him to shut up. Then they were heading down. Down and round and round and round. Eventually they reached the bottom and a similar corridor to the one at the top stretched away from them. Again, doors stood open, but this time they could see many of the rooms were occupied by bunk beds. Savage pointed down to the far end.

'There's a large briefing room. Kenny said we'd find what we need in there.'

Sure enough, at the end of the corridor double doors led into a larger room. There was a long table with several chairs clustered round it. At the far end of the room a number of blackboards had been fixed to the wall, rosters chalked across the boards.

'Holy shit!' Horton gestured across the room. 'Your Kenny's right about finding what we need.'

Savage stared beyond the table to where some sort of throne-like seating arrangement stood on a pedestal. To one side a trolley with aluminium trays carried what appeared to be surgical instruments.

'A dentist's chair,' Savage said, realising what the seat was. She felt a sudden chill and wondered what terrors had gone on down here. She quickly put the thought from her mind. They had work to do.

They pushed Kendwick forward and then turned him so he fell into the seat. Horton pulled the gun from her back pocket, checked the weapon and stepped back a few metres, holding the gun and aiming it at Kendwick's chest. Savage pulled the sack from his head.

'You fucking bitches.' Kendwick blinked, his right eye swollen and red from where Horton had hit him with the pistol. He glanced around the room and then spat at Savage. 'You won't get away with this.'

'Shut up!' Savage shouted. 'It's you who's not getting away with it.'

'I haven't done anything, I told you. I'm innocent.'

Savage ignored Kendwick and pushed his head forward so she could work on his arms. She took several lengths of rope and bound one wrist and then the other. She led the ropes to the arm rests on the chair and fastened them. Then she released the cuffs and tightened up the ropes so Kendwick was secured in place. She placed a third rope round Kendwick's neck and pulled it tight and tied a knot at the back of the head rest.

'Nice one, Charlotte,' Horton said. 'He's not going anywhere now.'

Savage moved round and examined the instruments on the trolley. There were scalpels of various sorts, a Stanley knife, a long screwdriver which had been sharpened and fashioned into a vicious-looking spike, a pair of pliers, a lump hammer, a hacksaw, a meat cleaver and a corkscrew. There was also a container of industrial concrete cleaner. Savage moved over and saw a big warning sticker on the bottle: hydrochloric acid.

'Shall we?' Horton had picked up one of the scalpels. 'I mean there's no point hanging around.'

'No, Janey.' Savage placed a hand on Horton's shoulder. 'This is something I have to do for myself. Let's say, it's out of your jurisdiction.'

'OK,' Horton said. She let the scalpel clatter onto the tray and then swept her hand over the array of tools. 'Be my guest.'

Savage ignored Horton and turned to Kendwick. 'Last chance, Malcolm. Where is Samantha?'

'I told you before, I don't know!' Kendwick struggled against his bonds. His eyes stared wildly round the room before meeting Savage's. 'I haven't taken your daughter and I haven't killed anyone.'

'Fucking lies, Malcolm.' Horton looked at Savage. 'Just like before. There's only one way to get the truth out of him, Charlotte.'

'Malcolm, we know you killed the girls in the US because we found your stash of souvenirs on the moor. Your lies are wasted on us, so just tell me where my daughter is?'

'I DON'T FUCKING KNOW!' This time Kendwick screamed out the denial. 'Please believe me.'

'You sent me a text from her phone warning me to stay away from the moor or you'd kill her. Did you really think I'd just sit at home while you did God-knows-what to her?'

'I didn't send a text. I've never seen your daughter. I don't even know what she looks like. Honestly, if I knew where she was I'd tell you.'

'He's lying,' Horton said. 'Look at his face. He had exactly the same expression when he told me he'd never met my Sara. This time there's no doubt though. The girl in his bedroom proves that.'

Savage felt her heart pumping. She opened her mouth and sucked in a gulp of air. Kendwick was a multiple killer, but he wasn't going to admit anything. She remembered reading about the American serial killer, Ted Bundy, how he'd had the chance to plea bargain for his life. He'd turned down the opportunity and later died in the electric chair. Serial killers rarely admitted their crimes as if, somewhere deep inside, even they couldn't believe how heinous they'd become. That didn't change the facts here though. Samantha was missing and Kendwick had kidnapped her. He was either keeping her somewhere or she was dead. Either way, Savage needed to know.

She moved to the trolley. There were implements here she couldn't even begin to imagine using on another human. Her eyes settled on the container of concrete cleaner. She reached forward and unscrewed the cap. Next to the container there was a cracked mug. She poured a good shot of fluid into the mug and then turned back to Kendwick with the mug in her hands.

'I mean it, Malcolm. I'm not mucking around.'

'I know you're not, but I didn't do it, I didn't do it!'

Savage felt a wave of anger rise inside her. She thought of Horton's daughter, abducted and brutally killed. She thought of the other missing women, their bodies found in the wilderness. She thought of the girl on Dartmoor who'd run in fear and died alone in a crack of rock. The girls attacked in the tent and the poor wretch lying in Kendwick's spare room. Then she thought of Samantha, her flesh and blood, terrified or even dead.

'You fucking bastard!' she said. And then she tipped the contents of the mug over Kendwick's right arm. 'Tell me where she is!'

For a moment nothing happened. Kendwick peered down at his skin where the liquid was beginning to froth and steam. Then he screamed as red welts began to pop up on his forearm. He writhed against the ropes and scrunched up his face in pain. Savage stepped away from the chair and stumbled across the room.

'Way to go girl!' Horton said with a whoop. 'Now we're really rocking.'

'Arrrggghhh,' Kendwick yelled. He twisted his face again and sucked in air. He let out another scream and then panted several gasps in and out. 'You'll pay for this.'

'Where is Samantha?' Savage stood a few steps away. She placed the mug down on the briefing table and clenched both her fists. 'You can tell me or I can start over with something else.'

'Don't you think I'd tell you if I knew?' Kendwick said, sobbing. 'Please don't do this. I'm not the person you think I am. I'm innocent.'

Savage felt the anger build inside her once more. She moved back to the tray and picked up the pair of pliers.

'Malcolm, you're going to tell me eventually, it might as well be now.' Savage took the pliers and opened them. She moved across and rested them on the arm of the chair, slipping Kendwick's little finger in the jaws. 'Where's my daughter? Tell me!'

'I don't—'

Savage squeezed the handle on the pliers until Kendwick screamed again. Tears flooded his eyes.

'I DON'T KNOW!' he sobbed. 'I DON'T FUCKING KNOW!'

'You idiot,' Savage said. 'Tell me now or else I'll let Janey take a turn.'

'Now you're talkin' girl,' Horton said. 'Let me at him!'

'For God's sake, I don't know where your daughter is. You have to believe me. I didn't abduct that girl on the moor. I didn't attack the women in the tent. I didn't torture the one in my bedroom.'

'Come on, Malcolm,' Savage said as she began to close the pliers once more. 'We caught you red-handed. Are you seriously suggesting somebody else snatched that girl and put her in your room? All without you knowing? Who was this person, your fairy Godmother granting you your heart's desires?'

'It was my uncle,' Kendwick said, tears now streaming down his face. 'He's behind all this. We dug up the bodies together, the ones you found in the boneyard. After I left the UK, he flew to the States on numerous occasions to visit me. He killed the girls over there. I only watched. He kidnapped the woman you found at my place. I knew nothing about her until he turned up in the middle of the night and dumped her on my kitchen floor.'

'*What?*' Savage released the pliers. 'Say that again.'

'It was my uncle. He told me he snatched the student from Plymouth and attacked those campers. Both those attempts went wrong which is why he picked up the prostitute and brought her to my place. He had some crazy plan to subdue her, to keep her still.'

'The dress, Malcolm,' Savage said quietly. 'The girl was wearing a dress you bought this morning. How do you explain that?'

'That was afterwards.' Kendwick began to sob again. 'I couldn't help myself. I'm sorry. So sorry.'

'He's talking crap,' Horton said. She shouldered Savage out the way. 'Let me have a go.'

'NO!' Kendwick yelled again. 'In the States I picked the girls up, I chased them, I had sex with them once they were unconscious or dead, but I never killed any of them and I haven't kidnapped Charlotte's daughter.'

'You believe this?' Horton turned to Savage. 'He's trying to spin his way out of the mess he's in. Total fiction.'

'It's how I was able to pass the lie detector test, Janey. Remember? My lawyer insisted on specific questions as part of the deal. Ones to do with the actual act of killing. I told the truth. I didn't kill anyone.' Kendwick sobbed as the words came tumbling out. '*Stay away from the moor*, that was the text, right? Well, my uncle's the one who lives on the moor. He's the one who gets off by spending time with dead bodies.'

'Where on the moor?' Savage said, her voice low but insistent. 'What's his name, his address? How do I find him?'

'Alan Russell.'

'The *park ranger*?'

'Yes. I told him that you'd assaulted me after I mentioned your daughter. He must have picked up on that. He must have taken her. He'll have her in his barn. We used to take the bodies we dug up there and lay them out on this big oak table up the hayloft. That's how it started. With grave robbing and necrophilia. Then, when I got fed up and told him I'd had enough of the night-time excursions, he kidnapped this girl from near Bideford and murdered her. The murder was the final straw and I fled to the States, only Uncle came after me and we started up over there.'

'I asked him about you in relation to another man. He said he'd only heard of you through the newspapers.'

'There you go! Why would he say that unless he was trying to hide the link between us?'

'Fuck.' Savage shook her head. Wondered about the kind of shit she was in. 'What about the boneyard?'

'Alan was the one who suggested it. He took the bodies there after we'd finished with them. I thought the boneyard was just a convenient burial site, but it wasn't. He got a thrill out of returning there time after time, even when the bodies had rotted away.'

'And Chantry?'

'Who?'

'Graham Chantry, the man who owns the boneyard.'

'Oh, him.' Kendwick shook his head. 'He had nothing to do with any of it. Uncle Alan concocted some story about a pollution risk. He told Chantry to stop dumping the cars to make sure nobody went there and that nothing was disturbed. He even invented a fictional scientist and waved some official-looking papers at Chantry. Chantry fell for it and promised not to take any more cars there.'

'And the one in the US?'

'We came across it accidentally while searching for a dumping ground, but as soon as we'd found the place, Alan said we had to use it. He had a fetish for the rusting cars and the bodies of the girls. To be honest, the thought of what he did made me sick.'

'Sick?' Savage half laughed at the irony that Kendwick – a self-confessed necrophiliac – could find anything beyond the pale. Then she shook her head and pulled Horton away and across to the other side of the room. She lowered her voice. 'Look, Janey, I need to try and find this Russell guy and see if he really does have Samantha. If Kendwick's lying, then you get another chance at getting the truth, until then I need you to stay here and watch him, OK?'

'Sure, honey.' Horton looked deflated. 'What about you? Don't you need help?'

'Yes, I'll get some back-up. Say I've received a tip-off or something. Meanwhile, you promise you won't touch him? If he's lying and he has got Samantha he might be the only person who knows where she is.'

'Promise. Cross my heart and—'

Savage put her hand up to stop Horton mid-sentence. 'It won't come to that, Janey. Just be careful. You know what Kendwick's like.'

'Don't worry about me. I can handle myself. But you take care too, huh? Now go.' Horton slapped Savage on the shoulder. 'And find your daughter!'

Savage turned and ran from the room.

Chapter Thirty

Chagford, Dartmoor. Monday 1st May. 2.15 p.m.

DC Enders' discovery of the car keys was enough for Hardin to authorise a lockdown of the area. A witness had seen Kendwick in town that morning and the proof of his trip came in the form of a receipt for a dress bought from a local boutique. Layton had found the receipt in the spare room alongside the drill and syringe. Since Kendwick's car was parked several doors along from the house, it was reasonable to assume he'd left on foot. The ambulance had arrived at a little after eleven-thirty. Was it possible Kendwick had seen the crew and then legged it out the back? Hardin seemed to think so. The only question was, who was the anonymous woman who'd phoned the emergency services?

Now, a couple of hours later, Hardin had arrived in Chagford to supervise the ongoing operation. Roadblocks had been set up on all routes into the town and members of the Force Support Group were scouring the surrounding moorland. NPAS 44, the police helicopter, had been in attendance for the past thirty minutes, but so far had spotted nothing. Riley stood alongside Hardin outside Kendwick's place as Nigel Frey explained that, for now, he was putting his trust in the dog team.

'They'll be here shortly.' Frey looked at his watch. 'The dogs should be able to follow the trail if Kendwick left on foot.'

Riley listened as Frey continued. They'd started with a five-mile search zone and were confident Kendwick was still inside. Once the dogs arrived, they'd flush him out.

'He might try to lie low until later, thinking he's got more chance after dark.' Frey gestured at the mid-afternoon sun. 'He'd be mistaken. The helicopter has thermal imaging so he'll stick out like a beacon once it's night-time. I'm confident we'll have him in custody today.'

Riley nodded and tried to appear enthusiastic, even though he knew the search would prove fruitless. Kendwick had left the area. And not willingly.

'Are all your officers armed?' Hardin asked. He glanced down at the barrel of the semi-automatic weapon which Frey wore on a shoulder strap. Frey nodded. 'Well, tell them to be careful. I don't want any cock-ups.'

'They'll do what's necessary.'

'That's what I'm afraid of.'

Riley's mobile rang and he muttered an apology and stepped away.

'DS Riley,' he said.

'Darius!'

'Ma'am?' Riley walked off at a brisk pace and turned his back on Hardin and Frey. 'Where are you and what the hell's going on?'

'Alan Russell, the ranger. Remember him?'

'Yes. I've just been with—'

'He's kidnapped my daughter. He's holding her captive.'

'Ma'am, you're not making any sense. Where's Kendwick? I know you've been to his house.'

'Stuff Kendwick, Darius, I need your help. Russell is

Kendwick's uncle. The two of them are involved in this whole thing. The boneyard, the girls in America, everything. Now Russell's got Samantha.'

'How do you know?'

'Kendwick told me.'

'Just like that?' Riley didn't believe it. Kendwick wasn't one for giving the game away so easily. Obfuscation was his middle name. Then he got it. The blonde woman Kendwick's neighbour had seen. 'Fuck, Charlotte, Officer Horton's there, isn't she? Kendwick didn't tell you anything. Not voluntarily.'

'My daughter, Darius. Didn't you hear me? Russell's got Samantha. What else was I supposed to do? You know about the girl in the bedroom. Kendwick and Russell drilled a fucking hole in her head. Look, Kendwick's sister promised to send me a list of relatives. Since I've been suspended I haven't been able to access my emails, but I bet if you check the list, Russell will be on it. I'm pretty sure Kendwick's telling the truth. Russell *is* his uncle.'

'Shit.' Riley thought for a moment about the circumstances surrounding the disappearance of Nina Staddon. 'The girl at Kendwick's place was abducted by somebody in a Land Rover. I thought it was Graham Chantry.'

'It wasn't Chantry, he's innocent. Russell has a Land Rover too.'

'You're right. Plus one of the campers said they saw a DPA vehicle at the first spot they went to. Russell could have eyeballed the girls and later gone in search of them.'

'And the tracks Nigel Frey discovered near where they were attacked. Made by a 4x4.'

'One moment.' Riley took the phone away from his ear. Savage's theory made sense, but what the heck was she playing at? She'd taken the law into her own hands and kidnapped Kendwick. He looked back towards Hardin and

Frey and cursed. It couldn't end well. 'Ma'am, I think you should reconsider. We need to make this official so we can mobilise all possible resources to find Samantha.'

'You're beginning to sound like the DSupt, Darius. Just listen: I know where Samantha is, she's at Russell's place. I need you to meet me there. We go in, get Sam, leave. That's it.'

'And what about Kendwick? How are you going to explain to Hardin that you kidnapped him?'

'Fuck knows.'

Riley stood waiting for something else but there was nothing but a crackling on the line. 'Ma'am?'

'Yeah, I'm here. Meet you at Russell's place in forty minutes.'

'No, ma'am, I can't—'

Then the phone went dead.

Savage eased her car through the village of Widecombe-in-the-Moor and then accelerated along the little lane which led towards Alan Russell's place. She breathed a sigh of relief as she approached. One of the pool Focuses sat on the verge next to the track which led to the farmstead.

She stopped behind the car and got out. DS Riley sat in the driver's seat staring forward. He didn't move for a second, but when Savage pulled open the passenger door and climbed in he turned to her.

'Ma'am, I really don't think this is a good idea,' he said. 'We should call it in.'

'No we shouldn't. And stop calling me ma'am. This isn't police business any more. This is personal.'

'OK, Charlotte, then.' Riley reached across and touched Savage on the arm. 'This could be the end of your career. It could be a disaster.'

'The only disaster will be if I don't manage to rescue Samantha.' Savage turned to Riley and briefly smiled. 'Anything else is a win, OK?'

'Still, we might need back-up.'

'Nonsense.' Savage gestured down the track to the farmstead. 'Russell's Land Rover isn't there. He's out. Kendwick said he and Russell took the bodies they dug up to the first floor of the barn. I reckon that's where he's holding Samantha.'

'OK.' Riley sighed. He pulled out his mobile and checked for a signal. 'But first sign of trouble we call for help.'

'Sure.'

Riley shoved his phone away and then released the handbrake and rolled the car forward. He turned right and they coasted down the track. At the bottom he swung round in front of the pretty little cottage. Across the concrete yard stood an open-fronted stone byre with three bays. The one on the right was empty, the one in the middle held a small trailer and the one on the left a pile of fence posts. At the far end stone steps led to the upper level. Riley stopped the car.

'There,' Savage said, pointing at the byre. 'Just as Kendwick told me.'

They got out and stood for a moment. There wasn't a sound.

Savage walked across to the barn. The steps hugged the interior wall and ended at a trapdoor in the ceiling. She nodded her head in the direction of the stairs. 'Come on.'

Riley followed as she went across to the stairs and began to climb. At the top she could see the trapdoor was secured with a bolt. She slid the bolt across and pushed up on the trapdoor. Riley moved alongside to help. The door swung up and then banged against a beam. Savage reached up to where a hook hung down. The hook latched to an eye on the door, holding it open.

She climbed the last couple of stairs and stepped into the space above. The room was long and thin, the roof slanting down so the eaves were at floor level. Piles of junk had been heaped against the eaves or hung from hooks in the ceiling. A scythe, dozens of huge saws, piping, lengths of iron, rolls of fencing wire, pots and pans, tools ranging from hammers to crowbars, car tyres, an oar, ends from a brass bedstead, several chairs in various states of repair, two copper bedpans, hanks of rope tangled like jungle vines, rusted tins of paint, buckets full of nails or nuts and bolts or gate hinges.

'What is this, ma'am?' Riley said. 'It's like one of those farm sales you get when some old bloke dies.'

'He's not old, Russell.' Savage moved between the debris. 'Probably fifty or so.'

'What's he need all this stuff for?'

'He's a hoarder. Can't bear to throw things away. No wonder his place is so neat and tidy, he keeps everything up here.' She tiptoed on, brushing away a sheet of cobwebs. A huge coil of firehose stood next to a door at the end of the room. 'This way.'

'Right.' Riley swept his hand at the cobwebs and then wiped the debris on the firehose. 'You think she's in there? Samantha?'

Savage nodded. There was a padlock clicked through an iron hasp. She jerked a thumb at Riley. 'Find something to open it.'

Riley walked back down the barn and retrieved a wrecker bar. He placed one end beneath the hasp and levered the metal away from the wood. It cracked off with a splintering sound and Savage pulled the hasp free, pushed open the door, and peered in.

'Mmmmmm!' Samantha sat on the floor in the middle of the room, her back to the corner of a huge oak table. A strip of material had been wrapped round her face to act as a gag, while a length of rope encircled her body, securing her to one of the table legs. 'Ummmmm!'

'Sam!' Savage felt her heart miss a beat. She rushed into the room and knelt beside her daughter. Within seconds she'd removed the gag.

'Mum!' Samantha wriggled free as Riley undid the rope. She flung her arms round Savage, burying her face in her chest. 'Thank God!'

'Are you . . . hurt?' Savage hugged her daughter and stroked her hair.

'I'm OK, Mum. He didn't do anything, but he said he would. He said he'd be back.'

'Ma'am?' Riley coughed from behind them. 'Probably be a good idea if we got out of here pronto. Before he *does* come back.'

Russell roared along the winding lanes from Chagford towards Widecombe. He was pissed off. He'd taken a girl to Kendwick's on Sunday night but the boy had let him down. He was a complete flim-flam. The girl had been *perfect*. *Ready*. At least she had been after a little surgery.

Russell couldn't help but smile to himself as he relived what had happened. Once he'd drilled the hole and injected the bleach, she'd just lain there. The screaming of earlier in the evening had ceased and the struggling had stopped. She'd simply stared at the ceiling, eyes wide. Waiting. Still. Just how he liked them. Just how all women should behave. The experiment had been a complete success. He'd got her clothes off and then fucked her, leaving her with the boy, hoping Kendwick would come round to his way of thinking. If the lad could see how easy this new method was then perhaps he'd want to help Uncle Alan with his project. Russell figured two or three would be about right. Two or three *each*. He could lock them up in the barn. They'd be so docile and compliant he'd be able to keep them as if they were pets. Hopefully for months. Perhaps even years. They'd need feeding, but he had plenty of scraps. They'd need bathing, but that in itself would be fun. Perhaps he could even have stuck them in the duck pond for a good wash down.

Fuck it!

Russell gripped the wheel, his anger rising once more at the thought of what he'd lost. He recalled the scene he'd just witnessed in Chagford. Kendwick's place had been crawling with police, the girl gone. *His* girl gone. Worse was the knowledge that his nephew must have either turned himself in or been caught.

Never mind!

He had an ace up his sleeve, didn't he? The young girl in the barn. When Kendwick had mentioned that Savage was on his trail and she had a teenage daughter, Russell knew what he had to do. He'd waited outside Savage's house and then followed her husband on the school run. Once the girl had been dropped off she'd been easy prey. Him in his DPA gear, official ID and all. Plus, he'd flashed the business card Savage had given him.

I've got a message from your mother . . .

The card had been enough to get the girl's attention and as she'd stood by the tailgate of his Land Rover, he'd lunged at her, hefted her up into the back and locked the chain round her neck. She'd screamed plenty, but Russell had jumped into the Landy and roared away. The whole thing had taken perhaps thirty seconds.

Up ahead a group of walkers thronged in the road. Russell

thumped the horn and put his foot down, the walkers scattering left and right as he ploughed through them. As he passed, one swiped a walking pole into the side of the Land Rover. For an instant Russell thought about slamming on the brake and reversing back down the road. He'd always hated walkers and the chance to kill or maim one or two was tempting. But no, he had more pressing concerns. Kendwick would be at the police station by now.

Russell didn't think that he'd break under questioning; Kendwick had endured far harsher treatment in the US. The issue was the lad's wiliness. He'd try to twist the police round his finger, but this time the evidence would prove hard to deny. A girl in his spare bedroom with a hole in her head? He'd struggle to explain that. Instead, he'd be forced to try a different tactic and Russell knew that would be to sell him down the river.

For years, he'd been able to manipulate the boy. As a teenager he'd done as Russell had asked. Accompanied him on grave-robbing trips. Then, when Kendwick had protested that he no longer wanted to be involved in digging up corpses, Russell had gone out of the way to please the boy. He'd snatched a girl from the streets. A *live* girl. At the boneyard, after he'd killed her, Kendwick had enjoyed the warm body as much as Russell had. Only then his nephew had fled to the States. Still, Russell had soon put paid to any crazy ideas the young man had that their partnership was over. He'd flown to the US and tracked him down. Told him the move was the perfect opportunity to start anew. No more graves, just fresh bodies, young bodies. Kendwick hadn't wanted to, not at first, but Russell told him he didn't have a choice. And, to be fair to the boy, once they'd begun he'd been as up for it as Russell had.

He smiled to himself, remembering the tall sequoia trees.

The summer holidays he'd spent hunting in the wilderness. The screams of their victims echoing through the woods. The feel of their flesh as they lay warm in the soft grass amongst the rusting cars.

He snapped back into the present as the Land Rover skidded on a sharp corner. He blipped the wheel into the skid for a microsecond and the vehicle straightened. Not long now. Once home, he'd make preparations. He'd seen how the police dealt with Chantry; well, they wouldn't take him so easily. He knew the moor like the back of his hand. There were plenty of places he could hide out for weeks on end, even with the Land Rover. He'd load up with food and supplies, take his shotgun, and head on out. He'd grab Savage's daughter from the barn and bring her along too. Be right cosy to have a wench out on the moor with him. Best pack a syringe, he thought. And some bleach.

'Uncle Alan's coming,' he sang to himself, his mood brightening. 'You can't hide from Uncle Alan!'

He pumped the brake pedal as he approached the turning to his house, and swung onto the track. Which was when he saw the Ford Focus parked smack bang in the centre of his yard.

Chapter Thirty-One

Near Widecombe-in-the-Moor, Dartmoor. Monday 1st May. 3.27 p.m.

They'd reached the trapdoor and were about to descend when Riley held up a hand. He cocked his head on one side.

'We're too late, ma'am,' Riley said. 'He's back.'

Savage heard an engine splutter and die. Then the clunk of a car door. She moved across to one side of the room where a patch of daylight showed through a cracked slate. She put her eye to the crack.

Alan Russell stood next to his DPA Land Rover with his hands on his hips, staring at Riley's car. He turned towards the barn, nodded to himself and spat on the concrete. Then he was jogging round to the front door of the cottage and disappearing inside.

'You're right,' Savage said. She stood still, watching the cottage. Seconds later, Russell emerged. Crooked under his left arm was a shotgun and he held a box of cartridges in his right hand. 'Shit, he's got a weapon. Time to call for back-up.'

Riley took out his phone. 'Going to be a while coming, ma'am. Even with Inspector Frey already on the moor, I can't see him getting here soon.'

Savage nodded. Russell had moved past his Land Rover and now stood over next to the pool car. He cracked the shotgun open and loaded it with two cartridges. Then he took aim at one of the tyres and fired. The tyre exploded and Savage involuntarily stepped back as the retort echoed round the farmyard.

'Sam, back in the other room,' Savage said. 'Find somewhere to hide and don't move, right?'

Samantha nodded and Savage kissed her on the forehead and ushered her daughter away. She moved towards the trapdoor. She unhooked the door and let it drop shut with a thud. Next, she began to move a large wooden chest across so it would sit on top of the door. Riley finished his call and came to help. Together they shifted the chest into position.

'No way he can get up here now, ma'am,' Riley said. 'Frey's on his way. We just have to sit it out.'

Savage put her finger to her lips. There was a sound from below, somebody on the stone steps leading up to the trapdoor. Then the room exploded.

She fell backwards as a huge chunk of floor burst up in a fury of splinters. Shotgun pellets spattered into the slates above, pieces of wood flying everywhere. She moved quickly down the room, scampering away from the trapdoor.

Bang!

Another shot rang out and another hole appeared in the floor. Savage sprinted through into the room where Samantha had been held captive. Her daughter stood in the corner, quivering.

'Up on the table, quick!' Savage pushed Samantha across and they both clambered up. The surface was oak and plenty thick enough to stop the blast from a shotgun. Savage swivelled where she sat and looked through the doorway. Riley had jumped up on the wooden chest and now lay on his side. He raised one hand, thumb up and shrugged. Then he put the other hand out and flashed his fingers, three times.

Fifteen minutes. Shit, they'd be lucky to last the next five.

She looked at Sam. 'It'll be OK, sweetheart. Help's on the way.'

Samantha just sat there for a second, expressionless, before turning her head slightly in the direction of the farmyard. Savage heard it too. Another vehicle coming down the track. There was the sound of tyres skidding on gravel, the vehicle's door opening, a shrill voice calling out.

'Whatever's going on, Alan?' the voice said. 'The police have taken away my Graham and now you're stomping round with a gun.'

'Get back home, you fat old crone!' Russell shouted. 'Get back to your bloody cake programmes.'

'Alan Russell, don't you dare speak to me like that. I won't have it, d'you hear me? I won't stand for it.'

'I pity poor Graham. All hot with desire for you and there you are getting excited about some B-list celebrity tart with a fucking sequinned dress. You women don't understand anything. Always denying us pleasure, withholding what's rightfully ours. If it had been me, I'd have told you to lie back, spread your legs and keep quiet.'

'That's it, Alan. You've gone far enough. I'm leav—'

Mrs Chantry's words ended with a bang as Russell discharged the shotgun once more. Seconds later the gun went off again, vicious shards of wood flying up from the floor not far from Riley.

'Mr Russell!' Savage shouted. 'It's no good. You might as well put down your weapon and give yourself up.'

Bang!

A hole appeared in the floor halfway down the room.

This time the shot dislodged a slate in the roof and a beam of light shone down.

The roof!

Savage looked over to Riley. The DS had rescued a man from a cow shed a while ago by breaking in through the roof. Savage pushed herself to her feet and then waved at Riley. She pointed at the slates. The pitch above Riley's head sloped away from the farmyard. If they could climb through they could slide down and drop off the rear where they could make their escape across the fields at the back.

'Mr Russell?' Savage shouted again as Riley stood and began to work on loosening some slates. 'How about we do some sort of deal?'

Bang! Debris flew up just a couple of feet from where Savage sat, the dust spattering down around her.

'I'll come down and talk to you. Face to face. We can try to work something out.'

Another shot rang out, this time Savage feeling an impact directly beneath her. Samantha flinched and huddled closer. Savage glanced over at Riley. He was beckoning her, daylight showing through a large hole in the roof above his head.

'Come on, Mr Russell. You want me to play dead for you, let you do whatever you want?'

This time the shot didn't come. Savage grabbed Samantha's hand and they slipped off the table and ran down the room. Riley had already pushed himself up through the hole and he reached back in for Samantha. Savage helped her as Riley grasped her hand and pulled her out onto the sloping roof. Savage followed, hefting herself up and sitting beside her daughter. Riley pointed towards the edge of the building. A small paddock lay beyond and past that a hedge and a larger field. From there they could make their way back to the road and Savage's car.

They eased themselves down to the edge. It was a two-metre drop to soft grass. Riley went first, turning so he was on his front and then letting himself fall. He tumbled over and then stood and beckoned Samantha. She hesitated, but then she copied Riley's actions, dropping down and rolling as she hit the ground. When her daughter was clear, Savage followed, slipping over the edge and landing awkwardly. She pushed herself to her feet, one shoe sucking off in a patch of mud. She left it lying there and then she was up and running alongside Riley and Samantha, half hopping, in seconds reaching an open gate to the next field. She pulled off her other shoe and they sprinted up behind the hedge. The field rose to the lane where another gate sat opposite the little pull-in where Savage had left her car.

'We're safe now, look.' Riley said as they climbed over the gate. He pointed down the valley. In the distance a police car swung round a bend, haring towards them with its lights flashing. Behind was the FSG van. 'The cavalry have arrived.'

'About time.' Savage turned to Samantha. She pulled her close and hugged her. 'Are you OK?'

Sam nodded.

'Sure?'

'Yes, Mum.'

'Good, because I'm going to leave you here with DS Riley. He'll look after you and sort all this out.'

'*What?*' Riley turned his attention from the oncoming vehicles. He looked bereft. 'You can't!'

'I've got to be away from here before Frey arrives. Plus, I need to get back to Janey.'

'But what about Kendwick, ma'am? What should I say happened?'

'Say what you want. Whatever you think is best.' Savage stepped forward and took Riley's hand. She leaned over and

348

kissed him on the neck. Then she gave Sam one last hug. 'Whatever happens, Darius, thanks. I owe you everything. Everything, understand?'

'Charlotte!' Riley said, grabbing her arm as she walked away.

'No time.' Savage slipped from his grasp and got in the car. She held up her odd shoe and then chucked it in the back. 'Cinderella, fairy Godmothers, pumpkins and all that crap.'

She started the engine as the patrol car drew up alongside. Riley turned to the car and as he did so, Savage floored the accelerator and roared away.

She swung the car in through the gates to the compound a little over three quarters of an hour later. She remembered she had a pair of walking boots behind her seat so she grabbed them and put them on over her muddy socks. Then she got out and entered the bunker, wondering how she was going to explain the situation to Horton and what the hell they would do with Kendwick. She trotted along the corridor and then went down the stairs, round and round until she reached the bottom.

'Janey!' she shouted out. 'I found Sam. She's OK.'

Savage walked towards the briefing room. The door stood half open but Janey wasn't answering. Halfway down the corridor Savage paused and listened. Nothing.

'Janey? Are you there?'

There was no reply. She tensed and moved slowly forward, keeping to one side of the corridor and edging towards the end. Through the door she could see half of the room. The other half, where the dentist's chair sat, was out of sight.

She took another step and stopped at the door. She felt her heart beating. Something was wrong. She reached out and pushed the door fully open and gasped at what she saw.

Janey Horton was slumped in the dentist's chair, seemingly unconscious.

'Janey!' Savage let out a cry and as she did so Horton moved slightly, her eyelids fluttering open and shut. She turned her head towards Savage.

'Charlotte . . .' Horton let out a wince. 'Kendwick . . .'

A click echoed down the corridor and Savage spun round. A few metres away Kendwick stood in an open doorway, the pistol in his right hand.

'Nice of you to drop by,' Kendwick said, smiling. 'It was getting a little lonely with just the two of us. And, to be honest, Janey is a bit of a bore. You, on the other hand . . .' Kendwick smiled and nodded down at his crotch. 'Well, let's just say things are looking up, know what I mean?'

'Malcolm,' Savage said. 'You were right. Alan Russell did take my daughter, but she's safe now.'

'Oh, that's great, Charlotte. Wonderful, even. I'm so pleased.' Kendwick made a waving motion with his left hand, as if dismissing the whole thing as a mere trifle. 'We can just forget what happened earlier. I mean, what's a brutal beating, kidnapping, and an hour or two of torture between friends? Hell, some weirdos pay good money for that sort of thing.'

'I don't know what your involvement was, but you can escape now.' Savage glanced back down the corridor to the stairwell. 'Samantha's safe, so I'm not going to stop you if you want to leave.'

'Why thank you, your Royal Highness.' Kendwick made a half bow. 'I'm so very grateful for your beneficence. I'm free to go if I want, am I?'

'Yes.'

'WELL I DON'T FUCKING WANT!' Kendwick spat the words out. 'Because you and that American bitch owe me and I'm going to extract payment in full. Now move.'

Kendwick waved the gun, gesturing down the corridor to the room he'd come out of. 'In there.'

Savage hesitated for a moment, but then she saw a glint in Kendwick's eyes. The man was close to cracking. She walked across to the room and entered.

A bare bulb glared from a length of wire in the ceiling. A single bed with a striped mattress lay with its head end up against one wall. Placed next to it was a small table. A large desk with a swivel chair was over in one corner and a filing cabinet stood alongside. Unlike the other rooms which had held multiple bunks, this was plainly a retreat for somebody with executive powers.

Savage moved into the centre of the room. Kendwick came in and pushed the door shut. For a moment there was silence and then Kendwick smiled.

'This is cosy, isn't it?' he said. 'Now then, I want you to take your boots off and lie on the bed.'

'Malcolm,' Savage said, holding her hands out in a gesture of resignation. She had to try and persuade Kendwick there was another option to what he had planned. 'I've been to your uncle's place. Samantha was in his barn like you said she would be. He hadn't touched her, thank God, but I'm sure he would have given the chance. You say he's guilty of the murders both here and in the US and I believe you. Alan Russell's not right in the head. He led you on, corrupted you, didn't he?'

'He certainly did that.'

'So there are mitigating circumstances to what happened. You're likely to get off with a reduced sentence. What you did to Janey Horton will probably be seen as self-defence. It's Janey and I who are in trouble. We'll be going to prison for a long time. But if this goes any further you're in danger of losing any sympathy and coming out on the wrong side.

351

Then nobody's going to believe it was your uncle who was to blame. Just think how it will look if you hurt us, if you do other things.'

'Oh, I do intend to hurt you. And other things too.'

'Please don't do this.'

'"Please don't do this,"' Kendwick parroted the words back at her, putting on a whiny little voice. 'Funny, where have I heard that plea before? I remember! I used the exact same words to you and Horton.'

'I was confused, Malcolm. I didn't know where the hell my daughter was. I did what any parent would do. I honestly believed you'd done something to her.'

'You're repeating yourself, Charlotte. Now I'm going to repeat *myself*: lie down or I'll bloody kill you.' Kendwick moved towards her. He transferred the gun to his left hand and then swung his right hand at Savage's face, slapping her hard on the cheek. 'LIE ON THE FUCKING BED!'

Savage recoiled from the blow. Kendwick had his mouth open and now he held the gun in both hands, legs spread in a shooter's stance. All of a sudden she realised he knew how to use a weapon. After all, he'd lived in the US, hadn't he? And the way he braced his hands on the pistol showed he was deadly serious about using it.

'OK, you win,' Savage said. She stepped away from Kendwick, bent over and spat blood from her mouth. 'Just give me a moment, right?'

Kendwick nodded. 'You've got sixty seconds.'

Savage took several deep breaths and then bent to undo her walking boots. She kicked them off and straightened.

'You're going to kill me like you killed them,' Savage said. 'Those girls in America.'

'No, I was telling the truth. I didn't kill anyone. I'd lure girls into my car and abduct them. Then release and chase them. Once I'd caught up with them, Uncle would appear and he'd slit their throats so we'd have a nice fresh body to use. So sad. If they'd kept still then maybe they would have lived, but they didn't. Once they were dead, we could do what we liked. There was plenty of time for that up in the mountains. Over and over. There was no one to disturb us, see? Just like here.' Kendwick laughed. 'You've badly miscalculated. You chose this place because it was secure and no one ever comes here. Nobody would hear me screaming, would they? But the reverse applies too. I'm going to torture the life out of Janey Horton and then I'm going to have you. I can't quite decide which I'm going to enjoy more.'

'Please, Malcolm.'

'They begged too. But it didn't do them any good.' Kendwick stepped across to the desk. The handcuffs Savage and Horton had used earlier lay next to a key. He picked them up and then waved the gun at her. 'Now, on the bed.'

Savage moved across to the bed. Kendwick threw the cuffs onto the pillow and told her to click one on her right wrist and then lie down. She did so and Kendwick moved across.

'My finger is squeezing the trigger on the gun,' he said as he reached for the loose cuff. 'One wrong move and it goes off. And guess what? I still get to have you while you're warm.'

Savage nodded as Kendwick led the cuff round the metal rail of the bed and locked it on her other wrist.

'Just get it over with,' she said.

'Oh no.' Kendwick laughed. 'You get to wait a while. I'm going to do Horton first.' Kendwick turned and walked to the door. 'And after I've left her to bleed to death I'm going to come back here and fuck your brains out.'

With that Kendwick turned and left the room.

Savage wrestled with the cuffs for a few seconds, but they

were secure and the bed frame solid. No way could she get free by breaking either. She'd been in some scrapes in her life, but mostly they had been ones where she'd had little time to dwell on what was happening. Now she did. Being chained to the bed made her feel incredibly vulnerable and the thought that Kendwick was just a few metres away, shortly to be inflicting untold horrors on Horton, was terrifying. And when he came back it would be her turn.

She wriggled again, turning on the rough mattress. Her movement caused the bed to scrape on the floor so she stopped, not wanting Kendwick to hear. Then came the first scream from Horton, a sickening, drawn-out howl which, when Savage shifted again, drowned out the noise the bed made. She turned onto her front so she could slip the lower half of her body onto the floor. As she turned she spotted something out of the corner of her eye. A glint of silver from the desk. The handcuff key!

To Riley's surprise, Alan Russell surrendered at a little before five p.m. He'd been inside his cottage, but came out with his hands held high, lying down in the yard when instructed to do so. A swarm of Nigel Frey's men converged on the ranger, pulling his arms behind his back and clicking handcuffs into place. A size eleven boot pressed his face into the ground as he was patted down and searched.

Riley walked across when Frey gave the signal that it was safe to do so, and Russell was hauled to his feet.

'Alan Russell,' Riley said. 'I'm arresting you for the rape and torture of Nina Staddon, the murder of Bridget Chantry and the abduction of a minor. You do not have to say anything, but it may harm your defence if you do not mention when questioned something which you later rely on in court. Anything you do say may be given in evidence.'

'It was the boy.' Russell spat dirt from his mouth and then bared his teeth. 'My nephew. He's a psychopath. He led me on from the start. Twisted everything. You've seen the way he is. Clever. Devious.'

'Malcolm Kendwick?' Riley said, making sure there was no possibility of confusion.

'The bodies, the girls. Everything. He's responsible, not me.'

'Right,' Riley said. He realised this was how Russell was going to play it. At least until Kendwick turned up. He gestured for the officers to take Russell away and then stood in the yard staring at the building where an hour or so ago he'd been holed up with Savage. Where was she now? And what about Kendwick? Riley shook his head and cursed aloud. 'Fuck it!'

'I know what you mean.' Frey moved across and stood alongside Riley. 'Shocking.'

'Huh?' Riley turned and stared at Frey and then realised the officer had misconstrued him.

'We should have put a bullet in the man. Saved a lot of heartache.'

'You think?' Riley gestured towards a squad car where Russell was being pushed into the back seat. 'Suppose he's telling the truth? Suppose it *was* all down to Kendwick?'

'What about her?' Frey pointed at the body of Mrs Chantry. She'd fallen face down on the ground, a gaping hole in her back where Russell had shot her at point-blank range. 'Murder, plain and simple. He can't blame that on Kendwick, can he?'

'No,' Riley said.

'Anyway, I guess we'll know when we find Kendwick, but I wouldn't mind betting he'll try to spin it the other way round.' Frey patted Riley on the back. 'Don't fret, we'll get them on joint enterprise. They'll both go down for the whole gamut of offences: murder, necrophilia, causing me to miss my dinner.'

Joint enterprise. The phrase almost caused Riley to miss Frey's quip about his dinner, but he managed to force out a laugh and then began to walk across to the squad car. He wondered whether he'd be liable for whatever DI Savage had done to Kendwick. So far he'd kept quiet. When Frey had first arrived at Russell's place, Riley had simply said that Savage had asked him to meet her, having discovered the park ranger had kidnapped her daughter. Frey had asked where Savage was and Riley told him she'd had an urgent call and rushed off. Frey had raised an eyebrow and looked over to the FSG vehicle where Samantha was sitting inside with DC Calter.

'I'll never understand what makes that woman tick.' Frey had shaken his head. 'Are you telling me, after all this, she *left* her daughter?'

Samantha had long gone now, Calter driving her home to Plymouth. Riley was relieved that she, at least, was out of the way of Frey's probing questions. In all the confusion, Frey appeared to accept Riley's account, but Riley was worried the lies were piling up. Sooner or later he'd be caught out.

He reached the squad car and stood by the rear door. He peered in through the glass at Russell. The man stared forward, muttering to himself. He stuck his tongue out and then turned and smiled at Riley.

'I'm bloody crazy, right?' Russell shouted. He flicked his eyes and glanced at the barn. 'Digging up corpses and shagging them? Spending time with all those bones? Well, what do you think?'

Riley didn't answer. It looked as if Russell was reconsidering his options. Since he couldn't blame Kendwick for the death of Bridget Chantry, he'd plainly decided diminished responsibility might be a better bet. Riley tapped on the roof and the driver started the engine. Russell grinned and began to rock violently back and forth until the officer beside him forced him to sit back. Then the car pulled off, leaving Riley standing on his own in the centre of the yard, shaking his head.

Chapter Thirty-Two

Ex MoD bunker, South Hams, Devon. Monday 1st May.
5.10 p.m.

Bit by bit Savage shifted the bed across the floor, timing each movement to coincide with one of Horton's screams. Between the screams she could hear her sobbing and begging for mercy. Savage just hoped Horton could hold out because if she lapsed into unconsciousness or died there'd be silence. And once Horton held no more interest for Kendwick he'd be back for the second course.

'Pleeeaaase! Nooo!'

Horton's voice came again followed by a screech. Savage shifted the bed a little more. She was close now, the head of the bed nearly touching the desk. The problem was Savage's arms were cuffed to the end of the bed and there was no way she'd be able to retrieve the key with her hands as it lay in the centre of the desk. She jerked the bed one more time and then swivelled herself round and clambered back on top of the mattress. She turned on her front, lifted one leg and eased it up and onto the desk. She brought the other leg up too and began to wriggle her feet across to the key.

Which was when everything went very quiet.

Savage stopped moving for a moment. Something clattered

in the distance. Metal falling onto metal. She heard Kendwick huffing and cursing. He was muttering something to himself but Savage couldn't hear the words. Next came a whistling and then Kendwick began to sing.

'Hi ho, hi ho, it's off to work we go.'

Footsteps echoed in the corridor. Kendwick was coming.

Savage looked across the desk and planted her right foot down, feeling the key beneath her big toe. She swept her leg back towards her and the key slid across the top of the desk. It fell from the desk and bounced on the side of the mattress before dropping to the floor with a little 'ding.'

'You fucking bitch!'

Savage swivelled herself round. Kendwick stood in the doorway with the gun in one hand and several pieces of rope in the other. He moved quickly over to the bed. He placed the gun on the desk and then grabbed Savage by her calves, pulling her legs straight and wrapping a loop of rope round her ankles. He secured the rope to the bed frame.

'Nice,' Kendwick said. He ran both hands up to her knees and pushed them apart. 'Like soft butter, you spread easily.'

'Let me go, Malcolm.' Savage squirmed against the rope and shook the cuffs. 'We can discuss this.'

'Let you go?' Kendwick cocked his head on one side. 'To be honest, I *had* thought of loosing you free and chasing you. Hide and seek. Forty-forty. Tag. I can see now that would be a mistake. You're much too clever. It's better you're tied up and all ready for action.'

Kendwick stood by the bed for a moment. He stared down at Savage and licked his lips. He slipped a hand onto her knee and then ran it up her thigh. Savage shivered. She'd met and interviewed many victims of sexual assault, but before this moment she'd never fully understood the horror, the feeling of powerlessness, the awful sense of violation.

She'd assumed much of the trauma would be physical, but now, even before Kendwick had done anything but touch her, she realised the mental burden would be much harder to bear. She swallowed and tried to put herself in another place, thinking of how she just needed to get through the next few minutes or hours or however long Kendwick would choose to torment her for. Beyond that, if she was still alive, there might be another chance to escape.

'You've got a great body, Charlotte.' Kendwick had moved his hand away and now he was pulling off his hooded top, revealing a black T-shirt beneath. 'You're a bit old for my taste, but youth isn't everything. There's something to be said for experience too, and I certainly intend to add to yours.'

Savage stared up at Kendwick as he tossed his top to one side. She had to get him talking, see if there was a chink in his armour, some small spark of compassion she could draw on.

'I thought they had to be blonde,' she said. She raised her head a little and shook her head so her hair spread on the mattress. 'I'm a redhead.'

'Blonde, yes, I prefer them that way. But there's been others as well, only the cops never linked me with them. I must say, Charlotte, it's shocking what happens over in the States. You can get away with murder. Literally. Not like here.'

'The other girls, how many were there? Tell me about them.'

'There's not much to tell. We just took them up into the mountains and killed them. We didn't bother with the bone-yard, these were quickies, ones we hadn't planned.' Kendwick paused and looked at Savage. 'As to how many, well I think there were another half dozen.'

Kendwick smiled and then began to remove his T-shirt.

'And the blondes, why the obsession with hair colour? Something to do with your mother?'

'My mother?' Kendwick scowled and shook his head. 'No, I'm not some sort of perverted weirdo who wants to fuck his own mum. This isn't Oedipal.'

'OK, then why?'

'It's a long story, Charlotte.' Kendwick pulled his T-shirt over his head and then gingerly slipped it over the arm where Savage had poured acid. He flinched. 'Too long for now, but let's just say it was to do with a girl who rejected me. I was young and vulnerable and she led me on. I fell for her and all she could do was leave me bereft. Then Uncle Alan showed me there was another type of woman. One who was compliant and still. Who'd lie there while I did whatever I wanted.'

'They weren't women, Malcolm, they were corpses.'

'Of course. To be honest it was sickening. Especially when Alan ended up turning to murder. When he did that, I decided I wanted a break and I took up a job opportunity in California. Which was when I was rejected again. I was well off with good prospects. I was handsome, intelligent, quite a catch, but this American girl, well we were engaged for a while and then she broke it off. Just like that. I wrote her notes, sent her flowers, tried everything. The answer remained "no". In the end she married somebody else and moved away.'

'So because of that you decided to take your anger out on random women. You chose victims with blonde hair and kidnapped and raped them.'

'NO!' Kendwick shouted the denial. 'You don't get it, it wasn't that simple. One night I met another girl at a bar and got chatting, we seemed to get on. Later, I gave her a lift home. Halfway there I stopped my car so we could do a little, you know, kissing. At first she was willing, but then as things began to get a little heavier she wouldn't have it. That bitch rejected me as well.'

'So you killed her.'

'I never killed anyone, that's the truth.' Kendwick smiled. 'It was Uncle Alan. I'd tried to keep him at arm's length, but he tracked me down. Being rejected yet again was the last straw and he found me at my weakest. He told me he could help. We went and found the girl I'd met at the bar and picked her up. The problem was she wouldn't keep still. That's all I wanted.'

'So that was the thing about killing them. You wanted them still.'

'Let's not talk about it now,' Kendwick said. He threw his T-shirt away and clambered on the bed and knelt to one side of her. Then he reached up and pulled his hair out of his ponytail, tossing the hairband away. 'Not when we're about to have some fun.'

'Malcolm,' Savage said, aware this was her last chance. 'You needn't do this. You can get away.'

'I've told you too much. Besides you haven't seen what I've done to Horton.'

Kendwick moved across and lay on top of her, supporting himself on his arms. His hot breath brushed Savage's face as he gazed down at her body. She realised that although he'd taken his top off, he hadn't yet made any attempt to remove her clothes. She knew some serial killers were often sexually inadequate. It either took violence to arouse them or they became angry when they couldn't get turned on physically.

Savage closed her eyes, feeling Kendwick's weight press down on her. She wasn't sure how to handle this. Lie passive and let Kendwick do whatever he wanted? Or fight like crazy, aware that resisting would probably make him mad enough to kill her?

'I'll keep still,' she said, realising what she was going to do. 'I'll be a good girl and behave like you want me to. Make it like your first time.'

'Huh?' Kendwick looked surprised, but then he bent to kiss her, his long hair hanging over her like a veil.

Savage jerked forward, smashing her forehead into Kendwick's mouth. A spray of blood shot out as he swung away, reeling from the pain.

'You fucking cow,' he screamed, spluttering blood from a split lip and then spitting a tooth free. He pushed himself off and his hands went down to her hips and grabbed her jeans. He ripped the button open and yanked them down to her ankles. 'Now I'm going to really hurt you.'

Savage twisted beneath Kendwick so he couldn't get hold of her. He leant forward again and swung a fist, catching her on the jaw.

'Lie still or it'll be all the worse for you.' Kendwick screamed and then his mouth was agape with surprise. He reached for the button on his own trousers. The violence had turned him on. He grinned. 'God, Charlotte. You're the first woman in ages who's made me this excited while they're still alive. I can see we're going to have a lot of fun in the next couple of hours.'

Savage swallowed. She was going to die, but first Kendwick would humiliate her. This wouldn't be over quickly. No, he'd want to draw it out, to get as much pleasure from her suffering as he could.

'Right,' Kendwick said as he pulled his trousers down and began to lower his boxer shorts. 'You're going to enjoy this.'

Then Kendwick flinched. He moved his hands to one side of his abdomen and stared down to where a trickle of red oozed from a hole on one side of his belly button. His mouth opened in shock and he gasped as a silver spike slid from the skin, blood slick on the metal.

'What the . . .?' Kendwick turned to peer over his shoulder, his face creasing in pain. 'My God, no!'

Janey Horton stood at the end of the bed holding the sharpened screwdriver. The right side of her face was a mass of blood and pulp and her top was ripped across the front. Beneath the top a great slash of skin hung down where her right breast had been cut open.

Horton yanked her hand back and the screwdriver slid out of Kendwick's body. He rolled forward onto Savage.

'Get off her, you fucking pervert!' Horton flung the spike away and stepped alongside the bed. She grabbed Kendwick, pulling him off Savage. Kendwick slid off the bed and fell to the floor.

'The key,' Savage said. She nodded her head to the other side of the bed. 'It's on the floor.'

Horton walked round and picked up the key. She unlocked the handcuffs.

'You OK?' she said. 'He didn't . . .?'

'No, but he would have if it hadn't been for you. Thanks.'

'I'm sorry, Charlotte. About what happened. Kendwick tricked me. He pretended to have some sort of seizure, put on a choking fit. I thought he was going to die. I was worried that if he did we might never find out about your daughter, so I loosened the ropes and he broke free.'

'Never mind me.' Savage sat up and looked at Horton. 'It's you I'm worried about. You need to get to a hospital.'

'I'll be fine.' Horton turned to where Kendwick had been. A trail of blood led across the room to where he now lay up against one wall. His tongue hung out from one corner of his mouth, blood dribbling down his chin. His hands lay on his abdomen where some sort of fluid trickled down his side. 'What about him?'

'I don't know.' Savage shook her head. Kendwick was badly injured, but not mortally so. They could hardly take him to a hospital though. 'I guess we'll have to leave him here.'

'CHARLOTTE!' A deep booming voice came echoing through the subterranean complex. 'YOU DOWN THERE?'

Horton whirled round, panic in her eyes, but Savage sought to reassure her.

'It's Kenny,' she said. 'Kenny Fallon.'

A few seconds later a figure stood in the doorway. Leather jacket over a bulky frame. He stared in at Savage, who was still sitting on the bed, working on the knots at her ankles. Then his eyes moved to Horton, finally they settled on Kendwick.

'You OK, Charlotte?' Fallon said. His brow furrowed as he looked at Savage again, taking in her bare legs, the jeans down by her ankles. He reached up and scratched his goatee beard. 'There's a joke somewhere here, isn't there, lass? Undercover cop or something. Agent provocateur. Perhaps best if I save it for another time.'

'I'm all right, Kenny,' Savage said. She slipped the loop of rope off her ankles and pulled up her jeans. Then she climbed off the bed and picked up Kendwick's top from the floor. She passed it to Horton. Horton folded the top and pressed the material against her chest. 'Janey needs to get to a hospital though.'

'That Kendwick?' Fallon walked into the room. 'The guy who took Samantha?'

'He didn't take Samantha. It was down to somebody else. His accomplice. She's fine now.'

'So what's the story with him?' Fallon stepped over to Kendwick. 'Looks like you need to take him to hospital too.'

'No, we don't. You see we tortured him. To find out where Samantha was.'

'Right.' Fallon nodded and bit his lip. 'These things happen, Charlotte. You've got to do what you've got to do. If it was my kid, believe me I wouldn't have played it any different.'

'Then he managed to get free and he hurt Janey and tried to rape me.'

'You can't blame him for that, though. Not if you tortured him.'

'He's a killer, Kenny. Janey's a cop too, from the US. She's been hunting him for ages.'

'Who did he kill?' Fallon turned to Horton.

'With his uncle, at least five girls,' Horton said. 'Teenagers, early twenties. Stephanie Capillo, Amber Sullivan, Chrissy Morales, and Jessie Turner.'

'That's four.'

'And Sara Horton.' Horton stopped. Looked over to Kendwick. 'My daughter.'

'I see,' Fallon said. 'Déjà vu, hey, Charlotte?'

'Not the same, Kenny.' Savage reached for her boots and began to put them on. 'Kendwick's the worst kind of sexual predator. He thinks nothing of the terror he brings to his victims and the pain and heartache he causes their families.'

'And you, what have you got to say for yourself?' Fallon half bent and sneered down at Kendwick. 'This true?'

Kendwick coughed and then spat a globule of blood and mucus to one side. 'It's lies. All of it. I never killed any girls, it was my uncle. These bitches tortured me so then I got my own back. Like you said, I can't be blamed for that.'

Fallon looked at Savage. She shook her head. Kendwick had said his uncle had been the killer. She wasn't sure if he was telling the truth or trying to save his skin, but it didn't

366

matter. He was responsible one way or another for the deaths of the five blonde girls and the others he said the police in the US had never found out about.

'It's Janey's call,' she said.

Horton took two steps over to Kendwick. She gazed down, her eyes blank and devoid of any emotion. Savage could see whatever had driven her this far had gone.

Horton opened her mouth to say something but then thought better of it. She turned and staggered from the room.

Fallon turned and stared across to the desk. 'That my gun? The one I gave you so you could deal with that kid?'

'Yes.'

'Spot of luck.' Fallon walked to the desk and picked up the weapon. 'Clean, if I remember rightly. Never used.'

'Please,' Kendwick said. 'You can't do this. You won't get away with it.'

'I've got away with far worse,' Fallon said, stepping back to Kendwick, the gun in his right hand. 'And believe me nobody's going to be shedding any tears apart from a few bleeding heart liberals. Charlotte?' Fallon nodded in the direction Horton had gone. 'Go and help your friend. I'll sort this piece of shit.'

'You don't have to, Kenny. We could just leave him.'

'Nah, can't risk it, love. Go on, skit. I'll see you up top.'

Savage glanced down at Kendwick. He was shivering, his eyes filled with moisture, but she felt nothing for the man. She'd never understood how people could bring themselves to campaign for clemency for serial killers. Perhaps they were better people than she was, but she didn't think so. They'd just never had to face the brutal reality of what these monsters were capable of. They'd never had to share in the grief of the relatives, never had to see young bodies lying on a post-mortem table, a pathologist detailing the horrific abuse the victims had suffered before they'd died.

'See you up top then,' Savage said, and she turned and walked from the room.

They'd just finished climbing the stairs when they heard the shot. The retort echoed through the bunker and Savage could have sworn she heard a scream which came just a moment before.

She put her arm round Horton and helped her along the corridor towards the slit of brightness where the door stood half open. They emerged into bright sunlight. Fallon's Range Rover was parked alongside the Galaxy and Savage guided Horton past the cars and towards a grassy bank.

Horton eased herself down and lay on the grass, resting her head on Savage's lap. She looked up and smiled.

'I'm glad I met you, Charlotte,' Horton said, her eyes misty and faraway. 'It's like I was meant to. Destiny or some crap like that.'

'And I'm glad you decided to come over here. Without you we'd never have got Kendwick or Alan Russell.'

A minute or so later Fallon came out from the bunker. He went across to his Range Rover and put the pistol in the boot.

'I'm going to get somebody to come and clean up and get rid of the body,' he said. 'Within a couple of hours he'll be fish food and nobody will be any the wiser. But, for the record, as far as I'm concerned I've never heard of Malcolm Kendwick and I didn't know you came here with him. All you have to do is get your stories straight.'

'Thanks, Kenny.' Savage looked up at Fallon. 'I owe you.'

'That you do, Charlotte, even more than before. But now's not the time to worry about debts, hey?' Fallon glanced back towards the double doors. 'I'll get this mess sorted while you get Janey to hospital. We'll catch up when this has all blown over. Work something out.'

Savage helped Horton to her feet and into the Galaxy. Fallon stood by his vehicle, speaking into a mobile. He waved as Savage started her car and pulled away.

'Where are we going?' Horton sounded groggy, her voice slurred.

'To get you fixed up. After that we're going home.'

'Home.' Horton closed her eyes, lay back in the seat, and smiled. 'Sounds good.'

Epilogue

Friday afternoon found Riley stuck in a briefing room which reeked of sweat and coffee. Jackets hung on the backs of chairs, paper cups littered the floor, and a pile of sandwich wrappings formed a mountain of detritus in the centre of the glossy conference table. At one end of the room, an easel supported a huge pad of paper, several sheets already flipped over. Riley propped his chin in his hands and tried to focus on DS Collier's presentation. A dozen other officers tried to do the same, but Collier had lost half the room and he'd certainly lost DSupt Hardin.

'This won't bloody do,' Hardin said as Collier made to flip over another sheet. The DSupt sat at the head of the table, nearest the easel, and he jabbed a finger at the mess of black felt-tip scrawled across the page. 'It's a hotchpotch of guesswork with a few facts thrown in to sweeten the bad taste. What has everyone been doing since Monday? We can't make a case out of this.'

'Alan Russell's not getting off.' Collier waved his marker pen at a series of bullet points. 'We'll get him for the murder of Bridget Chantry and the abduction of Samantha Savage. Plus his prints were all over the drill and syringe at

371

Kendwick's place so I'm hopeful we'll be able to charge him for the rape and torture of Nina Staddon too.'

'Hopeful? And that's good enough, is it?' Hardin swung his head round and glared down the table. 'What about Amy Glynn? The victims at the boneyard. Melany Lodwell. The poor lass bludgeoned to death in her tent on the moor. The girls in America. I want to know what we – no, what *you* – are doing about them?'

Riley coughed as Hardin's gaze swept the table and alighted on him. He'd been tasked with liaising with the US authorities over evidence concerning Russell's frequent visits to California.

'Homeland Security are reluctant to share the immigration data,' Riley said. 'But we do have details of flights from Russell's credit card statements and we know from the Border Force the dates he returned to the UK.'

'And the dates he was away match the killings?'

'Yes. For several years he went to the States at least biannually. Not only that, the statements show he rented a 4x4 on many of those occasions. If you remember, that was something missing from the evidence against Kendwick.'

'Well, I'm glad someone's been doing some work.'

'It won't wash, sir,' Collier said. 'Circumstantial. If they couldn't manage to bring charges against Kendwick, then they won't be able to make a case against Russell. I very much doubt a UK court would approve extradition on such flimsy grounds.'

'We're back to where we started, what, two hours ago?' Hardin glanced at his watch. 'Where the bloody hell is Malcolm Kendwick? Without him, we're buggered. Russell will keep on claiming Kendwick was the instigator. He'll try to pin blame on him.'

A silence followed Hardin's question until Nigel Frey

began to outline, not for the first time, the steps being taken to apprehend Kendwick, both locally and on a national level.

As the attention moved to the manhunt, Riley zoned out. He stifled a yawn. The past few days had been exhausting.

On Monday, after going to the station to deal with the processing of Russell, Riley had headed for DI Savage's place. On arrival, he'd found a patrol car blocking the driveway and an armed officer stationed at the front door.

'She in?' Riley asked.

'Yup. Been back an hour.'

Riley went inside. Voices floated from the living room. He poked his head round the door.

'Ma'am?'

'Darius!' Savage was sitting on the sofa beside Pete, but when she saw him she leapt up. She rushed across and ushered him in.

'I thought I'd better come round,' Riley said, nodding a greeting to Pete. 'Get a statement, that kind of thing.'

'Shit. A statement.'

'Yeah. Just to get things . . . um . . . *straight.*'

'Between us?'

'Between us.' Riley glanced at Pete. 'Yes. You, me, Pete, Janey, Samantha.'

'I'm out of here,' Pete said, standing. 'The less I hear of this the better. Tell me when you've agreed on the story, but leave Sam out of it, OK? She gets to tell the truth as she saw it.'

With that, he was gone, striding out of the room.

'He's right. Sam tells it as it is and you too.' Savage moved back to the sofa and Riley went and sat beside her. 'Now, how do we start?'

'Where's Kendwick?'

Savage shook her head. 'Wrong question.'

'He's not . . .' Riley half laughed, but then felt a wave of despair sweep over him. 'Oh fuck. Fuck, fuck, fuck.'

'He admitted he was involved in the killings in the States and told us about Alan Russell and how the two of them worked together.' Savage's words came tumbling forth as if she wanted to get everything out in one go. 'When I got back from Russell's place, he'd escaped. He attacked Janey and tried to rape me. Janey's in A&E at the moment. Beaten up, unconscious, in surgery. Christ, I hope she . . . well . . . I . . .'

'And Kendwick?' Riley ignored the stream of emotion and tried to cut to the facts. 'What the hell happened to him?'

'It was self-defence. Janey stabbed him as he was attacking me.'

'And he's . . . ?' Riley didn't finish his sentence but Savage nodded the answer. 'Shit.'

'We didn't have a choice, Darius. It was him or us.'

'You said self-defence, right? So we have to get John Layton out to wherever the body is so he can verify your story. With forensics on your side, you're sorted. There's a witness in Chagford who saw you leave with Kendwick, but his account wasn't very clear. You could say that Kendwick forced you to drive off. Your version could easily match his. Anyway, it would be the word of an officer against him. Two officers, if we include Janey.'

'Unfortunately, it isn't that simple. Kendwick was wounded first and then we shot him.'

'*What*?' Riley stared across at Savage. 'Are you telling me you *executed* him?'

'No, I didn't. Nor Janey.'

'Who then? Who pulled the trigger?'

'Kenny Fallon.'

'You're joking, Charlotte?' Riley shook his head. His despair had now turned to anger. 'This gets worse and worse. As if things weren't bad enough, you get involved with Fallon and let him do your dirty work for you.'

'There was no alternative. Anyway, Kendwick was a killer, a rapist. Are you saying he deserved mercy?'

'He deserved a fair trial. The application of the law.'

'Rubbish.' Savage paused and then reached out and touched Riley on the arm. 'He tried to rape me, Darius. The only reason he failed was because Janey regained consciousness and rescued me. In the process she stabbed Kendwick. He was going to kill us both.'

'That's all well and good, but you should have left it at that. You should have called an ambulance for the man, not let Fallon shoot him in cold blood.'

'You know why I couldn't get the authorities involved. There would have been too many questions.'

There was silence for a minute. Riley had stepped into the house as a police officer, but once inside the relationship had changed from professional to personal, from being Savage's DS, to being her friend. He realised the relationship was now in danger of collapsing completely.

Riley sighed. His disapprobation would do neither of them any good. They needed to find a way out of the situation.

'Where's the body?' he said.

'Fallon's taking care of the disposal.'

'Small mercies for that.' Riley gave Savage a smile. 'Fallon's a pro, I think we can safely say Kendwick will never be found. Now we just have to work on your statement.'

'So you're not going to turn me in?'

'No, ma'am, not this time.'

'Thanks, Darius. I owe you.'

'Well, you can start by making me a coffee.' Riley yawned. 'I've had about six hours sleep in the last two days and if we're going to get your story right we'll need clear heads.'

In the end, getting the story right had taken until the early hours. Eventually, they had something which rang true, something which Riley thought, if their luck held, they might get past DSupt Hardin . . .

'*Detective Sergeant Riley?*'

Riley jerked, back in the briefing room. At the far end of the table, Hardin leered in his direction.

'I *said*, what are your thoughts on Kendwick?' Hardin drummed his fingers on the table top and a couple of detectives sniggered. 'Where the hell could he be?'

'I don't know, sir.' Riley tried to compose himself. 'DI Savage's statement says he was wounded, didn't it? She stabbed him in self-defence and then drove off with Janey Horton, leaving him somewhere near Two Bridges.'

'Only she can't remember the exact spot and an extensive search of the area has revealed no sign of him.'

'That's my point. All this effort – the watch on the ports, extra patrols, the FSG combing the countryside – it could be a waste of time. My opinion is Kendwick may simply have crawled off into a corner and died. His body could be out on the moor, rotting to nothing but bones. And that would be an appropriate end to him, wouldn't it, sir?'

Several officers round the table flinched in expectation of Hardin's reaction, but the DSupt said nothing. Then he nodded and smiled, lightening the mood for a second before he spoke again.

'Well, Darius,' Hardin said, the smile all of a sudden gone, replaced by his regulation sneer. 'I don't know about "appropriate". More like . . . what's the word, Gareth?'

Hardin swung back to Collier, who, taken aback, dropped his marker pen. He bent to pick the pen up from the floor and then placed it on the conference table with a distinct *click*.

'Convenient?' Collier said.

'Yes.' Hardin swivelled his head again and this time the scowl on his face told Riley everything he needed to know. 'Very . . . *convenient*, don't you think?'

On Sunday afternoon, Savage went to Derriford Hospital to visit Janey Horton for the final time. The final time because Horton was due to be discharged the next day. Savage had been a regular visitor over the past few days and she'd seen Horton recover from a pale husk to the brash and confident woman she'd met at the railway station a little over a week ago.

'Hi, honey,' Horton yelled out as Savage crossed the ward. 'I'm just about ready to quit this crappy place.'

Looks of disapproval from other patients followed Savage as she walked over to Horton's bed and pulled up a chair.

'Chocolate,' Savage said, handing over a large bar of Cadburys Fruit and Nut. 'I know what you think about grapes.'

'I told you, flowers are for when you're dead, grapes for when you're ill,' Horton said. 'I'm neither. I've got a scar halfway round one breast, but other than that I'm fine. The surgeons did a pretty good job at sewing me up. My only regret is I didn't get them to give me a boob job while they were at it.'

They chatted for a few minutes, talking about the arrangements for the week ahead. Horton would come and stay at Savage's place for a few days, then she'd be flying back to the States.

'You're welcome to stay longer,' Savage said. 'You know that. It's not like I've got to work or anything.'

'No news on that front then?'

'No more than I'm on indefinite suspension until the circumstances surrounding our unofficial investigation have been fully investigated.'

'I gave them my statement. Wasn't the word of another law enforcement officer enough?'

'Apparently not.' Savage smiled. 'I guess your reputation precedes you.'

'I've got a reputation? Well, that's something I guess.'

'I meant what I said about staying longer.'

'I know you did, Charlotte.' Horton began to unwrap the chocolate bar. 'But I've unfinished business back home. There's folks who need to know what happened to their daughters. They need justice for their loved ones and that involves more than simply holding the perps to account. There's evidence to gather, a story to be told, endings to be written. Those parents sure can't rest until the final dot hits the page. I know I can't.'

'If then.'

'Yeah, if then. Still, I've got to try and help them.' Horton broke off two pieces of chocolate and handed one to Savage. 'Make amends too. If I'd gone by the book, perhaps things could have worked out differently. Perhaps those parents could have had a different kind of justice, a more complete one. For them, Kendwick's still out there, free.'

'We know different.'

'Of course, but I can't go telling them that, can I?'

'No.' Savage munched on her piece of chocolate. 'You'll come back though, to visit?'

'Hell, yes, and you'll come over, won't you? You and the family?'

'Of course.'

'Talking of your family, how's Sam?'

'Sam's fine. She seems to have got over what happened. At least on the surface. Pete's not happy though. This is the second time Sam's been in danger because of me and he's had enough.'

'He wants you to quit?'

'Quit or move into management away from the front line.'

'You're not going to do that are you, Charlotte?'

'I honestly don't know.'

'I do, honey. That sort of shit isn't for you.'

'You might be right.' Savage pushed herself up from the chair. 'Look, I'll see you tomorrow morning. Now I've got to go. I've got somebody else to visit.'

Horton nodded and reached out with both arms as Savage bent over. The American gave her a bear hug and then she was shooing her away.

'See you tomorrow,' she shouted, once again turning heads.

Savage waved as she left the ward and then went down two levels and wandered along a corridor until she found the area of the hospital she was looking for.

She peered through the glass panel into the high dependency unit. Nina Staddon lay in a bed by a narrow slit window. Monitor screens stood either side of the bed, coloured lines and figures dancing across black backgrounds. A breathing tube curled into the woman's mouth and to one side a drip line ran down to her arm. She looked unchanged from when Savage had visited several days ago.

On that occasion, she'd been standing at the glass window as Nina's mother and three-year-old daughter had arrived for a visit.

Mummy, wake up! Please wake up!

Of course, Nina hadn't woken. The doctors had put her

379

into an artificially induced coma with the hope her brain might recover from the trauma. As Savage had muttered her apologies to Nina's mother and made to leave, the woman had put out her hand and grasped her wrist.

'I just wanted to say thank you,' she'd said. 'Thank you for saving Nina's life.'

Savage shuddered as she remembered the mother's eyes. Blank. All hope gone. She blinked and for a second she saw Clarissa, her daughter, lying in the room. Clarissa had never come round from the hit-and-run and Savage and Pete had had to watch as the machines had been turned off and their daughter had drifted away.

'Can I help?' A consultant appeared beside Savage. The woman pointed into the room. 'Are you a relative?'

'No.' Savage reached into a pocket. She still had her warrant card. 'Police. What's the prognosis?'

'Well . . . Charlotte,' the woman said, peering at Savage's ID. 'I'd say a couple more days.'

'A couple more *days*?' Savage shook her head and swallowed as the memories came flooding back. 'And then you turn everything off?'

'Yes.'

'Christ.' Savage felt all her energy drain away. She put a hand against the glass to support herself. 'I . . .'

The consultant looked askance for a moment and then smiled. 'No, you misunderstand. We're turning everything off so we can bring her round. She had a scan yesterday and the indications are that there's been no long-term tissue damage. The brain is a remarkable organ, but in this case I must say Nina's recovery has been almost miraculous. We're very hopeful for her future.'

'Oh, God!' Savage laughed. 'I thought you meant . . . you know . . .'

380

'Are you one of the detectives who found her?'

'Yes.'

'The men who did this were animals, right?' The woman gestured at Nina. 'I don't want to believe somebody normal could treat another human being like that.'

'Worse than animals. Much worse.'

'Well, I hope you catch him soon, the one who got away.' The consultant wheeled on her heels, ready to go. 'And I hope he gets the punishment he deserves.'

'Don't worry about that,' Savage said, turning herself and catching sight of her reflection in the glass window. 'He will.'

Back home, Savage found Samantha slouched on a large beanbag on the front deck, enjoying the sun. A pair of binoculars sat in her lap.

'You OK?' Savage said.

'Yeah, Mum. Fine. Except for PC Plod coming round the back every half hour to check on me.'

Savage nodded. There was still a uniformed presence at the house. The fact pained her as it was illustrative of the resources being wasted as a result of the story she and Riley had concocted.

'Well, Sam, he's only there to keep you safe. Hopefully it won't be for much longer.' Savage paused and then gestured at the binoculars. 'Any sign of Dad?'

'Yes, you're just in time.' Samantha pointed out across Plymouth Sound. 'They're passing the breakwater right now.'

Savage squinted. Trying to make out anything against the glare from the sea was just about impossible, but then she spotted the small dot of white which was *Puffin*, the family's tiny yacht. Pete had been away for the weekend, taking Jamie for a quick jaunt down to Fowey and back. Ostensibly the trip had been for Pete to spend some quality father-and-son time with Jamie, but the real intention was for Savage and Samantha to be alone together.

'Got them.' Savage raised her hand to cut out some of the reflections. 'Looks like they're motoring in. Not enough wind. Why don't you give them a call? Tell Dad we'll meet him down at the marina.'

Samantha nodded, stood and handed the binoculars to Savage, and then grasped for her phone. Within seconds she was skipping off the deck and away across the lawn.

For a minute or two, Savage peered through the binoculars. She could just make out Pete and Jamie at the stern, Jamie on the helm, Pete's arms flailing, no doubt trying to impart various pieces of sailing knowledge to Jamie. Then she saw him reach into his pocket, answer his phone, and turn in the direction of the house.

She moved to the table and put the binoculars down. On the table lay a copy of Saturday's *Daily Mail*, Malcolm Kendwick's face smiling from the front page. A Post-it note partially covered the photograph and the newspaper's headline, black biro on the yellow surface: *Thought you might like to see this. Darius.*

Darius?

Savage hadn't seen DS Riley since Monday night. There'd been an uncomfortable silence as Riley had left and she hadn't been sure if the feeling of space between them had been down to stress and tiredness or something else. She knew Riley was shocked at what had happened to Kendwick, but she wondered if the visit to drop off the newspaper was an attempt at a reconciliation.

She removed the Post-it to reveal the full headline: *My Night of Passion with a Serial Killer*. She peered at the byline, smiling when she saw Melissa Stapleton's name, remembering too the words the reporter had used when she'd described the ramifications of Kendwick turning out to be a killer: it would be gold dust, she'd said.

Savage picked up the paper and began to read the article. Stapleton had certainly struck a rich seam and was mining it for all its worth. She claimed she'd been deceived by Kendwick's charming alter ego. He'd lured her into bed and it was only because his lust had been satisfied that she'd escaped with her life.

In an editorial to one side of the main piece, the paper performed a nifty volte-face. The notion Kendwick had ever been an innocent tourist was shamelessly discarded. Malcolm Kendwick and Alan Russell were monsters, pure and simple, and an illustration of the need for a reintroduction of the death penalty. The paper gleefully reported that an online petition had been set up and the number of signatories was rapidly approaching a quarter of a million. The vision of the baying masses calling for retribution disturbed Savage and yet, perhaps hypocritically, she felt no guilt for what had happened at the bunker.

Down at the far end of the garden, Samantha whirled round while talking to her dad, waving like mad in the direction of the Sound. Janey Horton's daughter, Sara, had been just a few years older than Sam, and Kendwick and Russell had snuffed her life out purely to satisfy their desires. They'd killed others, too. Now Kendwick was dead at the hands of Kenny Fallon and Russell would most likely be spending the rest of his life in prison. Differing routes to justice, Savage thought, but justice all the same.

She put the paper down as Samantha came running back up the garden. Her daughter tugged at Savage's arm.

'Come on, Mum,' she said, pulling Savage in the direction of the house. 'We've got to get down to the marina so we can take their ropes. We'd never hear the end of it if they got there before us.'

Savage looked out to sea where the little boat was now halfway across the Sound, a crystal wake behind the yacht glinting in the late-afternoon sun. She sighed. The scene was so peaceful, but the peace couldn't last forever. Tomorrow morning she had to attend a meeting with DSupt Hardin, where not only would he grill her on the statements she'd submitted, he'd also intimated he would be making a decision about her long-term future in the police force. Then there was the matter of a Professional Standards department investigation, not to mention the possibility of a parallel one by the IPCC.

'Mum!' Sam yanked her arm again. 'We'll be late!'

Savage took a final glance across the Sound and turned and followed her daughter into the house.

Stuff them, she thought. Stuff the whole damn lot of them.

'We're going to find them, sort them, pay them back . . .'

DI Charlotte Savage is back. And this might just be her toughest case yet . . .

'He could be out there right now. Passing you on the street. You'd never know . . .'

DI Charlotte Savage is back, chasing a killer who was at large ten years ago, a killer they presumed dead . . . Now he's back and more dangerous than ever.

'*Four murders in not much more than a week. Was that acceptable?*'

DI Charlotte Savage is back. And this might just be her toughest case yet . . .

'*A wonderfully twisted maze.*'

It's down to DI Savage to seek out a cold-blooded killer. Before it's third time unlucky. Before it's too late.